Also by C. H. Lawler

The Saints of Lost Things

The Memory of Time

LIVING AMONG THE DEAD

C. H. LAWLER

To Elizabeth,

C.H. Lawler

ISBN-13: 978-1544095400

ISBN-10: 1544095406

For Catherine, any roof you're under is home.

In memory of Bernie P. Landry, one of the finest carpenters and men
I have ever known.

"I believe that there is one story in the world, and only one. Humans are caught—in their lives, in their thoughts, in their hungers and ambitions, in their avarice and cruelty, and in their kindness and generosity too—in a net of good and evil. There is no other story. A man, after he has brushed off the dust and chips of his life, will have left only the hard, clean questions: Was it good or was it evil? Have I done well—or ill?"
— John Steinbeck, *East of Eden*

Dismissed from the University of Mississippi, second week of the fall term:

Samuel M. Teague, freshman, violation of the Honor Code.

Report of Right Rev. Nelson Hobbs, Dean of Students, University of Mississippi

Minutes of the Faculty Council, October 2, 1853

Those who are loitering about here when they owe
military service are hereby forewarned to look out
for squalls.

  -Opelousas Courier, September 17, 1864

Dear Mr. ~~Landry~~, Chip

I have in my possession the memoirs of John Simon Carrick, known in this city at the time of his death as Pierre Carriere. With the passing of his last surviving granddaughter, Suzette Carriere Laviolette, in November, they are now available for publishing if anyone so desires. After Mr. Carriere's death, they were held in a safe deposit box at the Hibernia Bank on Gravier and subsequently transferred over when Capitol One bought Hibernia after Katrina.

Mr. Bourgeois, the original custodian of these memoirs, and himself long since passed away, directed that a trust be set up, per the documents set forth by Mr. Carriere (Carrick) at the time of his death in 1925. You may remember the younger Mr. Bourgeois, who, when we began our careers in the seventies, was an old man himself. Old Mr. Bourgeois' law office stood on Canal Street. There is a Popeye's at that location now.

My secretary and I have read through the original manuscript and transcribed them. I have added footnotes here and there. Carriere's handwriting itself tells of his decline in his last days. Each entry becomes a little less legible. Toward the end it took the combined reading of my secretary, my paralegal, and me to decipher them.

I hope that these papers will see the light of day. Perhaps the Historic New Orleans Collection would be interested in publishing them. Please let me know if I can be of assistance.

I look forward to seeing you all at Endymion next week. Until then, my warmest regards to Celeste.

Sincerely,

Matt

Matthew Deville, Esq.

Take to Mr. Bourgeois on Canal Street.
Do not open under any circumstances.

Dear Mr. Bourgeois,

When you receive word of my passing, please come to my workshop behind the house here on Prytania. It is at the end of the alley past the port-cochere. The key you already have will give you access. My workshop is largely emptied except for a few projects that I will not complete. You may dispose of these as you wish. The storeroom is to your right as you come in the door. The second key, the brass one that I have enclosed, will open the lock. Once inside the storeroom, look to the left (as you enter the door). You will find it covered with a sheet of burlap behind the half-finished statue of an angel. My family does not know of its existence yet.

I remind you, though I'm sure I don't have to, that the documents I send you are to be kept under lock and key until the last of my grandchildren has passed. With any luck, that will be well after the year 2000. Just think of it, the year 2000! What sort of world will it be then?

Also enclosed with the key, you will find the memoirs of me, Pierre Carriere, which I have written in my own hand at my home here on Prytania Street, New Orleans, Louisiana. The events in these pages happened just as I state here, my failing memory notwithstanding. I apologize to whoever must read them. My handwriting was once a thing of beauty. Now, I'm afraid, it is barely legible. So it is for the aged.

Yours truly,

Pierre Carriere

1

On the day of the hanging, it rained, and when I say it rained, it came down a rain like pellets of white marble, crashing into everything, including his body as it dangled there from the rope and the oak beam. The rain ricocheted off the cross beam and the platform and the hood they had put over his head. It beat down on poor Prosperine and Te Jean, too, as he held her slumping body and they cried at the cold, hard end of things there on the scaffold. An end as cold and hard as the rain.

It was they who told me about it, though I also read the account of it in the Baton Rouge and New Orleans newspapers. That is because I wasn't there, and I carry that shame with me yet, even into my old age. He was my best friend, and I wasn't there. Oh dear God, forgive me, but I wasn't there.

I wasn't there as his old boots, three leather straps connected by a ring at the ankle on each side of each foot, old boots, well-worn boots that shuffled up the steps one at a time because his legs were shackled together like the hands behind his back, his hands so much like mine, like looking at mine in a mirror. Nor was I there as he turned in small steps to face the crowd from up there on the scaffold. Or as he turned to the hangman and asked him,

"You know what you doin'?"

It made the hangman pause, holding a limp halo of rope above the condemned man's head.

"Son," the hangman said, "I been hangin' folks since before you was born."

"Yes, I'm aware a that," he replied, "but do you know what you doin'?"

The hangman gave him this look, narrowed eyes, knitted brows, slightly canted head, a puzzled sort of look, then the man tells the hangman, "I want you to know I don't hold none of this against you. I know you just doin' what they tol' you."

"In thirty years a hangin'," the hangman says, "I ain't never had nobody say that. Usually they's cussin' or blubberin' or pissin' themselves. Twiced I had a man spit in my face."

"It's all right, then," the condemned said, and he bowed his head. The hangman slipped the noose over and put the knot under the chin so it would be quick.

The captain read the charges, John Simon Carrick, you have been found guilty by a military tribunal of insurrection and murder and this, that, and the other and sentenced to death by hanging. Then in his high-pitched voice, like the squawk of a gull, he asked the prisoner if he had any last words, and the prisoner just shook his head no.

The captain nodded to the hangman, who held the hood, just a dingy white sack, really, poised just over the prisoner's head. It was a sack much like we used to wear. The prisoner's brown eyes studied the hangman, who seemed to forget what it was he was about to do. Then he remembered. The hood went over the man's head, and I'm sure the world went black and the only sound was Prosperine sobbing and thunder in the distance. Then, as the floor dropped out from under his feet, there was another.

There's a sound a rope makes when a man's weight is suddenly applied to it, the sound of a piano string being tuned, a stretching, questioning sound. If you listen real close, you can hear it over the opening slap of a trap door (or the gallop of hoofs, if a horse is run out from under the man-how we usually did it). I wasn't there to hear it, but my conscience has played that sound for me regularly for sixty years now. I still wake up to it, sometimes.

The officer announced in a loud voice, so as to be heard over the thunder, "The crowd is ordered to disperse." The umbrellas sifted away like a garden of black flowers moving off on their roots. The muddy yard of the courtyard by the river was slick and brown, and the crowd of men and women picked their way through it carefully under a low, mismatched ceiling of black starbursts. The rain kept beating down on them, drumming like fingers on a canvas tent and splashing in small circles in the mud and puddles.

The rain had begun as he twirled slowly in the afternoon steam, a rain so hard that it struck the ground and then bounced up a good foot or so. There was thunder like the rattle of a sheet of tin or somebody pushing a big armoire across a plank floor. There was lightning, too, and it struck the belfry of the Episcopal Church, and the steeple fell.

The Yankee soldiers, black men with a white officer, stood by as the rain soaked everything and everybody. Their blue uniforms were midnight black from the dousing, midnight black men in midnight black uniforms. The dead man's pockets filled with water, and one of the soldiers used his bayonet to poke it so they wouldn't get the burial party more doused when they came under umbrellas to take him down. Another soldier used his bayonet to saw him down. It took a while, the dull blade singing and groaning in the downpour as it slid ineffectively against the rope. The officer in charge examined the bayonet and told the soldier, "This bayonet's got to be sharp, soldier, not like this. Sharp."

"Yussuh," the soldier said.

Then the other soldier, whose bayonet was apparently sharper, succeeded in sawing through the rope. The body splashed down into the mud under the platform. It landed in a heap as if the condemned were merely sleeping on his side.

Even after the crowd had evaporated away, a man on a black horse with a blonde mane was there, sitting tall in the saddle under an umbrella he'd taken from a Negro woman, leaving her to get doused in the rain. He was a tall man with sandy hair under a stovepipe hat. His swallowtail coat hung over the flanks of the black horse.

There was a crack of lightning that made the soldiers flinch, but the man only looked up slowly. And when he did, the flash revealed his eyes, the size and color of nickels. And what's more, the semicircle of a scar on one cheek, the scar he had gotten because of me.

The girl was there. She and her father watched with satisfaction as the body twirled slowly in the rain and then as it splashed in the mud. She and the man moved up, his arm around her under a simple umbrella. The sack was removed from the deceased's head. The girl looked from the dead man's blue face to her father's face and back again. Her expression fell from one of righteous satisfaction to perplexed, and then from perplexed to horrified.

"That's not him, Papa. That's not him. They hung the wrong man. They hung the wrong man, Papa." She pushed her head into her father's chest, and she cried.

"Are you sure?" her father asked.

All the girl could do was sob. She knew what I knew. They had hung

4

an innocent man.

This was all secondhand information relayed to me by Te Jean. The rest of us had gotten a demijohn of rum, and we drank it in the barn loft we were staying in at the time. It faced a field that spring had painted a fiery green, a bright green that glowed in the rain. The air had that metal smell, and the heavy drops of rain rattled against the shakes of the roof.

We got drunk and watched it rain. All these years later I can see them, dark shapes illuminated by the gray light of a rainy day. Te Jean sitting on the floor with his back to a bale of hay, his clothes soaked, his hair wet and matted down to his head. His legs were parted, the left one twitching, bouncing nervously up and down off the barn floor in small movements. He and Prosperine had been the only ones of us with the courage to have been there. The rest of us stayed behind and stared out the loft door at the rain streaking down. We were all crying in some manner, some silently, some sobbing, some with fingers laced over our foreheads as we studied the floor, some wiping at tears with the heels of our hands. We had seen each other laugh, dance, work, shout, sing. Never cry. Not before that day in the rain in the barn in the woods, when our terror held us captive in the loft. I, for one, had never cried so bitterly in all my life. Not as a child, and not as a man.

Across the pasture, cows were gathered under a live oak. Tails that were normally swishing at flies were limp in the rain as they gathered in a tight group to keep dry.

We weren't so much scared of the Yankees, who had put the prisoner to death, as much as we were of Teague. And I more so. I had fought the Yankees, but I had betrayed Teague. Really, I suppose, we had betrayed each other.

While we cowered in that barn loft, the dead man was placed in a simple box, the type that artillery shells came in, big enough to hold a man. The box was put in the wagon. The undertaker rode on the buckboard, pulling from a bottle that he tucked inside his coat pocket in between swigs. Prosperine walked along side of the wagon, pulling the hem of her dress above the muddy streets of Baton Rouge, past the great castle of a capital and down the levee where a boat sat getting up steam and waiting to head downriver, back to St. Matthew Parish.

Several burly Negro stevedores took the artillery box and its occupant, gingerly easing up the gangplank onto the boat ahead of the undertaker, who continued to reach in and out of his coat pocket. Prosperine waited on the bank as the big paddlewheel slapped at the water and the twin stacks belched black smoke into the air and the boat made the channel and bore away the body in the artillery shell box. Later that day, we put together our money and sent her downstream on the next packet. Money was tight for us just then, but we felt that one of us needed to be there when they buried him. And, besides, a woman was less likely to be arrested. We were wanted men in those days.

The undertaker was a St. Matthew Parish man whose name escapes me now, sixty years later, but it was widely known that the man liked to have a drink on days that ended in Y and if an eighth day had been added that didn't end in a Y, well, he would have given that day serious consideration also. After a three-day bender, a magnificent, rambling thing I'm sure, as I've had a few, some say he woke and found out that the coffin was empty. He was hungover and dry, embarrassed by his lapse and the lack of an occupant in the box. That's the story, but it's the kind of story that some believe and some don't. A Negro man who worked for the undertaker swears he assisted with the embalming and put the man's body in the casket. But the assistant was a man who was loyal to a fault, and it was widely believed that he would never say anything against his employer.

"Ain't no doubt," the assistant said. "I seen him. He was in there."

Prosperine went to see him the next day, hoping to bring a Rosary to drape it in the deceased's hands. The undertaker met her at the side door, dry and squinting, looking like some exotic bird with his white hair askew and a bulbous red beak of a nose. He was hesitant, waffling in that weightless space between drunk and hungover, I'm sure.

"Let me see him! Let me see *mon defan*,[1]" she implored.

"I'm sorry Madame, his face was so swollen, so blue. I couldn't do nothin' with him. It just ain't my best work. Best we leave the casket closed." He stretched out his hand, and Prosperine absently handed over

---

[1] My dearly departed

6

the Rosary. "I'll put it in there myself," the man said. "Drape it over his hands real nice, I promise." His hand perched itself on her shoulder in that way of undertakers.

They hurriedly placed the box in the crypt, a simple above-ground arrangement, devoid of any decoration other than a name. The men who bore the simple rectangular box said that it was heavy like it contained a man. Those who said it was empty said the funeral man had put sand in it, and those who said there was a body in it said no, there was someone in there.

Filled or unfilled, manned or unmanned, they buried it, and the undertaker avoided any embarrassment. In the days that followed, the question I went to sleep with, dreamed of, and woke up with was this: was the tomb with my name on it empty?

2

I've left directions through my attorney, Mr. Bourgeois on Canal Street, to see to it that these memoirs stay unpublished until the last of my grandchildren passes away, which, God willing, will be well into the next century.

My time, however, is short, and my mind is groping and grasping as if it were playing a game of blind man's bluff with my memory. Things that occurred decades ago are clear as a bell, but recent things are hazy as if viewed through steam, including who lives in this house with me. They all seem pretty partial to me. They bring me things to eat, sit me in a chair on the balcony. They take me by the hand and lead me on walks to places that also are vaguely familiar. They bring me pencil and paper, but seem doubtful that I write anything coherent. They humor me as if I were a child drawing fanciful pictures.

There is a woman who lives downstairs. Her name escapes me now. I know she's important to me, that she's played a very meaningful part in my life. But I cannot for the life of me remember her name. Perhaps she is my daughter or maybe a hired girl, though she can't be a girl or my daughter because I believe she's my age. My mind is failing, slipping slowly; I'm sure of it.

She takes me to Mr. Toussaint's barber shop on Napoleon Avenue where the men greet each other with a kiss on both cheeks and ask, *"Comment ça va, boo?"* and Mr. Alphonse cuts my hair as he has since old Jefferson Davis died and was paraded through the streets on the way to his judgment. The woman takes me there to get my haircut and sees to it that I'm fed and that I have clean clothes. I can hear her sing to children and shush them when they get loud, scolding them gently, "Shh, Papere's trying to make *do-do*, sha."

On days like today, with the wind coming off the river from the south, I can smell whatever they might be unloading at the Poydras Street wharf. The soft, sweet creamy smell of bananas, the sharp yellow tang of pineapples, the rich brown of coffee. I can hear the shouts and singing of the men who unload those ships, young men in their prime just as I was sixty years ago. The sounds and smells reach me on the south wind, to my balcony that looks over the brick walls of the Lafayette Cemetery, over the grove of monuments, many of which I have sculpted myself.

The smells of this city, delightful and generous, are a far cry from my boyhood, which was spent in north Louisiana, either Bienville or Claiborne Parish. My daddy always told the Bienville tax man, sent by the sheriff, that we were just across the line in Claiborne. Then he told the Claiborne man it was Bienville. Each left satisfied. Neither wanted to spend a moment longer at our place than necessary. The smell was horrendous, but, of course, we were nose-blind to it, the smell of my childhood.

My daddy was a tanner, a short, powerful man who kept a cigar to his lips and exhaled smoky curses with every other breath. The aroma of his cigars is also the scent of my childhood, just as his curses are the sounds. He knew the usual repertoire, but for variety, he would twist the Lord's name into all sorts of poses and shapes and brilliant, inventive combinations like an artist with a tongue for a brush. All without ever looking up from his work, scudding the fat off the underside of a cowhide or pig skin, launching into song, usually only a bar or two and always some bawdy saloon ditty. His suspenders hanging off his shoulders and down to

8

his thighs as limp as afterthoughts. We were two men, one grown, one his miniature, forced to be grown out in the midst of the wilderness. Two men, a man and his boy, who were obviously related by our black hair, though his was thinning to show a small plate of scalp at his crown. Mine has remained full even into old, white age, even now at close to eighty.

My name when I was born was Carrick. The way a leaf carries on the wind, I've ended up here in New Orleans, a city that changes itself from French to Irish to German to Italian every few decades, each group met by the Negroes and the Jews. It's a strange soup, this home of mine. How I got here, and how any of us arrive where we arrive, is strange and sprinkled heavily with chance.

A man named Carreagh in Queen's County, Ireland, kills his English landlord and then takes the first ship bound for anywhere. When it arrives in Wilmington, North Carolina, he drifts into the heartland like a vapor. Somewhere in the Appalachians, he marries a Cherokee woman and loses the Catholic faith, if he ever had it in the first place. They settle in Tennessee and then Alabama, moving, moving, restless. They have several children who, on coming of age, scatter into the countryside like dandelion fronds on a spring breeze.

One of them is a son who has lost the fair hair and bright eyes of his father in favor of the coal black eyes and hair of his Cherokee mother. Like his siblings, he sets off west into the wilderness. He spells his name Carrick now instead of Carreagh, the phonetic spelling of a semi-literate man. On wandering in north Louisiana, he meets a local girl, and she domesticates him. They settle in Bienville Parish. Or Claiborne Parish, depending on which tax man came to call.

Those two were my mama and daddy.

But I never knew my mother. She had almost died having my older siblings, who themselves died soon after birth. They were all boys except for one girl, those brothers and that sister that I never knew. Then, when I was born, my mama died and I lived. It seemed that someone was to die in the process of being born, as if there were only room for one more Carrick in our little clearing, and if one was born and stayed, well, then one had to be swapped out. All my life, I've tried to imagine my mother's face and wondered if she spent her last lucid moments looking at my little, pudgy round self, swaddled in amongst blankets. I've wondered if she had even a brief tear of happiness before she departed this world. My curiosity has forever spun on itself, never finding satisfaction.

My daddy was a man who would return from market with the wagon empty of hides and pockets almost empty of money, hungover and dry from spending what was supposed to have been our sustenance. He would sway on the buckboard, the reins loose in his hands, singing one of his favorite songs, sometimes the one about the amorous antics of "Dear Old Aunt Mabel," every other line rhyming with "able"-table, and so forth-I'm sure you can guess the rest. The other tune was one about "Ol' Toothless Nell," one I never heard in its entirety because Daddy would always break down in hilarious, gut-splitting laughter halfway through it, usually the verse that went "shaped like a bell, and she'll never tell..."

Our place was really in Bienville Parish, a place where the rocky red earth had tried to push up into mountains and either failed or became disinterested, leaving only a few dozen square miles of knobby hills and the people like us that inhabited them. Those hills were just big enough to exert pressure on the earth, to coax out little unreliable springs, flailing, faltering trickles that tasted like warm, liquid iron. We had one, though in the summer, just like the earth below it, it either failed or decided to take its water somewhere else. We had a cistern also, for times such as those. We made it ourselves, my daddy and me, a skill essential to men who lived apart from society. My skill with carpentry would alter my course in life.

The only intrusion into our clearing was the arrival of my Aunt Cora every Sunday afternoon. She was my mother's sister, maiden name of Driskill. They were kin to the people who the mountain is named for, the Louisiana earth's best, though failed, effort to reach heaven.

Aunt Cora was the wife of one of the professors at the college in Mt. Lebanon, a gracious woman who felt an obligation to me, her nephew. Every Sunday, she brought a satchel of books, all sorts, mostly Horatio Alger-type nonsense in which Dick pulls himself up by his bootstraps and forges on to a self-made fortune through honesty and rectitude and the tutelage of a kind father-figure. I read them all, most of them ten times or more, though I could never see how they had anything to do with our stinking outpost on the road between Mt. Lebanon and Athens.

"Working on the Sabbath again?" Aunt Cora would ask my father as she alighted from the carriage she had driven up the five miles from her house.

"Why not?" Daddy would say. "Got to eat on the Sabbath, too, don't a man?"

She always let it go. She had argued the point before but had gotten nowhere, since in the end, Daddy had refused to recognize the authority of the Bible, Aunt Cora's trump card. ("Written by men who didn't wear drawers," he would say.) I'm sure she was glad that she hadn't come upon us when one or both of us were leaning against a tree in yellow, arching midstream, as she sometimes did, her bonnet looking away with her hand poised there as a shield, extra insurance against an unwanted sight.

She stood there every Sunday as I scudded hides side by side with my daddy, until finally he would look up at her and then at me and say, "All right. An hour."

The hour would fortify itself with another hour and another as Daddy ate the meal Aunt Cora brought and then as he napped in the shade of the back porch. Meanwhile, I would read to her and then practice my penmanship on a sheaf of papers she brought, a pen and a glass inkwell full of black ink. Despite all the washing, the side of my hand always left a shadowy imprint, a set of lines like wavering furrows on a hillside. She always said I had the hand and eye of an artist, a fine hand for someone who did such hard labor preparing the skins of animals. She would trace out a delicate letter, and I would copy it curve for curve, line for line, my tongue tip at the corner of my mouth in extreme concentration. *Excellent*, she would say in a low voice. To see my handwriting now, you would have a hard time believing it, but it was once beautiful and flowing, the hand of an artist.

My Aunt Cora cut a corpulent figure, her skirts fanning out a little to the horizontal until they fell over her hips and headed to the ground like the shape of a bell, like Ol' Toothless Nell. She always wore a double dose of rosewater, and I suspect now that it was to hold back the smell of the Carrick and Son tanning yard. An hour was all she was allowed, and an hour was probably all she could stand, but, for my betterment, she held on longer. God bless her.

Afterward, she would vault back up into her carriage, a nondescript black thing pulled by a dappled mare whose hide flinched away flies as if reminding my daddy *stay away-I'm still using it.* She would bid my daddy farewell, and he would grunt back to her without looking up. She visited us, just me, really, for years that way, cold, rain, heat, sun. I never thanked her, and I never thought of thanking her until it was too late. It has been the second biggest regret of my life, right after failing my best friend with my absence on the day they hung him.

And when Daddy would go into town, Shreveport, usually, he would leave me with Aunt Cora, and I would get a chance to play with the town boys, though Mount Lebanon was just a small college town then. My visits would begin with a series of baths. For Aunt Cora, the finishing point for me was when the cat no longer found my scent interesting. Then I was clean enough.

The town boys knew all sorts of mean names to call me and all sorts of jibes to try on me, the worse being that out where my daddy and I lived, we had to break wind to get fresh air. I bore their insults so as not to be a poor guest. It was when they made sport of my Aunt Cora and her tremendous girth that I resorted to my fists. I was good at it, naturally good at it, and there was no more teasing about our smell or about Aunt Cora.

I did, however, return to my Aunt Cora and Uncle Horace's house with a big lip and bloody knuckles. Uncle Horace was an esoteric man who could quote Latin (correctly, as opposed to Sam Teague) and who, for fun, worked algebra and geometry problems. He was not a proponent of fighting.

"While you are in our house, there will be no tolerance for pugilistics," he said as he smushed his lips together in a look of exasperation that drew the ring of his whiskers tighter around his face.

"Yessir," I said. I didn't know what pugilistics were, and as long as I could fight when I needed to, I didn't care. When I finally came to learn that pugilistics was a fancy term for fighting, I still was not ready to give up. I was not about to let the town boys insult me or my daddy or my Aunt Cora. Uncle Horace, though, would've been fair game, but they seemed uninterested in him.

The visits to Aunt Cora's grew fewer and fewer until finally the only times I would see her were on her Sunday visits, and then those became equally as rare. I had become a young man.

3

I awake to see the child. He's sitting on a chair at my bedside, his hands tucked under his legs. He swings them, and his feet bounce lightly off the chair. He's young enough to still wear knee pants. When he sees me awaken, he hastily takes off his cap and puts it in his lap. He knows it's what a gentleman does, he takes off his hat indoors. I want to smile at him but the apoplexy, or whatever it is, won't let me do it. I just look at him. I know my mouth is drawn down into a frown. It betrays my inner emotion, joy at seeing the young fellow.

"Good morning, Papere," he says.

"Ger-ming," I say back, all I can say. Thankfully, I can still write, or else these memoirs would go unrecorded.

"Mamere made *tarte bouillie*. Do you want me to get us some?" he asks.

I grunt and give a slight shake of my head. He stares at his shoes. He is six or eight. An auto mutters outside the window, followed by a brass band and a bass drum, slow, sorrowful music. A funeral procession is approaching the cemetery on Prytania just across the street.

The boy looks over his shoulder and then gets up from the chair. He holds his hat in his hand, a brown tweed cap that matches his knicker pants. He watches the procession out the window and down below. His attention spins as he loses interest in the mourners. He turns around, and he asks a question that I've been asked before. Sometimes they ask me in English; sometimes they ask me in French.

"Papere, how you lose your finger?"

Dozens of children have asked me this, and it's always been a great source of amusement for me to make up answers. An alligator ate it. A bear bit it off. The Rougarou pulled it off. The pirate Jean Lafitte cut it off because I refused to tell him where I had buried his treasure. All

13

foolishness, but each fib was believed for a time until each child grew old enough to know better. None of them ever got the truth.

The truth is, when I was a boy, about ten or so, I cut my finger with a knife. I had disregarded the advice of my daddy: never put your hand in front of a blade. I was trimming some fat from the underside of a cow hide when I got a little too close to my finger. I didn't even feel it when it broke the skin.

Not until the next day when I woke with the finger as red and angry as an erection, weeping yellow pus and as painful as all get out. I showed it to my daddy who told me to go and "warsh it real good." I did, but that night it was worse, and I felt achy and tired. My daddy examined it in the firelight and pressed hard on it. *Mashed on it*, as they say in north Louisiana.

"Shit-fire!" I said, and he chuckled over my mastery of one of his favorite phrases.

He put me to bed, thinking that a good night's rest would aid its healing, but the next day I woke up in my Aunt Cora's spare bedroom. I vaguely remembered someone sitting on me as I lay on Aunt Cora's dining room table, and someone else holding out my arm as a doctor used an instrument to remove the finger. She was there that day, my Aunt Cora was, a short, immense figure tilting forward and back in a rocking chair as her voluminous skirts rustled with the movement. She smiled at me, a smile of wholesome goodness, cheerful kindness. I went to scratch my cheek with my finger and found a bandage-covered emptiness instead.

In the great scheme of things, it was not a great loss, as I had nine spares, and I always shot a gun right-handed. I could hold a scudder and a knife, though now I took great care to keep everything behind the blade. I could plant and harvest, dig potatoes, husk corn, wring a chicken's neck. I could chop and saw and hammer. I could scud and trim a hide. The middle finger fell right in for all the chores the index finger had taken care of.

But the loss of that index finger would incriminate me years later. All for the careless nip, the inattention of a ten-year-old, a fraction of an inch.

4

Boys are playing out in the street with that oblong ball that is becoming all the rage now, this football, they call it. The little fellows dream of playing for Tulane on Saturdays. I watch them from the balcony as they run and tussle. I think it is the kind of game we would have enjoyed back in the days of Mount Lebanon and visits to my Aunt Cora and the town boys. It is a game, as I understand it, that is played on a big rectangular field and involves trying to advance the ball while the others try to keep you from doing so. Down there on Prytania, the boys are content with the narrow street. They pause when a wagon or an auto passes, one boy with the ball under his arm as the boys all huff and puff from their exertions. When the street is clear, they line up again.

The years that I was their age passed by in a whirlwind, and I grew up as boys do when they think no one is looking. When war broke out, Daddy couldn't understand how I would want to join up and leave what he considered a twisted little patch of paradise out in the woods, a colony of lucrative rancidness where a man could pause from his work, produce himself out of his trousers and urinate without ever having to so much as step behind a tree, a free and easy lifestyle. Perhaps he didn't think there was anything better out there in the world. More likely, I understand, now that I'm a father, he knew I would never come back.

"Mark my words, son," he said as he straightened up from his work, putting one hand on his hip while the other pulled the stub of a cigar from his teeth, "At the end of this thing, if there ever is an end, it won't be one side or t'other that wins. It'll be the man what sells the guns to 'em both. He'll be the winner."

He stood there with a scudder in his hand, holding it limply at his side. I stood there with a sack drawn up on a stick over my shoulder. Neither of us said anything. Neither of us looked at the other.

To have told him that I was proud of him would have been a lie. To have told him that I loved him would have been closer to the truth but just plain odd and not in keeping with how we conversed. So I just said goodbye, turning from him and the smell of his cigar and the yellow-brown stench of the tanning yard, turning to the rocky red earth and the orange cinders of the Mt. Lebanon-Athens Road as it ascended a little rise of a hill. When I got to the top of it, I turned around. He was a small figure on the edge of the road in front of our place, looking back at me with his hands on his hips. I waited for him to acknowledge me, a wave, perhaps, but he hastily put his cigar to his mouth and turned back to his work. I wonder now if he felt I had betrayed him.

In camp, in Minden, I fell in with Re-Pete. Oh, but if I could remember his name. He was an earnest, excitable boy who spoke nonstop, and we became good friends because I listened to him nonstop. We studied the tracts that they gave us, the New Testament, *Hardee's Tactics*. We listened to the preaching and watched the baptisms of those whom the prospect of death in the coming months had converted into religious men. Then, after a week or two of the tedium of camp life, Re-Pete and I visited the traveling wagons and discovered the double-jangling bounce of being ridden by a Dutch gal, the burn of whiskey, whether a flush beat a straight. We decided that this soldiering thing would be first rate.

And I excelled at being a soldier. I bested the drill sergeant in hand-to-hand, I could rapidly stab the manikin, a shirt stuffed with straw, and my marksmanship was superior to any other.

Marching I did not care for, nor did any other soldier. We endured it, but no one enjoyed it. It was only made bearable by singing. Lift up your burdens with singing, Honoré always said, though this was in the time before I'd met him.

We soldiers learned and sang all the marching songs, and then we invented new ones and sang those. Re-Pete and I sang some of the bawdy saloon ditties I knew courtesy of my daddy, and, when our company picked them up and gave them a big voice, our officers shushed us with threats of punishment. They did not want to allow such vulgar merriment to sully the sacred business of training to kill others.

And then one day we began marching, and it wasn't just our company or our regiment. It was the whole Confederate army. We camped at night, and marched and sang the next day, and the next and the next. We marched singing through Arkansas, clear through to Missouri. And then the officers had us stop the singing. We were told to be quiet.

When morning broke, we marched a little more and then we waited. We could hear them. Maybe they could hear us. The drums were the first sound. And then the drums stopped, and there was silence again. And then the preparatory clicking of thousands of men loading. And then the roar of gunfire and the flash of muzzles and a cloud of sharp-smelling smoke. Men fell, and the ones who didn't rushed forward.

I found that I was very good at it. Killing is what I mean.

Cain slew Abel in a fit of rage and jealousy. And I imagine once he'd done it, once he'd seen his brother lifeless and bloodied on the ground, rather than feel remorse, he'd had a thrill that made him feel the equal of God. We, Cain's descendants, have been doing it ever since. Perhaps Abel was the more peaceful, level-headed of the two, and if he had lived, we would have been more like him.

But in our camp at night, I dreamed of it the way some men dream of cards or the drink or women or home and the smell of their mama's cooking. My mind practiced it, over and over. Rip open the cartridge. Tamp down the powder and the bullet with the ramrod. Place a percussion cap. Shoulder the weapon. Aim. Fire. Rip-tamp-cap-shoulder-aim-fire. Rip-tamp-cap-shoulder-aim-fire. Over and over until it was second nature. A cause for excitement, an intense, perverse pleasure.

Weeks and months would go by in which there were no battles, only the drudgery of camp life, picket duty, bad, monotonous food, stale jokes, packs of stained and bent playing cards, all played to the tune of the army cough rippling over a hillside of tents and campfires.

The prospect of the next battle was the only thing that kept me sane. As we marched through the dust and then the rain and then the mud, my mind fixed on it, the wealth of blue, brass-buttoned targets. I never once had the thought that they could shoot me. It was as if I had discounted the fact that they might have guns, too.

To see a man far away, to see his chest burst or his shoulder give way, or best of all, his forehead sink in as his hat flies off, well I tell you, it's a rare kind of thing; nothing breathes the air of immortality than assigning another man his mortality. A man develops a taste for it, like some men develop a taste for whiskey or cards or women. To see it from far off and know you did it, or could have done it, as they [sic] are men all around you doing the same thing, loading and firing. Some were scared of getting hit themselves, and it was them that tended to catch it. I was never scared of that; I was too wrapped up in the pure animal joy of hunting the other man.

The other ones, the scared ones, would frequently jam two cartridges down at one time or leave their ramrod in. It would fly off between the lines when they took a shot, and then they would scramble through our lines, stepping over our dead and wounded, looking for another ramrod. Things like that would get you hit. Inattention could be deadly.

I was grazed a few times, lightly singed by the whizzing heat of a bullet while men around me fell. My eyes and my mind were on the lines of men in blue across from me. My heart was pounding for the next shot and whatever it might reap. Some fellows shot for officers, but I made no distinction. I always went for the one I saw first, usually a private. There were so many more of them, you see.

It was in Arkansas that I got my nickname. We had a lieutenant that liked to give them out. Well, I was friends with a boy from Natchitoches, and we went everywhere together, played cards, visited the sutlers' wagons, shared mess together, laughed at the men who passed out religious tracts, visited the tents of the women who were called camp followers. All those soldier things. The lieutenant started calling me Pete and him Re-Pete. We were good friends, messmates, he and I, and I find it strange now in old age that I can't remember his real name.

One day during the siege at Vicksburg, Re-Pete and I were talking. The sharpshooters, ours and theirs, were taking shots. You might hear three or four bursts in a morning, just infrequent enough to put your hand on top of your hat and squat down, which became a reflex. The weather was getting hot, and rations were getting smaller. Water was scarce, and we were all thirsty. So very, very thirsty, so dry that it was hard sometimes to form words. We waited in the heat for something to happen, though whatever that something was, it was bound to be unpleasant. Our coats were stretched on sticks over our heads to give us a little patch of festering shade.

Re-Pete was talking about digging a well. It was a fanciful idea that would have been fruitless, for if you were to have dug a well, the filth of the trench would've just quickly run down in it. But the way he was talking about it, the water we would get out of it would be as pure and clear as the water that Moses knocked out of the rock with his staff. Across the way, I'm sure boys just like us were engaged in the same sort of whimsical young man talk, except that they had plenty of water and food.

He paused for a moment in his description of our desert oasis. I looked over, and Re-Pete is looking up to the sky. His eyes were open as if he were looking at clouds and trying to make them into shapes of things, and I caught myself wondering if my Cherokee grandmother had ever been able to conjure the rain.

I followed his eyes up into the sky and to prod him I said, "Now couldn't you just drink a whole tub of that crystal clear water right now?" When he didn't say anything, I looked back down to him, and he had the same expression on his face. I took off his hat and there it was, just over the ear opposite me. A dark red hole that had trickled out dark red onto his neck. I found out after the surrender that it was probably ol' Coonskin[2] what had done it.

Well, you, like everyone else, knows the story of Vicksburg. Our Righteous Cause was defeated by Their Righteous Cause. We ran out of everything, food, water, men. The only thing that stopped me from fighting was that we ran out of cartridges. And the only thing that we didn't run out of was men in blue to shoot at. It was the only thing that would have stopped me. I will tell it to you plainly; I had developed a passion for killing.

Pemberton surrendered us, and, in truth, most were relieved, but as for me, it broke my heart. We stacked arms, and, though I didn't cry, I looked sad enough for one of their officers to put an arm around my shoulders and say, "You've done your duty, soldier." But I didn't care about duty. I was sorry the killing was over. I would never again be engaged in The Great Hunt, or so I thought.

They gave us rations while they paroled us. Men were eating like wild

---

[2] Second lieutenant Henry C. Foster, otherwise known as Old Coonskin, was a sharpshooter with the 23rd Indiana Infantry Regiment. He was famously deadly from his perch atop a stack of crossties across from the 3rd Louisiana Redan at Vicksburg.

animals, dull tapping, scraping tin spoons on tin mess plates while the Yankees watched us. Some of the looks were pretty horrified. We were thin as scarecrows, an army of rattling, loose-jointed skeletons.

They lined us up, all of us as dry and thin as a September cornfield, and they went down the roll. The Yankee officer had a voice that was eat up with New England, a voice like the sound of a nail being pried up out of a plank. Men had trouble recognizing their names, and the man, sitting there with the list before him, was getting exasperated having to repeat himself. At last he came to me.

"Carrick, Simon." The officer made a face as his tongue probed his teeth for a stray remnant of the boiled beef they'd fed us.

"Carrick. John Simon." He looked over the ovals of his wire rimmed spectacles.

"Carrick! John! Simon!"

With that last one, the Boston really came out. The officer's voice cracked as he raised it. It was sharper, angrier, impatient. See, I was used to my army nickname, Pete. I stepped forward.

"Yes sir."

"Raise your right hand," he said mechanically. His pen hovered over the parole papers where my name, *Pvt. John Simon Carrick*, was written in a flourish, as if on an invitation to some fancy ball. "Do you swear (*sway-uh*) never again to take up arms (*oms*) against the United States?" He yawned and smacked his mouth in the aftermath of it.

"I do, sir." And I took the pen and signed the oath.

But what's an oath to a man like me? Or, I should say, a man like I was?

5

The weather is hot today, but as I do not move much, it does not affect me as much as it does other, more energetic people. The dog sits out here on the balcony with me, yawning and panting away at the heat. Clouds are forming, rolling in from the south and the Gulf, as big and white and billowing as the face of God. It will rain again this afternoon, as it always does this time of year, and we will have half an hour of respite before the heat regroups. So it was that summer in Vicksburg.

We were supposed to have reported to parole camps to await some sort of bureaucratic procedure, but most of us had had enough of that kind of foolishness, be it Union or Confederate. We decided that we'd just furlough ourselves. We had our parole papers. That was all we needed. It was probably a good thing. Some of the men were marched off to Meridian and Demopolis, and some went to Camp Martin[3] in Indiana and didn't come back for quite some time.

We crossed the river in groups of fifteen or twenty or so in a boat about as big as the porch out here. Thing had a steam engine that clattered and belched. It was the second time in my life to cross the river, but not the last. The river was low, and the heat was on, baking the mud flats at the water's edge into a cracked mosaic. My friends and I alighted and left the river and Vicksburg behind us, traveling back into Louisiana through fallow cotton fields choked with weeds and last year's crop still on the boll. One by one we fell out, bidding one another adieu, those left telling stories about the departed as if they had died, and we would never see them again, which was likely.

Then it was my turn, and I turned on the Mount Lebanon-Athens Road and headed up home, wondering what tales they were telling about me, dearly departed Pete. What would they say, knowing they would likely never see me again? That Pete sure could kill a man, now couldn't he? Or, remember that time he and Re-Pete and them two bawdy gals had themselves a time? What about that time the sergeant challenged him and what did Pete do? Well, he threw that cocksure bastard to the ground and put his bayonet to his throat, now didn't ol' Pete! Yes sir! Would've gotten strung up if we hadn't vouched that he was challenged.

Vouched for him. If they hadn't vouched for me. The same thing I failed to do. Will I be damned for it?

The voices of my friends drifted away down the road to Minden as I

---

[3] Camp Morton, Indiana.

walked in the red dust of the road home. When I got there, I was surprised by the absence of any stench, the odd fragrance of home. All I smelled was the green of the woods, pines and pin oaks. I thought perhaps I'd gotten use to the bad odors of camp life, the sweat and funk of thousands of unwashed men, and that the old smell of home was still there, just so far back in my mind as to be lost in the background.

The door was partially open, and I pushed on it, and it complained. The waddling scurry of a possum flashed. It paused to hiss at me, small-toothed, beady-eyed, pink-mouthed. I suppose he said all he had to say, and he ambled off into the woods. I beat on our beds, first mine, then my daddy's, to scare off any other creatures. There were none. The cast-off quilts that Aunt Cora had given us were dusty. The roof had leaked, and a green ring of mold had taken hold on the corner of one of quilts.

I stood and listened to the howling silence. Gradually, like I was underwater, I began floating around our old home, the womb of my first memories. My hand reached out and picked things up, my mind thinking, "Is this the last time I'll hold this pan? Is this the last time I'll walk through this door?"

In that hour or less, I haunted that house, a silent being that coasted from one end of the cabin to the other. In the cupboard, I found penmanship papers I had done with Aunt Cora and figures I had carved in idle hours by firelight and by sunlight. A bird. A bobcat. A horse. My daddy had saved them there in that simple pine cupboard. It was only then that I knew how proud he was of me. He had never had the words to tell me.

There was also half a jug of whiskey, an old brown jug with the stopper still in. I pulled out the stopper and took a swig. If I had been the kind of person who cries, I would have. But I wasn't, and I didn't. I took another swig and surveyed our home, the tannery outside with several hides still hanging, nailed to the pines, the flies long since given up on them.

Then I went down to Mt. Lebanon, looking for Aunt Cora and Uncle Horace Sims. The college was a hospital now, and a sign read, *Classes suspended, students all off to war.* Aunt Cora's house, a nice little cottage once lined with blue and pink hydrangeas and orange daylillies, was populated with men in linen pajamas on the porch, smoking and talking quietly and waving away flies. Flowers in pots had been placed, a desperate attempt at cheerfulness amid the misery.

A man on duty, an old man whom I remember to be the druggist in Mount Lebanon, was managing the hospital.

I asked him, "Can you tell me where I can find Cora Sims?"

"You Simon Carrick?" he asked me. He had a beard like a goat and small round spectacles. His shirt sleeves were rolled up against the heat. A little, wiry, bespectacled goat.

"Yessir," I said.

"Quit Louisiana for California, she and her husband the professor. Left you a letter."

He got up slowly with a long scrape of the chair legs against the floor, an old man pressed into the work and pace of a young man. I know that feeling now. He looked under his spectacles at the rows of vertical slots on his desk and pulled one out, looked at it, pushed it back in, then another and another. At last, he said, "Why, here. Here it is."

I recognized the graceful characters of my Aunt Cora's handwriting, sweeping, curving, arching vowels and consonants. I'd kept the letter for years, but I've also lost it for years, and I wonder if anyone will discover it among my things after I'm gone.

I read it, and the beautiful characters rendered the stark news to me. My daddy had been beaten to death by a mob for refusing to hurrah for Jeff Davis. Daddy had told them that a war had never been fought for a sorrier cause and, as my Aunt Cora tactfully put it, "of a certain intimate activity they could do to Mr. Davis and his horse."

Years later, as Mr. Davis' funeral cortege was making its way down the streets of New Orleans, I smiled to myself, knowing exactly the unvarnished thing he had said. Aunt Cora said the men had pressed him, and that he'd refused to take it back, which is exactly what I would have expected of him.

I looked up from the letter as two Negro orderlies carried a litter down from upstairs, the form of someone departed pressing up under a sheet. The men carefully watched their footing as they negotiated the stairs. They made the first floor and Aunt Cora's parlor, and the druggist asked them, "McInnis?"

"Yessuh," one of them said.

The druggist peered under his glass ovals and the thin brass wire that held them together and made a line through an entry that said 'Private Horatio B. McInnis.' Then he got up to open the door for the litter bearers.

The men made their way through sunlight and shade to the burying ground where Private McInnis would be fed to the earth. I tucked the letter into my knapsack, the one that the Confederate Army had so thoughtfully given me in exchange for my youth and innocence, and I went back to our clearing and packed up some things.

What do you take from your childhood home, when it's your last time there? What's important? Do you take the practical? The nostalgic? Or do you just leave it all and let time and mother nature devour it slowly, silently? Let the rain dissolve it? Let the crows and the mice come and gather what bits of it they please to make their nests with? Let the Virginia creeper vault over, around, and through it like green fire?

The weight of nostalgia and unwanted emotion was pressing on me, so hurriedly I took Daddy's tools, a hammer, a saw, a pair of planes, a drawknife, a bit brace, all with our name CARRICK, carved in them. A block plane, a set of three chisels. A workman's apron. The rest I left for the woods, which were already testing the edges of the tanning yard with leafy green fingers.

But the things you choose to carry with you get heavy, sometimes, so heavy that you have no choice but to stop and rest from time to time. And where you stop sometimes determines when you move on.

6

This house is on Prytania Street. This I know. And there is a woman who lives here also. Her name, I do not know, but I have lived here a long time, and she has lived here a long time, too. I wish I could remember her name. I think she is Mexican or a Cuban or maybe a Tagalog.[4] Or a Syrian. No, not a Syrian.

Her hair is gray now, though I know it hasn't always been, the same way mine hasn't always been. Her eyes are her striking feature, green and luminous and round. Those have not changed. People who meet her always remember her eyes. To them, she is "the green-eyed woman" or "that pretty older lady with the green eyes," not "that woman with the tan skin" or "that Indian woman" or "that mulatto woman."

She comes from downstairs when she is finished doing what she does down there, still keeping a house, a house where a dog barks greetings to the visiting children and adults, merry canine shouting. She and the dog come upstairs and sit with me, she patiently crocheting or tatting lace while I write or nap. The dog sleeps at the foot of my bed, and the woman fusses at him to get off. But the dog just rolls on its back and makes its comical smile, eyeteeth protruding like a dragon's. It is male, but I don't remember the dog's name. I should because I named him.

The woman and I once shared a bed, I think. Perhaps. No, I'm pretty sure we did. And when I say once, I mean it could have been for a night or for a few nights or for a few decades or longer. The memory of it scurries across my mind like a mouse might do when you're sitting up reading at night, a brown flurry, a flash that makes you look up and then it's gone and you wonder if it was ever there at all.

The woman and I no longer share a bed because the loss of my faculties no longer makes me good nighttime company. Now I only share a bed with my conscience, and that is a very restless bedfellow.

I had a friend from the old CSA days who lived in St. Matthew Parish, a young man who described it as green, leafy paradise, bayous filled to the top with fish, the sky filled with ducks, beautiful brown-eyed women who laughed easily and smiled even more easily. The boy had been one of the ones to march to the furlough camps. I had no attachments and no place else to go, and I was determined to see this place.

Though I had no map, I knew that if I followed the big river and took it all the way down to Bayou Lafourche, I could find it. So, on a warm

---

[4] A name commonly given in the 1920s to someone from the Philippines.

summer morning, I set out. The horizon wavered as if it were behind blown glass, and I followed it. And as I followed it, the heat of late July traveled with me on the dusty roads, down through Catahoula Parish. I wandered through a countryside that had been sapped of all virility and vitality. The dusty earth spoke in wisps of red dust, and every afternoon a rain shower squeezed itself out of the sky, and I took refuge under the skirt of a tree, the dense leaves of a live oak, if I could find one. Then, after what should have been enough rain to turn it all to mud, the dust returned, turning the dark green leaves of deep summer to paler, pastel versions of themselves. And the Louisiana heat returned.

The foliage opened up onto a clearing, the sky leaping up in hot blue with a sun that throbbed at the world. My feet scuffed the powdery lane as a tunnel of dust trailed behind me. Ahead was a place, not a grand plantation home but not a farmhouse, either. Corn had been planted but never tasseled, and only the ears near the house had been picked. Dry yellow, spindly weeds sprouted up from within it. The cornstalks themselves were skeletal, beginning a slow slide from green to dry yellow.

I was still thirsty; I stayed so thirsty in those days. No matter how much I drank, deep inside, I remained dry, like water poured into desert sand and quickly disappearing. Perhaps it was the memory of those dry days on the bluffs of Vicksburg. I felt as though I was made of paper or straw.

The yard of the house was knee-high in weeds. A shutter hung askew along the bank of windows that looked onto a sagging gallery. In the yard, a carriage was knee deep in weeds, the shafts declining toward the ground where the traces and horse collar all rested in dried mud. There was no sign of any horse. The air clicked and buzzed. A breeze would have been welcome, but this was not a place accustomed to breezes. This place was dry and hot and windless.

A chicken came bobbing and clucking from around the back of the house, followed by a lady in black who was chasing it. The bird, a speckled hen, ducked under the carriage with each circling pursuit of the woman. Insects hummed at the edge of the clearing and from the fields surrounding the house. The woman stopped when she saw me, and the chicken strutted under the house.

"Ma'am, may I trouble you for a dipper of water?" I asked her.

She pointed to the well, and I approached it. From behind a veil of dense black lace, she watched me as I laid down my satchel of tools. She watched me as I lowered the bucket into the well. She watched me winch it up and take the gourd and dip it into the bucket. I drank carelessly- I was thirsty, powerfully thirsty. Those were some hot days. The heat made the distant tree lines shimmy and waver. The water from the dipping gourd wet my face and beard and darkened my shirt front. I poured a dipperful on the back of my neck, and it ran down my back, cooling the hot sweat and making my shirt cling to my body, which was so different then in my youth- firm, wiry, muscular, the body of a man used to long days of physical labor.

I drank again, aware that she was watching me. At last, I had drunk all I could. I laid the gourd in the bucket and reached for my satchel.

"Thank you, ma'am," I said as I hoisted the strap onto my shoulder.

"You're welcome," her voice said behind the veil of black. I turned to the dusty road and paced away from the clearing. My back was already hot again. I was to a point almost out of sight when she called to me.

"Wait," she said, her voice made small by the distance and the black veil. "I have some things I need done around here. Are you handy?"

I stopped and turned around. I knew the answer to my question before I asked it, but to be clear, I asked it anyway. It was a question that had to be voiced.

"Your husband can't do it?"

"Went off to the war," the black veil said. "Tennessee." There was a pause. "He's not coming back. Why I'm in black. Why else would someone wear black in this heat?"

"What you need done?" I shouted down the dirt-baked path. A mockingbird swooped into the branches of the myrtles. Frilly pink and white blossoms fell from it.

"Cistern leaks. I'm afraid of the well going dry." Her hand was to her forehead which gave a shadow of complete blackness over her face. "And there's a hole in the henhouse. Chickens gettin' out, and possums and coons gettin' in."

I turned and went back.

She could not do anything, unless you count playing the pianoforte or embroidery. Everything else, anything useful, anything pertaining to her daily sustenance, was as foreign to her as a Turkish bazaar. Even my Aunt Cora, my refined, erudite, esoteric Aunt Cora, could dispatch a chicken and get it ready for the table.

But the widow was different. As far as I could tell, all she could do was fry an egg and draw water from the well, and I imagined that all she'd had was water and eggs since her Negro servants had run off with the Union Army.

I worked that day for her, and, when the sun fell low, she brought me quilts to make a pallet on the porch. The next day, as I prepared to take my leave, she came up with other chores for me. She promised to pay me, but over time, I began to doubt her ability to do so. I finally abandoned any notion of payment for my labors.

Over the next week, I did one task after another, like something out of a Greek myth. The cistern. Replace the staves of the pigpen. Repair the floorboards on the back porch. Every time I went to leave, she would have another chore for me, all the while watching me in her mourning clothes like a sentinel of death. At night, I slept on the back porch, aware of the slow parting of the curtains every once in a while, a small movement in the gray moonlight. Her face indistinct in the crevice between damask cloth and wood frame, and then the curtain would close again.

I tried to get a look at her face, her figure. She was a little older than me, but younger than my Aunt Cora, I gathered. I believed she was a beautiful woman, beautiful for this remote place and beautiful for any place, for New Orleans or Memphis or Natchez. I, a young man starving for female attention, longed to see her without the veil and without the rustling black cloud of bombazine she wore.

At last, a cool night arrived, one of those rare August nights in Louisiana when the air thins a little and the temperature relents a little, but you dare not get used to it for you know it will still be another month or more before you get another. She had me light a fire, but smoke billowed into the room and made a haze around the lamplight until I had her bring me a pitcher of water to put it out.

"Chimney's not drawing," I said up into it. "Blocked."

The house filled with smoke, and we waited in vain for a breeze to

28

push it out and away. It was well past dark and still smoky when finally, I said to her in the twilight, "Ma'am, don't think it's gonna clear."

So, she had me fetch extra blankets from a chifforobe upstairs and bring them downstairs. We arranged pallets on the porch. The moon was big in the sky, and as I went to sleep in the light of it, I could see her propped on one elbow watching me.

The next day, I woke before she did. On her end of the porch, she was a tousled heap of blankets and blonde hair. I rose and set a rickety old ladder against the chimney and carefully ascended the top. A wren had made her nest there and then vacated it, leaving only the woven circular mass in the way of the chimney, an obstruction like a crown of briars dotted with feathers and lint. I cleaned it out, tossing the nest out where it fell with a quiet crunch on the ground below.

On looking down, I saw the small figure of the widow there. She was adjusting her dressing gown, the creamy white of her cleavage catching the sun as she tugged at it. Her chin was on her chest as she judged it, for subtlety of presentation, I presumed. As she looked up to me, I quickly looked back to my work.

Later in the day she appeared, not in mourning clothes, but in a light, white linen dress like something coming alive in the spring. Her figure was an hourglass, though you could tell it had once been a little fuller. Her clothes hung on her a tad, like curtains falling loosely over a window. The veil was gone and her face was apparent, a lovely face, round blue eyes, long lashes, a finely shaped nose, though it was a face worn with care, care about her dear departed husband, lost, having fallen into the grinding gears of the machinery of war.

The smoke cleared from the house, and she adjourned to her chambers upstairs. She offered me a room inside, but I declined, still holding out for some sort of night breeze to wash over me. But the night stayed vacant and inert. Nothing moved anywhere as the insects in the night trees sang a hymn to the vacuum.

The next day, as I split wood for a winter that seemed impossible to ever exist, they came with a clopping of hooves. There were perhaps six or eight of them, lanky, dingy men on horseback. They sat and appraised the house.

We said nothing to each other, and they did nothing. But their eyes roved the clearing, pausing at the hogpen that I had neatly repaired. The hog slept in the small patch of shade, its hide pushed up in hairy furrows between the slats of the pen.

The men looked to me and asked for water. And I showed them the well like the widow did for me that first day. And they drank deeply and sloppily like I did. Their glances examined the house and the yard again. I had been a soldier once. I knew that if they had been hungrier, they would have taken whatever they wanted, but like sated wolves, they had no need or desire for anything of ours. But their glances said, *next time, yes, next time.*

The widow came outside as the clatter of hooves disappeared in a cloud of sandy dust. She looked at me with blue eyes. I answered her unspoken question.

"Thirsty men," I said.

Later that day, she came to me as I was finishing up with the chicken coop. Coons had pried back the wire again, and I was determined to keep them out. She came stepping through the yard, watching her footsteps, holding a box in her slender, pale hands. I twisted a wire to bind the seam of six-sided rings together.

With a little effort, she lifted the box as if presenting me an offering. It was fancy, with a delicate 'L' on the lid. I opened it, and there it was. A Navy colt revolver. Her late husband had left it behind for her to use but had neglected to show her how to shoot it.

"Mr. Carrick," she said as if she were giving me with another chore, "I would like to learn how to fire this weapon."

I left the chickens muttering in the shadows behind the wire hexagons. We went off to the edge of the corn where a fence sagged, another of the endless projects on my list.

I set a can on a post and marched off about twenty paces or so, about as close as she might need to shoot if a robber or worse might try her home when I was gone. I showed her how to load, to cock the lever, how to hold the gun at shoulder height and prepare for the kick. My hand was behind hers, her hand holding the gun, her finger on the trigger. Waiting, watching with one eye, breathing, waiting for the sudden, cracking report of the gun, the smell of rose water on her neck, the rise and fall of our breath, our bodies close, the zinging song of insects in the weeds, the watery heat in the distance, the can waiting on the post, my hand cradling the back of her hand, rose water, breathing, hand cradling hand.

Then the sudden kick, the slap of recoil, the gun pointing into the hot blue sky through a cloud of bitter smoke. And the mocking can still on the post.

We laughed as we caught our breath, our ears ringing as we realized that we had both been holding it. The smell of powder, sulfur burning, and rose water and the green tang of the weeds at the edge of the clearing. We loaded again.

"Aim low," I whispered into the sweet fragrance of her neck. "A little lower." The back of her hand seemed to reach out for mine as she raised the Colt to shoulder level. She gathered my free hand with her free hand and set it on her waist.

"Steady me," she said in little more than a whisper. I did, and I could feel the swale of her hip, the shape of a woman, a real lady, not a quarter-a-ride camp follower. I could feel myself stirring, and what's more, I could feel her stirring.

Her breathing quickened and pulled mine along with it, each inhalation of sweet rosewater. My palm pressed into the back of her hand, and I felt her finger caress the trigger lightly, more sure of herself. She wet her lips, and I could hear her do it. It was so quiet.

And then the Colt erupted, and the recoil pointed it up to the sky and the smoke. The can jumped and flipped and fell, and the widow shrieked and jumped and laughed.

"Mr. Carrick!" she exclaimed. "I got it! I hit it!"

"Yes you did," I said quietly. "You sure did." And I think I smiled, and she glanced at me, and it was like a small, pleasant electric shock.

The tinder of a moment like that catches fire easily, and you find yourself engulfed in it. The world is covered in smoke, and you realize that it isn't the smoke from the Navy Colt. You realize that the world has a certain fuzziness. Passion, lust, call it what you will, but it clouds the air, and it clouds your senses, and while it does it, your body does what *it* will.

There was something inside her, buried deep, fathoms underwater, something that came up clawing for the surface, unloved and friendless, a

31

loneliness that held its breath and imagined each moment as its last but instead found each moment to be the first in another string of quiet, endless moments.

My old mind still remembers my young hands on her breasts, the weight of them in my hands, the broad, flat nipples of them cradled in the arc of flesh between my thumb and forefinger. The gaze of her sultry eyes, lids drooping with the enchantment of desire, the press of the tangled hair into me, the sway, the sway, the arched back, the sway, the sounds she made like something dying and being reborn. Sixty years hence, my old mind remembers. There was no tenderness to it, none at all. It was more like two animals hurriedly slaking their thirst from the same puddle of rainwater.

And so we fell into the same bed, and I thought that perhaps this might be a fine place to stay a good while or longer.

She was older than me, perhaps ten or maybe twenty years. But her body was youthful in its response to mine, and the gift of it, presented to me on the breath of a hot, gray summer night, maddened me and made me think of nothing else. I took up any chore for her, any task was worth doing so that it pleased her, so that she would come to me in the chirping night air, naked-pale in the grainy light, hovering over my youthful body, kissing it, tasting it.

And it wasn't just in the night. The afternoons, too, when the heat of the day made her call to me, "Mr. Carrick, you'll catch your death in that heat. Come inside for a spell, I've got you some cold water in here. Certainly you must need a drink of clear, cool water, don't you, Mr. Carrick?"

I would go inside, and I would drink from the wooden bucket that she had pulled from the well, the bucket that I had fixed so that the seams were watertight. I would drink panting in between deep draughts and then drink again, and she would watch my youthful body heave with drinking and breathing, and, when I put the dipper back in the bucket, she would push my sweat-soaked shirt off my shoulders as her shaking hands unbuttoned her blouse, and we would fall into madness again.

So it was on such an afternoon that we heard the knock on the door, an insistent, firm knock.

"Anyone home?" a man's voice said.

The widow slipped her day dress over her naked body and padded to the front door. Had I not been so exhausted, I would have followed, as I should have if I had been serious about being her protector.

The man's voice again:

"Ma'am, the army of the United States requests the use of your hog, ma'am." He said it as if they would return it after they were done with it, as if they were only going to use it to pull a wagon or a plow, and not for the true and accepted use of a pig.

"My husband will be quite annoyed with you, sir. Robert?" She called to me in the afternoon shadows of the house. I hastily dressed, shouting to the front room as I laced up my boots, "Yes, dear?"

"Visitor," she said.

When I appeared on the porch, the officer asked me, "Not away at war, sir?"

"War's over for me. Paroled at Vicksburg," I said.

"Papers? Parole papers?"

"Inside," I said.

I scrambled through the house, trying to remember where I put them. In every window, I could see a Union soldier, posted lest I try to run out the back door or crawl through a window. I checked my trouser pockets, the settee in the hall, the sideboard, every drawer.

At last I found them in a drawer in the bedside table. I came out on the porch where the widow and the officer in charge sat in the wicker chairs contemplating the heat but saying nothing. I gave him my parole papers.

"Robert? Says here you're...John. Simon. Carrick." He looked at me for an explanation.

"Robert's what I go by," I said.

He chewed on that as he considered the house. He looked as if he were trying to fit the next piece of the puzzle.

"Private?" He snorted. "Awfully nice house for a private."

"Thank you, sir," I said.

"What regiment were you in?" he asked.

"Third Louisiana."

"Third Louisiana," he repeated, as if trying to taste it for truthfulness.

"Commander?"

"General Forney."

"General Forney," he echoed me, pursing his lips as if trying to smell the upper one.

"Well," he finally said, "We had quite a time blowing you fellows off that redan, didn't we?"

"Yessir." My mind reached for something else to say, but all it found was, "Reckon you did."

At last he was satisfied and gave me back the papers. He stood up as if we had just been chatting about the weather or some other light topic.

"Now about that hog," he said. He descended the steps from the porch and turned, shielding his eyes from the glare.

"You'll not take our hog," the widow said.

I knew the way of these things, having been on the other side of the issue.

"Best let him take it," I whispered to her.

"What will we eat come fall?" she asked either me or him, or perhaps both of us.

He produced a slip of paper and used the flat of the bannister to write out a note. An army promissory note. A worthless IOU.

"We'll soon have the rebels beaten back all the way to Alexandria. You'll get a new hog then. A whole pen of them."

"I protest, sir," she said.

"Best we let him take it," I said again, through my teeth and under my breath. And as I said it, we heard the squeal in the side yard.

They boiled him, scraped him, left the parts of him they didn't want unburied at the clearing near the cornfield. And then they carried him off and away down the road, on a pole with his small pig-hooves tied together, swaying the marching steps.

That night we lay in the afterglow, the moonless night dark and the small night sounds buzzing through the windows somewhere. She was tracing her fingers on my chest, the soft tips describing arcs and circles and fancy curves. "What happened to your finger?" she asked.

"Shot off in a battle," I lied, not knowing why I lied. I just did, just lied. I thought she would ask about the hog, but the hog was forgotten.

34

We didn't speak of it again.

A few days later, I was splitting wood for a winter that seemed no closer. I was imagining a cold night with the widow Lowe in front of a fire. The blow of the axe cleaved the last log along the grain. I had made up my mind to go inside to see to the widow. When I looked up, I saw them.

They were the scraggly band of men that had come before the Union men. They had no set uniform, a set of stragglers riding a hodgepodge of horses. They sat on the horses as tails swished and hides flinched away flies. I stood with the axe in my hand and wiped the sweat away from my forehead with my forearm.

"Help you?" I asked.

"Thought y'all kept a hog."

"We did. "

"Well? Where is he?"

"Yankees took it."

"Took it?" He spat and wiped his mouth with the back of his hand. "Took it, or you give it to 'em?"

"Took it," I said. "I'd never give away something like that." I added to make sure he knew we were on the same side, "Not to a Yankee."

They took a couple of chickens instead, spindly clawed feet lashed to saddle horns, a flurry of beating wings. The widow awoke and came out onto the porch. She was livid, and I had to restrain her from going after the men and her chickens. The men laughed at her from atop their horses, rifles pointed downward and unthreatened. They tipped their hats in a gesture of mock gratitude and rode off. One day I would become someone much like them.

7

From the balcony on which I write, I see a wagon approach from the uptown end of Prytania headed downtown. It is the Negro man whose family has a laundry down on Magazine. He stops at our house, and the woman brings out our laundry, a white sack that bulges with the clothes of a household. The man waves to me and shouts, "Mornin', Mr. Pierre!" before meeting the woman at the gate. She lifts the bag over the fence, and he hands her a bag with clean clothes in return.

"You want me to set this on the porch for you, ma'am? No trouble, now."

"Oh, thank you, I've got it," she says as she lifts the clean bag over the fence.

The laundry man pauses to wave to me again. I raise an old hand to him, the one with four fingers and not three.

"Don't you get you-self in no trouble now, Mr. Pierre!" he yells up to me, and then he is on the buckboard again, and there is a wave in the leather of the reins. The mule tries to glance beyond his blinders and then takes a tentative step. There is another and another and then the clopping recedes downtown with the dirty laundry, the unpleasant business of households. I don't remember the name of the laundry man, but he remembers mine. But I do remember when two Negro men delivered some unpleasant business to the widow and me.

It was on another afternoon as we lay exhausted in the bed, the afternoon sunshine falling outside the window and creating shadows inside where we lay behind the lace curtains. I was trying to think what day it was, trying to figure if it was September yet.

It was in that afternoon silence, before the electric evening song of the insects. Everything was still except for the breathing of the widow as she fought sleep, her head on my chest, her hair loose and blonde and tousled up over my neck and down to my stomach. Our creamy nakedness intertwined and draped over the wetness of sweat and passion.

Through the window and the trees, there was a sound, a quiet shout of a driver speaking encouragement to his team. There was silence again, and then the click of a tongue and the rattle-and-snap of leather and then the quiet voice with a muted shout, 'mon hyar.

I rose from the bed to go to the window, and the colors of the wagon filtered through the yellow and green and brown of nature until it made the lane that led up to the house. Under the small yellowing leaves of the

36

myrtles and over their pink and magenta fancy blossoms, the wagon creaked and a harness jangled slowly.

The wagon had rubber-shod wheels that spooked up wisps of dust in the hot road. It stopped, and two Negro men got out. One climbed in the back under the canopy. For a moment, I covered myself with the curtain, and, in the bed, the widow sat up and covered herself up to her neck with the sheets. It occurs to me now that it was probably much in the same way that Adam and Eve covered themselves when God came to visit them in the Garden.

She slipped her dress, a light blue skirt with a darker bodice, and went out on the porch to greet them.

One of the Negro men approached and removed his hat, an old slouch that was dark around the base of the crown. Dust rose from the part that wasn't wet.

"Ma'am, you be Misrus Octavia Lowe? Wife a Cap'n Robert Lowe?"

"I am." She paused. "I was."

"This is a happy day, then," he said. He returned to the wagon, and together the two men carried something in a sheet like you might carry a hundred-pound sack of flour like the army did. The widow reached down to pull back the sheet and instantly put her hand to her mouth. She followed the men up the steps where they set the sheet and its contents in one of the wicker chairs.

The sheet fell back onto the chair to reveal a man. I say a man, really he was the shell of a man, the way a locust might crawl out of its wrappings and fly away. A husk with his arms folded over his chest like an Egyptian mummy.

The widow stood stunned for a moment, her eyes squinted with her hand still clasped to her mouth. She shook, and her cries were muffled by her hand. She kneeled before him and embraced him, and I felt an odd sensation of jealousy, though as I've gotten older I realize I should have felt shame. She held him and rocked him, and he smacked his lips like a dog does when he is petted into contentment.

"Oh Robert, my Robert, my love. I thought you were dead. Oh, I thought you were dead." She nuzzled her face into his chest as if she were trying to breathe him.

"Praise Gawd," one of the men said as he took off his hat again. "Back to life like Laz-rus. Show is."

"Now, he got a tenancy to mess hisself," the other said. "He gone be a handful."

I took a closer look at Robert. One side of his head showed the indented pucker of where a bullet had pierced him. And his left eye was missing. His lips smacked and ground as if he were trying to gather enough air to say something.

"Oh, my Robert," the widow said, though the widow was not a widow, and her late husband was not her late husband. And I was not Robert.

The Negro men left in their wagon, the colors of the wagon and the sounds of the wheels and the harness and the clop of the horses and the singing of hymns fading back down the lane of myrtles and into nature. Leaving the three of us. The spokes of the wagon twirling into a blur.

Whenever the widow, now Mrs. Lowe again, I suppose, whenever she went to the privy or napped or did any other private errand, she asked me to watch Robert, though it was certain he wasn't going anywhere on his own. I would sit on the porch with him and try to imagine him before he was ruined and came back a shell, a shadow, a husk. He must've been a brave man. Certainly, he'd been an unlucky man. He sat there napping on the porch, the sun encroaching on his shade as he slumped in the cane-bottomed rocker. Flies lit and flew again from his skin as he sat motionless. His eye seemed as if it were locked on the last thing he saw, maybe a wave of blue soldiers, or a cannon or a cloud of gray smoke.

As night began to fall and cast shadows on us, the question of what would happen next fell on us as well. It was apparent that Robert would not make a very good bedfellow for anyone, so we moved him into one of the spare bedrooms and tucked him in as if he were a child. Mrs. Lowe went to bed, and I sat up in the parlor. After an hour or more, I heard her footsteps on the wood floor and smelled the rosewater. I looked up and saw that she held a candle, and the light turned her eyes from blue to golden. Her hair was down, falling over the collar of her nightgown.

"Are you coming to bed, Mr. Carrick?"

It was an odd moment to say the least. But I rose and went with her.

And I got in her bed with her. And we satisfied our thirsts. And then she lay with her head on my chest. My younger body made no exceptions when it came to its desires.

"I can't manage him by myself," she said. "I can't. I'd rather we both die. Both of us. If you leave, I don't know what I'll do, but I can't manage him by myself."

I felt her shake, and I felt her tears drip onto my bare chest.

"You'll not leave us, will you, Mr. Carrick? You'll not leave Robert and me, will you?"

"No ma'am," I said.

"Do you promise?"

I promised.

I lied.

That night, I got out of her bed and tiptoed past the room where her husband slept, though even if he were aware of it, he couldn't have said a thing about it. I packed up my things, taking with me two silver candlesticks, as payment for my weeks of labor, I suppose. Then I snuck away, pressing down lightly on the front gallery with each hovering step. In the half-moonlight, I turned to the road, a stranger to her and to the world ahead of me. And to myself.

I got to the lane of myrtles, colorless in the pale night, and began running. I ran as the sack of my daddy's tools and the candlesticks clattered together and bounced off my back and side and my breath huffed and my feet drummed on the lane and the thousand eyes of the night watched me from the woods on either side. I ran until I made the open night sky over empty, fallow cotton fields and I could see Venus, the morning star in the eastern sky. I followed it, leaving behind the awkward obligation.

I ran for reasons then unknown to me, though now in old age I know why I ran. I was disgusted with myself.

I would later be blamed for what happened, incriminated by the candlesticks I had taken from the Lowes. And the finger that had been taken from me.

8

By the milky pink sunrise, I'd made Harrisonburg and the Ouachita. The morning sun of August glowed angrily in the dusty sky. The town was awakening in that same dust and the distant bark of dogs in angry conversation, the rattle of a wagon somewhere up the road, the pop of wheels in hard dry ruts of the main road down to the ferry.

The ferryman sat on the railing of his raft. The towline dipped down into the brown water for several yards before reemerging across the river where it was tied to a willow. He was an older man with several teeth missing, a jack-o-lantern face that watched his hands plow tiny crescents of dirt from under his fingernails.

"You lookin' to croth?"

"Yessir."

"Quarter to croth, kind thir."

I was still dressed in the captain's burgundy waistcoat and gray linen britches and jacket. I'd kept my old slouch hat. The summer sun was just too hot to leave it, but I left my army clothes with the widow.

"All I got's this," I said.

I produced a silver candlestick from my satchel and handed it over to him. They were heavy, and I was tired of carrying them. He canted his head and narrowed his eyes as he took it.

"Juth how many timeth you need to croth?" he asked.

"Just once," I said. "Afraid it's all I got."

"All right, then," he said with a trace of doubt. He set the candlestick down and picked up the towline and pulled it up out of the river. The water dripped clear brown drops as he retrieved it, hand over hand. It took us a minute or less to cross, short, easy work for a silver candlestick. The lazy water of the moss-green Ouachita slipped under the raft with only the slightest push against it.

We slid up on the opposite bank, and the ferryman quickly picked up the fare and tucked it into a sack, afraid, perhaps, that I would renege on our deal. His shirt and the waist of his trousers were already dark with sweat, though the day was just starting. He noticed my hat.

40

"You a tholdier?" he asked as I alighted from the planks of the ferry.

"No sir," I said. "Not no more."

"Well, they'th a-plenty of 'em down yonder toward the big river, Natcheth. All Yankeeth. Dreadful full of 'em." He cackled through a smile that was missing half its allotment of teeth.

"Yes sir," I said. "I expect there are."

"That how you lotht your finger, tholdierin'?"

I didn't answer him. I just pushed my hat down on my head and scrambled up the tree roots that spread over the embankment leading up from the river. As I disappeared from him and the river, he wished me a "nithe day."

I didn't cross at Natchez. I turned south at the big river and followed it down to the Red. I traded the other silver candlestick to the ferryman there, a man named Bordelon who used a long oar perched in a Y shaped log to push the cinnamon-colored water behind us. As garrulous as the Ouachita ferryman was, the Red River man was just as tightlipped. He reminded me of the ferryman on the river Styx, the story that my Aunt Cora said was just an old fairy tale like an Aesop's fable, on account of it not being in the Bible. The ferryman Bordelon grimly plowed at the water, lips pursed against the wet splash of the oars over the smooth sheen of the river.

I offered the other candlestick to the man, who only said, "*Merci, monsieur,*" as he tipped his hat before rowing back to the shore we came from. I gingerly stepped off on the muddy landing as his oars slapped at the current. He coughed and hocked and spat and then left only the watery pace of the oars to diminish by itself in the distance.

I walked the road, my shuffling feet kicking up a long, dry tunnel that expanded and dissipated into the trees. I stopped once or twice to look back at it, the dust of August hanging in the air and concealing where I had come from in a hazy beige. And when it was clear again, the dust having returned to the earth that had shrugged it off, I turned and proceeded south again.

At the river across from Bayou Sara, I stopped and pondered the town. I felt that I had been there before, an intense sensation that spoke silently of great significance. The town was golden in the failing light of

41

day, the sunset reaching over my head and the river and making the town glow. I could imagine myself on the other bank, watching myself. As if time had bent on itself and was showing each of us, present-self and future-self, one to the other.

As night fell, I slept in a pecan orchard, the hard, green pecans still in bitter husks and a month or two from being edible. They pressed up into my back, no matter how much I cleared the ground of them. At last, I slept with my back to a trunk as the summer lightning lit up the night sky without any noise whatsoever.

In the morning, I stuck to the river road, walking along the levee. Cattle grazed on its crest and slopes, but as the day wore on, they adjourned to the shade of the random oaks to escape the heat. Boats passed in the river, steamboats and occasionally a Union gunboat, a twin-stacked thing, hunched down low on the water. Sailors dotted the deck of it, lounging around and waiting for a breeze to blow across the river.

And then across the river, there was Baton Rouge and the capitol, the castle that Twain hated so much. "So, that's where the mischief was done," I thought. A group of men inside had worked themselves up into a frenzy that had led to the deaths of so many, my daddy and Re-Pete among them. I kept walking.

I walked for another two days, passing the grand mansions and those less grand. Castles with columns and dark green shutters. Steamboats to my left, fields to my right. Towns slept in the heat and waited on the afternoon rains. Signs were both in English and in French now. And I kept walking. And then there it was, nestled in between Bayou Lafourche and the river.

Donaldsonville was a place where the dogs of the town no longer barked at loud noises or strangers. The former because of two years of fighting and two attacks on the town, and the latter due to the constant influx of men. The dogs simply wandered the town with their tails and ears drooping, which is the greeting I received when I arrived in Donaldsonville, the late summer of 1863. I'm sure that to town dogs, I was just another shadow, a silhouette set against the afternoon sun.

The town had been the capital once, for a short time, until it was moved to New Orleans, then to Baton Rouge, then to Opelousas, and finally, on a tidal wave push of blue uniforms, to Alexandria and Shreveport, well away from any blue uniforms. Several months before, there had been an assault on the Yankee fort there, a night assault that had failed when the Texans who attacked it encountered a wide ditch they hadn't expected. Our troops had been driven back all the way down Bayou Lafourche to Brashear City[5]. Now the town, Donaldsonville, was full of soldiers, navy blue caps and uniforms with brass buttons on every street, bored young men, many of them Negroes, all wiling away the hours, some on edge in anticipation of an attack. But most of them bored.

A couple of the soldiers were flying a kite with some little boys on the levee, running the length against the backdrop of an indifferent river, the tail of the kite snaking and shimmying up into the sky. A cap flew off of one of the soldiers, and one of the local boys retrieved it. The faces of them, all of them boys, really, tilted up to the sky to see the kite get smaller and smaller on the breath of the southern breeze. Against the race of a cloud-streaked sky, the jangle of harnesses and conversations of men, French and English, English and French, the clop of hooves, the low shouts of drivers, the occasional slap of paddlewheels in the river against the current and the belch of smoke in the blue sky. And then just the silent water and the silent sky.

On the levee, two men sat their horses and talked, though they were perhaps twenty or thirty yards from me and I couldn't hear them against the quiet sounds of life in a river town. One of them was a Union officer, a squatty man in a blue slouch hat, a colonel by the insignia on his shoulders. His dappled stallion pulled at clumps of grass on the crest of the levee as the two men spoke, looking in different directions, at the river, at the town, down the levee, at the river again.

The other man sat on a black mare with a striking blonde mane, a magnificent, shining black horse, a horse as dark as the inside of a tomb. She shook her muscular neck and snorted, lifting her hooves slightly. The man paid her no attention. He was tall, and even taller in the saddle, a man in a gray swallowtail coat and top hat, sandy brown hair. The Union officer had a neatly trimmed beard; the tall man was clean-shaven.

At last, the conversation on the levee came to a close with a handshake

---

[5] Later named Morgan City

at horseback level. The officer carefully stepped his horse down the decline of the levee. A cigar, clenched in the man's teeth, protruded from his beard like a small, horizontal chimney. When he got to the street at the base of the levee, he cantered the dappled horse down the street and away.

The tall man on the top of the levee threw his cigar toward the river and wheeled his horse around, the blonde mane whirling with the circle of motion and the shake of her head. He looked at me with nickel-gray eyes, eyes that saw me and no one else, though there was the usual coming and going of people that the front street of a river port has. There was no careful stepping down the levee, only a sudden blur of motion and the clatter of hooves as the man passed me and took off into the town.

That man was Sam Teague, though I didn't know it then.

Along the front street, a crew of men was resurrecting one of the buildings that had been taken down when Farragut bombarded the town two summers before. Hammer blows clopped against the sunshine as saws huffed through boards. The sound of the hammers was familiar to me, the sound of a nail driven home, click-click-click-clack-thump. Click-click-click-clack-thump. The cadence of the blows spoke of the confidence of the men hammering. I heard them before I saw them.

One of those men was Honoré Mouton, though I didn't know that then, either.

I turned my back to the river and Donaldsonville and headed down the bayou, Bayou Lafourche. Corn was tall on either side of the road that paralleled the bayou, but, when I looked closer, there were no ears on it, no tassels, only stalks, and I shook my head at such a waste of land, producing cornstalks but no corn. I didn't know it was sugarcane. They looked so much the same to me then, corn and cane.

Alligators sunned their evenly-rowed, knobby hides in the sun while wary herons, some dull gray and blue, some brilliant white, inched their way along the bank, yellow eyes big and beaks ready for the shadows of fish. Clouds were building, and I was beginning to be able to tell time by them: cloudless mornings, the sky half-filled at noon, completely filled at three in the afternoon, and then rain that crashed to earth as if it wanted to go straight through it and come out the other side.

It took me the better part of a day before I reached St. Matthew

Parish, just as an afternoon shower boiled into the sky and a wind pushed the cane tops in a wave of swaying green. I was only in the rain for a few seconds, but it was sudden enough and heavy enough to douse me thoroughly so that I was dripping and cold when I stepped onto the front porch of a dry goods store called Aucoin's, not the young man who owns it now, but his grandfather, Monsieur Hypolite, they called him.

On the front gallery of the store, a man sat reading a copy of the St. Matthew newspaper, which came in two versions, the French version, *Le Boussole de St. Mathieu*, and the English version, the *St. Matthew Parish Compass*. It was a two-pager that had since dispensed with publishing the proclamations of President Davis and now broadcast the words of Union commander Benjamin Butler and President Lincoln. The English version came out on Fridays, as I recall, and the main version, the French version, *Le Boussole*, came out on Saturdays.

I sat on the rail of Aucoin's, dripping, waiting for one of the men to be done with his paper, hoping to find an ad for work, possibly a harness or saddlemaker or something similar. The Frenchman finished his paper first and left it on a barrelhead. I slid into his spot on the bench and picked it up. My French was no good then, and only a word or two made any sense. *Catahoula* was one, I was just there, where the widow lived. *Confédéré* was another, the French name for a Confederate soldier.

I gave up on trying to gather any more information, and looked up from the French paper. Across Bayou Lafourche, the green leafy wave of cane tops was glistening in the sun that had suddenly appeared after the shower. Steam was rising from the road and the bayou.

And then, nailed to a post, I saw the announcement. A place called Mount Teague plantation was advertising for help in its cooperage, preparing barrels in anticipation for the upcoming grinding season. Interested persons should apply in person at the place on Bayou Lafourche south of Napoleonville, it said. I had no family and no prospects at the time, and so it seemed as good a place as any.

I set the copy of *Le Boussole* on top of a barrel. The edges of it were darkened where my wet fingers had held it. I folded it over where the headline of the main story stood firm in big block letters:

Despicable Assassiner Double !

Part II:

In which I work for Sam Teague as a cooper and other sundry tasks

9

People who see things like Niagara Falls or the Grand Canyon for the first time seldom forget it. They remember who they were with, what they were wearing, how the air smelled, the weather. Places like those chisel the memories deep on some flat surface inside us like an inscription in white marble. Memories like that do not fade. Nor does my first memory of Mount Teague.

It spread out before me like Pompeii before the eruption, Atlantis before the flood. Those places and hundreds of others like them had long since been obliterated, but Mount Teague was still there, and still is, and likely always will be. Majestic, stately, an island nation in a sea of cane. Smoke rose from hearth fires in the dwellings large and small, as well as the work sheds and kitchens and forges. Treelines were distant, carefully standing aside and giving way to the thousands of acres of sugar cane that fueled everything.

Dotting the landscape were dairy barns, chicken houses, grinding sheds, boiling sheds, all neatly painted white and trimmed in black and dark green. The cooperage where I would spend that fall was there, open-sided with a forge at one end. And, of course, out front and down the bayou road a little ways was the commissary. Here prices were inflated so that no one ever left, despite the presence of the Union Army. It was said that in one lifetime at Mount Teague you could accumulate enough debt for two lifetimes. The commissary was the anchor that kept the hundreds of workers of Mount Teague from drifting away.

The commissary may have been the anchor, but the crown jewel of it all was the big house, Mount Teague.

It was relatively new then, probably ten years old or so, twenty at most. It had been built by a man named Savoie. He and the rest of his family had perished in an epidemic of yellow fever, and in the absence of any other heirs, the place and its inhabitants were sold at a sheriff's auction, an event advertised in the New Orleans papers. Apparently talk in the city then was of little else, and that talk caught the ear of a young man who had just arrived in the city after leaving the University of Mississippi. That young man was Sam Teague, the son of a wealthy planter in north Mississippi somewhere. Using his daddy's money, Sam Teague bought the house for a song and renamed it from its original name, *Bon Sustance*.

On that day that I arrived, the live oaks that flanked the lane up to the house were all smaller than they are now, only a foot or two around. When I returned years later, they were many times that size. But the house was already a colossus and a reflection of the owner.

On that day, I stood there looking at it through the rows of growing live oaks. It was the biggest-no, the *grandest* house I'd ever seen, grander than the mansions on the bluffs of Vicksburg. Massive columns, long, airy galleries, shaded against the evening sun that glared against the façade and made it glow an angry orange in the sunset. The sea of leafy green cane all around it was paying homage to it, murmuring and rippling in the slightest of breezes. From the upper balcony, you could watch it and imagine yourself floating over all that green, green that would be ground down into the white gold that nourished the house and its occupants. It was said that the very top of the house was the highest point west of New Orleans and south of Memphis, proving that, despite the broad, flat terrain, the house had been renamed properly: Mount Teague.

I paused for a moment watching the house glow in the setting sun. I had brought my satchel of tools, my daddy's tools, and I set it down to take off my hat and wipe my brow. The bayou and the bayou road were behind me, the croak of bullfrogs and alligators in the approaching twilight. My shadow preceded me, the darker image of me leading my way to the golden pillars of Mount Teague, the windows being lit by a shadow inside, first one room, then the adjacent one. I approached, and I could see her, the outline of the servant, a woman stretching tall with a taper. Her face concealed from me by the darkness and the shadow and the distance. I was mesmerized by her like a moth drawn into light. Her figure was lean and pure, even under her skirts and her blouse and her apron. She was lithe with a grace of movement that was poetic.

She completed the lighting of the windows into tall rectangles-within-rectangles that glowed as the front of the house fell into purple-tinted nightfall. Then she moved to the back of the house. It was the first time I saw her, but it wouldn't be the last. No, it wouldn't be the last.

As I neared the front door, I suddenly heard a scream, the shriek of a woman. It had come from the rear of the house. I ran down the lane, my leather satchel of tools slapping against me, my shadow ridiculously long and bounding. The scream sounded again, somewhere off to the left of the house. I ran past the big house and down toward the source. My chest rose and fell as I listened for another scream and wondered if anyone in the house had heard it. Surely they had, but why weren't they running out to investigate it?

I stood there in the deepening twilight, blue light and black shadows, looking and listening and wondering. Off in the trees was a building, made of some kind of stone. As I approached and saw the rusted wrought iron fence, I recognized it as a mausoleum, a family crypt. SAVOIE was chiseled into white marble. The sides of the tomb, as big as a small cabin, were stained green and black from moss. There was a sign in front of it that proclaimed, BEWARE OF DOG, and as I read it, I heard the barking and liquid growls in the dark. It was nearby, within ten yards or so. I stood perfectly still. The dog was uncomfortably close, a sputtering, slobbering snarl. When the silence fell, I moved slightly, only to disturb the dog again into a throaty warning.

And then he was there, the smell of cigar smoke and the glowing ember like an immense orange firefly. He spoke, and hazy blue smoke clouded out into the night air.

"What business do you have here, sir?" His voice was very much like north Louisiana or Mississippi or Alabama, the same plain southern accent I had heard since my boyhood and my time in the army.

"I heard a woman scream," I said.

He laughed, a derisive laugh that ended with another bright, orange glow of his cigar, and he exhaled a reply. "Peacocks. Peacocks sound like that to those unaccustomed to hearing them."

The firefly glowed orange again. It was higher than my head; the man was quite a bit taller than I was. He exhaled a question.

"And I ask you again, what business do you have here, sir?"

The dog barked again, and I heard the rattle of his chain as he launched against it in the dark. He gurgled angrily, hollow and wet. The man clapped his hands once, a powerful clop, and the dog was silent.

"Serbus!" The man shouted with the clap. The dog whimpered an apology.

"I come to see about the cooper job," I said.

A breath of smoke and the pop of his lips on the cigar leaked out into the night and the silence. Night things began to chant, a zinging, buzzing night song.

"Come inside, then," he said with a little more gentility.

He motioned me to walk in front of him, and we walked to the front of the house. Insects were haphazardly orbiting the lanterns flanking the front door. When the man and I arrived on the porch and in their light, I saw him. He was the man I had seen on horseback talking to the Union officer.

"Sam Teague," he said as he extended his hand.

I took it in a firm shake. It was soft and fleshy like the underbelly of a catfish.

"Pete Carrick," I said.

We passed into the central foyer of the house, into a world of opulence. It made my Aunt Cora's fine house in Mount Lebanon seem like a privy. The floor boards were wide planks of cypress, the molding at the floors and ceilings ran in elaborate, stair-stepped courses that caught the light and made shadows that doubled and trebled the contours. Heavy damask curtains in rich colors fell from the molding to the floor and were held back by velvet rope ties.

His tone was one of a simple man, while the trappings of Mount Teague spoke otherwise. All the other plantations I had passed had fallen to the depredations of the armies in one way or the other, but Mount Teague was unscathed.

An unfinished portrait sat on an easel. A cut-glass decanter sat on a mahogany sideboard in the central hallway, and a set of matching glasses sat next to it. I was looking at all the finery when Teague's voice pulled my attention from it. He had gotten up and was at the sideboard. He turned with two tumblers of whiskey and gave one to me. The subject of the painting had Teague's long chest, but the face was unfinished. He saw me looking at it.

"It's yours truly, only the artist was forced to leave on account of the war starting. Philadelphia man, one of the best. Only the best here at Mount Teague."

Only the best here at Mount Teague. It was an expression you heard constantly. If there had been a company song, "only the best at Mount Teague" would have been the refrain of it. Looking back, I'm surprised there wasn't a company song. Perhaps they have one now.

But back then, as I looked all around me, I could see he was correct. Crystal chandeliers, intricate molding, ornate curtains, cupboards with fine china and silver. All in the midst of a war that had ruined every other plantation along the Mississippi and Bayou Lafourche. Somehow, Mount Teague had been spared. What sort of luck could accomplish something like that, spare this particular place in the midst of so much desolation?

There was a shriek from the yard again, and it startled me.

"Peacocks," Teague said kindly, reassuringly. "They sound like a woman shrieking." An image seeped into my mind in runny watercolors, an image of Octavia Lowe discovering that I had fled in the night.

"The peacock's plumage, when it's unfurled, is like a thousand eyes. A thousand eyes that see everything, that nothing escapes," he said as if he, too, could see everything.

"I need a man in the cooperage,"[6] he said. "You up for that kind of work?"

"I am, sir."

The truth was, I had no place else to go. Mount Teague was as good a place as any, good and out of the way.

"You read and write?" he asked me.

"Yessir," I said. "Read anything I can get my hands on."

It was true. I had read an old copy of the Memphis paper so many times while we were under siege that I thought I could still recite it. I told him so, and he laughed. The whisky was taking its effect, and I was thinking that there might be something likeable in this fellow Sam Teague.

"Well, perhaps you could read me some things from here," he said. At the time, I thought he was testing me. Looking back, I know it was this,

---

[6] Area designated to make barrels, in this case, for the transport of sugar.

and that it was something else, something I came to realize later. He handed over the latest edition of the *St. Matthew Compass*.

"Read for me, if you would," he said as he lifted his chin in that look of skepticism waiting to be put aside.

There it was, the English version of *Le Boussole de St. Mathieu*, and the article in French that I could not understand, now here in English and blatantly understandable:

Despicable Double Murder!

The headline screamed. I read on evenly, as I used to read to Re-Pete (as he couldn't). But as I read, I paused and looked over the paper to Sam Teague, who was lounging back in his arm chair, eyes closed, tumbler of bourbon in his hand.

Catahoula Parish planter, an invalid CSA veteran, was found dead with his wife at their home eight miles west of Harrisonburg on the Winnfield Road. The two were discovered by a Union soldier bringing a pair of replacement piglets.

My hand rattled the paper with a tremor as I read on:

Robert Lowe, lately a captain in the Confederate army, Catahoula Rifles, and his wife Octavia, formerly of Port Gibson, Miss., were found dead in their home in Catahoula Parish. The committee of gentlemen investigating the scene say that on cursory inspection, it appears to be a murder-suicide.

And then something about gunshot wounds to each of their heads. While it bore the marks of a murder-suicide, the article said, there was no note. Furthermore, it concluded, it was inconceivable that a woman could handle a pistol such as the Navy Colt found at the scene. Nor could her invalid husband, the late Captain Lowe.

"My, my, my," Sam Teague muttered and tisked. "What is this world comin' to? Gabriel come blow your horn!"

He noticed my pause and then gently urged me, "Go on, son."

And then I read the part that changed things completely for me.

The authorities are looking for a man, possibly a paroled Confederate soldier, who paid for ferry passage on the Ouachita and Red River ferries with each of a pair of silver candlesticks believed to have been taken from the Lowe residence. The Ouachita ferryman, one R. B. Braun, states that the man was lacking his left index finger and seemed to be flustered or generally in a hurry.

The paper rattled lightly in my hands, enough to make a small noise, enough to make Teague open his eyes. Enough to make him look at my hands, one of them missing a finger and holding the *St. Matthew Compass*, a two-sheet paper with lists of eastern war dead and wounded, ads for tonics and Union army notices and horse collars and blacksmith services. And a bombshell revelation that had landed at my feet.

Teague looked at my hands that were holding the paper, especially the one with three fingers that now felt to me as oddly as a claw. Then he looked at me, and it was as if he knew everything. He rummaged through a drawer and produced a pair of kid gloves and tossed them to me. It was both comforting and incriminating. I felt hemmed in, pursued. I felt that this was a refuge.

So I put the gloves on. Later I would stuff the limp, vacant index finger with Spanish moss. I took the gloves, and I took the job making barrels for Sam Teague and his sugar, for ten dollars a month, plus room and board in the garçonnière. He produced a ledger, and I signed my name in it, John Simon Carrick. I was now employed by Sam Teague, the de facto ruler of St. Matthew Parish.

Thus, I began my new life in the Mount Teague cooperage. Death would graduate me to the house.

10

There is a man who visits me here quite often. Other than the handlebar moustache he wears, he reminds me so much of myself from twenty years ago. His skin is just a shade darker than mine, a light café-au-lait color. I think he is a Spaniard.

Until recently, when my health was a little better, he would take me on walks down to the riverfront where we would watch the boats being loaded and unloaded, by Negroes and Italians, mostly. On some days, I would spot them, barrels from upriver with the mark on them: *Mount Teague Sugar, Sweetest-Purest*. They're still making sugar at Mount Teague. I suppose they will until Judgment Day.

We would sit in the breeze, he and I, and enjoy the smells of the things being unloaded and the songs of the men moving up and down the gangplanks. Sweating in the summer and bundled up against the winter. Ships coming in on sail and then steam, and then going out with something new in their holds. And the river sweeping time out to sea.

Finally, the man with the moustache would say, "Well, Pops, you ready to head home? Mama ought to have supper for you by now. And if I wash my hands real good, maybe she'll make me a plate." Then he would laugh and put his arm around me and kiss the side of my head. With time, he has had to lead me by the hand. Now, perhaps, they must think I'm too old to take the trip on the street car to the Poydras Street wharf.

But the barrels with the mark on them, *Mount Teague Sugar, Sweetest-Purest*, always kindled a memory for me. How many did I make in my time there that fall? Hundreds? Thousands?

It was on that first day of autumn, not by the calendar, which in Louisiana frequently lies about fall's onset, but on the day that the temperature drops and the slightest of breezes whispers, "all right, that's enough, I won't bake you this year." I was brought around by Old Mr. D'Ormeaux, who was the overseer at Mount Teague. I stood there with my satchel of tools with CARRICK stamped on them as he introduced me to the other men in the cooperage.

They paused only briefly from the rasping of saws and the beating of hammers. And then they all smiled and lifted their hands or their chins in greetings before resuming the work of making barrels, the symphony of wheezing saws and clopping mallets. It was an hour before sunrise, the usual start of the workday at that busy time of year. The bruised eastern horizon was blushing in bright blue and pink and orange pastels.

They all greeted me except for one. He was the Mount Teague

blacksmith and perhaps the largest, blackest man I have ever seen in my life which is now eighty years. I have seen larger men, and I have seen blacker men, but never in this combination. His name was Etienne, but everyone called him Big Eight. There was another Etienne who, though he was normal size, was called Little Eight.

Big Eight was not a friendly man, not at all, but rather surly in his work, with a brisk economy of motion that afforded him a chance to sit on the brick hearth from time to time and wait for us to catch up in our supply of staves.

On that day that the other men raised hands with tools or staves in them to greet me, Big Eight only gave me a momentary glare as he heated a strap in the fire to a molten, glowing orange. Then, he plunged the hot strap into the water trough as steam drifted over his image, and he gave me a scowl that could wilt a rose or knock over an elephant. He did not like me, perhaps for my skin, or perhaps for any number of other reasons. Or, perhaps, he just didn't like anyone.

It made me no difference, as friendship with anyone was not on my list of things to do. I had lost Re-Pete and half a dozen others, and I didn't see the point in expending energy on the practice of friendship, when all it led to was loss and heartache.

It was good, hard, repetitive work. Ripping the staves with a saw, angling them with a drawknife and a plane, fitting them in the iron hoops of three sizes, a big one around the middle, two smaller ones on either side of that one, and then the smallest ones at the end. I was one of the men who put an angle on the staves so that they would fit around into a barrel shape. The cypress shavings would curl off the wood in a pleasant shimmer, as Big Eight beat on red-hot metal, down to a tapping and then the sizzle of the metal as it hit the trough of water to cool and become black again.

An hour or two after sunrise, she would come, the woman Mathilde, with a basket of biscuits filled with ham or bacon. The heat was returning by then, and our clothes would be clinging to us as our hands stayed busy, moving as if we weren't even connected to them. The sounds of hammering and the scratch of saws and the whisk of planes and drawknives would pause for a moment. All the tools would rest, and we would rest as we gathered around her. She was tall and pretty, in an exotic way, caramel-colored with green eyes. Her hand, lithe and light brown, would part the folds of linen and then our hands, all different, black and white and shades in between, would reach into the basket.

She was an angel of prompt succor, sent from the house. We worshipped her, all of us. It was as if in the heat of midday, the rustle of her skirts brought cooling breezes, and in the cool of the twilight, her smile warmed and sustained us. And when her basket was empty and we were full, we watched her, all of us, as she returned to the big house, carefully pulling up the hem of her skirt to keep it just off the ground. Our masculine eyes, half-feral, half-tame, watching, waiting, looking, hoping for a glimpse of her sweet café-au-lait ankles like penniless boys staring into a confectioner's case.

We dreamed of a night and a day and another night with her, though generally by tacit agreement among us, these desires were left unspoken. We could see it on each other's hearts and faces, the silent idolatry each of us had. When the door closed behind her and it was clear that there would not be an encore showing of her face and figure in a window, only a pause would be left until finally, the cooperage *chef d'equipe*, Monsieur Lapeyrouse, would mutter, "All right, you stud mules,[7] let's make Marse Sam some barrels."

And then hands would find tools again, and the work would begin again. I'm sure each of us was thinking of the garden of delights beneath the mantle of skirts, bodice, and shawl. Such is the way of things; beautiful women have had multiple suitors since the days of Cleopatra. But we were not the only ones. There was another with whom none of us could compete.

During this time, the story of what was now firmly believed to be the double murders in Catahoula Parish was beginning to become the fascination of the lower Mississippi Valley.

Anyone who's ever observed a pack of stray dogs knows the way of these things. One dog finds an object on the ground and sniffs it. Another of the pack notices and sniffs it as well. A third stops to see what the first two dogs are interested in. A crowded circle of wagging tails forms, small

---

[7] This is Mr. Lapeyrouse's joke. Mules are sterile and hence cannot be 'studs.'

dogs, big dogs. Whatever the thing, it is grasped with the shake of a furry head, and another muzzle snaps at it and another grasps it and the thing is launched a little way into the air and falls among the pack where the center of the circle reforms.

And so it was with the news of what was now, without a doubt, considered to be the double murder in Catahoula Parish, the demise of a defenseless invalid hero of the failing cause and his equally defenseless wife. The newspapers, like a pack of dogs, flipped the story back and forth with a lot of printed yipping and growling. It was nipped and shaken by the Natchez, Memphis, and New Orleans papers, and finally, by one of the smaller dogs in the pack, the *St. Matthew Compass*. It was the talk of the town, an outrage so bright that it eclipsed the tens of thousands of deaths that were occurring weekly, elsewhere on the continent.

Every crime needs a villain, for without it there can be no play, and attention soon focused on the man who was dressed in the fine burgundy waistcoat, the man who paid for his ferry passages, first the Ouachita and then the Red, with silver candlesticks taken from the Lowe place in Catahoula. The man with nine fingers.

I seldom went anywhere without my gloves. I had shed the burgundy waistcoat of poor Robert Lowe and taken on the plain dungarees issued by the Commissary, which the French speaking workers called *la commissaire*, or, more commonly and more aptly, *l'ancre*, the anchor. Even after the freeing of the slaves, few if any left. For some, the reason was a connection to the land. For some, pure inertia. But for most, the main reason was the millstone of debt generated at *l'ancre*.

I was glad for the anonymity of the cooperage, one of many men, working like automatons in the production of Marse Sam's barrels. The cane was growing well over a man's head, even taller than Teague's head. He and Old Mr. D'Ormeaux would ride the fields. I would see Teague's head bobbing over the cane, and it would appear that he was talking to himself. But when he emerged from one of the lanes that ran between cane rows, there was old Mr. D'Ormeaux next to Teague, Teague on the back of his shining black, blonde-maned mare and D'Ormeaux on the back of a white mule. They looked like Don Quixote and Sancho Panza.

They stood their animals at the edge of the cane, pulling in on the reins against straining necks whenever the mule or the horse tried to reach over and nibble a stalk. Though our work continued, all eyes in the cooperage shed were on them. Finally, the two mounted men shook hands, and the signal was given.

A large bell on a post near the house rang in hard metal waves that buffeted everything for miles as Mr. D'Ormeaux cantered the white mule to all points of Mount Teague, at last passing by the cooperage with the message: Form up in front of the boiling sheds.

Teague emerged from the big house in a dark swallowtail coat. He mounted the black mare, who was being fed handfuls of oats by a Negro attendant. The bell rang again, and the crowd of us fell from a roiling murmur into silence.

And then from atop the black mare, his hand holding the reins nestled in the blonde mane, he addressed the dozens of workers, perhaps a hundred or more, giving us an exhortation that made it seem as if the earth was created for this very moment and this very purpose, to bring forth white gold from green stalks, all for the grandeur of this place, this garden of Eden, this Mount Teague.

The bell rang again, and men went forth in wagons, each drawn by a tandem of mules. From that hour of that day, there was a steady procession of wagons, going out empty and rattling and returning heavy and creaking, shaggy with stalks and higher than most houses in St. Matthew Parish. The whole process was man-and-mule powered, the cutting, the grinding, the boiling, and, of course, the making of barrels to put it in.

11

I can hear the sound of my workshop across the yard being cleared out. They are leaving the larger pieces of my unfinished work for now, but the smaller chaff is being gathered up. Marble chips fall into wheelbarrows to be carted away, along with drawings and sketches. Marble falling like that day of the hanging. The other people in this house have made the decision, and I know it: I will never work again.

And that is a sad day in a man's life, when he is no longer deemed relevant, when he is no longer someone who operates upon the world and becomes someone whom the world operates upon. The loss of a finger is nothing compared to the loss of relevance.

How many blows of the chisel have I made in my lifetime? How many times have I taken up a mallet? How many evenings have I passed sharpening my tools by a lantern light? The monuments across the street in the Lafayette Cemetery bear witness to that infinite number. Angels, crosses, plinths, columns, pilasters, so many of them the work of my hands. How many blows of the mallet does a man make in a lifetime, I ask you? Perhaps God has counted them, and they are in St. Peter's book. A column recording blows for good, a column with blows for evil. What is at the bottom of my balance sheet? I shudder to think of it.

My gloved hands were busy that fall in the cooperage, but my mouth was silent. There was perhaps half a dozen of us, some white, a couple of them Negro. The air would fill with a song or a shout and then only the hollow sound of wood staves rattling as they were tossed to the ground. The days were sliding into autumn, and the cypresses that lined the bayou were rusting from green to orange. The air was taking on the scent of dying leaves and burning cane stubble.

Old Mr. D'Ormeaux' son, Eugene, worked in the cooperage with us. He had a mop of straight auburn hair, not red and not brown and not copper, but somewhere in between. His face was full of freckles and pimples and blemishes that were presided over by an upturned, blockish nose such as a turtle or a boxer dog wears. He was excitable, and, like most boys his age, had a head full of boyish dreams and notions. He was too young to serve in the army, but just old enough to *want* to serve. He was also too young to lie about his age and get to go, and when the time came that he appeared old enough, the Yankees had retaken St. Matthew Parish for good. The poor, lucky boy had missed his chance to join the circus and "see the elephant." The circus and its elephant had left without him.

He hounded me for questions about battles and army life, prancing around me like a small dog trying to get the attention of a bigger dog. He would stop midway through a stave, his saw poised in the thin kerf, and ask me things like, "Is it true that during battle you can scarcely hear yourself think?"

"Sometimes," I would say as I curled off a shaving with a drawknife. "Mr. Sam's paying me to make barrels, not tell war stories," I would tell him. And Eugene's saw would resume rasping and my drawknife would continue its *shick-shick-shick*.

Our work was feverish, beginning in the cool of the mornings, progressing through the warmth of the day, and extending until the cool of the evenings and into the night. The open shed that was the cooperage was lit by torches and by Big Eight's forge and resonated with the clank of his nine-pound hammer on the anvil and the sizzle of the cooling trough and the saw and scrape of staves taking shape. Sunrise-morning-noon-afternoon-evening-night, over and over again like the rotation of the planets, all punctuated by the blessed appearance of the beatific angel, Mathilde.

The apparition of her was a distraction to us as we searched for it in the windows on that side of the house. Our tools seemed to work themselves as we watched for her. Silently, we all tried to gauge the angle of the sun, the length of shadow around the cooperage, trying to determine how long it would be before she would appear again to see to us. And as we looked back to our toil, we would catch Big Eight scowling at us. At the time, I couldn't tell if he was angry with our inattention to our tasks, or our attention to Mathilde. I found out later.

For Mr. Lapeyrouse, our *chef d'equipe*, it was our diminished production that was the problem. To remedy this, he had us stack our finished barrels in a growing wall between the cooperage and the house to keep us from becoming distracted by looking for her apparition in the windows on that side of the house. The reason was an altercation that lead to a dismissal.

Mathilde had come out to minister to us, and, as usual, there was a pause in the process and we stopped to silently adore her as she made her way to the house. There was a man everyone called Old Tuck because he had been sold down the river from Kentucky. He was a lidder, a man who made the tops and bottoms of the barrels.

Well, Lapeyrouse, who was apparently immune to Mathilde's charms, says, "All right. Let's have them bottoms, Old Tuck."

"Now they's a bottom I wouldn't mind havin'," Old Tuck said with a nod of his head to Mathilde, who was slipping back in the door of Mount Teague. He began doing a suggestive dance, his hands cupping and fondling an imaginary bottom, then cupping his own bottom through his baggy trousers. He shifted from foot to foot, humming a little tune and wiggling the tip of his tongue.

We all guffawed, and each new move by Old Tuck brought another gust of laughter from us. All of us except for Big Eight.

He became enraged, incensed. If he had secretly thought of Mathilde as his, now it was no secret. He pointed to the house and Mathilde and said, "My, sir!" And then pointing to his chest, "My, sir!"

He threw his nine-pound hammer against the hearth where it knocked out a chunk of the brick with a chalky sound and the deep-throated ring of metal. He fell upon Old Tuck, who was still facing the house with his shoulders shaking, laughing with us at his own joke. Big Eight's big, dark hands encircled Old Tuck's little brown neck. Old Tuck made a sputtering sound, his hands clawing at Big Eight's enormous black fingers, each as big around as a link of boudin and as black and hard as wrought iron. Old Tuck's eyes lolled in his head. His tongue was forced out of his mouth, the sputter trailing off as the air choked within him.

The little man fell to the dirt floor of the cooperage, and Big Eight straddled him like an eclipse blotting out the sun. Old Tuck's eyes were completely white as if he were trying to examine the inside of the top of his head. The little brown man was beginning to turn blue.

There was one thing I was always good at, and that was a good old-fashioned scuffle. To look at this old, broken, dilapidated body, you would have a hard time imagining it, but when I was in the army, I had bested our drill sergeant at Camp Moore when he challenged one of us to come at him, the only one in our regiment, the Third, to take him up on it. I did, and I took him straight down. And it took all of fifteen seconds.

Well, it took less than that to subdue Big Eight. Looking back, dissecting it, it's all a matter of physics and geometry. A small force placed here on a man defeats the advantage of his larger force. A twist in such a manner there exerts more than the force applied. And a razor-sharp drawknife at the throat holds a larger man in place.

He laid there under me, his red eyes angry and feral as I held the shining arc of my drawknife blade at his throat. Our chests rose and fell together. Tools fell as the other men came to subdue him, after I had. Mr. Lapeyrouse fired a shrill whistle through his teeth, and more men came to the cooperage. Big Eight was led away still wearing his blacksmith apron and carrying the armload of tools he was allowed to take with him. The next day he was gone, and I never saw him at Mount Teague again.

His replacement, Auguste Favorite, was also a big man. He had been the blacksmith at Hollyfield, a place that was struggling. It was no small miracle, and inexplicable to me, how Mount Teague could prosper while the neighboring places struggled. I didn't understand it at the time, the cunning, the subterfuge. I was simpler then, in those days, still a believer in the Horatio Alger stories of my Aunt Cora, that success was always gained by the high road, and the low road eventually ended in misery. My understanding of human nature is more complete now.

The new blacksmith was as jovial and merry as Big Eight had been sour and dour. He sang little ditties in French to himself and us, and the tune of one of them was oddly similar to "Old Toothless Nell." I've always wondered if it was the French version of it. The clink of his hammering kept time with his full-chested singing. Whenever Teague would drop in, the new blacksmith would cry out:

"Cet homme-ça a jamais travaillé un jour de sa vie." [8]

The French speakers would shout out, *"Ah-ee!,"* and *"Oui, monsieur!"* And I would, too, not knowing what any of it meant at the time. Such is the way of soldiers: understanding has no value, your purpose is to fall in and go along.

The first time Teague heard it, he turned to Monsieur D'Ormeaux and asked him, "What's he saying?"

Mr. D'Ormeaux knew that blacksmiths were in short supply at that time of the year, and he knew that to fire this one would have been ruinous when there would be so much sugar to get to market. So, he told Teague, "He's saying, *'Here's to a bountiful harvest!'*"

---

[8] "That man there never worked a day in his life!"

Teague smiled and clapped his hands lightly and nodded his head to Favorite, who won Teague over that day with a cheer. Without ever looking up, the new blacksmith struck the red-hot metal and the anvil under it with two quick clink-clinks and shouted out:

"*Vive le baws-man!*"

"*Vive le baws-man!*" we all shouted in reply.

12

It was after the scuffle with Big Eight, but before the arrival of Auguste Favorite, that I was summoned to the big house. The lady of the house, Mrs. Teague, met me at the door. She always kept to the house, and I hadn't seen her enough to notice, but she was expecting, and noticeably so. Mrs. Teague was a kind person, as far as I knew her, which wasn't long. She had an easy rapport with the workers of Mount Teague. Frequently, I would see her shelling peas with Mathilde, or planting flowers with the albino gardener whose name escapes me now, if I ever knew it at all.

When Mrs. Teague answered the door, it startled me. I was expecting to see the housekeeper. In truth, I suppose I was looking forward to seeing the housekeeper. My face must have betrayed it.

"Mathilde is getting the girls down," she smiled as she let me in. Mrs. Teague was an intuitive woman who understood the fascination that Mathilde conjured in the hands of Mount Teague. "Sam is in his study."

It was odd to hear him addressed as "Sam" and not "Mr. Sam" or "Mr. Teague," or, the most common, "Marse Sam."

I followed her down the central hallway, past the unfinished portrait of him, to his study. Mrs. Teague put her hand to her waist and exhaled. She inhaled again, deeply and deliberately. This was in the days before I'd been around an expecting woman. It was that walk of someone whose feet hurt, someone whose condition had long since lost its novelty.

"Sam," she said with the next exhalation.

There was a book on his desk, not anything weighty but instead something much more elementary. Looking back, I'm almost sure it was the *McGuffey's Primer*. He sat there studying it, his finger tracing the letters, his lips tracing them. I cleared my throat. He jumped and put a copy of the *St. Matthew Compass* over the book.

"You called for me, sir?"

"Yes, I did Carrick. Let us adjourn to the gentleman's parlor, shall we?"

He rose and put his hand on my shoulder and escorted me down the hall. Pausing at the sideboard in the central hallway, he poured himself a drink of whiskey and without asking poured me one, too.

"What's this I hear about a certain...altercation in the cooperage?" he asked.

"Yes sir, I do apologize," I stammered.

"No need, Mr. Carrick. Sometimes force is called for. For certain people. In certain situations."

A hard silence fell between us as we each contemplated our tumblers. He was tilting his, this way and that, watching the amber fluid sway as if it were some sort of magic trick.

"The boys in the cooperage were impressed with your skill. Tell me, Mr. Carrick, have you ever killed a man?" He asked it in a carefree manner, as if asking me if I enjoyed checkers or was planning on attending the church social. It was so nonchalant, so casual, that I answered truthfully and right away.

"I have. In the army, I mean."

"Bother you to do it?"

"No sir."

That, of course, was the truth. The purer truth was that it gave me great pleasure.

He smiled as if I had given him a good answer. He was looking at my missing finger.

"Ever killed a man, Carrick? Outside of the army, I mean?"

"No sir, I have not."

He chuckled. "Of course you haven't," he said, in that way of someone excusing a jest, pardoning a lighthearted fib. He sipped from his tumbler which dazzled in the lamplight. I don't think he believed me. No, I *know* he didn't believe me.

"You know anything about this man and his wife up in Catahoula?

65

Anything that hasn't been in the papers?"

I regretted that I had been so forthcoming in my answer about killing and not being bothered by it. I felt like I had told him too much, as if a hook had sunk deeper into me, the barb plowing into the flesh of my soul.

"No sir." I hesitated a little. "Only what I read."

"Well, sure. Of course not," he smiled a smile that dripped false sincerity. He sipped the last of his drink and got up again. "May I replenish your glass, Carrick?"

Before I could reply, he did it.

"Let me be frank with you, Carrick. I have certain errands to attend to on certain, special nights. I need stout-hearted men to come with me." He sat again in his Campeche chair, careful not to spill his tumbler. I took another sip of mine. It was smooth. This wasn't backwoods popskull or army camp Oh-be-joyful. This was good stuff. The more I drank it, the more his proposal made perfect sense.

We were laughing, and I think we told some jokes, and I'm almost certain we sang a few bars of "Dear Old Aunt Mabel" which he says he heard in his days at Oxford, the one up in Mississippi, and that he would show those bastards one day for what they did to him, yes he would, and at some point Mrs. Teague came downstairs, heavy with child, and my dear friend Marse Sam Teague told her to be careful with my boy in there, woman, that he was destined for great things, and she kissed him on his forehead and whispered again for him to keep it down, that the girls were sleeping upstairs, and pretty soon the tumbler was almost empty again.

Before I knew it, he was seeing me to the door and we were shaking hands, my rough hand squeezing the soft fish-belly of his. Sometime during our talk, I had taken off the kid gloves and laid them on the side table. He handed them to me, and I stumbled out into the night.

13

Across the way from my balcony, in the Lafayette Cemetery, a family is tending to a grave in the early morning cool. It is a recent internment, and I've noticed that the more recent graves get attention more often than just the traditional day. That day, of course, is the first of November, All-Saints' Day, a day to clean graveyards, whitewash tombs, place fresh flowers and so forth. I've watched many an All-Saints' Day from up here, always glad to see the work of my hands lovingly restored by families that are laughing and telling stories about their departed and maybe crying some. I watch them from this balcony every year, cheered by their devotion to those monuments and to the memory of those they represent, those touchstones for their grief that I have made for them.

All-Saints' Day was observed at Mount Teague as well, though it was a day that was grudgingly allowed, about the only day of rest during harvest season, other than the Sabbath, which was composed of services in the morning and something called Panama in the afternoons.

Those who supplied the work, the cane cutters, the grinders, the boilers, the house staff, the coopers, the drivers, the cooks, all of us were allowed half a day on Sunday for worship each week, if we chose. Then Sunday afternoons were reserved for horseraces and prizefights, one plantation competing against another. Mount Teague always won. The Mount Teague racehorses always wore dazzling livery. Only the best at Mount Teague. The only other day given during cutting-and-grinding season was All-Saints' Day.

And so I saw her there that day in a *garde-soleil* bonnet, pulling weeds around the Savoie mausoleum. What caught my eye was that Serbus was fast asleep, his chain slack and curled on itself as he snored in front of the tomb with SAVOIE chiseled over the door. Beside him and the rusted wrought iron fence, BEWARE OF DOG warned passersby of what this dog could do, were he not sleeping.

She had a small stool, and the way she was sitting on it, the hem of her dress rose and a thin strip of her skin showed, a dark tan. I approached Serbus, cautiously looking at the sleeping dog, an immense pile of brown fur as big as a bear. I threw a rock and it bounced in front of his snout. Still he slept. Finally, I got the courage to pull up an eyelid. A blank pupil stared back at me. The dog's snoring continued.

"Pork chop *au laudanum*," she said from within her bonnet. "With chloroform for an after dinner *digestif*." She smiled from under her bonnet, a sunrise of a smile. A brown bottle and a rag were under the stool on which she sat. A handful of weeds crunched away as its roots surrendered the earth. I took to my knees to help her pull at the weeds that rose from the base of the crypt. If need be, I would have wrestled the dog to stay in her vicinity.

"The Savoies were good people," she said. "They treated everyone like family."

"What happened to them?" I asked as I tossed a handful of weeds behind me.

"Fever. All of them within a month." She shook dirt off spindly roots and flung them away. "I nursed all of them, from the youngest, who went first, all the way down to Madame and then Monsieur, who was the last to go. Such a shame. Treated us like family," she repeated.

Serbus was sitting up now watching the ground in front of him with a befuddled, bemused expression. Mathilde rose from her seat and took the bottle and rag. She splashed a small amount onto the cloth and held it under the big dog's nose. He swayed for a moment and then collapsed on his side again and resumed snoring.

We spent the afternoon that way, quietly pulling weeds around the perimeter of the tomb, then whitewashing side by side and then planting flowers along the sides. With the help of laudanum and *Dr. Pecot's Chloroformium*, Serbus napped all afternoon. When the work was done and the sun was low over the bayou and the bayou road, we paused side by side and looked at the tomb, a happier place now.

"*Merci, monsieur,*" she said.

"You're welcome," I said. I walked away and left Serbus sitting up, staring off blankly. He yawned a large canine yawn of pink and black gums and smacked. He saw me and tried to snarl but only yawned again.

Mathilde had gathered up the tools, buckets and trowels, chloroform and rags. She scratched Serbus' head the way one might pet a toothless tiger or bear at a sideshow, and then she polished the sign that said in big block letters, BEWARE OF DOG.

As we walked away from each other, we both looked over our shoulders. Unable to do otherwise, I turned and watched her as she gathered a handful of her hem and hurried to the big house.

I have always wondered about her. What sort of life did she have?

Did she marry, have children? Surely she is long since passed on.

14

A woman comes to read to me. I think the other woman, the one downstairs, sends her. I also think they are related, either mother and daughter, or sister and older sister. They resemble each other strongly, except that one has green eyes and one has brown.

The younger one, the one who reads to me, usually reads from *National Geographic* or some similar work. Today she reads an article from the *Times-Picayune*. A schoolteacher in Tennessee is on trial for teaching that men are descended from monkeys.[9]

I have my doubts about this. We are pack animals. We desire to go along with authority, to subjugate ourselves to it, to follow it blindly, wrong or right, and in doing so, impress others in the pack. If Darwin had studied the matter a little closer, he may have theorized that we are descended from wolves. And if he had ever met Sam Teague, he would have been certain.

Teague called the certain, special errands we were going on "coon hunts," but we had no dogs. This was perplexing. The hunting of coons is sometimes called a poor man's foxhunt. Teague's could have been called a rich man's coon hunt.

We used to coon hunt, my daddy and I, and an old Negro man I called Uncle Ransom, though, of course, he wasn't my uncle. But he was kind to me, and I think my daddy enjoyed his company, perhaps the only other human being on the planet that my daddy ever did. I knew that to hunt coons, you needed dogs and a lantern. Whiskey was also good to have, and sometimes my daddy and Uncle Ransom had some and sometimes they didn't.

We would meet under a red oak tree and a full moon where Uncle

---

[9] This gives us a clue as to when theses memoirs were written. The Scopes "monkey trial" was held in the summer of 1925.

Ransom would have his dogs. One was a blue dog named Maybelle, I do remember that. Well, the dogs would be straining at their leashes, and Uncle Ransom would be straining at the other ends of them, holding his balance with a smile.

"Well, Mr. John," Uncle Ransom would say, "these here hounds ain't gonna wait much longer, now."

I would take their leashes, always making sure that I had Maybelle's, and my daddy and Uncle Ransom would clasp hands in a hearty handshake, and, if there were a bottle or a jug, they would pass it back and forth a time or two, and the hounds would bay and strain, and we would be off into the woods after our quarry. A poor man's foxhunt.

And when we were done, we would sit down at a table with our quarry having come to its final resting place amongst a bed of sweet potatoes, and we would laugh and Uncle Ransom and my daddy would tell stories, and the dogs would sit on their haunches and wait for the bones. Those are among my fondest childhood memories.

Sometimes I dream about Uncle Ransom. We're usually coon hunting in City Park or cooking whiskey in the neutral ground of St. Charles Avenue or some other implausible errand in some preposterous setting. His brown hands are braced on his skyward-pointed rifle as we sit in the firelight and listen for the dogs. Or those same brown hands calmly work a pine paddle, turning the bubbling mash over and over as the inexplicable street cars squeal and squeak past us on metal rails. In those dreams, we are happy for each other's company. He doesn't ask me why I never came back to see him again after I left for the army.

But that kind of coon hunt had nothing to do with the kind we went on that night with Sam Teague. Except for the part about drinking whiskey.

We were furnished mounts from the Mount Teague stables. Mine was a fractious gelding, a nervous animal that pranced back and forth with me in the saddle. It was me and the boy Eugene D'Ormeaux, Virgil Reeves, Maurice Berteau, and a couple of others whose names I can't remember and whose faces I never really saw very well, anyway. Some of them worked at different places at Mount Teague, some of them didn't.

As soon as the sun was low, we gathered under a live oak out away from the farthest outbuildings of Mount Teague on the border with Hollyfield, the neighboring place. I believe one of the Parris men was with us, now that I think about it. We were about half a dozen or so. Teague came up from the big house, the hoof beats of that black mare rising like an approaching waterfall, shadow of horse and rider stretched out long behind them. He pulled up, and we all sat up straight.

He said a few hollow words about honor and duty and fortitude. Then he produced a bottle of French cognac from his saddle bag and raised it to us. We sat our horses in a small semicircle, their tails and hides swatting at flies, and he proposed a toast to us, some snippet of mispronounced Latin, "Audacious for tuner you bet."[10]

The bottle was passed around, the younger men (boys, if the truth be known) making faces as the cognac went down. When it got to Eugene, he coughed and retched, finally vomiting the toast into a spattered shape on the dry earth. It brought a disapproving scowl from Teague.

"Go back home," Teague snarled. "You waste good liquor like that, go back home. Go back home and don't come back until you grow a little hair on your nuts."

Eugene was wiping his mouth with the back of his hand. He gave a surprised look at Teague, a look that questioned the sensibility of the demand.

"You heard me," Teague said again. "Go back home and come back when you stop shittin' your drawers."

Eugene was on the verge of tears. He looked at each one of us, as if we might intercede for him. With a clicking sound, he wheeled his horse, a white mare, and headed back toward the gleaming buildings of Mount Teague, first at a trot, then at a gallop. His face was contorted; I'm sure he was crying.

When the rolling sound of the gallop had faded off, Teague wheeled the black mare around so that the blonde mane whirled around. He took off into the setting sun, and we followed him.

We swam our horses across Bayou Lafourche and then back across the fallow cane fields of a planter that didn't seem to share the same luck as

---

[10] Probably "*audaces fortuna iuvat.*" Fortune favors the bold.

Sam Teague. After a mile or so, we came upon a Union sentry, a bored-looking young man eating a peach. He stood up, still holding the half-eaten peach, though limply at his side like he was trying to hide it.

"Halt," he said to us.

Teague raised a hand in salutation, and the boy-soldier absently raised the peach.

Then the soldier gave the whimsical sign, *"How much for that shovel?"* and Teague gave the equally ridiculous countersign, *"Long live the king."*

The soldier took the last bit of flesh from the peach and threw the pit into the woods. Then he nodded, and we advanced.

We moved on into the swamp. The air was cool, and our breath steamed out into it. Moss hung from ancient trees, and things moved in the places far off where there were shadows. Horses and riders picked our way through the night, where birds made high-pitched, fluttering calls, and bullfrogs and alligators grunted.

After a couple of stream crossings that left us chilled, there was a light up ahead, a small speck in the gloom. As we approached, it became a campfire with the faces of three men illuminated in it. When they heard us, they reached for their rifles and filed in behind trees.

"Abe Lincoln!" one of them called, the shadow of his face only a bulge in the bark.

"Hang 'im at dawn!" Teague called out.

"Forward, then!" the man said.

"Texans," Teague said over his shoulder to us.

You couldn't tell it by their mismatched uniforms, but it was something that I hadn't seen in months: Confederate soldiers.

The men formed around Teague, and he reached down and shook hands. Then Teague showed him a paper that he produced from the inside chest pocket of his swallowtail coat. This was not the immense Confederate Army that had camped before the enemy at Iuka and Vicksburg. This was a ragtag collection of sundries, an irregular outfit.

The night's work began. We made our way quietly on a road that followed a bayou. I don't remember the name of it, if I ever knew it at all. Steam rose from the glass-flat surface of the water, into the cool night. There on the bank was our objective, a two-story house built in the style of

72

the area, stairs on the front porch going up to the second story, like a loft, almost.

Teague put up his hand, and we reined in our mounts. Then he wheeled around and got close enough to whisper.

"A couple of you go around back, look for anybody to make for the woods."

Virgil and I went to the back of the house, sitting them quietly next to a clothesline with a couple of men's trousers, two pairs, and a woman's dress. A barn slept restlessly out beyond the back of the house near a clearing. Virgil eyed the barn suspiciously, spitting between his teeth. We could hear Maurice speaking in French to the woman on the front porch.

The door shut to the house, and Maurice trotted around to the back of the house to Virgil and me. I don't know where Teague was in all of this.

"She says her boys are off in Virginia with Robert E. Says she hasn't seen them in months," Maurice said. He seemed satisfied with the woman's story.

Virgil wasn't. His lazy eye was still on the barn.

What an innocuous thing a bottle is. An empty bottle, whether it was once filled with whiskey or rum or cognac, expensive or cheap, is a simple, innocent thing. But fill it with kerosene, halfway, and put a strip of torn linen in it, say, one you might tear from a dress on a clothesline, and light it. And then take it and throw it through a barn window. Well, then an empty bottle becomes something else altogether.

As the flames multiplied in the barn, figures ran out, flailing arms in longjohns, legs pumping toward the woods behind the barn. We pursued, ducking limbs, quartering our horses. Virgil was a much better horseman than I was, and I lost him. Then I heard him again, shouting to me to come here. I shouted back to gauge where he was. When I found him, he had a carbine leveled at the two boys. Their hands were up, their long handle drawers wet from sweat and sticking to their bodies. Their chests rose and fell, their hair was long and matted over their heads. Adolescent whiskers were scattered over their faces.

Virgil made a motion with his head, and we marched them back towards the light of the barn, and orange cube glowing around the red hot bones of beams and trusses. The family milking cow stared wild-eyed within it, lowing anxiously. Chickens roosted in trees in the firelight.

Then, suddenly and without thinking, I ran into the barn. Glowing orange timbers were beginning to fall. The cow glowed in the heat as well. Her nostrils flared, her eyes were glassy. She would not budge at first. I slapped her flank with my hat and finally she trotted out of the intense heat and to a tree near the house. I tied her up and returned to where Virgil had the boys cornered.

Virgil gave me a look of stupefaction. "What'd you do that for? You coulda gotten kilt," he said.

The mother emerged from the back door this time, her hands in her hair and then to the night sky and the light of the burning barn, crying, asking, begging. She fell to her knees. Maurice was mildly effected by it, her supplication, but Virgil was as cold as stone.

"Tell them to come with us," he said to Maurice, about the boys.

There was a pause, and with a sideways hitch of his head, Maurice told the two boys, "*Allons.*" And then they walked before us down the bayou road. Their mother begged us, "*S'il vous plait, sil vous plait. Je suis une veuve. Une veuve. A wee-dow.*" She beat her chest, "*Wee-dow.*"

She ran to her boys, kneeling at their feet, hugging their legs, one and then the other and her palms pressed together like a church steeple, her face wet in the radiant crackle of her barn. I thought perhaps someone in our group would have a change of heart, that we would have pity on this poor woman and speak up for her. But no one did.

We marched the boys away from the house and the burning barn and the lowing milk cow. Fifty yards from the house, we met Teague. He appeared as an ember and a wafting vapor of cigar smoke.

"What do we have here?" he said, though I'm sure he knew.

"Dodgers," Virgil said.

"Well, no man can shirk his duty in this time of peril," Teague said. In the dark, high on his horse, his lips popped on his cigar and the ember glowed. His face was indistinct. "Suppose we should turn them in to the Texans, as there's a bounty on men such as these."

Maurice gave a command in French. Down the road and in the night, their mother wailed for her lost children.

We marched them through the night on the road that paralleled the bayou to where the Texans were. An officer was with them now. After a brief, heated conversation, Teague took a handful of bills but gave them back with an angry shout. The officer wanted to give Teague Confederate scrip, but Marse Sam insisted on specie. They complied, a heavy sack of gold and silver coins that Teague himself inspected. When he was done counting, the two boys were marched, shivering in threadbare long-handles that were darkened with their sweat, into the darkness of the swamp.

I've often wondered what happened to those boys and their mama. I like to think that they were spared the war and made their way back home. But it is just as likely that they were pressed into service, or worse, shot for desertion. Those boys and their mama, those strangers whose names I never knew.

I like to imagine the reunion they might have had. My imagination makes it a brisk, clear day. There would be gumbo cooking on the stove somewhere inside, or a sauce piquant. The boys' mama sees them approach on the bayou road. She's on a stool milking the cow. She dries her hands on her apron as she stumbles out to the road. She shouts their names in questions. The boys pause as if not believing that they are home. She runs to them, falling to her knees and hugging her returning boys, now with beards grown into manly fullness, but healthy and whole, unmarked by war. She embraces their legs and weeps tears of joy and gratitude, and raises her hands to heaven and thanks the God she has been begging constantly for their deliverance, "*Merci, mon dieu, merci.*" The boys put down their CSA knapsacks and help her up, telling her, "Get up, mama, get up. We're home." I have thought about that little family quite a bit. Quite a bit. It is a good day that I don't think about them. It is also a rare day.

But back to what certainly did happen. A fog rolled in that night as "thick as mashed taters," as my daddy used to say. We were all clustered in it. I still smelled like smoke, and the hair on my arms was singed. In the rolling sphere in the fog, just the rump of Teague's black mare was visible to us. I asked the Gordon boy what time it was. Teague overheard me and sniped back, "You got somewhere to be?"

The boy pulled a watch out of his vest pocket and whispered, "Two-thirty."

We straggled apart in the fog and after a while, I was separated. I lost my companions, and I lost their sounds, and then I was just plain lost. It was terrifying, being alone, perhaps because I was alone with myself in this world of white fog and wet sounds of bullfrogs and crickets and grunting alligators. I shouted out, "Virgil! Maurice!" but the fog absorbed my shouts. They were somewhere else. I did not call out for Teague, for fear that he would answer and shower me with caustic derision.

I passed the same forked tree several times and finally resolved to wait until the sun came up. The fog was glowing white now. I tied my horse to a cypress tree and waited. I leaned against it and napped, hoping that when I woke the fog would have thinned out some. The smell of smoke clung to me, and I waved at it as if it were a cloud of invisible insects. But each time, both it and the fog seemed thicker. Birds called in the night in watery warbles.

Sometime in the early morning, I became aware of a large presence. The horse was aware of it, too. Its eyes widened, its hooves stamped quietly, nervously. Whatever it was, the shape moved in the distance, smoothly like the shadow of a cloud. Small sticks broke out there, somewhere. I turned my ear to pick it up, to verify that it had been there, but then it would be gone. If I had known of the legend of the Rougarou then, I would have been even more scared than I was. I thought I could see it, or the movement of it, enough to cause a swirl in the mist, like when you move your hand in water. But then it would be still again. I could not see it, but I knew it was immense and dark.

"Virgil! Maurice?" I called out again, but, once more, there was only silence. The charred smell of the fiery barn still adhered to me, my clothes, my hair, even the inside of me, it seemed. Shapes moved in the fog, blurred, distorted. I closed my eyes to them. If I could have, I would have closed my ears to the wet sound of things sliding into and out of the water and the warning calls of birds and the buzz of insects.

I napped again, and by midmorning, the fog had lifted into a cotton mist that floated around the brown and orange tops of the cypresses. I was no more than fifty yards from Bayou Lafourche. Across it was Mount Teague, as plain as day in the morning sun.

15

The woman downstairs, who I think may be a hired girl, has brought me *pain perdu* and molasses. She dusts it with powdered sugar. This has always been a favorite of mine. She must be aware of it. Perhaps someone has told her. It is a small act of love to be brought food by someone. Other love acts are for the young, those in their prime, but the gift of food is love presented from the first day of life to the last.

Downstairs, someone is practicing the piano. The tinkling notes are tentative, pausing and tracing back over themselves. The sound of someone practicing a musical instrument, a child, most likely, brings me back to the days when I was a young man and quartered in the garçonnière at Mount Teague.

It was not a piano, but instead, the scratching sounds of a violin played by the Teague girl somewhere inside the house. Ba-ba-black-sheep-have-you-any-wool? A pause. Have-you-any-wool? Have-you-any-have-you-any? Have. You. Any. Another pause. Yes-sir-yes-sir-three-bags-full. The strings sing it again, Ba-ba-black sheep, and I imagine the look of concentration on the pretty face of a head with sandy brown hair and a colorful bow put there by her mother or the woman, Mathilde.

My mind sees her again, yellow-brown and lithe Mathilde, bringing me a tin pan of food. On that autumn night, the sky was moon-washed and star-crystalled, and crickets sang in blue and gray shadows. The lights in the children's rooms were extinguished after the music lesson and the dutiful practicing of it. Dew was on the ground, dew that would become the first frost of the season the next morning.

I was on the verge of sleep. A dream was toying playfully with me, a dream about my daddy and Uncle Ransom pitching horseshoes that Big Eight was forging. They would bare-hand the red hot shoes, unbothered by the heat, talking about some other thing and preparing for their next toss. All of it taking place in my Aunt Cora's front yard where fresh rectangles of red earth were lined up in rows and columns.

"*Monsieur*," someone whispered, and at first I marveled at that.

"Aunt Cora," I said to the dream voice, "I didn't know you could speak French."

"*Monsieur*," she said again, and I opened my eyes to see the woman Mathilde through the window, a shadow among shadows.

"I brought you something to eat. To thank you for your help with the mausolée."

She passed a tin plate with a tin spoon, the kind the servants ate from.

"What is it?" I asked as I took it, though it didn't matter. I was nineteen then, and after two years in the army, I would eat anything.

"*Couche-couche*," she whispered. "To thank you for helping with the tomb."

I ate the *couche-couche* hungrily, hastily, in the style of a soldier. I watched the profile of her shadow, too. The only thing that could catch light in that twilight were her green eyes. She spoke as my spoon pocked against the tin bowl.

"Have you heard anything of Etienne, the blacksmith?" she asked, and I realized her visit had as much to do with him as it did with the mausolée. She was looking at me, the way she might watch Serbus eat a laudanum-spiked pork chop.

"No ma'am," I smacked. I swallowed like a dog gulping. My eyes were on the plate she'd brought. "He special to you?" I asked.

"Yes, very," she smiled wanly. "I miss him. I worry for him."

So they were romantically involved after all, I said to myself. It made perfect sense to me.

She straightened her skirts. She seemed tired, breathless. I assumed at the time that she was worn out after a day of tending to her family.

"The men, the others, said you could have killed him," she said.

"Big fella oughten jump a littl'n like that," I said, scratching the bottom of the metal bowl to get the last bits of *couche-couche*. "Ain't a fair fight."

"No, my...Etienne, he's always had such a temper. Thank you for sparing him. I know you could have...could have...killed him."

I handed her the empty bowl. "Welcome," I said. "I had no intentions of it."

She was sitting on her hands, warming them in the night chill. She

78

took the tin bowl and rose.

"Thank you," she said, and then, after a pause, "If you hear where he is, you'll let me know, won't you? If one of the men in the cooperage says something, you'll tell me?" She seemed on the verge of tears.

"Yes ma'am," I said.

"Well, *merci*, and, *bon nuit, monsieur*," she said. She rose and floated back to the big house. And I watched her. Yes, I did.

16

The Spaniard has a new motorcar. From the front balcony, he shows it to me. It's parked on the curb under the shade of the oaks. Across Prytania in Number One, the sleepers are unconcerned and unimpressed. He grins from ear to ear as he tells me, "What you think, Pops? Brand new Chevrolet!" I think it's the first one he's owned.

The people of this house ease me downstairs and then out onto the porch and then down the steps. They open the door and help me into the thing, which gleams black in the dappled shade and the morning heat. A group of boys stand around with their hands in their pockets admiring it. I sit on the front seat with my cane between my legs, and everyone piles in around us, the Spaniard and me, including a couple of the neighborhood boys who were watching us. We are so close, we can hear each other's breathing. Everyone is excited.

The Spaniard pushes something and the auto grumbles and then ticks out a rhythm, and I'm sure we all feel the leather beneath us vibrate. The little girl, the one whom the woman sometimes calls *pichouette*, is next to me, and she shrieks a tiny, happy shriek, a small whoop, and leans into me. Her sandy blonde hair is wiry like cotton candy and pulled up in a red bow that strains against its fullness. I am happy, but my locked-in face won't tell anyone, and then I am sad a little. We lurch forward, and the Chevrolet chuckles.

We turn on streets until we are on St. Charles. The auto gives us a breeze and then takes it away again when we stop for the street car headed uptown. We cross over the neutral ground, and a bump over the rails is added to the stirring vibration of the leather seats. The little girl pressed in next to me giggles and holds my hand. "Hold on, Papere," she says. We are all perspiring, but no one says anything because we know we are bonded by the scent. Perhaps it is what a mama cat or dog sniffs for in her kittens or puppies, a reassuring scent that says *you are mine and I am yours.*

The dog is in here with us, too. He is sitting near the window, wind blowing at his ears as he barks in glee at people and rival dogs whom he perceives as now being slower than he is. The Spaniard smiles proudly as his gloved hands grip the wheel and our shoulders press into one another and the wind winds in tendrils around us and the woman who lives in our house sits on the side of me and holds my old hand and the little girl she sometimes calls *pichouette* and other times Suzette and other times *sha-beh-beh* sits on the other and the dog smiles into the breeze. And the Chevrolet trills and mutters beneath us. The big houses on St. Charles slip past us unconcerned in oak shade.

"Maybe we can get you to Mass on Sunday in this thing, Pops," the Spaniard says over the steering wheel and the rattling purr of the engine. We pause to let a mule pulling a cart canter by. "Lot easier than the streetcar, no? Maybe take you to see them Tulane boys play football in the fall."

The woman who lives in the house, who is not the hired girl, now that I think of it, smiles and squeezes my hand. Her hand is old and tan, a mild, soft beige, the same color as the spots on mine, the hand with three fingers. My gnarled hand that held the chisel and the drawknife and the mallet. One of a set of gnarled hands that in their prime fought on Sundays for Sam Teague.

The only regular day of rest at Mount Teague was Sunday. Teague and his family attended the Episcopal church, sitting in a pew that I'm sure he considered the center of the church, the true altar of the place and he himself the icon on the altar, never mind the Sufferer hanging from pierced hands behind the vicar. I marvel yet that Sam Teague could sit there Sunday after Sunday with a straight look on his face and listen to the preposterous story that someone other than him had dominion over the

80

world. I'm sure it took great restraint for him not to jump up, point an accusing finger at the vicar, and shout, "You're a goddam liar! I'm in charge here!"

Perhaps Teague had his mind on Panama, like most of the other men of St. Matthew Parish. It was a spectacle that he had come up with himself. The full name of it was "Panama Sir Kansas," or something close to that, another example of some corrupted Latin something-or-other that he had gotten from Mrs. Teague's reading of Riley's *Book of Latin Mottoes and Maxims*. Everyone else called it simply "Panama."[11] During the meeting to discuss the nightly soirees that Teague called coon hunts, I had agreed to something that I didn't remember agreeing to. After services at the Catholic, Episcopal, and Baptist churches, and noonday Sunday dinners, the plantations sent their champions to a field along the Twelve Arpent Canal for the events of "Panama Sir Kansas," or, more simply, "Panama."

Virgil Reeves had been the Mount Teague champion earlier in the fall. He was not a particularly big man, but, pound for pound, he was one of the meanest men I have ever known. He had been drummed out of the Confederate Army for attempted murder of one of his messmates and wound up here at the perimeter of the world, working, like me, for Sam Teague.

He worked in the dairy, Virgil did. He was a ruddy-faced man with a lazy eye that seemed to be searching cautiously, as if someone were trying to sneak up on him. Auguste Favorite liked to say that Virgil could milk a cow and watch for the cat at the same time.

But Virgil and his lazy eye had been disqualified from Panama after pulling a knife, something that was clearly against the rules. Some said that he did it on the suggestion of Sam Teague; some said he was just that mean. At any rate, the other plantation owners refused to send in a man to fight him because of it.

So Teague had replaced him with Big Eight. By all accounts, he was an indifferent warrior, fighting like a bear slapping away at a yapping hound, eventually landing a final, annoyed blow that won the bout through sheer strength. And when I defeated him that day in the cooperage, he departed

---

[11] This may be Teague's corruption of *Panem et circensis*, Bread and circuses.

Mount Teague for good, and the job of champion fell to me.

On those Sunday afternoons, announcements were made, proclamations, toasts, rules were delineated, and, after a few more toasts, wagers were made.

I fought two men that day and licked both of them. One was an Irish wheelwright from Hollyfield. The other was an enormous chocolate brown cane cutter from the Parris place. Neither was much of a contest, though the cane cutter did give me a black eye.

The highlight of the day was the horse races, the horses and riders thundering down a cane row by the Twelve Arpent Canal as men waived money and women waived handkerchiefs, and the late autumn sun blazed against the cold and hoofs sprayed back the black earth and the smell of burning cane hung in the cool, crisp air.

The horses won, and I won, and everyone was elated and the big bills building up at *la commissaire* were forgotten for a time, and everyone was proud to be a part of Mount Teague, proud to be part of a winner. Through the power of Panama Sir Kansas, we were euphoric and connected and would have marched into battle against cannons armed only with sticks and cane knives to defend the honor of dear old Mount Teague.

Mount Teague pigs were roasted, and we smoked cigars that week in the cooperage, courtesy of *le baws-man*, in honor of our victories the Sunday before. The men in the stables got them, too. It had been a clean sweep, victories by both man and beast, all the king's horses and all the king's men. And at the end of the day, Sam Teague made a pretty penny off us, and we were delighted to have rendered the service. *Vive le baws-man*.

I found myself walking back to the big house among the throng of people, some clutching money from side bets, money they would feed to *la commissaire*, a monster whose appetite would not be sated by the small sum, a drop in the ocean, but still a drop. She fell in beside me, a warmth on a cool afternoon. My sweat from the fight earlier in the afternoon was beginning to chill me.

"Etienne was our champion. Before." Her words trailed away without completion. Then I saw it, the hint of it, the delicate swell of her stomach under her skirt, as subtle as the curvature of the earth. The blush of her skin, her breathlessness. She was carrying a child.

"Well, then," I said. "This victory is for him, then."

She smiled, and the world was illuminated.

"I can wash your things when we get back to the house," she offered.

I didn't say anything. I may have won handily, but I was still tired. The next day would be a long one, filled with barrel staves, lids, and bottoms.

When we returned to Mount Teague, I took off my sweaty clothes in the dark of my room in the garçonnière and passed them through the window where she stood in the dusky yard, respectfully looking away. I washed in the basin on the nightstand in the dim light of a fall evening and went to bed. From my window, I could see her shadow in the window shade of her quarters, upstairs in the rear of the house. I pretended that her silhouette was looking at me.

17

She's sitting near the window where a thin strip of sunlight pierces the curtains that are drawn against the afternoon heat. Children are playing in the yard. Some are the children of this house. Some are neighborhood children. The sounds of their shouting float up through the window and are muffled by the curtains.

The woman- who is the daughter of the woman downstairs, I'm sure of it- sits and reads from an old issue of *National Geographic*, her eyes scan the page as she reads to me like she will read to the children outside when they come in from play and lay quietly for their naps on the shady back porch, each on a pallet and listening sleepily and waiting for a breeze off the river to bring in a mellow calliope song from one of the departing steamboats. They say the days of the steamboat are numbered. Trains will carry the load from now on.

She reads to me from an article about wolves. It seems a pack of gray wolves can have a territorial range of several hundred miles, more than that if prey is scarce. I lay and listen to her and remember the days that I was a wolf, part of a pack.

We went on rides with Teague once or twice a week, these rich man's coon hunts. Not only did we cross over into Confederate territory, we frequently made the rounds in Union-held land. It made no difference to us, except that on those nights in Union land, we wore sacks over our heads with openings for our eyes and our mouths. As a common soldier, I was used to standing in the line of battle in the daytime, waiting to face the blue line of danger across a field. This was different. We were the danger. And before us were lambs for the slaughter. It was one of Teague's favorite quotes: "East nun come molest 'em loophole," he would say.[12]

We stole hogs. We stole chickens. We stole horses, mules, wagons, silverware, pewter plates. A pianoforte once. A violin, a scythe, framed daguerreotypes of a man's grandparents. Washboards, irons. The only thing we wouldn't steal was a red-hot stove, though it was probably just a matter of time before Teague would figure out how and then have us do it. He had no need for any of it. I think it just irked him to know that someone else owned something. Those who put up a fight, enough of a fight, were shot. Or hung.

Some of it he would sell in the Mount Teague Commissary. Some of it he would have us dump in the Twelve Arpent Canal or in Bayou Lafourche. Some of it, he would give to Yankee officers, who then never seemed to show any interest in investigating the complaints of the conquered people who had been victims of masked robbers in the night.

"Probably Confederate raiders," they always said. "We'll be on the lookout for them." It was all in that way of giving a small child a glass of water and a pat on the head before putting them back to bed after a nightmare.

But I would see him from my window, that man Sam Teague, a shadow among shadows moving out in the yard at night, ducking under the gray beards of moss hanging from the oaks. The dog, Serbus, would

---

[12] Chip, remember this is from our days at LSU? Virgil's *Aeneid*: "*Est nunquam molestum lupo quot oves exsistant.*" "It never troubles the wolf how many the sheep may be." We had a professor who would say it as he passed out our exams. What was his name?

challenge him in the night with a single bark, and Teague would answer with a single, low, shrill whistle. The dog would whimper and cower his head and wait for the fleeting rub of the man's fingers on the dog's wide head. And after a rattle of a key in a lock, Teague would disappear into the crypt with something, a satchel, I believe it was, the satchel. He would only stay a minute or so, and then the lock would rattle again and the dog would whimper again and Teague would duck back under the hanging moss, as gray as everything else in the shadow-world.

He would smoke a cigar on the back porch, a shadow pocked by its ember, glowing and fading. I could only faintly smell the smoke of it. Then the ember would fly out into the bloomless azalea bushes, the back door would open, and the world would descend into a deeper level of stillness. The nights at Mount Teague were darker and stiller than anywhere else I have ever been. On those still, dark nights, Sam Teague would deliver his tainted riches to the keeping of those who had no need or desire for it, the dead.

The days, however, were filled with honest industry. After a night spent on hunts that had produced everything except a coon, I would frequently fall asleep and get poked awake several times by Mr. Lapeyrouse, having fallen asleep with my head on a barrel, my drawknife limp in my hand. *Réveillez*, he would say to me in French, and then in English, *wake up. Get to work, stud mule.*

Meanwhile, the cane cutting was in full tilt. I will tell you that I have seen soldiers complete fifty mile marches or all-day battles in the heat. I've seen stevedores on the levee here in the city, rolling big barrels and toting monstrous bales up and down gangplanks all day in the hot sun. But I have never seen men as exhausted as those poor Negroes cutting cane at Mount Teague.

They would ride out in empty wagons drawn by mules, the men quietly jostling as they sat on the floor of those cane wagons. There was no laughter, no levity, only the grim knowledge that it would be a long, sweaty day of toil. They would alight from the wagons, cane knives in hand, and trudge to the edge of the cane fields, spread out in a line, and begin hacking away. Younger boys and the very old would gather the cut cane, tossing great armloads up into the wagons where another man would lay it down carefully so as to get as big a load as possible.

Every so often the men with the knives would retreat a sudden few steps with a shout, scattering from the edge of cane rows. Then the *chef d-equipe*, the foreman, would raise a shotgun and blast at something in the cane rows. A snake, always a snake, usually a rattler.

Then when the wagon was tall and shaggy with a heaping load of dull green-and-beige cane, the mule team would pull it back to the mill, hooves straining in the black soil against the weight, and an empty wagon would fall in line. And so on and so on and so on, men and mules working from can to can't, as they used to say. Bringing in the thousands of acres of white gold that was, and is, Mount Teague. All the while, everyone wearing invisible shackles to *la commissaire*.

My days were still spent in the cooperage getting barrels ready for the white granules that would come from the grinding and boiling. But more and more, I would be summoned from my work to Teague's study. He would say that he had misplaced his glasses or that his eyes were tired or that he had a headache that was made worse by reading. It was easy work, the reading, and it got me out of the heat and into the cool cross-breezes of the house. And it got me away from Eugene D'Ormeaux whose non-stop rattling had even eclipsed Re-Pete's. If there is such a thing of dysentery of the mouth, Eugene D'Ormeaux had it.

On the day that the papers reported the battle of Chickamauga, which had occurred over a month earlier, I was summoned again to the big house by Mathilde. In the gentleman's parlor, a bespectacled fellow waited with bolts of fabric. His mouth was under his face like a gaspergou, a goo-fish, as Uncle Ransom used to call them.

I found Mrs. Teague reading to her husband from the book entitled, *Dictionary of Latin Quotations.*[13]

Mrs. Teague's swollen belly held the book, which her unseen occupant jostled from time to time. Teague was stretched out on his chair with his hand on his forehead and his eyes closed.

"Vennie, Viddie, Veesy,"[14] Mrs. Teague drawled.

---

[13] English scholar H. T. Riley first published *Dictionary of Latin Quotations, Proverbs, Maxims, and Mottos* in 1856 and again as a second edition in 1860.
[14] *Veni, vidi, vici-* Julius Cesar

"Vennie, Viddie, Veezy," Teague repeated through closed eyes. "What's it mean?" he asked.

"I came, I saw, I conquahed."

"Hm," he said, "Vennie, Biddy, Peachy," he repeated with his finger waving like a band leader marking out a jaunty tune. "I came and saw and conquered."

"May I retire, dear?" Mrs. Teague said as she rubbed her stomach.

"A little more," Teague said. Then, when he saw me, he said, "No, that's alright."

Teague rose and took me into the hallway and introduced me to the man waiting there.

"This is Mr. Craps," Teague said.

"Kratz," the man corrected Teague, his mouth working from under his face.

Teague stared at him. And stared at him. And stared at him. The hallway clock was ticking. Kratz wore the expression of a dog pinned by another dog.

And then Teague said, slowly and deliberately, "Mr. Craps will take your measurements."

Teague returned to his study where the Latin lessons continued.

"I am really quite exhausted," Mrs. Teague said in there.

"Yes, I'm sure. A little more."

Mr. Kratz silently began measuring me as, in the next room, a clearly exhausted Mrs. Teague kept reading Latin to her husband.

"*Oderant dim metuant,*" she sighed.

"*O'durnt dumb mesh-want.*" Teague repeated. "What's it mean?"

She sighed again.

"Let them hate so long as they…" she yawned loudly, "…fear."

"Hm," Teague said. "I like that one. Let them hate so long as they fear. How do you say it in Latin again?"

Mrs. Teague exhaled forcefully, the kind of exhalation that would be lethal if it were a gun.

"*Oderant dim metuant. Caligula.*" She pronounced it Callie-Goola. And then, so did Teague.

"O-durnt dim meshint. Callie-Goola. Let them hate so long as they fear. Why, doesn't that just say something?" Teague said genially, as if discussing a line of scripture with the vicar.

The tailor's scissors crunched quietly through fabric, and I waited while he worked in the lamplight, foot kneading a treadle-powered sewing machine, glasses poised on the tip of his nose. His needle dipped and dove through the fabric of the cuff, a thin silver flash in the black gabardine.

The reason for my new suit was a ball to be held in celebration of what looked to be a banner harvest. The beginning wisps of cold were floating in on northern breezes, and the floor to ceiling windows were open to welcome them. Cane stubble was being burned in sulphurous flames, shapes of men like lesser demons silhouetted as they tended the blazes through the night. As these shadows attended the fires, the guests arrived by carriage and lamplight.

I felt ill-at-ease at first. I had never attended a soiree such as that, had never expected to, never even dreamed of it, never knew what one was, never knew that they were necessary. The lights were low and boiling, conversation rumbling. My new suit pulled and pushed against my body, coaxing it into unnatural postures. My collar teased my throat, pretending to choke me, then relaxed and did it again when I wasn't thinking about it. My new shoes squeezed my feet, jamming my toes together, rubbing the back of my heels. My new silk socks slid down my calves, my cuffs jammed themselves against my forearms. My new suit felt more like my new costume.

Mrs. Teague stopped me in the hallway and retied my tie, a black silk cravat. She smiled at me and said, there, and patted my shoulder. I kept looking for her among the bubbling of conversation about race horses and cane prices and politics. She would smile at me, a friendly, reassuring smile from the ladies' parlor adjacent to the men's, a place where more refined things were discussed. Her dress was rounded with her condition, and she would wince when her baby, the little boy so longed for by Marse Sam, jabbed at her from within. Her frown would dissolve, and then she would smile again. She was a woman of natural kindness who was struggling in her present condition to remain good-humored.

In the gentlemen's parlor, Teague held court, taller and louder than the others. The men were smoking cigars and drinking port, while the women visited in the adjoining parlor. The rumbling conversations of the men were a contrast to the higher pitched chatter of the women. Teague's baritone sounded the cadence in our room. When he spoke, we were all to listen.

"People down here speak that French jabber. If they had any sense, they'd speak English like we speak up in Mississippi and like Christ himself spoke."

Two of the Union officers exchanged glances, trying to decide if this was a joke and polite laughter was in order. At last, they decided that a neutral smile would be sufficient. One of them gently swung the conversation around, by proposing a toast.

"To friendship and reconciliation, let enemies become brothers again."

"Hear, hear!" went up with glasses and nods.

Then there was talk of Hollyfield and its fate. The men of Hollyfield were said not to be coming back from war. Someone said, isn't that a shame? And someone else said that the word was, the man's widow would have to sell out.

Teague pretended not to be concerned, but this is something I came to find out about Teague: the less interested in something he seemed to be, the more preoccupied with it he was. He sat and stared as the other men uttered regretful, rueful phrases. Teague looked like a man figuring out a problem or a puzzle, his tongue probing the inside of his cheek. I don't think he could listen and think at the same time, though, then again, maybe few can.

Raindrops of champagne fell and gathered into rivulets of whiskey which ran into gullies of wine and creeks of cognac and at last, rivers of port. All very good stuff. Only the best at Mount Teague. My clothes were very comfortable now; I scarcely felt them at all. I had struck up conversations with several of the men and their wives, the men finding me a "capital fellow" and the women finding me "absolutely *chahming.*"

I thought of a joke that my daddy and my Uncle Ransom used to tell. It was obscene, but to my daddy and Uncle Ransom, it was decidedly funny and at that time and in my condition, I was sure the men and women gathered there would certainly enjoy hearing it. Luckily, someone interrupted, and the conversation took some other path, away from the joke that I was about to tell, about an island composed entirely of shipwrecked men and a barrel with a hole in it set up on a hill. It was just as well.

The liquor milled about in me and then began to paw at the door to be let out. In those days, I was unaccustomed to indoor toilets. Indeed, few homes, if any, had them, and my memory can't recall if Mount Teague had them in that day and time. I had been raised by a man who himself was content with the outdoors for that sort of thing, and army life had only reinforced the habit for me. So, after several rounds of port, I staggered out the back door of Mount Teague to one of the live oak trees there.

As I stood there, I heard the door open and close and then from the other side of the tree, a conversation. One was the blaring drawl of Sam Teague, trying to contain itself in hushed tones. In the dark, there was the sound of the flare of a Lucifer match, a sound much like the strop of a blade being sharpened, and then another voice.

"I've got us round about a thousand bales from up in the north part of the state, middlin grade or better," Sam Teague said.

"That so?" the voice asked. It was a northern voice, the kind of accent that southern boys are raised to believe the devil uses.

"Yessir. How much is cotton going for now?"

"Let's just say we're setting on a pretty penny."

"Well, it's just a matter of getting it to market, now ain't it?"

"Oh, don't worry about that, Mr. Teague."

"Sam, please. Sam to my friends and trusted business associates."

"Sam, then. Don't worry about getting it to market. The army's got the whole river now, and it'll just be a case of getting our product to New Orleans and then on ships to Manchester and Liverpool first. They're so starved for cotton that we'll fetch top dollar if we get there first."

"Hot damn," Teague said, "I like how you think, Colonel."

I felt it was a conversation I shouldn't be a part of, and I had long since buttoned up and was leaning tightly into the other side of the live oak. My palms were imprinted with the pattern of the bark. Their voices receded with the cigar smoke, and the sounds of revelry broadened with the opening of the door and then narrowed again as it shut.

Still the night carried on, unable to stop itself and in danger of plowing into morning. I looked into the ladies' parlor searching for the reassuring sight of Mrs. Teague. I found her sitting down and being fanned by two other ladies. I walked over toward her.

"Go and fetch Mr. Teague, would you?" one of the ladies said.

I staggered up the stairs, which seemed steep and more like a ladder than steps. I wandered the upper halls looking for Sam Teague. All the doors were shut. Several of the guests had indicated that they would be staying overnight, and I was reluctant to knock on doors and disturb them. I paused in the hallway, held back by drunkenness and inertia. I was pondering going downstairs again when I heard it.

The sounds of passion murmured behind a door. The thump and squeak of a bed, the grunting and moaning. I waited, unsure of what I should do. Should I go downstairs without bringing Teague with me? But drunkenness makes little problems big, and big problems little.

And then there was a grunting crescendo and then silence and then the shuffle of bodies rising.

The door opened, and, in a floor-length dressing mirror, I caught a glimpse of green satin skirts lifted in the air and falling over the crinoline hoop skirt of a copper-haired woman whose face I didn't see. And then the mirror was filled with the tall figure of Sam Teague pulling his suspenders over his arms and onto his shoulders. He quickly shut the door so I couldn't see who his paramour was. The door shut on her as he put on his swallowtail coat. He cast me this grin, this menacing smile and whispered-no, it was more like a growl.

He said, "Don't let your tongue cut off your head."

And then he patted my cheek with his big, soft hand. It smelled like sex.

Downstairs again, the party quickly wound down as Mrs. Teague took to her room in anticipation of a long night of labor.

Colonel Hutchison left, wishing Sam Teague well in the new addition to the Teague clan and joking that he should name it after him, the colonel, if it was a boy. The men laughed at that, as the colonel had some sort of odd family name, an albatross of a name that had been handed down a few times more out of obligation than anything else.[15] At the door, Teague

---

[15] Chip, this is probably C. W. Hutchinson, Colonel of the 54th Wisconsin Infantry. The C stood for "Cassiopius."

planted a demur kiss on the white kid gloved-hand of the colonel's wife. A copper-haired woman in a green satin dress.

18

The mailman is delivering along Prytania. He sorts through letters as he walks, shuffling them into order, alighting onto porches, then down to the street, then the next house, shuffling, sorting, one house and then the next like a bee sampling flowers. His satchel catches my eye and stirs my memory. He waves to me, and I lift an old hand to him. Across the street in Lafayette Number One, the residents have no mailboxes and no need of mail.

It is something to be entrusted with correspondence, notes containing expressions of elation and sorry, sadness and happiness. News such as, *Your aunt is very ill*, or *Father has called for you, buy a train ticket and come at once*, or *you have a new niece, we are naming her after Mother*. Or, news as mundane as *the weather here is nice, though we could use some rain*, or *Grandpa has put in two more rows of peas*. Still, it is an honored thing, to be put in charge of such news, be it ordinary or momentous.

And so, that is what I thought when I performed the task for Sam Teague. He asked me into the house, through an invitation brought by the albino gardener. I could hear the Teague girls upstairs, arguing over something, and one of them crying, then the heavy steps of an adult up there. Downstairs, there was no sign of Mathilde and no sign of Mrs. Teague, who had not gone into labor and who was upstairs resting.

There was just Sam Teague in his study. He was tracing things onto a slate, a tangle of nonsensical lines etched in chalk. When I appeared at the door, he hastily put it away.

"Good morning, Carrick," he said with a lift of his gaze from his desk. "Please, sit down."

I sat in a plain Windsor chair.

"I have a task for you. I need you to ride up to Donaldsonville to carry a satchel to the colonel there."

"Yes sir," I said.

He patted his shirt pocket and then made a show of looking through the cubby holes of his desk.

"Carrick, I seemed to have misplaced my glasses," he said. "Do you think you could compose a note for me?"

"Yes sir," I said again. How many times, I now wonder, did I tell that man yessir? More than I should have, I'm thinking.

He cleared his throat. And then he looked at me with those nickel-gray eyes, and he said, "This is to be discussed with no one. No one, understand, son?"

He frequently called me son, though he was nowhere near old enough to be my father. It always irked me; it did. He cleared his throat again.

"Yes sir," I said, one of a thousand times, a million times, *yes sir*.

"Now," he said as he shut his eyes in thought. "To Colonel C. W. Hutchison. Enclosed is the amount we discussed. I have retained my share. You are, of course, enjoined to keep this in strictest confidence. Signed, Samuel M. Teague."

I wrote it out and showed him.

"You have quite a hand, Carrick."

"Thank you, sir," I said. "Do you want to sign it?"

"Oh, no," he said. He was momentarily off balance, it seemed. "I mean, you have such a beautiful hand. Just put, *Samuel M. Teague*."

I did it.

"Now," he said as he rose. "I'll need you to take the note with this satchel up to the colonel in Donaldsonville."

We walked out onto the porch where a horse was tied to the railing, nosing quietly through the azaleas, lips pulling at the leaves and finding them inedible or unworthy. I placed a boot in the stirrup and pulled myself up. He handed the satchel up to me.

"Do not look inside this satchel. For any reason," he said as he held onto it for a minute. He only let go of it when I responded, "Yes sir."

I worked the strap over my head and onto my shoulder. Teague untied the horse and handed me the reins.

"My regards to the colonel," he said. "He should send you back with a note to verify his receipt."

"Yes sir," I said, once again. How many times? A million?

The ride along the bayou road was pleasant in the crisp fall air, the smell of wood smoke and cypress and cooking. The fields of Mount Teague fell away, teams of Negroes hacking away at it, some singing, most not. The bayou was wooded in stretches, then fallow fields of other plantations where cane should have been, and then more woods. Towns, Plattenville, Paincourtville, Napoleonville. And then above a levee, smokestacks: Donaldsonville.

There were blue coats everywhere, and it still gave me a start to see them. I still imagined that I was behind their lines and would be taken prisoner.

I stopped one of them and asked, "Where might I find the colonel, Colonel C. W. Hutchison?"

"Mississippi Street," he said, his bored face looking up with a bored look from the boring work of garrisoning a bored and conquered place. Surely it was also so for the Romans in Judea.

The flag of the United States also gave me a start. It was flying over the office on Mississippi Street, a breeze off the river rippling the stripes, the stars lapping and overlapping each other. It took me years before I could finally look at it and not sense danger. The door to the office was open, and a young aide-de-camp was hunched over a desk writing something. I knocked on the door jamb.

"Yes?" he asked in an annoyed tone down to the report he was writing.

"Delivery for Colonel Hutchison," I said timidly as I lifted the satchel.

"Set it there," the man said. He still hadn't looked up. The jacket hanging on his chair had lieutenant bars on it.

"I'm to give it to him personally. It's from Sam Teague, down in St. Matthew."

The colonel himself emerged from the back room.

"I'll take that," he said. He was in shirtsleeves, too. The coolness that the early morning had promised had been a ruse. It was warm again and inching toward hot. The colonel struck an odd figure, a thick head of perfectly fixed hair like a lion's mane with a thin, angular face and neat beard under it. He took the satchel and said, "Thank you…Carridge, was it?"

"Yes sir," I said. It was close enough. He shook my hand and noticed the missing finger. He smiled at me, and I wonder if his mind was making connections between a dead man and woman in Catahoula and this nonexistent finger. Surely he had seen hundreds of men who were missing things, not only fingers, but arms and legs and hands.

"Good to see you again, Carver," he told me.

"And you, sir," I said.

Then he said to his aide-de-camp, "Peabody, no more visitors this afternoon. I'll be going over…correspondence in my office."

"Respectfully, sir, I still have this report to finish."

"Pish-posh. That will be all," the colonel said pointedly, and then a little softer, "That will be all. Your hard work is appreciated. But hard work and no play makes Jack a dull boy."

Peabody gathered the coat with the lieutenant's bars on it and shoved the report into the drawer of his desk. He and I exited together.

"Shut the door behind you, Peabody," the colonel said.

19

The girl has come to visit. Not the little girl, but another, one whom I remember when she was small like the little girl. Now she is older, tall in that sudden way, gangly legs and arms with knees and elbows that are wide places on them like the nodes on a twig. Her face is bespectacled, oily, and randomly pocked with pimples and blemishes. She is in that painful era, not a girl and not a woman, that uncertain, awkward stage. Like the other girl, the little one who is her younger sister, her hair is blonde and wiry. But she has cut it into a bob, abandoning the longer hair of childhood, something that was once combed and petted by older girls and mothers. They both remind me so much of the girl Prosperine Billiot whom I knew back in St. Matthew. I catch myself wondering again, what ever became of her?

The girl who comes in today asks me, "What will we read today,

Papere?"

She holds up a book, *Ivanhoe*, and I shake my head. She holds up the *National Geographic*, and I shake my head. My fingers tap the newspaper she has brought. On the front is a photograph of rows and columns of peaked hats, an oblong, regular mountain range of steep summits, or a set of funnels like a baker might use to spread icing. Over them is the old flag of a defunct nation that Jefferson Davis himself said, "Died of a theory." Behind them is a contrasting shape, the dome of the United States Capitol.

The headline in the *Times-Picayune* proclaims, "*Klan Marches in Washington*," a fact that is evident in the photograph of pointy heads in pointy sheets, men who march anonymously under the stars and bars, men who are afflicted with the same national madness that we were afflicted with sixty years before. But these men were not even alive then, when we were marching under it, and these men are not starving, thirsty, scared, dirty, or sick from coughing and the runs.

After their morning exercise, the Kluckers will listen to the vitriol that the speakers have for Nigras, Jews, Papists, and all the other common enemies. After all, it is common enemies that make uncommon friends. Then they will take off their hoods, for I'm sure those heads must get hot under there. Then, only in their robes, they will look more like members of the choir after Sunday services (as some of them may very well be), and they will go back to their hotel rooms in our nation's capital, to clean up for dinner and perhaps a trip to the part of town where love can be bought by the hour.

The girl who reads to me today isn't aware of the way of these things, the deeds that men commit secretly under sheets. I wouldn't tell her if I could. It is not my place. And she will find out soon enough. Let her live in a world that is still beautiful while she can.

Today's headline is the Klan, though tomorrow, something else will take its place. Such is the way of the news: it is what the men at the newspapers say it will be.

That fall the news of the double murder in Catahoula Parish was quickly washed out, diluted by news of other deaths by the thousands in Virginia, Tennessee, and Georgia, a small drop of red in a bucket of blood,

96

a tiny smudge of darkness in a bigger darkness.

I was beginning to breathe a little easier, relieved and hopeful that the deaths in Catahoula would be forgotten, upstaged by a bigger show. I still wore the patent leather gloves, however, to hide my missing digit whose place was taken by a wad of gray moss. But I was becoming careless, and it was a carelessness that would later cost me my best friend. It would be one of the biggest regrets of my life. Forgetting to wear a glove.

Mrs. Teague had taken to bed, at last refusing to sit and read to her husband, tired of Latin, tired of English, tired of her relentless condition, and just plain tired. She waited for labor the way that the bored and condemned wait for the lash: it will hurt, but at least it will be done.

Because of it, I was spending more and more time in the big house, taking dictation for Marse Sam and reading to him, and going on errands into Donaldsonville with the satchel that I was now sure held the filthy proceeds from a tainted enterprise. The men in the cooperage would tease me calling me, "Marse Sam's new housecat," but I didn't care. I could hear them out there when the breeze was right, the monotonous rattle of staves and straps and lids and bottoms, over and over, ending in the hollow growl of a finished barrel rolled on its side to join the others in their wait for sugar.

As I mounted my horse with the satchel, Auguste Favorite would see me and shout, "*Garde-la ba*s, boys! Marse Sam's house-*cat*!" The men of the cooperage would meow derisively at me and say, "Here, *minou, comme ci, sha minou!*" I would give them a crude gesture, and they would laugh and I would laugh, and I would be on my way to Donaldsonville and the colonel.

The Mount Teague satchel and I became regular traveling companions. I was happy to be on horseback, cantering along the bayou road under the rusting cypresses and the cool blue or gray sky. The countryside bounced past me in time to the clop of my horse, fields with houses with crooked chimneys and lines of cane cutters and sagging cane wagons. Turtles on logs in the bayou, snowy egrets on bandy legs staring carefully into the sheen of the green water. Mist on the mirror surface of the water on those cool days. All of it wavering, scrolling by to the gallop of a horse and the sway of its rider.

And then the sleepy bustle of Donaldsonville, the dogs who were learning to bark again at strangers. Union soldiers, both dark and fair, milling around, some feeding the dogs scraps. Steamboats in the river, towering stacks, taking soldiers away and bringing more. And my well-worn path in the muddy streets to the office of Colonel Hutchison who now greeted me like an old friend.

I would give the colonel the note, the one I had written and signed, "Here is the amount you were expecting. I have retained mine. Respectfully, your obedient servant, Samuel M. Teague."

"Excellent, Carson," the colonel would say, and then he would give me a letter of receipt. Afterwards, I would pick about town for a while, visiting the shops, reading the paper silently on the porches, and then ascending the levee to watch the water whirl by slowly on itself, downstream, off to the right, down to New Orleans and the Gulf. I thought how I would like to see it one day, the Gulf, an immense beast that slept most of the time, but occasionally woke in a rage and bounced on itself, slapping the shore and its inhabitants, each having gotten too close.

When the falling angle of the light changed the water's color from brown to blue to black, I would saddle up and return home, back to Mount Teague looming in the dark and the shriek of the peacocks in the chill air.

20

Across the street in Number One, a woman who is advanced in her state attends a grave. It is a monument that I did for them, though I cannot remember the name. It was Galjour or Galloway or something like that. I don't remember the name, but I do remember that it was very sad, something unexpected. They've come to me at times like these, when death has appeared suddenly, and at other times, when death had been expected, a welcome companion come to guide an old one home. They've come to me for a monument to commemorate a life, long or short, but still a life.

And they've come to me when the business of the appearance of a new life took a dangerous turn. It was so common then. My motherless upbringing can attest to it.

Mrs. Teague's time for new life came. Her low moans were, at first, hard to distinguish from the playful singing of the children. The moans deepened into groans, and then into throaty howls. The servants scurried around the house, up and down stairs. One of Marse Sam's drivers took the girls to a neighboring place. I believe it was Hollyfield, though my recollection has a hole in it here, as in other places. The younger Teague girl was carefree, but her older sister had a look of worry about her. She looked back to the house one more time before climbing into the carriage. I remember that part so well. Big sister sat in the back seat, one made of tufted black patent leather, and put her arm around her younger sister.

Upstairs, the storm raged, as turbulent as an angry sea. An afternoon of it passed, and the doctor in Donaldsonville was sent for. He arrived in a horse and buggy, alighting from it with a black bag, tossing the whip up onto the seat like a black snake. Mathilde met him at the front door, wiping her hands on her apron and ushering him upstairs.

Around sunset, the others began to arrive, by the special invitation of Samuel M. Teague, Mount Teague Plantation, St. Matthew, Louisiana. That's what he had me write on them. He treated it like a cocktail party, only Mrs. Teague herself could not attend as she was indisposed, preoccupied with the body-splitting business of delivering a child.

Those in attendance, however, included the vicar, Colonel Hutchison, and his red-haired wife, Polly, I believe her name was. She was a buxom lady with creamy skin and red lips and green eyes, very fetching, but in a Northern way, a woman who was used to long nights and a great deal of time spent indoors. My young mind immediately flashed to the sight of her pale thighs under the crinoline cage awaiting its mantle of green skirt.

There were a few others there, Monsieur D'Ormeaux was one, the others I either didn't know or can't remember their names. Men gathered in the parlor, waiting the news if it would be a son, the thing Teague dearly wanted, the only thing he wanted more than his next dollar.

While his wife wailed upstairs, Teague appeared unconcerned, smoking cigars and sipping bourbon, making small talk about the war and the cane crop. He was dispassionate to her shrieking, as if it were just another peacock cry in the night.

Sometime in the night, after several rounds of port, a baby cried upstairs, the great, nervous, gulping for air, one yelp after the other and then the other. We men in the parlor looked at one another, and Teague received our pats on the back and handshakes with a smile, though he was holding out for better news, the thing he had been waiting for, the thing that had eluded him for years. As the baby repeated its blustery cry, the servants listened for the sound that was lacking: the great sobbing laughter of a happy mother.

The doctor came down with his shirt sleeves rolled up and mottled with blood. He paused halfway down the stairs. Behind him, upstairs somewhere, the newborn was heaving air in and out of its little lungs. The doctor braced himself with one hand on the bannister.

Teague looked up to him in the yellow gaslight and asked the question, waiting for the answer that had escaped him for so long.

"Well?" he said.

All eyes were on the doctor poised there. He swallowed hard and gave the announcement.

"Another girl, Sam."

Someone said, "Ho-Ho! There, Sam! Another Teague princess!"

Teague raised his glass with the rest of us, and took a sip with the rest of us, and then he kept his glass raised as he contemplated it. His face went from a neutral expression to a sour scowl.

And then with a lunging motion, he threw it into the fireplace. It popped against the marble and then the shards tinkled and the alcohol ignited into a brief flare. Everyone was silent as Teague excused himself from the circle to go out on the porch and stare out onto the moonlit lane of oaks. As he left, we heard him exclaim quietly to himself, *Goddamit*.

One of the men there asked the doctor, who was turning to ascend the stairs again, "Doc, how is Mrs. Teague?"

He paused on the stairs and spoke down to us, "I'm afraid it's grave."

Our congratulations fell like kites in a downdraft, into a hard silence that was broken only by the ripple of the fire as it calmly clamored for more whiskey and more glass and the clock in the hallway patiently counted off the seconds in our lives. The reverend was there, the vicar of the local Episcopal church (Daddy always called them pissers, mostly to get Aunt

100

Cora's goat-she was herself a pisser). Teague returned from outside, still fuming but better composed. The reverend put his hand on Teague's shoulder and said, "Mr. Teague, shall we pray?"

"That ain't gonna help," Teague said, and he wrenched his shoulder away. "Prayin's about like beggin', and Teagues don't beg."

Some men left, some slept in chairs and then left, drifting away one by one. I stayed, and perhaps it endeared me to Teague. I said little or nothing, offering only my silent presence. The health of the patient upstairs faltered slowly but surely, like something sliding down a hillside. A wet nurse was sent for the baby, the little girl named by the house staff, as Teague took no interest in the child. When the doctors, from Donaldsonville and then Thibodaux and then Baton Rouge, could do no more, the reverend from the Episcopal church in Napoleonville was sent for again.

The hearse came with a coffin, and she was placed in it. Then, the box was driven through the lane of oaks as the lines of house staff and field hands removed their hats with the passing of the glass-sided carriage with black curtains drawn back with thickly braided satin cords. The spokes twirled into a circular blur.

The hearse with its cargo of sadness had scarcely cleared the lane of oaks when Teague said something that surprised and appalled me, even coming from someone like Sam Teague.

"Maybe now I can get me one what can give me a son," he said into the distance.

We put on our coats to ride to the cemetery. She had chosen to be buried with "her people" in Thibodaux rather than at Mount Teague. I couldn't fault her for that.

21

The woman spends the afternoon with me today, knitting something or tatting lace. I've never been able to tell the difference between the two. She sings to herself, and sometimes she talks to herself, even canting her head slightly when she makes a point. Her green eyes follow the needles, the tips dancing a minuet, one over, one under, and reverse. My eyes follow them, too. They are graceful, soothing in their play. Certainly, it must have been so for Mrs. Teague.

The scene she was embroidering was left in its small hoop on the mahogany sewing table in the ladies' parlor, next to the book she was halfway through, *Sense and Sensibility* by Jane Austen. Both were kept just as they were. Mrs. Teague's death left a vacuum in the house, and I was pulled into that vacuum because of something I could do and Teague couldn't.

The day-to-day was still in the keeping of the house staff, particularly the tall mulatto woman, Mathilde. After Mrs. Teague died, that woman Mathilde raised those girls. Any sense of love, any sense of belonging, any sense of tenderness, all was due to her efforts. Thanks to her, they wore clean clothes, were well-fed, took their lessons dutiful from the tutor who Teague had hired. She kept the other house servants working like a conductor leads a symphony. And Teague stayed out of her way.

She flitted from room to room, cooking and cleaning with her hair up in a tignon and the baby wrapped up against her chest, or rushing into the nursery when the little thing woke up fussing. She would shift from foot to foot and sing to the baby, sweet, French songs that never failed to quiet the little girl.

In the evenings, after I had washed, I would eat with Teague, who ate separately from his girls, whom he treated as some sort of slag heap of his procreative efforts, failed byproducts in the quest for a male heir. He did see that they were formally schooled, and paid a man from Thibodaux to come up and educate them, which included lessons on the viola. The hesitant scrape of "Ba-Ba-black-sheep-have-you-any-wool?" wafted through the house as well as the "Alphabet Song," and other simple ditties. If they had ever learned the ones about Dear Old Aunt Mabel and Toothless Nell, well, I would probably have sung along. I suppose it's just as well that they didn't.

When we were done eating, I would read the paper to Teague. If there was something that interested him, he would have me read the article twice or three times. If there was a word that was unfamiliar to him, he would ask me, "Carrick, what do you suppose that means, *abrogated*?"

I would read for the better part of two hours, first the papers, and then something weighty like *Rise and Fall of the Roman Empire* or Darwin's *Origin of the Species*. Darwin was a favorite, as Marse Sam was a devout believer in the survival of the fittest, but invariably he would fall asleep in his leather Campeche chair. I would stare at him, not wanting to leave without his permission and not wanting to wake him, which, in the end, I did.

He would rejoin the world, smacking his lips and blinking his eyes.

"Yes, yes, Carrick." A scratch of his head, sandy hair beginning to thin at the temples. "That will be all," and I would adjourn to my quarters in the garçonnière.

After less than a week, I became more and more certain of something.

Sam Teague couldn't read. Not one lick. He was a refined man who could dance the waltz and the quadrille. He knew which fork to use. He could flirt, he knew when to kiss a lady's hand, when to shake her husband's. He dressed himself, and dressed himself well, a great sense of style. He was tall and even taller in the saddle of his black horse with the blonde mane. He only had one shortcoming, and it was a source of great frustration for him. He couldn't read, as much as he wanted to, it escaped him. There were whispers that he had been dismissed from the school in Oxford for it, for that and the fact he had cheated to try to cover it up.

The written word was a collection of mute shapes, tight-lipped consonants, smirking vowels. A jumbled tangle of twisted, nonsensical lines that held a secret that the printed characters would perhaps share with others but not with him. He only knew three letters. One was the line with a face on it. That was P. One was S, which he never made the same way twice-backwards, on its side, skinny, fat. The only other one was a line with another line on top of it. That was a T, and T stood for Teague. He knew that one, too. The rest of the letters were mere marks, like random scratches in the bare earth of a chicken yard.

He once hired a tutor who patiently sat with him in his study as his fingers followed the parade of letters that were little more to Teague than hieroglyphics. Every time, Teague would falter and claim a headache or strained eyes. Or he would rise frustrated and show the young man to the door and decline to pay him for a service that had not been rendered.

The spoken word, however, was a different matter altogether. He could speak fearlessly, especially to men, and especially from horseback. All because of his wife, and later his daughters, who read to him. His children became great scholars because of him, reading the New Orleans and Baton Rouge papers to him patiently as he sat with his eyes closed. He would stop them and say, "But what does it say about such and such" or "read that part again."

No, he couldn't read or write, which eventually became common knowledge, but my, how he could talk, especially in public to a group of men. He could get them to do anything. Men would run through burning buildings to retrieve unstolen silver, climb up trees draped with moccasins to scout the countryside, wade among alligators to collect unstolen hogs. All for that man, that man Sam Teague.

He was illiterate but still thirsty for knowledge. He knew that knowledge was a key that would open many a treasure house, and oh how he loved his treasure. He's been dead these many years, and now as an old man I can say it plainly: Sam Teague was the kind of man who would screw you over, ask you if you enjoyed it, and then be genuinely hurt if you said you didn't.

And he could screw you royally.

22

The issue of our floundering neighbor, Hollyfield, was one that most certainly preoccupied Teague. He would pretend not to care, or give only a token of mild concern, but he couldn't hide it from me. I was his source of information. I suppose I could have read to him that men from the moon had landed in St. Matthew Parish or that a sea monster had smashed a paddlewheeler in the Mississippi or that the South was enjoying stunning success and had Washington encircled. He would never have been able to check it for himself. Thus, the power of reading.

But that would have been a short-lived, whimsical amusement. I knew enough of men to know that there were some you did not trifle with. Thus, the power of Sam Teague, *le baws-man.*

Each Friday when the *St. Matthew Compass* came out, he had me scour it.

"Any word on Hollyfield?" he would ask, the benign tone in his voice a ruse for his real intentions. Like a buzzard circling in the sky watches a limping animal, he was waiting for Hollyfield to collapse so he could rush in. But, like most predators, he lacked the patience that carrion-eaters have. And at last, he could wait no longer.

He found out that the widow, who was trying to run Hollyfield after the demise of her husband and sons in Virginia, had gone to New Orleans to beg credit from one of the banks there. So, the next day, a Saturday, he gathered us up, his usual soldiers, along with a couple of wagons, and we headed off to pay a call on the Hollyfield field hands.

There in fading sunlight, in plain view of the widow's home, Sam Teague stood up in the back of one of the wagons. And he gave a speech that was so smooth, so persuasive, that I swear if Jefferson Davis himself had heard it, he would have vaulted into the wagon, picked up a cane knife, and shouted *vive le baws-man!*

For one thing, he offered two dollars a day, an unheard of wage in those days and certainly more than the Mount Teague hands made. He offered them Sunday and Saturday off, discounts at *la commissaire*. A whiskey bottle was passed around. Everything made perfect sense.

After the conclusion of his pitch, Honest Sam Teague said, "Well, let's get you people situated in your new quarters."

One of them, an old gray-headed man who was the butler at Hollyfield, said, "We can't leave Miss now, how she gonna get along without us?"

"She just gonna half to shift for herself," another said. "We gettin' two dollars a day. Two dollars, Clarence! They's white men ain't makin' that kinda money!"

One man went to get his wife and baby, another went to get his mama.

"You all damn fools," the old butler said to those getting in the wagons. I got the impression that if he wouldn't have been so old, he would have physically prevented them.

"Fools for what?" Teague snapped, "for wanting to make top dollar? For wanting to get ahead in this new world, where a man gets honestly paid

105

for his labors?"

There was something my daddy told me once when I was a boy that I didn't understand until that day: dangle a dollar in front of a man who doesn't have one, and he will do a backflip.

Well, the Hollyfield hands, the ones who chose to come, were doing everything but. As night fell, they filed up, Sam Teague himself shaking hands with them and helping them in. When they were seated, a whip cracked on the backsides of the mules, and the wagons they pulled trundled forth, filled with merriment, smiling faces singing songs made up on the spot about a change in fortune. The bottles of cheap whiskey made their rounds as the singing and laughing continued in joyful noise. It rose as we approached Mount Teague.

It slowed down as we passed it.

It stopped when Mount Teague disappeared behind us.

The Negroes in the wagons looked one to the other. When one of them proclaimed that he was going home, one of us, Virgil Reeves, I believe, said, "No you ain't," and pushed the man by his chest back to the center of the wagon. The rest of the men in the wagon looked up at the night sky and down at the hands they were wringing.

We turned down a road I had not seen before, little more than a lane, so narrow that only one of us could ride on either side of the two wagons. There was a signal, and men came out of the woods. A lantern was struck. Dirty white faces entered the lantern light as it rose suspended from dirty white hands, holding them up to look into the faces of those Negroes. I had seen men like these before, the lowest sort of men. They were slave drivers, merchants whose goods were other human beings.

One by one, the cargo was unloaded, almost all men, but a couple of women, one with a baby. Teeth were examined. Hands held out. Grips tested. Stand up straight, there, boy. Mm-hm. All right. One of the women had her breast grabbed and shaken. All she could do was clinch her jaw and shut her eyes.

"A thousand for all twenty."

"You must be out of your god-damned mind," Teague grumbled.

"Two thousand," the head man said.

"Five," Teague said and spat. His hands were gathered on the blonde mane of his mount.   He was looking up into the night sky as if disinterested.

"Five? You're crazy. Three."

"Four and no lower."

There was a heavy pause. Things moved in the shadows. Birds maybe. Then the baby cried.

"Shut that baby up, or I will," Teague growled.

"All right," the head man said. He took one more look at the cargo. "All right," he said again, "but for four thousand dollars, they better be able to fly and do handstands."

The people were taken out of the wagons and shackled together with leg irons.

"We free men," one of them contested.

"Don't look like it to me," one of the slave drivers said, "Nor will you be in Texas.[16]"

Rifle barrels poked into ribs, and feet began stirring in a common shuffle, like the clanking march of an enormous centipede or one of those Chinese dragons they have at festival times. Black hands braced themselves on the shoulders ahead of them as the chains jangled into the dark night air, and lantern light yellowed the ground and the bare, black feet. The look of betrayal etched on those black faces was something searing, like looking into a black iron skillet and sensing an intense heat.

The next day, the widow of Hollyfield returned from her trip to New Orleans and the banks without the credit she had sought. And so, with cane still in the fields and an insufficient number of hands to cut it, she had no choice but to sell out to the incredibly lucky Sam Teague. For two dollars an acre.[17]

A little under four thousand dollars.

I only saw him twice after that evening, the old gray-headed butler

---

[16] At this point in time, the Confederacy still held Texas.

[17] Chip, the last time I was in St. Matthew Parish looking through conveyance records on a probate case, I searched the courthouse records for this sale. Sure enough, there it was in a dusty ledger, "*Remitted from Samuel M. Teague, $3, 987.12 in payment for 1,866 acres and all buildings and emprovements* [sic] *of Hollyfield Plantation, to Mme. Marie Falgoust, this 13th day of Novbr, 1863. Witnesses: J. L. D'Ormeaux & V. Reeves.*"

who had had the courage to speak up. The first time was when we were moving Miss's things out of the big house at Hollyfield and putting them on wagons to be taken wherever she was going. He had tears in his eyes, as she did. It was apparent that they had an affection, a respect for one another. They had grown up together, not like brother and sister, but as something a lot like it. It was also apparent that she could not take him with her to that place, Wherever She Was Going.

The second and last time I saw him, he was in an old flannel coat, out near the Twelve Arpent Canal, a cane knife in his hand in a line with other men with cane knives in their hands. He was with a crew that was cutting the last of the season's sweet stalks, working for his new boss, Marse Sam. I had ridden out to bring a message of some sort to the *chef d'equipe*.

The old man stood up from his stooped posture, cloudy-eyed under a cap to keep his gray head warm. He looked at me, and I at him. We looked at each other, and in that fleeting second, he recognized me, and I thought his stare would bore a hole clean through me. I had to look away, and when I looked back, he had stooped again. His knife was violently chopping at the cane.

23

There is giggling on the landing outside my room. The door wheezes open and a sheet with two girl-sized lumps in it feels its way in. One of the lumps bumps against the wall, and the sheet giggles some more.

"Whooo, Nonc Pierre," one of the lumps says.

"No, he's sposed to be Even-easer Scroosh," the other lump hisses.

"Whoo, Even-easer Scrooge, we ghosts come to haunt you."

The other lump forgets her line, and there is whispering under the sheets.

"Are they no prisons? Are they no workhorses?"

"Work-*houses*," one of the ghosts whispers to the other, and there is a pause and fluttering laughter like a spring shower.

There is some sort of poking under the sheet, and the production they stage falls apart in belly laughs hidden under the sheet. If only I could smile, or better yet, speak. I would yell, "Bravo! Bravo!" when they conclude their performance. But I can only tap my palms together, so lightly that there is no sound, no applause. That is enough for them, and they bow and curtsy.

Afterwards, they sit on a chair at my bedside as I write. Their ghostly raiment is spread across their laps as they eat satsumas, chattering in little-girl talk and taking turns peeling and feeding each other sections. Brown fingers, white fingers. I get the idea that they have no idea that they are different colors, or, at most, that it is a small matter, a trifle. The world will teach them differently. With time, I am afraid it will.

But for now, the little ghosts sit on the same chair, their little legs swinging off the edge of it as they chatter in that little girl manner.

I do not believe in ghosts. You may find that astonishing, coming from someone who has lived the better part of his life in a city that is supposedly replete with them. But I have never seen so much as a passing shadow on a door or a squeak in the night that I have suspected as being one. Nor have I heard the wind howl through a small crack in a window and quivered at the thought that it might be the moan of some undead. Perhaps ghosts exist, and I am just blind and deaf to them.

The girls get up from the chair, suddenly distracted by some other enterprise. Before they leave, they kiss me on my grizzled face, two smacks on each cheek. "Au revoir, Papere!" And "Au revoir, Nonc Pierre!" Like blurs they make for the stairs and their footsteps thunder down. *No running, children*, the woman downstairs scolds. And I am left to think about ghosts.

But who needs ghosts when one's own vivid memories are terrifying enough?

A week later, after the disappearance of the Hollyfield hands, the slave traders were found in the swamp by an old woman who gathered roots and herbs there. One had had his neck snapped. The others may have had the same thing happen, though it was hard to tell after the mischief that the alligators had visited upon them. They were a mismatch of the macabre, an arm there, a torso here, a bashed head with a face still wearing a look of frightened surprise.

At first, the Negroes were nowhere to be seen. Through some trick, some magic, they had lost their chains. A couple of them, the old cook and her son, a cane cutter, would only say that the Rougarou got the men, though they had not looked. The common belief then was that if you looked at the Rougarou, it would affect your luck the rest of your life. And they felt pretty lucky to have been spared Texas and a life of slavery again. They were unsure if they would be getting any more of it, luck.

We continued our "coon hunts" once, sometimes twice a week. Sometimes there were a dozen of us, but usually less, maybe a half dozen. When we worked Yankee territory, we wore sacks over our heads, tied at the neck with eyeholes and a hole for the mouth and nose. When we crossed over into rebel territory, we didn't need them but with the progress of the war, rebel territory was receding away.

There was a man named Boutte who lived down below Mount Teague, almost to Thibodaux. The rumor was that he had served with the pirate Jean Laffite, or that perhaps he was Laffite himself, having staged his own death, taken on a new name, and come to live out his last years in peace in a tranquil backwater.

Teague was convinced that Old Boutte was the man Jean Laffite, and he thought we should ride out and meet him. And while we were at it, maybe Boutte would say a word or two about things like buried treasure. Perhaps there would be a map or something, somewhere in the man's humble abode, the small shanty that was the perfect disguise for a rich man who wanted to remain anonymous to the rest of the world.

What he found was not a dashing, Douglas Fairbanks, Hollywood pirate, but a short, pudgy, balding man who spoke good English, though he preferred French. He was clearly a tinkerer. The yard of his little place was filled with gewgaws and ornaments hanging from tree limbs. We sat our horses around him in the night air.

"You're quite the *artiste*," Teague said as he palmed one of the figures.

"For the chirren. They like to come out here and fish in the summertime."

"Listen, Mr. Laffite. I can call you Mr. Laffite, can't I?"

"That ain't my name. My name is Boutte. B-O-U..."

"Of course it is. But you can level with me, with my friends here,"

Teague gestured to us on horseback. "We're all gentleman, now, aren't we?"

I looked around. Virgil and Maurice were missing from their saddles. We chatted in the cold air, the rest of us, Boutte showing no sign of fear. Perhaps he had been a pirate; he was unafraid or had an air of being unafraid.

Virgil and Maurice appeared from within the cabin empty handed. Instead, they led Boutte's swayback nag. When they reached us, Virgil growled to Boutte, "Get on it."

Boutte looked calmly from one of us to the other. Maurice laced his fingers together for Boutte to step up onto his horse. Virgil, rather than give the leader to Boutte, simply let it drop.

"Where we goin'?" the old man asked. To his credit, he remained calm, but certainly he must have known what was about to happen.

"Tell us where it is, Laffite," Teague growled as he pulled a revolver.

Boutte looked straight at Teague.

"Ain't never been no treasure, if that's what you askin' after. Lafitte and his brother, they stayed their whole lives in debt. They died in arrears to their creditors."

"So you knew them?"

"*Oui*, I knew them. I knew them both well, Jean and Pierre."

Teague produced a rope from his saddle bag. He tossed it to Maurice, who fashioned a noose with it and threw it over a limb while Virgil tied Boutte's hands behind his back.

"Did they ever leave, say, a map?" Teague asked.

"Ain't no map, ain't no treasure," Boutte insisted. "Their household goods were sold to satisfy their bills." He spoke his facts calmly, as if he didn't care one way or the other.

Teague himself put the noose around Old Boutte's neck. The old man's wrists were bound together with rope, his hands were clasped together behind his back as if in some sort of backwards prayer. The flanks of Teague and Boutte's horses were next to each other but in opposite directions. The horses' tails swished in silent equine conversation. Teague pulled the noose hard around Boutte's neck.

"Last chance, my dear sir," Teague smiled.

111

"I die with a clean conscience, *monsieur*," Boutte serenely explained. "You will live yet, with a fouled soul." And with that, Boutte spat in Teague's face. And Teague's face contorted into a look of such anger as I, a veteran of the bloodiest conflict in the history of mankind, had never seen before.

Teague held the gun under the old man's jaw, thought for a moment, and then withdrew the gun and fired a shot in the air. His own horse wheeled around on hind legs like you might see on a monument somewhere. Boutte's horse took off into the night. And the old man swung in a series of circular arcs as the rope sang the sorrowful, stretching note.

I looked over my shoulder as we rode away from the scene. Boutte's feet tapped out a final rhythm. We left him hanging with the baubles and ornaments he had hung from the trees for his grandchildren, all backlit by the cheerful glow of his cabin.

His ghost does not haunt me, only the memory of his dangling form among the things he made for his grandchildren. Who found him up there, after we left that night? I hope it was a kind stranger and not his grandchildren.

I wake again after dreaming of Old Boutte. My neck feels tight, and I realize that I have forgotten to breathe again.

24

Today must be Sunday, as the house is quiet after a hubbub of activity as the people who live here prepared for Mass. Later, they will return with the priest, who will have the Eucharist for me. I will attempt to stand, or at least sit, and he will hold the wafer in front of me and say Corpus Christi. For lack of speech, I will nod yes, and he will lay God on my tongue and I will chew Him and swallow Him. There will be a big production of getting me downstairs, and we will sit at the table in the *salle-manger* and the people and the priest and I will have Sunday dinner, a roast by the smell of things.

I will eat very little and the woman will gently scold me like she does the children, and then she will cut a small bite of beef or perhaps some carrots and put it in my mouth.

By my own hazy calculations, I have outlived three or four priests. One of them may be the same man, just an old and young version that my decrepit mind has spliced together.

And I've confessed to these men the same crime hundreds of times. They sit there behind the lattice work prepared to hear the same litany of impure thoughts and petty crimes, lying and taking the Lord's name in vain and coveting thy neighbor's goods and so forth. What they've all gotten was so big, so horrendous, that there was a pause the first time each heard it.

When you kill someone, you take their life.

When you rape someone, you take their soul.

It was on a night when we went on a coon hunt, as Teague called them. We were riding along at a slow canter in Teague's wake, several paces behind him. We had six or eight chickens with their feet tied together. Sam Teague had no need for chickens. He only had us take them because he didn't want anyone else to have them.

We had taken off our hoods and tied them to our reins. Our heads were sweaty. We had a sack of persimmons and were eating some of them and throwing the rest at each other. We laughed and flinched away a shoulder with each wet thudding blow.

Up off the road, we saw the lights of a cabin. Something was cooking inside, an agreeable smell that seeped into the surrounding woods and onto the road. Virgil made a motion with his head, and Maurice, Virgil, and I pulled off to see about the smell.

A girl was cooking. She was about our age, a pretty girl with dark hair and lashes. She was singing to herself, a quiet, soothing song in French. We watched her through the window as she tapped the spoon on the skillet and wiped her hands on her apron. Virgil left the window and opened the door, and the three of us went in. The girl jumped when she turned and saw us.

"Well what have we cooking in the kitchen?" Virgil asked as he

113

looked in the pot. Maurice translated the question.

"*Lapin*," the girl said distrustfully, looking in a sideways glance to Virgil.

"Well, lap-pan!" Virgil exclaimed in mock surprise. He was looking in the pot with one eye while the other looked at the girl. With his lazy eye, he could do that. "And what else good might you have for us?"

He put the lid back down. He drew near her and palmed her breast. She pushed his hand away, and he grabbed her through her skirts and her apron and pushed her down. He leaned down and grabbed her head and kissed her roughly. She tried to get to her feet but got no closer than a sitting position, which she held for only a second. Over and over, she said, "*Monsieur, monsieur, s'il vous plaît...*"

The swing of the door startled all of us. It was Teague, who had come in from the night. We all looked to him, and I, for one, waited for him to admonish us for what was happening. I waited for him to say, "What's this nonsense?" I waited for him to say, "Virgil, son, you leave that girl alone!" I waited for him to say with a tip of his hat, "We got what we were after, now let's be on our way. Sorry, ma'am." But my short wait was in vain.

"To the victors belong the spoils," was what Teague said. And he disappeared into the night.

Virgil threw his suspenders off his shoulders and lowered his trousers. Her skirts rose up over her white linen drawers. And then they came down.

"*Monsieur, monsieur*," she whimpered, and then she began crying, sobbing, disconsolate. Then Virgil fell on her there on the floor of her dwelling, an act reserved for love twisted into the violence of a cudgel. Her bare legs, uncovered from their skirts, kicked at him, pale and flailing, heels gouging his thighs and calves.

When he was done, he nodded to Maurice. I cannot imagine but that it was his first time with a woman. It didn't take him long. And then it was my turn.

And I took it. Oh, dear God, I took it.

"*Monsieur-monsieur-monsieur, s'il vous plaît, monsieur, s'il vous plaît.*" The wind whistles it to me on nights when it comes from the south. When I was in better health, I would get up to close the window, trying to block it out. But I would still hear it.

How similar those two faces are, agony and ecstasy, though they are as different as the twin masks of comedy and tragedy. Hers could have been either, just like the widow Lowe's face of extreme pleasure could just as well have been that of overwhelming pain. The girl's face was furious and spitting, crying red-cheeked like a newborn, as we held her down by her shoulders, shrieking as she rocked side to side on the floorboards, wide-eyed, searching for a way out. Her scream scraped against my puny conscience, an accusation that reverberated against the only thing within me that was true and just. It pierced me.

My hand clamped down over her mouth to cut the splitting noise and reduce it to a low, primal scream, the sound of something being severed from her, something extracted from her and leaving her empty or beyond empty. She bit my hand, her teeth sinking through the leather and into the flesh of my palm. I pulled off the glove and looked at my hand, and she looked at it and saw the missing finger and the bloody palm. A crescent of scarlet indentions. And then I put it over her mouth to silence the screaming, the high-pitched lady-shriek of a peacock.

I perched atop her as the demons howled within Virgil and Maurice and me, and she screamed in my face and Virgil and Maurice hooted, and I found that the act could not be completed, that this was an act of violence and aggression and not passion. I pretended to spend myself, and when I withdrew, I stumbled out onto the porch of the house. I vomited off the side to the sound of sobbing inside, the sound of feminine despair. The sick-sweet smell of yellow-orange persimmon juice on my clothes.

I wish now that I could beg her forgiveness, that poor, broken girl, that girl that I helped break. If St. Peter opens the gates and she is paraded silently before me, mute testimony to what I did, what I participated in. And I see her and I'm denied admission, dismissed to spend eternity in fire, I will have no answer for him and he will close his book with a slap and a scowl. Her face haunts me as I'm sure our faces haunt her, our slack, huffing, smirking faces, her despairing face. Oh dear God, is there any such thing as forgiveness? For one who is truly sorry and has no means to ever make it right again?

I can write no more. Perhaps tomorrow.

25

I fell again today. I woke to what I thought was the wind taunting me, but then I realized it was that radio.

The woman and the Spaniard bought me one of those things, those wireless contraptions that gather waves from somewhere and turn them into sounds. I had no say in the matter, as nowadays, I have no say in any matter, no say at all.

Maison Blanche sells them now and has a radio transmitter that sends programs to it. Every so often, some fellow by the name of W. S. Emby comes on to announce himself.[18] The damn thing sits on its perch and squawks and mutters and whistles like a parrot in a wooden cage. It plays that colored music that they shut down Storyville for.[19] It tells us what soap to use, where to buy our automobiles and our shirts, where to eat Sunday dinner. I say give it time and it will tell us who to vote for.

I had had enough of it, preferring the silence or, at most, the sleepy background sounds of Prytania Street. I got up to turn the damn thing off, and my legs stayed in bed but the rest of me hit the floor.

The little girl found me. The woman rushed upstairs and said, "Pierre, you shouldn't get out of the bed without help."

My eyes posed the question to her, and then I wrote it.

How can I ask for it?

"*Pauvre bête,*" she whispered.

Then she held me, and I smelled her scent, sweet and pure, the smell of home on a cold winter day. I cried, too, no sobbing, just a slow leak from my old eyes. She dried them and kissed my forehead. She separated from me and held me at arms' length and looked at me with those eyes. Every time she looks at me, I feel as though she sees me for the first time. Perhaps that is how love is. And perhaps she loves me. Yes, she does. Of course. I can forget everything else, but I cannot forget that.

All through it, the radio played.

---

[18] Very likely station WSMB.

[19] Storyville was shut down in 1917, largely for prostitution.

The woman settles me back in bed, and hands me my pencil and paper after I pantomime for it like a mute. Which, I suppose, I am.

I began to think of reasons not to go on any more of Teague's raids. I would feign illness, having knowledge of just about every disease known to the army malingerer, runs, coughs, itches. Sometimes, I would just hide, lurking behind sheds or in storehouses or within castles made of barrels that waited the boil of the stalks and the sugar that would come from it.

The whole business of these raids, these coon hunts, was beginning to bother me, though, I'm ashamed to say, not because I thought it was wrong, though that may have been part of it. The main reason was that I thought I would get caught by the Yankees and hung for violating the terms of my Vicksburg parole.

I think Teague sensed my lack of enthusiasm. I think he knew that I wanted out. But such is the way of dirty business: you do not retire from it. Once you know too much, you cannot un-know it. There is only one way out, and it is not pretty.

He would come out to the garçonnière, a thing he had never done before.

"We missed you last night," he would say. "You're not getting cold feet are you?"

I would offer flimsy solutions for his puzzled looks, and he would at least pretend to believe me. He seemed content to allow my absence from the coon hunts, but there was one thing he needed me, and especially me, for, one thing I could not hide from.

What I could not hide from were deliveries to the colonel in Donaldsonville. I was Teague's scribe, his reader, his delivery boy. The trips into town with deliveries were weekly affairs, and sometimes twice a week. At the time, I had no idea what was in the satchel, or, I should say, how much was in the satchel.

Teague would visit the mausolée early in the morning. Serbus would bark at the tall man's shadow, and then grumble a liquid growl, then pant and whimper anxiously when he recognized Teague. Then I would be sent for, hoisting the satchel up on my shoulder as soon as I was in the saddle.

The last delivery I made was in a cold, driving rain, a rain like the crash of chains, a rain that said, "Keep your coat handy, yes, summer is truly over." Teague sent Mathilde out to the cooperage where the rain formed curtains and our breath steamed out of us into the cold. She scampered out to us, holding her hem up out of the splash, trotting under an umbrella, her own breath visible to us. What was also visible now was her secret, the one that was beginning to push out against the bodice of her dress. If anything, it only made her more lovely. I thought of Big Eight, a thought tinged with a pinch of sympathy, an odd emotion for a man like I was. I tried to justify it to myself: anger can get a man in trouble, I said to myself, the same as passion can get a woman into trouble.

"Monsieur wishes to speak with you," she said as she stepped under the eaves of the cooperage shaking out her umbrella. It scattered drops like a dog shaking off water.

The rest of the men paused only briefly from their work to enjoy a quick glance of her. We were in the homestretch in our production of barrels, the quota set by Mr. D'Ormeaux and Mr. Lapeyrouse almost filled. We could smell the finish line. The rapping and sawing and clinking barely hesitated.

I lay down the plane I'd been using. Yellow-brown curls of cypress littered the ground at our feet. She raised the umbrella again, and I stepped under it. We moved out under the eaves of the cooperage. The rain drummed on the umbrella, a starburst in simple black, and we shared the intimate cylindrical space under it, a quiet space, a sacred space. She put her arm in mine to bring us closer together under it. It was ecstasy.

We walked back to the cooperage, stepping around puddles, winding our way to the house. My Aunt Cora had always spoken of heaven in such a way that it led me to believe it was a big place, an expansive and grand place where the sun was always shining on endless orchards of perfectly and uniformly ripe fruit and the temperature was neither too hot nor too cold and everything grew like wildfire even though it never rained. My beliefs changed that day. I now thought that heaven might fit under an umbrella in the cold rain.

We alighted under the eaves of the back gallery of Mount Teague, and I shook the umbrella out and handed it to her. And then there was a pause, and an intense silence against the breaking-glass patter of the rain. She looked at me and I looked at her and I think in any other circumstance, we would have kissed.

And I think she knew it. And I think she also knew that it would have been wrong, disastrous, in fact. So, she only said, "*Merci, monsieur,*" and went in the house, leaving the door open for me. I set the umbrella by it and went in. I found Teague in his study, looking out the cold-misted window pane.

"Carrick," he said out to the rain. The lamps were lit against the dark of the day. I could see the reflection of his face in the window. He stared out into gray. Out the window and across the way, at one of the barns, a wagonload of field hands pulled up, and they jumped out to find shelter. The cutting wasn't stopped because of human discomfort, however. It was stopped because fully loaded wagons would get stuck in the wet earth.

"Carrick, I need you to ride up to Donaldsonville, to carry the satchel to the colonel."

"On a day like today, sir?" I asked. As I said it, I realized I should have said, *yes, sir,* which was always the correct response. I braced for a scolding, but instead, he was amiable, downright hospitable.

"Yes, I know, but I'm afraid it's somewhat urgent." He turned around and forced a smile. "Here, let's set for a moment and have a refreshment first. Perhaps the rain will abate."

We sat in his study, and he poured two glasses of amber whiskey. He lifted his and I lifted mine and we nodded slightly in a silent toast. We talked and sipped and watched the rain. Mathilde came in to tend the fire in the fireplace, and we watched her. With the passing of Mrs. Teague, she was the sole feminine presence in the house, other than the Teague girls, who were upstairs playing. Their chatter up there mingled with the sound of the rain.

After two or three refreshments, Teague said, "Well, the rain seems to have slackened, hasn't it? I suppose you can be on your way."

In truth, it had not lessened one iota, but the whiskey refreshments made it of no consequence, and so I gave the correct reply.

"Yes sir."

My mount had been patiently waiting for me under the eaves of the porch. My foot swayed as it sought the stirrup, and at last I found it and pulled myself up, almost going completely over the side. Teague chuckled. He handed me my hat, which I pushed down on my head like a circus clown. The rain was falling so hard that in a few seconds, I was already soaked. Then he reached down on the porch to get the satchel, and he handed it up to me. He used two hands to lift it.

"Careful," he said. I took it. It was much heavier this time. He looked up at me with those nickel-gray eyes. Despite the liquor, there was a seriousness to him. He gave me an earnest warning.

"Carrick, do not look in this satchel for any reason," he said.

"Yes sir," I said. "I never do. I never have."

"Good man," he said. "Now go. The colonel is expecting you."

I trotted down the lane a few yards, then turned around and returned when I realized that I had forgotten my gloves.

"Where are you going?" Teague shouted to me through the rain as I approached.

"I forgot my gloves, sir."

"No time," he said as the back of his hand shooed me. "Go ahead. It will be all right."

I turned and trotted down the lane of oaks and the bayou road and up toward Donaldsonville.

The satchel was definitely heavier this time and seemed to contort and twist and shift like the bowels of a gut-shot man. Teague had sent me with a small flask which I emptied by the time I reached Paincourtville. The weight and shape of the satchel lost any importance. Cotton must be doing well, I thought.

When I arrived at the colonel's office on Mississippi Street in Donaldsonville, the door was open to the porch and the rain. Framed within it, the lieutenant was once again hunched over his ledger.

"Here to see the colonel," I said. "He's expecting me."

The aide said, "He's down at the livery getting his horse put up."

I sat and waited while the young officer scratched in his ledger, dipping his quill into the inkwell and giving me a quick, disapproving glance before writing again. The rain let off for a minute or two, and I got up to look at it, but I sat back down again when it resumed. When I did, it seemed as if the satchel at my feet had changed shape, a little shorter and fatter. After half an hour or so, the colonel reappeared in one of those blue dusters that the Union army officers wore. Despite the rain, under his hat, his lion's mane of hair was near perfect.

"Crowder," he said. "I wasn't expecting you on such a day as this."

"I have something for you," I said. I stood up and lifted the satchel from the floor. I gave it to the colonel. In taking it, it sagged to the floor a little. In fact, he almost dropped it.

"Well," the colonel smiled and chuckled. "It's heavier this time."

He shook my hand and noticed my missing finger.

"How'd you lose your finger, Crosby?"

"Mumblety-peg," I said.

"Yes, we used to play that game when I was a young man in the Mexico War. I never lost like you apparently did," he laughed. His eyes were straying in anticipation to the satchel, which he was holding like you would hold a newborn baby.

"Peabody," he said to the young lieutenant. "Why don't you and Mr. Curtis go have yourselves a drink? Have Mr. Gonsoulin put it on my tab."

Peabody huffed a small huff, laid down his pen on his ledger and gathered his jacket. We exited the office as Colonel Hutchison shut the door behind us. The bolt on the lock clunked heavily.

I did not go get a drink with Peabody. The whiskey was fading, and my head was beginning to hurt and my mouth was dry. My clothes were wet, and I just wanted to go back to St. Matthew. That apparently was fine with Peabody. He left to go back to his quarters. I don't think he had any desire for my company, anyway.

When Peabody came in the next morning, the colonel was already dead.

They estimated there were at least four or five moccasins in the satchel. The aide used his sidearm to dispatch the two remaining snakes, one curled up under the colonel's desk, the other sunning himself in a patch of sunlight by the window. There must have been at least a couple more, judging from the bloated mass of scratches that was now the colonel's face. The others must have crawled off somewhere.

Those who saw him said that the colonel looked like he had run through a patch of dense nettles. His face was swollen to twice its size, covered with twin bite marks so numerous that it looked like a case of measles. He looked like he had fallen out of a locust tree and hit every thorn and branch and limb on the way down.

When asked if the colonel had had any visitors the day before, Lt. Peabody said that he was sure that the last visitor of the day was a messenger from Mount Teague. A man missing a finger.

26

The Spaniard takes me in his motorcar down to Café Du Monde for coffee and beignets. We sit there with the ceiling fans churning away at the heat as he holds a conversation that involves him speaking and asking me yes-and-no questions, or, at most, questions that I can answer with a gesture. A few people come up to greet us, some I remember, most I don't. Many thank me for things I don't recall doing, causes I can't remember contributing to.

Thank you, Monsieur Carriere, my mama 'n 'em would've been evicted that winter without you, and, *God bless you, Mr. C, my boy just graduated from Tulane wit' his degree. He told me to send along his gratitude next time I saw you.* The Spaniard glows with pride each time, reading the confusion on my face and reminding me who each person is.

I spill my coffee, and as the waiter goes to get me a replacement, a group of men come by in white seersucker suits and Panama hats and wingtip shoes. I recognize one of them as old Burman. He shakes a few hands and pats a few backs. It seems he has been mayor forever, though I think he was not mayor for a while and then was mayor again.[20] My mind used to be keen on things such as that.

Such are the politics of this place, my home, New Orleans, Louisiana. This place where foolishness is an art, care is not cared for, a place where

---

[20] Mayor Martin Behrman. He was mayor from 1904 to 1920, and then again from 1925 until his death in 1926.

laughter is crying and crying is laughter. A place that is always celebrating something and always mourning something. Mourning, of course, has made me a good living here. Like New Orleans, there are places where men rule for decades, and countries where power is held for generations. St. Matthew Parish was a place like that and perhaps still is.

St. Matthew Parish received a new ruler that winter, dispatched from Washington like the Cesar dispatched a new governor from Rome. He was a man named Potts who had commanded a gunboat on the river and was now given shore duty. He was a Navy man, a short, stumpy, headstrong man with a laurel wreath of white hair around a bald dome of scalp. He was straight as an arrow and refused to give in to bribery, graft, persuasion, flattery, whiskey, or any of the other tools. He could smell a rat, and he smelled one down the bayou at Mount Teague. And he was a terrier when it came to rats.

Union soldiers began patrolling up and down Bayou Lafourche, and especially St. Matthew, both day and night. They lounged about like dairy barn cats waiting on mice, loitering in the shade of trees on sunny days and under the eaves of roofs on rainy ones. These men that I once considered blue-woolen, brass-buttoned targets were everywhere, and there was little I could do about it.

Nor could Teague. It may be that it never troubles the wolf how many the sheep may be, as he toasted us more than once. But hunters are another matter. Hunters are not sheep.

When a wolf is trapped, the girl read to me from the *National Geographic*, he will gnaw away a limb to escape. So is his animal nature, his desire to survive. And Teague saw me as a limb that was snared in the jaws of the trap of the occupying Union Army. He had no qualms about gnawing me off to survive. He called us into a meeting, during the day, a rare thing.

"Close the door, Mr. Reeves."

Virgil got up and closed the door.

"Our circumstances have changed, I'm afraid. Due to our unexpected guests, we won't be able to get out and see to the countryside at night like we've been doing."

He said it as if we had been a bunch of kindly caretakers.

"Furthermore, I'm afraid you boys might get hung for your trouble. So, I suggest that you keep quiet about what we have done. If asked, your work has been confined to daylight hours. What you have done at night has simply been your business. I will deny that I sent you, if I myself am asked. If you do not keep quiet, then you will be risking your own neck and not mine."

His voice was low, but it rose from him like something pressured out by the geology of the earth, a steaming hiss:

"You are to keep your mouths shut, all of you. Do you understand? If anyone, Yankee or otherwise, uniformed or otherwise, asks you, you are to keep your mouths shut. Not a word to a soul. Not to a man, not to a woman, not whispered into the ear of a mule. Understand?"

We nodded, looking down and around to each other, then looking down and nodding again. No one said anything. Outside, off and away, the silence murmured with the creak of a grinding wheel and the smack of a switch and the bray of a mule. With the burning of the cane stubble, the air was smelling smokier every day.

"Well, then," Teague's genial demeanor had returned. "Let us all go about our business."

We filed out. I was the last of the dozen or so in the room. Teague pulled me aside. The others clomped down the steps, and I wished like anything to follow along with them. But Teague held my arm and shut the door. He snarled a whisper into my ear.

"If you say anything about deliveries or satchels or money to a soul, you'll regret it only once, and that will be continuously."

His nickel-gray eyes were on me, so I said what I had to say.

"Yes sir."

"Well, let's shake on it," he said. But instead of shaking my right hand, he shook my left. And at the end of the shake, which to me lasted a second too long, he raised my hand with his and showed my three fingers to me.

"After all," he said, "the Yankees are looking for nine-fingered men such as you."

He let my hand drop, and I let my hand drop. He opened the door, and I backed out of it, stumbling over the threshold and onto the porch. My hat fell off, and I stooped to pick it up. As I replaced it on my head, I saw him looking at me, a look as cold as steel on a winter night up north. I hurried down the stairs.

We finished our quota of barrels that week, a fortress of them waiting for the grinding and boiling to finish, a process that would take weeks and months, well into the winter. We spent the day rolling them down, watching Auguste Favorite stamp them with the brand, *Mount Teague Sugar, Sweetest-Purest*, and then restacking them. It was heavy work, but mindless work. To the rumble of empty barrels, Eugene D'Ormeaux babbled on about roast goose and oyster dressing and café brulot and other holiday delicacies. It was getting to be that time of year.

For me, there were no more deliveries, no more colorful fall rides along the Lafourche, no more strolls along the muddy streets of Donaldsonville, no more gazing at the river and the water that pushed by with a weight like a crowd, anxious to see the show, the big water, the sea. The deliveries stopped with the murder of Colonel Hutchison. It was as if they never happened.

Union men came down one day to see to reports of the nine-fingered delivery man who worked at Mount Teague, but no one seemed to know him. It helped that Teague had met with each of the men in the cooperage and the stables and explained that there was no one who worked there who fit that description. The blue-coated, brass-buttoned investigators left with no leads concerning the murder of Colonel Hutchison.

Teague let it be known that he had done me a favor, that he had died a little for my sins, and that I owed him for it. So there was no arguing that I should continue reading to him. And I did, the *St. Matthew Parish Compass*, Riley's *Latin*, Dickens. I read until I was hoarse. I read until I wanted to say, *why don't you read to yourself?* That, of course, would have irked him, as illiterate as he was and as proud as he was, and I knew that you do not irk a man like that. So, on I read. The Memphis paper, the New Orleans papers. The New York *Herald*, The London *Times*, which we could now get, though it was usually several months old.

And so it was, one day in the New Orleans *Bee*, an article appeared about a man in St. James Parish who claimed to be the last surviving member of Laffite's gang, a man who had clerked for the attorney for the pirate brothers. He had married a St. James Parish girl and moved to start his own practice when he passed the bar. Now he had retired to the countryside to assume the role of gentleman farmer. It was a short piece, just a paragraph or two, tucked in between the jokes and aphorisms that newspaper men put to fill the space between the weightier articles.

To Teague, however, it was as if I had rung the plantation bell, and only he could hear it.

"Read that again, Carrick," he said.

I did.

"Does it say where?"

"Vacherie," I said. "A place called Vacherie."

"Hmm," he said, opening one eye. "Have a family?"

"No sir, says he's a widower."

Outside, the grinding wheel squeaked and grumbled as it turned. And I thought I could hear Teague's mind do the same.

That afternoon, the sulfur smoke of burning cane stubble filled the clear afternoon air and a gauzy gray cloud began to hang in the bright sky. With our work complete, those of us in the cooperage were watching the mules pull in circles in the grinding wheels, men with switches following them around the arc, waiting for them to balk at any more labor. When the beasts tired to the point of no longer responding to the lash, another beast was brought in to wear the traces. Men held armloads of stalks that disappeared into the maw of the machinery like the chewing mouth of an insect, the boom sweeping around like the hand of an enormous clock that faced heaven.

A bottle was passing between us, man-to-man, back and forth, hand-to-hand, the backs of those hands wiping our mouths as the mules paced all afternoon and got nowhere, and the men paced with them, the switch sparking off bobbing hindquarters whenever the animals slowed.

She came out to where we leaned against the rail fence that delineated the grinding yard. The men feeding cane into the grinder looked up as she approached, ducking only when they felt the slow, sweeping nudge of the boom.

"Monsieur would like to see you," she said with a hand on the swell of her belly. I assumed there was something he wanted me to read to him. I knew that my words would slur. I also knew that I was drunk enough that I didn't care, and that I was almost drunk enough to tell him of a certain intimate activity that he could do to himself and his horse. What if I had, I often ask myself?

But I followed her, careening into the banister of the back steps, up to the gallery where Teague sat in a chair with his feet on a rail.

"Carrick," he said. "We have work to do tonight."

Looking back, the sober me would have declined, perhaps, asked for my pay, and left to seek a life elsewhere. But the drink decided for me, and my drunken mind agreed for me, and my drunken mouth spoke for me, the correct reply for the hundredth, thousandth, and last, time.

"Yes sir."

That night, we donned our sacks and peered out at the world and each other from the eye holes in them. There were no puffy toasts in twisted Latin, no berating of the one perceived as the weakest. We simply joined up quietly, smaller groups coalescing into larger ones.

In the night, along the bayou road and in charred cane fields, Union Army campfires shimmered, and shadows warmed their hands over them, and northern laughter rippled into the night. I had sat around campfires much like these. It was the only other part of army life that I had enjoyed, the night times of comradery spent around a camp fire, telling stories and sharing mess. We watched them as we sat our horses in night shadows and listened to the northern men. Someone in the distant bivouac pulled a bow across a fiddle, and a sad song, a lament squeezed out and into the night air. We listened to it, we hooded men, we shadow-men. It was sweet, bittersweet.

"Well, ain't that purty," someone said quietly from within their hood. I recognized the voice as Eugene D'Ormeaux. I should have; I had heard it enough. Teague had finally allowed him to ride. I guess Teague had judged that Eugene had finally "grown a little hair on his nuts and stopped shittin' his drawers."

No one said anything. Instead, we listened as the fiddle played and the men at the distant campfire sang. We swigged from a passed-around bottle through the mouth holes in our dirty canvass hoods. When the bottle was empty, the last man threw it off into the darkness where the hollow glass sound of it tumbled away. And then we were off.

We shook our reins and nudged our heels into our horses' flanks. We skirted their camp, and made our way into the night, looking for a little hamlet called Vacherie where this man, this Monsieur so-and-so, lived alone. Or perhaps, where he lived with a chest that contained the belongings of a dead pirate.

I looked over my shoulder at the lights of Mount Teague. I had spent my last night there, though I did not know it yet.

27

I sit on the balcony in the late evening watching the moon. My daddy said that his Cherokee mother told him the story of the moon, that he hides his face when he nears the sun out of shame for something he did. Gradually, his face becomes a rim and then disappears.[21]

Tonight, it is a waning moon, just like that night so long ago, a winter night when the moon was slipping away into a crescent and the rain was pushing through on the breath of a southern wind. It was that same moon more than sixty years ago, a thin sliver, a shamed thing.

The deeds done on nights like those, like most of the charges we made during the war, were conceived after a vigorous dose of alcohol. It has been so throughout history, I suppose, with endeavors like those, enterprises in which courage is needed and lacking. Men pass a bottle up and down a trench or behind a redan, or they share a goatskin flask in the shadow of a castle, or they pull from a jug behind the pointed posts of a stockade, waiting for the impossible to seem the reasonable. Such is the

---

[21] According to Cherokee tradition, the Sun was a young woman who had a lover who would come to her each month in the dark of the moon. She never saw his face, and he never said who he was. Finally, to find out who he was, she put ashes on his face. The next night, she saw his face and realized it was her brother. Having been found out, the moon hides his face as he nears the sun.

way of drinking. Bad ideas become good ideas. Stupid ideas become clever ideas. Preposterous ideas become plausible ideas. All conceived behind a liquid fortification.

That night with the sickle moon above us in the cold sky, we would pause and pass a bottle among ourselves and soon it all became possible to us. Yes, of course, we thought with every swig: crossing a countryside filled with Union men looking for us is an easy, natural thing.

A couple of times we left the road to let a handful of Union cavalry pass. They clopped by in the dark, quiet conversation going with them. We were riding in the night without the required passes, skirting campfires and the distant conversations of the men that ringed them. Their northern faces were bright in the glow, yet too distant to make out their features.

The moon hung over our shoulders, glaring a dim light on our backs before the clouds gathered quickly to shut the moon out. I knew that the moon rose in the east and that the little hamlet of Vacherie was there. I had looked at it on the map that Teague kept in his study, patiently pointing out the place names to him. But we were now headed west. We were lost.

We were also sloppy with the drink. Someone in our hooded group began softly crooning a carol to our objective, singing it to the tune of "O Tannenbaum":

"O, Vach-er-ie, O, Vach-er-ie, O-where-the-hell-are-you-oo?"

We all guffawed and someone belched and Virgil Reeves shushed us and called us a bunch of peckerheads and there was quiet and someone belched again and we all wheezed and chuckled. The night was turning cold but we scarcely felt it. We were content in the warmth of each other's drunken company.

The shadows of farmhouses careened by to the tune of horse hooves on the wet earth. The lights were all out, the people inside fearful of people like us. And, of course, the lights were also out because the occupants were fast asleep in there, dead tired from a day of the type of work that was required merely to survive. We let them pass by, those small blocks of shadows, smaller shadows beside them, silhouettes of smokehouses, outhouses, chicken houses.

A rain began, a cold, dense, Louisiana rain, and we adjourned to a barn behind one of those obscure farmhouses. It roared on the roof of the barn until it finally slackened to a steady patter. Our voices remained raised, though, as if the rain still thundered. Someone made some comment that would otherwise not have been funny, but we all laughed. Virgil shushed us again, and we all laughed again, and Virgil growled low.

"This ain't like before. They's Yankees all around here. You gotta keep yer mouths shut. *Shut!*" he said.

On the porch of the house in front of the barn, a dog barked. A light came on in the window, the slow evolving, amber shine of an oil lamp like we used in those days.

"Set still," Virgil whispered.

We did. We fell silent, even Eugene. Our eyes blinked white in the dark.

A man's outline came out of the back door of the house, pulling up his suspenders and shouldering an old musket that must have been a hundred years old. The man himself was only a little older than me, a man, I imagined, with young children inside. He moved as a dark shape through the rainy yard, pausing to open the door of the outhouse and level his gun quickly into the empty space. He moved on to the other outbuildings, a corncrib, a smokehouse. He was moving toward the barn. In the house, a baby began crying.

He approached the barn. He was close enough that I could hear his steps in the patter of the rain. The barn door opened, and his outline was clear against the rain-scored opening. I could feel us all holding our breath. The earth was turning slowly under us. The man shouted in French, *qu'est là?*

I was more scared than I had ever been in battle, scared not of a company or a regiment or a division defending the sanctity of the union of the United States, but of this one man with his one rifle defending his one family. I panicked.

I raised my rifle and I shot him. And I know for a fact that I killed him. Men do not survive wounds like that. He was the last man I ever killed.

A woman ran out of the house in a nightgown, clutching a bundled baby to her chest, running in thin fabric washed a thousand times, the rain thinning it further into a second skin. We galloped out of the barn and past her, the dog running with us and nipping at our heels. We hit the main road in a full-blown panic, the hoofbeats against the garbled barking, until the dog pulled off and returned to the little farmhouse and the cries of the young wife. And though I did not hear her cries that particular night, I have heard them every night since.

We rode haphazardly to the shouts of the dogs of other farmhouses along the road. We cut through burned cane fields, withered corn fields, side yards, snagging clotheslines and casting off the sheets and drawers and blouses on them amid cursing. And riding on without direction. If Teague had been there, he would have admonished us, called us a bunch of bedwetting cowards, a pack of limp men. But he had had enough sense, to stay at home with a tumbler of bourbon and a warm fire, staring at nonsensical lines on a sheet of paper, trying in vain to decipher them.

We, however, his pawns, were in a cold rain, panicked into random movement by the threat of an ant colony of Yankees that we were sure we had stirred up. It was just a matter of time before we encountered them.

"Halt," the voice said. "Who goes there?"

We did not pause. We veered off in different directions. And then, in another direction, there were two more of them. I could see them clearly in the firelight. They wore the uniform of western men, Indiana or Illinois, most likely.

"Halt," one of them said, "I'll fill you fulla holes, I swear to Christ I will."

We did not halt. We could not. Rain was falling and it was cold and we had no leader. Terror was leading us.

Muzzles flashed a split second before I heard the shots, which was a split second before I felt one of them. I often wondered how it would feel to be shot. Would it be like a knife? A slap? A burning, searing pain?

It was more like a punch, followed by a warmth. I fell forward onto my mount, which continued to gallop away, eyes wild and nostrils flaring. At first, the slap of my shoulder into his neck was only a little painful, but after a hundred yards or so, it became more and more painful, and at last it became unbearable. The horse ran in a frenzy, off into the swamp, carrying me away and into darkness. I felt myself slipping as the horse quartered around live oaks, the wet beards of Spanish moss brushing my face. I was hugging his muscular neck, struggling to stay mounted. I could hear the drumroll of hoofbeats under me, and some behind me, and I wondered if the soldiers were following me.

The horse ran through water, and gave another, last turn. I slipped and fell, landing in the mud. The horse galloped off, snaking around trees and splashing through water and splashing out on the other side of it. I rolled over with a moan that sounded faraway. There was a brief silence and then other hoofbeats that got louder. I waited for the Yankees to come and take me, to send me to their hospital where I could recover so they could send me to their gallows.

Then, I saw them towering above me on horseback. The rain had pushed through, the night clouds were rushing by above them. There were two of them.

"Shit, Virgil," a voice said. It was Eugene's. "What we gonna do now? Shit, shit."

"Don't think he's gonna make it," Virgil said, and he spat. "I mean, Christ, Eugene. Look at all that blood."

I could feel it, my blood, matted and wet and sticky on my shirt and my shoulder and my arm. I held my hand up in the dim moonlight. My glove was dark with it. I could smell it, the smell of metal, the smell of iron like the rusty water of my youth. I felt weak, short of breath. *Swimmy-headed*, as Uncle Ransom liked to say.

"Can't do nothin' for him," Virgil said at last. I could hear the shouts of men in the distance. Northern voices.

"We gonna leave him?" Eugene said in disbelief.

"We take him, we get caught. We get caught, we get hung," Virgil said. They were talking about me as if I wasn't there. "I don't think he's long for this world, anyhow."

Then Virgil made a clicking sound and whirled around his mount. Eugene lingered a moment, and Virgil said, "Come on. Leave him be, and God rest him."

"Teague's gonna be fit to be tied." Eugene said. His voice was weighed down with the fear of displeasing Teague. It sounded like pleasing

132

Teague was what Eugene lived his life for. I had not noticed it until then.

"Ain't nothin' we can do," Virgil said. His horse nodded and snorted, the big block teeth clacking against the metal bit. Virgil and Eugene cantered their horses for a few yards, either out of respect for me or their consciences. Then the horses drummed against the earth in a cadence that picked up and diminished into the distance.

The rain had said what it had to say, and a hard north wind was clearing the sky. The wisps of white clouds parted on the midnight blue to reveal a sliver of shameful moon.

I was alone like on the night of that first raid. The same night creatures conversed in watery howls and calls. The tops of the trees swayed against the wind-driven sky, the crescent moon flying by over white clouds. The air was considerably colder, but every time I hugged myself against it, my shoulder screamed in agony and I moaned in response. Who will find me if I die here? I thought.

I stared up into the night sky, cold and brittle, the black outlines of oak leaves and cypress spires. My eyes faltered into feverish dreams, and I struggled to open them again. The thousand eyes of the night kept their death watch over me. My shoulder throbbed, and everything smelled of mud and decay and blood. The moon smirked down at me, and I squinted to see the ashes in his grin. I moved to try to sit up, and my shoulder howled at me, *no! You'll kill us both!*

I reclined back, and the mud smacked under my back. My hood twisted and blotted out the world. The night sounds seem to grow louder, and I tugged the sack around so I could see through an eyehole. Something swirled in the water, the steps of something large or the splashing entry of an alligator, or two alligators or an entire riverbank of them, each of them, all of them, keen on the same scent. Whatever it was or whatever they were, the movement pushed waves of frigid water up onto my feet. I began shivering, which was exquisitely painful, and strained not to move, not an inch.

But then a shadow blotted out the dark blue sky and I did move, lifted up by a dark shape, a cloud. I thought it was death, coming to collect me with his scythe balanced in one hand. Or maybe it was the Rougarou, preparing to carry me off deeper into the swamp to devour me at his leisure and leave the rest for the alligators like he did the Texas men.

Whoever or whatever it was, it pulled the sack from my head and threw it into the water where it made a light, slapping splash. I stared into the black outline, the night sky behind him, or it, the sharp burning points of stars in the company of the sickled moon. The outline tilted its head to each side, like a dog might when perplexed by something.

He draped me over his back, holding me like a sack of laundry or cotton or potatoes. He was cold and dark and immense. He took me into the cold water, wading with me up to his waist. My arms were outstretched, and my hands trailed in the water. My gloves were missing. And then the water receded as he walked out of it and onto dry land. My shoulder hissed with pain, and I struggled to keep my eyes open. I was convinced that if I closed them, I would never open them again. And then they closed by themselves.

28

The woman downstairs sits with me today. She murmurs the Rosary, her head canted a little, her fingers grasping each bead as if it were a child. *"Je vous salue, Marie, pleine de grâces, le Seigneur est avec vous, je vous salue…"* ten times, and then, *"Gloire au Père, au Fils et au Saint-Esprit…"* and then, *"je vous salue, Marie…"* Over and over, like a lullaby. The first time I heard it, in French or English, was in a carriage house on a cold winter night.

When I woke again, I was in a building, a stable. I could smell manure and hay. It was still nighttime. My head swam, and it was hot, unbearably hot. Perhaps I have died, I thought, and this is my reward. Why is there hay here? I thought again. Everything was burning and not being consumed, like Moses and the bush on the mountain. If Moses is here, then it is heaven, I thought, but why is it so hot?

The figure of a woman was there, wearing a hood like we wore. She pulled it from her head, and dry brittle blonde hair fell from it like straw. It was the widow Lowe. She turned her head, and blood trickled down from a hole on the side of her head. Her blue eyes turned golden.

I have a few tasks for you, Mr. Carrick, she said in the same sultry manner as before, on those afternoons when we drank deeply of each other and satisfied our thirsts. *No,* I tried to say, *you are not a widow.*

Are you sure? she cooed as her pale fingers stroked my shoulder. I swatted at her hand, and it vanished. I struck my own shoulder and it howled and I howled.

Then, I saw the devil there, pacing back and forth, rubbing his hands together, turning at the end of each series of steps, the swallowtails of his coat whirling as he turned, his face in shadows. My head whirled as I counted his clopping, cloven-hoofed steps-one-two-three-four-five-six-seven-eight-turn, a blur in the shadows, eight more steps. *Hurry up boy, and be done with it-I ain't got all night. Hurry up, dammit.*

And then in the darkness, there were faces lit with amber light, golden faces in an ochre darkness, like a Rembrandt painting, beatific, halo-crested. The faces contemplated me, and if I had had the strength, I would have contemplated them. But my eyes watered feverishly, and my shoulder wailed in pain as one of the faces looked down his nose through narrowed eyes and probed the tract of the bullet, the bullet that felt as big as a cannonball as it pushed out against my flesh and my bone, burning hot against my body.

He began a noiseless chant, a prayer, the shape of a sing-song melody that the woman downstairs still recites. I watch her lips, and I know it now as the Rosary in French. One of the other faces raised a lantern over my shoulder. The man braced a hand on my shoulder and used the other hand to wield a set of pliers or tongs that probed the hole the bullet had made. Something trickled down my chest and under my arm. His prayer intensified, silent and pressured. His clenched teeth gave his face a look of pure determination. The Rosary whistled silently through it. The devil and the widow Lowe melted back into the darkness behind the glowing faces of the men. Their faces were shining, glittering in the gloom.

The man's face looked like it would collapse on itself, and the bullet relented with a sucking noise and his face relaxed. He sat back on his heels and looked down, and his hair fell forward over his face. His chest rose and fell as he put his hands on his thighs. They were wet with my blood and left palm prints on his legs. I didn't notice the detail of their imprint then.

A second man lifted him up, and they staggered away together to another part of the room. Another one of them knelt, lifting a jug of water, cool, clear water. My lips searched for it like the mouth of a newborn, and my mouth pulled at it eagerly, sloppily, wetting my face. When I had drunk as much as I could, he stoppered it.

My lips formed a single, fragile word.

Who?

He looked back to where the man who had pulled the bullet from my shoulder slumped by the doorway with his head in his hands and his chin on his chest, the panting, slouching body language of an exhausted man. The first light of day was beginning to glow. The man who was now attending me looked back at the doorway and then down at me and said,

"C'est traiteur."

Part III:

In which I work for Honoré Mouton

29

I wake this morning with the dog snuffling my face and nosing into my neck. He wants to play, like we used to, but I have no capacity for that now. He slaps his front paws on the floor and grabs his plaything, a knotted rag, and eyes me. His gaze challenges me, but I can only gaze back. Finally, he gives up on me and sniffs his reflection in the mirror, and when he realizes that it is only himself, he yawns in exasperation and lies down. Poor fellow, I wish I could.

There is a mirror on a stand in my room. Most rooms have them now, but back in those days they were scarce, considered a luxury item. I peer into that mirror, and I see an old man. I raise a hand to him, and he raises one to me. I still don't believe he is me. He needs a shave, his face ticked with whiskers like thin, hairy grains of rice. Perhaps he has someone in that mirror-world who cares for him. In the days of my youth, a man seldom saw his reflection and had little idea what he looked like.

My mind and body were strong in those mirrorless days, but my French wasn't what it is now. I didn't understand what a *traiteur* was. A treater, a healer.

He would come see me several times a day, Honoré Mouton, flecked with sawdust, looking down at me. His face was etched with the exhausted worry of a parent for a desperately sick child, an expression that I remember seeing on my Aunt Cora's face the night I lost my finger. He would look into me, looking for something, his hair falling around his face, his brown eyes narrowing, his hand tugging thoughtfully at his beard. And then I would sleep again, and when I woke, he would be gone.

There was a carriage in the room with us, the simple sort of rig that a country preacher might use. I woke once to see him perched in it, head down, hands in his hair as if he were carrying the weight and worry of the world on his shoulders, as if heaven and earth were upon him and were squeezing him hard. He looked up at me, and in that brief, lucid moment, he smiled at me. It struck me as a smile that had the attitude of grace and beauty that I'd always imagined my mother having had when she looked down at me, if she ever did.

Then I slept again, for a day or a week. Sometimes he was there, and sometimes it was one of the others. And then, one day, I woke again in the daylight, the cold air of a cold day hanging sharply. The man Honoré Mouton was asleep in a feed trough, one that was made from a whole log hollowed out. His arms and legs splayed out in different directions with all the grace of an octopus. He rose from his slumber with yellow straw in his beard, and he gave me a befuddled look. He scratched his head and smiled and brushed straw off himself.

"Good a place as any to make *do-do*. He ain't got a horse no more. *Les hommes de nuit* take it. Them night men," he said. He walked his fingers in the air. *"Pauvre Pere, partout à pied a partir d'ici."*[22]

And then I remembered it, that place. It was on the night that we burned the little church of St. Lazare. We took the horse, and Sam Teague sold it to the army, the Union Army in this case. The priest, a fat man whose belly tented out in a mound against his cassock, begged us not to take his old mare. I think he was more worried about the horse than the church. In the end, there were no deserters or dodgers or runaway Negroes inside the church, just charred icons and a priest who stood angry and helpless in the smoking cinders.

So that's what they called us, I thought, *the night men*.

We had neglected to fire the stable, sidetracked by our drunkenness or the lure of a bigger prize down the road, and now the man Honoré Mouton and I were in it. He was sitting back on the feed trough like you might sit in an outhouse, slouched, relaxed. He stood up, and I saw the handprints on his faded dungarees, the blood dried to black. There was one on each thigh, my blood imprinted there. The imprint of his right hand, outlined on his right thigh, had a finger missing.

Outside, there was no hammering and sawing today, and something was cooking. The air was still and clear of the noise of work but brimming with the aroma of something good to eat. Men were laughing and singing outside in the brightness of a winter day and the smell of smoke and meat. One of the other men came and said something to Honoré Mouton in French.

---

[22] Poor Father, everywhere on foot from now on.

"*Merci*," Honoré replied, "*Et joyeux Noël!*"[23]

He turned to me and told me, "*Joyeux Noël, monsieur.*" Then he joined them outside.

A fiddle sounded, and there was singing of French carols, and then the music stopped and then utensils rattled and pans clattered. Then I could hear them settle down. I felt alone, and I was afraid that they had left me. I struggled to my feet. Straw clung to my hair and my beard, and I made no effort to remove it. At the barn door, the bright sunlight flashed in my eyes, and I put my hand up to shield them from it.

Men were sleeping, scattered around the campfire where the carcass of a pig still hung from a tripod. One of the men shifted in his sleep, from one side to another. The fire glowed in orange cubes over white ash. A mule was tied to a tree, eating from a generous stack of hay. And also eating from it was my mount, the one loaned to me from the Mount Teague stables. Side by side, tails swishing, necks craning and lifting, stony teeth grinding. I went back inside and I slept, too.

Later, the men brought me food from outside. I began eating and sitting up, but I spoke very little. I still slept a good deal. My dressings gradually changed from red-tinged to yellow to pink and then hardly anything. On cold mornings, I would wake with an old blanket over me. On warmer mornings, there would be a jug of water.

One morning I woke in the stable to the banging of the *to arms* signal of a drum, or at first that's what I thought it was. The rap-rap-rap that meant get ready, hell is just across the way. I waited for a moment, still confused by half-sleep. Then I realized they were hammer blows and not a drum.

I stumbled to my feet and staggered to the door of the stable. There in the brilliant chill and wood-smoky air, men were working up in the beams and rafters of a building. Thin clouds of breath drifted out of them as they hammered and sawed and balanced and passed boards one to another.

The man Honoré Mouton stood with his arms stretched out. He took a nail out of his mouth and held it in his hand as he demonstrated the

---

[23] Merry Christmas.

desired length to them, *un douze poutres, comme ça.*[24]

He was supervising the raising of one of the foundation sleepers to be used as a ridge beam. It had been burned, but the charred outer portion was largely scraped away to reveal the beautiful flowing grain of the cypress. The joist hovered high in the air near the apex of the church, every man straining under it.

"Bear the weight," he said in encouragement. "Bear the weight together." His fingers jiggled palmward, upraised to coax his men forward with the beam as he peered into the gap. Finally, he held up his hand and said, *droit-là.*[25] The sleeper, now a ridge beam, sat perfectly above the rafters.

Honoré scratched his head when he saw the beam was too short. I looked up to where he sat astride the ridge. He looked around the clearing as if searching for the answer. Then he looked down at the beam again.

"*Trop cort,*"[26] he said as he eyed the gap. With his hands, he measured the span where the beam had fallen short.

"*Mais, j'ai la coupee deux fois...*" Honoré muttered down to the end of the beam.

"*...et toujour il est trop cort,*" another man replied with a chuckle at some worn out joke.[27]

Honoré vaulted down from the rafter with the agility of a monkey. He paced around the worksite, lifting pieces, sighting down their length for trueness and wind, and letting them fall into a hollow, wooden sound. At last, he found the one he was looking for, the suitable one, the mate, the extension.

And then the housejoiner, Honoré Mouton, executed the most perfect scarf joint I've ever seen. It took him at most half an hour, and when he was finished, it was seamless. He drove the square peg home with three or four hollow raps. He called this version a *trait de Jupitre*, because it looked like a bolt of lightning.

They raised it and hammered it into place. The rest of the men trusted it so much that they walked upon it without a testing foot first. Later, they

---

[24] A dozen beams, like so.
[25] Right there
[26] Too short
[27] "I cut it twice...and it's still too short."

would put a coat of paint over it. No one would ever see it, that work of a master carpenter. Such is the way of a craftsman: though no one would ever see it, he would know it was there. Hidden, solid perfection.

A nail sunk into the cypress, clack-clack-clack-clock-whump. And then another as he set them sinking into the other side of the joint. He lifted himself, straddling the short distance to the next cross member. When he saw me, he took one of the square-headed nails we used then out of his mouth and exclaimed, "*Garde-donc-ça!*"[28]

I stood looking up at him and the sun behind him. It felt as though I'd been asleep a million years. The light was bright, and the sun made him an outline. Then it brightened as he put the nail back in his pouch and climbed down to ground level to speak with me.

What do you say to someone when they save your life? Are they the same tired words you use when someone holds a door for you? Is it the same ancient phrase you might use when a Yankee soldier offers you half of the boiled beef from his tin plate and water from his canteen? I could think of no others at the time.

"Thank you," I said. The words felt foreign in my mouth, like rocks or cotton or marbles. They were words I was unaccustomed to saying, but I had to say them again. "Thank you."

His smile fell, and he raised a finger.

"You don't never thank me for things like that," he scolded. "It's not me you should thank." And he pointed to the sky. He turned and walked back to his crew. Beams were being clacked into place. He took a handful of nails from a keg and put them in his apron. He pointed to the horse with his hammer.

"You friend, *mais*, he come back for you."

Honoré vaulted up to the ridge-timber and straddled it again. He rapped in a couple of nails and then scooted down the beam. I admired the joy with which he went about his work. The rest of the men had it, too. He was their heartbeat, their light. A man needs a purpose to feel like a man. My daddy always told me that, not in words, but in actions. And I never understood it until that moment.

"I can help you," I called up to him. "I can work."

---

[28] Well, look at that!

"For true?"

He swung himself down from the beam again and landed on both feet, pausing for a moment to regain his balance. He approached me, and I saw him clearly for the first time.

"You help us, *mon ami?*" he stood and asked me again, quieter, face to face, just the two of us. He was everything good in the world, everything that shines, everything that nourishes. In short, he was everything I was not. Unworthiness pecked away, somewhere inside myself.

"I got a past," I said.

He shrugged his shoulders and tilted his head. He was still holding a hammer at his side.

"I don't care about your past, no. We all got a past, like we all got a future. All I need to know is, can you can swing a hammer? Push a saw?"

My shoulder was still sore. He gave me a nail, a small square iron nail, and had me hammer it. I expected my shoulder to sing with pain, but his smile nudged me on. After three raps, the nail was flush. And something else, there was no pain in my shoulder. None. None whatsoever.

I was dumbfounded. My shoulder had never felt better in my life.

Next, he had me saw through a four-inch square post, the sweet whiskey smell of cypress escaping with the fine yellow-brown lint of sawdust. The kerf of the saw was true and quick, and the small square off-cut fell after no more than ten passes.

I looked up to him, and he canted his head a little and smiled.

"I guess I can," I murmured.

"Then your past, *mais*, it don't matter, no."

As we stood there face-to-face, the hammering up in the skeleton of rafters came to an end, one blow, then another, until a final blow ricocheted off the distant tree line. He turned to the crew, who were waiting on his direction, men poised with hammers, saws, chisels, timbers, boards. The rasp of a saw came to a stop. Hands with hammers wilted to their sides. Jaws dropped from gaping mouths. One of the crew finally muttered what they were all thinking.

"*Sont jumeaux.*"[29]

It was true what the men said of Honoré and me. We both had jet-

---

[29] They're twins.

black hair, were both the same height and build, both with dark eyes. And we both had missing fingers.

But it did not slow either of us down. I never knew how he lost his, though he loved to make up stories for the children on how he did, everything from biting his nails and forgetting to stop, to sawing it off, to our mule, "All Tom," aggressively nibbling it off for desert after the offer of a carrot.

He would give us simple words of advice as we went along in the day. "A man's only sharp as his tools." "*Measure deux fois, cort une fois.*"[30] But his favorite was one we began every day with.

"Ton travail est ta prière."[31]

"Your work," he would say as he pounded home a nail and pulled the next one from his canvas apron, "Your work is your prayer. Every blow of the hammer, every pass of the saw," he planted the next nail and tapped it. "*Mais*, it's your prayer. Your gift." He didn't say if it was a gift from someone or to someone. It was simply a gift.

I worked that first day, but I tired by noon. He had been watching me all morning. I would catch him pausing in his work to gauge my endurance and my strength. As my work slowed, he put his arm around my shoulders.

"That's enough, *mon ami*," he said.

"Pete," I said.

"Pete," he repeated. "Get some rest. Tomorrow, eh, Pierre?"

From that day forward, he began to call me what I've been called the rest of my life, Pierre. I don't think he ever knew my last name. If he did, he never called me by it.

The next morning, I was up before everyone else. The sun was blanching the eastern sky, and some farmer's rooster crowed in a distant, small voice. The church was beginning to take shape; you could tell that it was a church and not a house or a barn. The horse and the mule ate together in the morning shadow that stretched west to the stable. And then the others began to arise.

Several fixed breakfast, bacon and some sort of corncake. It struck me that it was much like life in the army, a group of sleeping men who ate out

---

[30] Measure twice, cut once.
[31] Your work is your prayer.

of a communal pot. We worked all day, and I listened to the songs and laughter and rapping of hammers and the rasping of saws and a pause for a joke in French that I did not get at all, but I laughed anyway. Such is the way of laughter.

And at night, we sat around the fire as our work cast shadows of rafters and beams up to heaven. There was quiet conversation and eating and a jug that made the rounds as we all contemplated things. It was in that firelight that Honoré Mouton began to find my purpose.

30

From this front balcony, I look out over the cemetery, and I see them. So many of the monuments in that city of the dead are the perfect work of my imperfect hands. Angels, crosses with flowery vines, columns with volutes, reeded columns, Ionic columns, Doric columns, stags for the BPOE, logs for the Woodmen of the World, Masonic calipers. I have done them all, and not just for Lafayette Cemetery, but for numerous ones in the various St. Louis Cemeteries. I've chiseled the commas and dots for the Hebrews, epitaphs in French and English. I have even prepared my own. This is largely due, perhaps solely due, to Honoré Mouton. He saw my talent and coaxed it out of me like a gardener coaxes a seed out of the soil.

It began when we were relaxing by the fire at night, our hands and our bodies aching after a day of labor. The advancing skeleton of the church we were building was in the firelight, and so were we. I was whittling a small figure. It was a bobcat about four inches long. Honoré was watching me as my knife pulled away curls and made stop-cuts in the cypress. The sweet whiskey smell of the cypress mingled with the smell of the fire.

"Let me see that, Pierre," he said with an outstretched hand. His head tilted as he looked down his nose at the little carving. I'm sure that if he had ever gotten old, he would have needed glasses. *"Mais, garde donc ça."* He turned it over in his hand, examining it from several angles. *"C'est chat-tigre."*

"Pierre, you think you could do a carving of the Blessed Mother, *comme ça?*" He marked off in the air a woman about shoulder height to us. I said I believed I could.

"*Mais*, if you believe you can, then you can."

The next day, he selected a post about five feet tall and a couple of feet wide. We looked at it, standing on end, with our hands working our beards, as if the answer might fall out of them. At last, he said, "*Bien, allez!*"

I started slowly, sawing away the profiles, first from one aspect and then from another. I began to see it. I used a drawknife to soften the edges. Then I saw more of it. I used a chisel, a knife. I could see the image trapped in the wood. She called to me silently, begging me, *let me out, give me life.* I worked quickly, as if she were trapped in rubble. I chipped away the lie from the truth, the quick from the dead, the repulsive from the beautiful, working always down the grain, across the line of the wood.

The rest of the crew adjourned for lunch and then resumed. I kept working. Her veil, her hair, her hands held up in prayer, her shoulders sloping gracefully, her breasts mounded diminutively. And then, there she was, wood colored, the cypress smelling as sweet as apples at Christmastime.

I was unaware that the sounds around me had stopped. I looked around, and the whole crew was there. One of them made the sign of the cross. Another said quietly, *Garde là!* And another, *Jolie!* They assembled two more cypress logs. The woman I had carved seemed to say to me, *There are two others. Please rescue them.*

I began in the same manner. Night fell, and I continued by firelight. It was chilly. The men watched me. One offered me his coat, but I could not stop long enough to put it on. My breath drifted out into vapor in the cold night air. The men kept the fire fueled. The rafters of the church rose behind it.

The figures emerged from the huge chunks of cypress. A bearded head. A robe. A hand held in benediction. A sash at the belt of the robe. Sandal-clad feet. And then on the smaller block, a round, cherubic body, a swaddle of diaper, a beatific smile. And then there they were, Joseph and his son, the carpenters of Nazareth.

The fire crackled with what the men called *les boutailles*, the offcuts, the waste. We looked at the figures. We ran our fingers over them. I did not sleep that night. Even after the others went to sleep, I could not.

The next day, André, our best painter, painted them, the Blessed Mother in light blue and white, Joseph in a brown robe, the Christ child in a white wrap and wavy blonde hair. André had the narrow brushes that an artist uses and daintily touched the statues here and there, dipping the brushes, dabbing them on an old rag, and applying the paint. He spent most of the day dipping and dabbing, but when he was done, we all sat back in the dim light and waited for Jesus, Mary, and Joseph to speak, to hear what wisdom they might give us.

When the new church of St. Lazare was completed, we installed the statues on the altar in alcoves we had made, and Honoré shook hands with the parish priest, the one I remembered standing in the blackened skeleton of the prior church. The priest, a somewhat disheveled old man looked around himself with a stunned expression, as if he were suddenly in St. Marks in Venice or St. Peter's in the Vatican. He walked through the pews, his hands feeling along the backs of them. At last he made his way back to the altar and its centerpiece.

"It's beautiful," he said. "Who rendered the Holy Family?"

Honoré put his hand on my shoulder, *"Cet homme ça."*

The old priest grasped my hands in his and kissed them, remarking as he let them go, "Your finger, child. God bless you." He kissed my hands again and said, "God bless you."

Then, the new church was toured by the parishioners, mostly women and the very old and the very young, as the men of the place were either in the army or hiding from it. Everyone was ecstatic to have something nice, something new, highlighted by the full-sized icons. A party was planned for the next day.

It was the day that I met that woman.

31

The woman from downstairs is in my room, cleaning. She rummages through the top of the armoire and finds the box. Looking over her shoulder, she smiles and returns to her cleaning. Her duster shakes its tailfeathers all over the room. When she comes to my portion of it, she catches me picking my nose with a shaky hand and a wavering finger, and she produces a handkerchief from her apron and she wipes each nostril, folding over the linen to repeat it. Then she kisses me on my forehead and resumes her work.

She is lithe and caramel-skinned, a pleasant tan, the color of fresh cut cypress and the sweet scent, too, with green eyes. I try to remember the first time I saw her, but I can't. How old was I? How old was she? Where were we? It was a beautiful moment, but I can't remember it, can't even imagine it, but I yearn for it, I want to relive it. I knew when I first saw her that I would see her many, many times again. From that day forward, every other woman would seem doughty and plain to me. Ordinary.

There's something that passes between a man and a woman the first time they see each other. The world falls away, and nothing else exists except the two of you and the moment, and then the moment slips in your pocket and winds up in your soul and you couldn't get it out of there if you tried. It gnaws at you, it sings to you. On cold nights, it warms you, on hot nights it cools you, but it never leaves you, that moment.

Whatever became of her, that girl, that woman, that I met long ago? As my mind has slid into its decline, I have wondered it like a pain that is forgotten in sleep and remembered again on waking.

The day after we completed the church of St. Lazare, a *fête*, a celebration was held. First, there was an open house. The congregation filed in, a few at a time, marveling at the beams and columns, even though they couldn't see the detail like I could see, the bridle joints, the pegged tenons, the *trait de Jupitre* that Honoré had executed. They only saw the beauty. They could not see the strength behind it. They genuflected and kissed fingers in front of the Holy Family, the cypress having been transformed into something mystical and holy.

A banquet was held. Hogs were summoned from the swamp where they had been taken for safekeeping from men like me. As the hogs were rolled over and over and basted with a mop, children were summoned from tag and blind man's bluff to engage in rendering the other portions of the pig. Nothing was wasted.

Everyone ate, including the old priest, who was a little late since he was *a pied*.[32] French was everywhere, and I was as good as deaf in the babble of it. The laughter I could understand. Laughter and smiling are the same in any language. It was a cold day, but I felt as warm as if I were under a quilt or two at my Aunt Cora's house.

And then I saw her. She spoke very little but listened a lot. Her vacant eyes gazed at the foreheads of the speakers, a spindly old man with a long white beard like a tail of Spanish moss, and his wife, a portly, jolly woman with a bosom that lounged in the bodice of her dress like two fat, sleeping housecats. The man leaned on his cane, a jagged, gnarled thing that he had obviously crafted himself. He said some French something to the girl and the woman, and, having made his point, leaned back and tilted his head with a look of mischievous authority. The old woman huffed sarcastically, and the girl tilted her head back in a broad smile.

The old couple stood up and went to find a plate, leaving the girl alone, and, as I was alone myself, I thought that perhaps we could be alone together, she and I.

"*Bonjour*," I said.

She looked up to where she thought I might be.

"*Bonjour*," she said to the top of my head. She said something to me in French, a rambling reply that overwhelmed my understanding. I stopped her.

"I'm sorry," I said. "My French isn't that good."

"We speak *anglais*, then," she said. She put her hand up, not in a greeting, but in a request.

"Permit me, *monsieur*, but I can't see." Her hand probed the air. "Where you face?"

Her fingertips found my cheek, and then her palm found it, and her fingers appraised my forehead, my eyebrows, the bridge of my nose.

"You and Monsieur Mouton, you brothers, no? You look the same."

"No, I just work for him," I said in wonder, astonished how this woman could see me with her hands.

"*Mais*, you could pass, you and him."

Her eyes were gray and filmy, clouds in the sky of her face. Her hair,

---

[32] On foot.

blonde and wiry like the straw of a broom, was drawn up onto her head, but stray strands of it fell onto her neck. She had a lovely, serene smile that often and easily flashed itself into a wide grin with two flanking dimples. Her skin was tan like someone who worked outside or like an Indian or both. Her hand rested on my cheek, and I wished she would put her fingers in my hair and that her palm would slide down over my ear to my neck and that she would draw her lips to mine. I wished it just then. I wished it more than anything.

But she smiled off into the distance behind me, the distance that neither one of us could see. Her hand withdrew, and I heard the other conversations, the French ones, and the laughter at French jokes and the barking of dogs as they shouted merrily in French barking at children who played with them, shouting commands and endearment in French. The smell of woodsmoke and food cooking returned, and the chill of the air returned and I saw her there before me again. She was wrapped in a brown woolen shawl over a simple dress.

"You got a name, *Monsieur Anglais?*" she asked me.

"Pete," I said. "But Monsieur Honoré calls me Pierre."

"Pierre? *Mais*, that's a good French name for an American boy.[33] You work for *monsieur?*" she asked.

"Yes," I said. "Do you have a name, Miss Français?"

"Prosperine," she smiled. "Billiot."

She was the kind of woman that if you saw her, it was hard not to sigh. And she had no idea how beautiful she was. Prosperine Billiot was not, and could not be, a slave to her own vanity.

We chatted the afternoon away, and my French began to grow from a small village of words, words like *merci*, and *bonjour*, to a small town of phrases. The shadows were getting long, and the air was darkening into a nighttime chill. And then I learned a new phrase.

Allons dancer.

It was a dance held in the stable of the rectory. The carriage held a chaos of coats and shawls and hats. Children slept together in the loft. As

---

[33] Chip, it was common in those days for the French people to refer to non-French as "Americans," even though they themselves were also Americans. I can remember my grandparents doing it. Maybe you can, too. -Matt

the night proceeded, teetering mothers and fathers would go up the ladder to check on them, whispering, "Time to make *do-do*." And the children slept, which was a small miracle among the fiddle scratch and the hand clapping and the clomp of boots on the plank floor. But they all had to be got to bed before the dancing could begin. And it was Honoré who did it. It began with a prompt from one of the women.

"Honoré! We want music. Them chirren, they need to make *do-do*."

"Chirren," Honoré said, "I can tell one more story."

They were drawn up around him. A little boy about eight or so raised his hand.

"Monsieur Honoré, how you lose your finger?"

"Well, it was the Rougarou. He came out the swamp, and I had to wrestle him. Yes, I did."

"What did he look like?" a little girl whispered.

"Well," Honoré thought. "The front half was green and scaly. The back half? Well, brown and furry like a wolf...or a bear. He had hisself big fang-teeth, *comme ça*." Honoré gestured two big fang-teeth. The children squealed with delight.

"*Monsieur*," one of the mothers scolded. "Them chirren gonna have bad dreams, them."

"But mama," one of the little girls said, "We gotta find out about that Rougarou."

"Well, the Rougarou said, 'Honoré Mouton!' I want you for my stew-pot. Get in this sack here, and I'm gonna take you back to my camp."

"Well, I wasn't ready for no stew-pot, me. So, I wrestled him. And I pinned him. And just before I threw him back in the bayou...well, he bit this finger. *Pa-ya!*"

"Did it hurt?"

"*Mais, oui*, it hurt. But I told that Rougarou, that's all you gettin'. And I threw him in the bayou. And he sank to the bottom. And he can't get nobody for his stew-pot no more."

The little boy and girl faces looked up in the lamp light. All were wide eyed.

"And as he sank to the bottom..." Honoré looked both ways. Even the grown-ups were listening. "...the last thing he told me was if good chirren don't go to bed, then I come back and I visit them and that's for

151

true."

The children scrambled up the ladder to the loft. One of them sat on the edge, and Honoré raised his hands like paws and bared his teeth and the boy scrambled under the blankets with the others.

As soon as the little boy was out of sight up in the loft, Honoré picked up his fiddle and plucked it into tune. He stood on the carriage and played each string to check it one more time.

"Learn to play your own fiddle, Pierre," he told me, his hair framing his forehead as it fell parted loosely in the middle, "Or you always gonna be dancin' somebody else's tune."

He scratched across the fiddle (the *violon*, he called it), and it rasped out a pleasing sound. The women clapped their hands in glee, and as Honoré played a song, some of them went to retrieve their men from a bourré game that was being played by lantern light. A woman in a bonnet nursed a baby in a similar one. The baby's bonnet shook as the little head inside rooted through the blouse of its mother. The mother's fingers parted layers of fabric, and then she looked up with a smile to watch the dancing.

And then the dancing began, and it lasted well into the night, and then the courting began. And I sat with Prosperine Billiot and watched it all. And she sat with me and listened to it all.

32

Downstairs, the telephone blurts out a sputtering, bicycle-bell ring. It only rings once, so I know the woman is in the kitchen. The telephone is there also. She answers it.

"*Bonjour, qu'est-la?*" Whoever it is, she is glad to hear from the person. She chatters, listening and talking in turn, her side of the conversation punctuated with *ah*, *sha*, and *pauvre bête*. When she inquires about the health of someone named Ulysse, I know she is talking to our friends in Côte-Française.[34] That means that it is long distance, and that means it is a special telephone call.

---

[34] Chip, I believe this is the old name of French Settlement, but I may be mistaken.

When the woman finishes her call, she comes up the stairs. She is as old as I am, but her steps are spry and rhythmic on the steps.

"Pierre?" Her voice is quiet as it probes the silence to see if I am awake. "The Heberts send birthday wishes to you."

Another birthday. I had forgotten. It is simply one of many. A drop in a bucket of birthdays, a bucket in an ocean of birthdays. There was a day when a birthday was a grand celebration. Today, there will be cake, perhaps, and they will put a little hat on me and sing happy birthday to me and the woman downstairs who is not the hired girl will feed me meager forkfuls and I will wear a collar of crumbs on my shirt.

After our celebration, the bishop came to consecrate the church of St. Lazare. It was a ceremony, I'm sure, full of fluff and pomp. We had moved on by then, following the siren call of work. There was plenty of it in those days.

The earth was tilting back to the sun. Nature emerged in green and gold, and flowers bloomed in joyful colors of life and sex and abundance. The rusted cypresses threw off their brown needles in favor of bright green ones. Cane grew knee-high to belt-high. Tools were loaded up and then unloaded again as we traveled job-to-job. There was so much rebuilding to be done in the scorched wake, the blackened path of war. We followed the work. And Prosperine Billiot came with us.

Her mother was a dissolute woman who went through men almost as quickly as she went through liquor. She was a woman who at times made her daughter the center of the universe and at other times would stagger past her without notice, sometimes holding the hand of a new gentleman admirer, who was usually as inebriated as she was. The girl would sit in her forever dark and listen with keen ears at the grunting huff and shrieks of ecstasy that may have been in the next room of their shanty and may have been in the very same room.

Prosperine had a boy she had been interested in, but he had been lured away by ten dollars of enlistment bounty and swept off in a tide of men marching off to adventure and glory. They had been sweet on each other, but his departure caused a rift. Still, her voice quieted when she talked about him, only referring to him as *mon beau*, though a time or two she referred to him as *"Leesie."*

Whether he was coming back or not was no small question to me, and I refused to give myself the hope that he wasn't. Perhaps I was growing a small sense of decency then, to put myself in this poor blind girl's place and hope with her for beau's return. And besides, the widow Lowe situation taught me that anything was possible and not to get my hopes up. I am ashamed to say, however, that I've never wished someone so dead in all my life.

I adored that blind girl, though silently. Her eyes slept under the callouses of her blindness like the blooms of flowers under a snow. I wondered what color they might be. Her figure, tall, lean, a statue, perfectly formed, at least in my imagination. I imagined its perfection, curves, points, dips, swells. I dreamed of her body the way Galileo must have dreamed of the heavens. Only for me, neither the earth nor the sun were the center of the universe, she was. I thought hard for the word in French that would make her love me and give up hope for the boy who had gone off for a soldier. A spoken key that would open an invisible lock. A word, a phrase, perhaps, that would make the eyes of her soul see me, and see me in a new light. And see no one else ever again.

She followed us, the girl, the young woman Prosperine Billiot, riding high in the wagon pulled by the mule that Honoré called Ol' Tom, which sounded like "All Tom" to me. Her blank eyes looked for the sound of the breeze, searched for the smell of the cedars and cypresses and flowers, and the scent of the sleeping earth reawakening in the Louisiana sun.

She cooked for us, hands and nose patiently examining each onion, each measure of meal, each cut of meat. And once a week, on Saturday, we peeled off our clothes for her to wash by feel over an open kettle stirred with a cypress paddle. We moved around half-naked as if she wasn't there, unthreatened by her sightless glances. Her lithe, olive-skinned hands would wring them dry and hang them on a line in the lilting wind, a small tinkling bell hung on the line to direct her back to it. She would visit it through the afternoon, her hands feeling for dryness as we waited in our underclothes on Sundays.

In the meantime, they taught me French. *Marteau* was hammer. *Scion* was saw, except in the case of the big, two-man saw, it was a *pas-de-deux*. They taught me detail, taught me craftsmanship. They taught me joy, laughter, camaraderie, forbearance, encouragement. We could put together a pretty nice house in two to three days, a barn in a week, a church in a couple of weeks. Only the most regal of buildings gets its own name, like that new Hibernia Building on Gravier. But the simple buildings built by common men remain anonymous. There is no glory in the construction of a house or a simple country church or a warehouse or a barn. There is no glory, but there is plenty of honor.

All the while, I worked with borrowed tools and wished for the only heirloom that I had of my daddy's, his tool satchel and the tools it contained. I would call them all by their French names, if only I could find them. But they were somewhere at Mount Teague, kept or thrown away or re-sold at *la commissaire*.

We spent a summer, fall, and winter rebuilding the countryside. So much of it had been burned or bullet-pocked or cannon-blasted or consumed in the campfires of armies. During that time, the Union army took Opelousas and Alexandria and Natchitoches. They threatened the capital in Shreveport but were turned away. And all the while, we built things. We re-built things.

And Honoré would practice his other craft, a wart here, a headache there, a heartache, a stomach ache. Pleurisy. Dropsy. A *coup de soleil*.[35] Poultices, salves, *un cordon*, a knotted string. Always with the restless breath bearing a silent prayer.

We were working on a house, I don't remember where, somewhere along the river, because I can remember we would all pause and watch the steamboats go by, tall stacks belching smoke. I thought of what Monsieur Lapeyrouse would say, *all right, you stud mules, back to work.* But Honoré would watch with us, all of us fascinated like boys at the sight of what was then the highest fruits of technology and industry, churning by with the great beam of an arm pushing the slatted wheel in a circle.

"We ought to make us one of them," one of the men said.

Honoré laughed. "We could sail it all the way to Cuba, all the way to Havana."

The rest of us laughed at the thought of all of us, carpenters turned sailors. We watched the sternwheeler plow upriver, and we turned back to our work.

---

[35] Sunstroke

Then a man came running. Honoré and I were each lugging a hogshead of nails from the wagon, when the man arrived panting.

"*Monsieur, c'est ma fille*,"[36] he said.

We ran down the road that paralleled the river and found her in the yard of the house. She had been drawing water from the well when she collapsed. She was in her teen years, a freckled face with a head full of thick brown hair, suddenly thick, like girls get at that age.

Her neck was craning back, her eyes blank-white. As we watched her, her head twisted to one side, and she gurgled a strange sound. Her chin pointed to the sky. A crowd had formed around her.

"Maybe she got a devil," someone said. "Maybe it's a *gris-gris*."

"No, she ain't got no devil," Honoré said. "And she ain't got no *gris-gris*."

He looked thoughtfully at the girl, whose torso was arching up away from the ground. He used his large, rough hands to open the girls mouth, like you would do to a horse to look at its teeth. The girl flapped and bounced on the ground, and the people of that little precinct held her arms loosely. They all seemed so helpless. Honoré eased a finger between her teeth, good, strong, young teeth that in any other circumstance would be a beautiful smile. He saw what he was looking for, and he swept it out. A piece of an apple. And then we saw what he had seen. The rest of the apple on the ground a few feet away, one large bite taken out of it.

"She ain't got a devil, no. She got an apple," he said. She was still contorting, but he relaxed the smallest bit, and in that brief split second, she bit him on the hand.

"Ay!" he exclaimed. He pried her mouth open again, and stepped away shaking his hand. Dots of blood were beginning to run, and he wrapped his hand in the carpenter's apron he was still wearing. But he was smiling as the girl opened her eyes. They were heavy-lidded, but they were opened, and she was looking up at all the faces looking down at her.

The girl's mother brought him a small towel and wrapped his hand in it. Honoré himself laughed off the wound. The girl was sitting up now, leaning back against the well, and the old women of the place were fretting over her. The attention suddenly seemed to embarrass the girl. She tried to

---

[36] It's my daughter.

stand, and the women all cooed, *no, sha*.

The father offered Honoré a small sip from a jug, liquor, I presumed. He took it and made a face and smacked his lips in the aftermath of it.

"*Merci, monsieur*," the girl's father said. "*Merci*."

"*Non*," Honoré said sternly, shaking his head.

When we left the clearing to return to the worksite, the people of that small hamlet walked with us for a short distance. We still had our carpenter's aprons around our waists, square-headed nails quietly jingling in them. Honoré was holding his hand in the white linen towel. He turned to give the woman her towel back.

"Keep it," she said.

"*Merci*," he said back lifting the towel and the hand in it.

And then the daughter was there, beautiful now in that way of the women in that area. She ran and stopped in front of Honoré. Raising up on her toes, she put her hands on his neck under each of his ears, and she kissed him on each cheek, not a peck, but something longer, the kind of kiss that can become a prelude to other things. The crowd crooned a collective blush, and Honoré kissed her back on her forehead and smoothed his thumb over it. Then we turned and began walking, he and I, leaving the people and the well and the apple and the pretty girl. We headed back toward the afternoon sun and the work we had to do. From time to time, he would unwrap the plain, blood-mottled towel and examine the ellipse of red punctures.

33

There is a man who comes to read to me sometimes. He looks like the Spaniard, but is fairer and younger. I think that they are father and son. He calls me Gramps. He sits and reads to me from the Bible, as he has done before, usually the New Testament. If I could speak, I would tell him that I prefer the Old Testament, though purely on sheer entertainment value. The Old Testament has more action, sword fights and chariots and horn-blowing and walls coming down and so forth. The young man seems rather religious, something with which I take no issue. Religion, like drinking and swearing, causes little harm if practiced in moderation.

He reads to me from John's account of the passion of Christ. It was always one of Aunt Cora's favorites, the gospel according to John, and she would sometimes have me copy it in fat, flowing vowels and great leaping consonants. It is the part in which Jesus tells his mother, "Woman, behold your son," and then to the apostle John, "Behold your mother." I always felt an odd pang of regret that I could never behold mine.

As he reads on, I daydream of my daddy. I see him standing behind the chair by my bed here in my room. A woman is sitting in the chair, and he has his hands on her shoulders. She looks exactly like the woman I carved from the block of cypress wood for St. Lazare. They are wearing clothes of the last century. I've always thought that I look like my daddy, but my resemblance to this woman is uncanny.

Your mama wanted to come see you, my daddy says.

Why haven't you brought her before? I ask.

Well, son, time gets away from us where we are.

I look to the mirror to check my reflection, to see how much I resemble this woman. But she has no reflection, nor does my daddy. Only the man who reads. But I think this is only my imagination. I put my hand to my brow and massage it. Still, it is troubling. But then I forget about them.

I wake up, and the young man with the Bible is gone, and I am alone with my memories again.

Honoré once told me that people tend to confuse God with Papa Noël. They expect that He will give you everything you want if you ask for it earnestly enough. And getting everything you want is probably the worst thing that can happen to you, even if it is something you want dearly and need exquisitely. Or think you need.

Honoré's hand healed, leaving an arc of white dots, and we completed the house and set off to another job. "All Tom" pulled the wagon patiently as Prosperine rode in the back of it with the tools and cooking things and spare lumber. Her arms stretched out along the sides of the wagon as she turned her face to the sky, her senses straining to fill the space vacated by her sight. Everywhere, spring was throbbing joyously, and she could not see it.

We stopped at a small farmstead and put up a barn for a man. It took us about a week or so, and afterward the man and his family celebrated with us. The family had a small horde of children, all seemingly born nine months and ten minutes apart, but one of them, something had happened to him. I think it was something from birth, but I didn't ask and anyway, my French wasn't that good. But the little fellow was enamored with Honoré, sitting in close to him as Honoré sat on a haybale and fiddled, tapping his boot in time to the shuffling of dancers and the music. The little fellow had a misshapen head and odd looking eyes and low ears. His parents tried to pull him away, that poor, ruined boy, so as not to distract Honoré from his music. But Honoré stopped-in the middle of the song-and told them to leave him there, that they were enjoying each other's company and that he was no trouble. Honoré played until the little boy's eyes slackened with sleep and his little body slumped against him. Honoré's *violon* squealed and crooned, and the boy was oblivious.

When the dance was over, he picked up the child's limp, slumbering body.

"*Pauvre bête*," he said, and he kissed the boy on his forehead before giving him over to his mother.

The mother gathered the boy, whose name was Alcee, I believe, but that is no matter now, and she took him in the house and put him in the bed with his siblings. Honoré was putting away his *violon*. The little boy distressed me. He did.

Can you change him? I thought, but I changed my question. "Can he be changed?" I asked Honoré.

"Not everything must be changed, Pierre. Sometimes things are like they are in hope that the world, or at least a small part of it, will change. In the meantime, this poor boy here is a soul just like you and me. And our souls don't toil or spin. They got no color, *sont pas homme, sont pas femme.*[37] But make no mistake. They are us. They are more us than we are us."

He clasped his hand on my shoulder.

"*Allons, eh?*"

---

[37]They're not male or female.

34

There are children in this house this evening, though this is nothing unusual. I hear the slap of water in the bathtub down the hall, and the rush of water poured over soapy heads. The woman downstairs, who is not the hired girl but a woman that I have shared a bed with many, many nights, she speaks to the children and sings to them in French, and they sing along with her, *Frère Jacques, frère Jacques, dormez-vous? dormez-vous?*

There is the flashing tumble of water and a dripping sound, and the dog barks happily. And then there are thudding steps running down the hall and into my room, the young girl and a young boy. They are four or five or so, the boy a little older. They are brother and sister or cousins to each other, but they are naked, running with their hands in the air like a couple of monkeys walking a tightrope at the zoo.

"Papere, we're naked!" they exclaim and they run through the room, their nakedness identical except for below, which for them is just an interesting novelty. The dog comes in shouting merrily, perhaps saying, "Look at me! I am naked, too! Why, I am naked all the time!"

The woman appears with towels, laughing as she corrals the boy and girl up in them. Then, they sit wrapped up as the light fades outside. The boy sits under his towel with his hands beneath his legs and contemplates me like one might watch an animal at the zoo. Next to him, the woman combs out the wiry, wet straw-colored hair of the girl, and it makes the girl's eyes as large and green as the woman's eyes.

At last clothed in pajamas, they kiss me on the cheek and tell me, "*Bon nuit*, Papere." And I am left with a lilac soap-scented memory.

The weather was warming, and the cane had grown waist-high. Elsewhere, the Confederacy was slowly being rolled up like a gaudy red and gold carpet. The Union Army was on the move up the Red River toward Shreveport. And we were on the move all through St. Matthew Parish, and the neighboring parishes, Iberville, Ascension, St. James.

The weather was getting hot, and the nights were doing little to slacken the air after the hot days. We were working along Bayou Pigeon, rebuilding houses, barns, and a church. I did a Holy Family altarpiece from cypress for that church as well, a new one as they had not had one before. It was far superior to the one I did for St. Lazare, but it was still not the best I would ever do, not even close. I was discovering my gift.

It was at the end of the day. Sunset was getting later every day, and the nights were pleasant. I was sitting by a tree whittling small figures in the firelight of our camp when Prosperine appeared, feeling her way. She had a towel over her arm.

"I could hear your knife, Pierre," she said off into the distance. The firelight cast her shadow up and into the trees with her gaze.

"You have good ears, then," I said down to my figure, an owl. I held it up to the firelight, turned my head, and cradled the owl again to make another cut.

"Pierre, will you come with me? I need to bathe and I need someone to look out *pour les cocodries*.[38] She asked me timidly, in French. "But promise you won't look, will you?" she added in English.

I led her by the hand down to the bayou, and then looked away as she shed her clothes. The water murmured as she entered it. And then the scent of the memory, the soft, sharp fragrance of lilac soap. Crickets chattered in rising and falling waves in the dark shadows. The water gurgled in pleasure as it moved around her, caressing her body.

I could look away no longer. I saw her head just above the water, her hair wet and close to her head and a foam of suds on the surface, all in shades of silver in the moonlight. She moved her arms in the water, the slow beat of angel wings.

"You can come in, Pierre. If you're shy, I can't see you anyway."

I could feel myself teetering into temptation, and I took off my clothes. I made my way between the low knobby spires of cypress knees, still looking for the lumpy heads of alligators. She craned her head to the sound of my entering the water.

We swam and we talked. Mostly in English, though in French, some. Wordlessly, sightlessly, she held out the lilac soap, and I took it and I scrubbed with it. I put it back in her hand, that small weight, but she said she was done with it. I tossed it onto the bank. We swam and talked some

---

[38] For alligators.

more.

At last, we became chilled and adjourned to the grassy bank under the stars. I led her by her hand around the cypress knees and back up the incline. The grass was cool under our backs, and I laid her clothes out for her. We made no effort to conceal ourselves. I'm sure she knew I was looking at her.

She asked me what the stars looked like, and I told her, small and bright and sharp in a blue-black sky. She smiled and said, "*Oui*, I can almost see them." The crickets trilled like bells, and frogs grunted. There were no other sounds. She fed me a few more words. *Etoile*, star. *Lune*, moon. *Rosée*, dew.

I became so bold as to turn on my side and prop up on an elbow to look at her. The moonlight kissed her all over. Her blank stare and her smile looked up into it. The smooth contour of her, the small wispy cloud of hair at the base of her stomach, straw-colored, I imagined, but now only gray in the moonlight. Her hair slicked back and over her ears. Hard points of her breasts in the chill air. Crickets chirping in waves, up and down. Far away, the sound of Honoré's *violon* and the laughter around a campfire that was only a small yellow point in the distance.

I thought perhaps I should move over to her, and take her hand, or maybe even hover over her and lightly kiss her and wait for her lips to rise up to mine. The thought of it made my body tense, and the sight of her made it ache. It would be bold, but, yes, I would do it. My body was moaning, yes, do it, yes.

But as I shifted slightly to begin my advance, she began speaking of the boy she called Leesie. One moment she was angry with him for going off to war, and the next she was tearful for his safe return. With the change in the tack of the conversation, I began to feel more like a brother or cousin than a potential lover.

I excused myself for a dip in the cold, black bayou water. I waited there, up to my waist, waiting for the cold water to quiet me. I emerged from it, still aching for her. She was spread out on the bank in the wash of moonlight. She sat up and reclined on her hands. Her breasts changed shape as she sat and ran a hand through her hair. It was beginning to dry and become wiry again. The seeping light had turned it from blonde to white.

Her hand patted the ground, and she found her clothes, her fingers appraising each garment, identifying underclothes, blouse, dress, stockings. I put my clothes on. We said nothing. The crickets had quieted. She put out her hand, and I took it and helped her up. Up in the sky, the ash-splashed face of brother moon looked down on us.

35

The *Times-Picayune* says that a boy was bit *[sic]* by a snake in the lagoon at Audubon Park. They took the poor fellow to Dr. Touro's place, and he is expected to recover well. The article, which runs on page two next to an ad for hair tonic, ends with an admonition to be vigilant around the water this time of year, as there are all sorts of creatures in a state of agitation from the heat.

That is good advice. Not only do snakes and alligators get more agitated in the heat, so do wasps, bees, and yellow jackets. People may also be added to the list.

The summer that I worked for Honoré Mouton was hot and wet, and the cane was quickly waist high and chest high in places. Prosperine and I swam a few more times, and in those naked soirees I became her confidant rather than her lover, listening to her speak, more and more in French now, about her troubles with this Leesie fellow and her yearning for him and the lack of letters and her fear that he was in trouble, or, her lip would quiver into a pause, dead.

There were no alligators and no snakes at first. It was still too cool for them to appear at night, though during the day, they would crawl sluggishly onto logs or the far bank, or the knobby black heads of alligators would cut Vs in the water. We stopped bathing in the bayou and left it to the other creatures. And that was unfortunate, for the heat was becoming unbearable, and a dip in the water would have been welcome. It was so hot that Honoré insisted that we take a longer break at noon, to be made up at the end of the day when the evening was cooler.

We were working near the Yankee fort in Donaldsonville[39] for a Union captain named Harris, putting in a smokehouse and a couple of other outbuildings. It was noon time, and we were napping in the shade. Some of us were in the shade of trees, and about five or six of us were under the wagon. All of us were waiting for a breeze to stir up off the river. Bayou Lafourche begins there, off the river, and we could hear children playing in it, shouts and shrieks and splashes.

There was another splash, and then there was a scream. We thought it was just a girl who had gotten scared in jest by a playmate, but the screaming continued. Those of us under the wagon crawled out from under it and started running down to the bayou.

A girl of about ten was struggling in the water, each roll revealing a tangle of scaly gray tails. I waded down in the water and pulled her up on the bank. She had about four or five moccasins on her. Apparently, she had stumbled into a nest of them. They hung onto her, twisting like the hair of the Medusa. She screamed and screamed, her hands slapping ineffectively at the serpents, which writhed and twisted as their mouths hung tight to the girl's flesh.

Suddenly, Honoré was there, grabbing the small fist-like heads and squeezing so that the bite was released and throwing each snake back into the bayou. The men shot at them as they cut S's across the surface of the bayou. With the shots, the captain himself came running, the brass buttons of his uniform undone. I think he had been napping like us while his children swam. The girl saw him.

"Papa," she pleaded. She was breathing heavily, her chest heaving in and out desperately. Her eyes searched all of us, as if one of us had an answer to a desperate question, and she didn't know which one of us did. The captain knelt and stroked his girl's head. He looked to Honoré.

"What can be done? What?" he asked. "Please. Please."

"Captain," one of the soldiers said. "Surely it's too late. She's been bitten quite a few times. Let's just keep her comfortable."

Honoré was looking over the girl. He had taken off her dress down to her underclothes. They were wet from swimming and had small, watery blood stains where she had been bitten. She had marks all over her body.

---

[39] Fort Butler

Honoré produced a knife and made cuts over them. There were plenty of them, legs, arms, torso. Maybe a dozen or so, some single punctures, some double. They were beginning to swell a little.

"Kerosene," Honoré called out loudly. "And I need cobwebs and two or three cockroaches. Alive or dead. But not too dead. Not dry."

Roaches were everywhere then as they are now. The items were sent for and brought back. The girl was lying on the bank of the bayou. Someone brought a quilt to put over her. Her eyes were wide with terror, pure terror. Her father, the Union captain, paced, while the girl's mother knelt at her daughter's side with Honoré.

"I'm afraid," the girl said.

"*Tracasse-toi pas*,"[40] Honoré said to her in a small voice. "Fear ain't no good, no. It don't help at all. Don't be afraid, daughter."

When the kerosene arrived, he pulled back the quilt and washed the wounds with it and applied a rag to keep them soaked. Then he made a paste with the roaches and the cobwebs. He picked it up with his fingers and applied it. He was silent, but his lips were moving, and I knew he was praying.

The girl's eyes were narrowing. The lids hung on them as if they were sliding down. Still, Honoré was silent, his eyes closed, his lips forming silent words. He picked her up and walked down the bayou road with her. The crowd followed him and the limp bundle he carried. They approached the house where the captain was billeted. The captain opened the door for him, and he eased inside with the girl.

We waited through the warm, muggy night. A lantern was kept burning in the window. Occasionally, a shadow would obscure it, sometimes the mother, sometimes the captain, sometimes Honoré. We waited in the gray light.

At last, the sun put the eastern sky ablaze in orange and pink, then rose over the bayou and the bayou road and the little house. And the girl came out and sat in the morning sun.

---

[40] Don't worry. Literally, fret yourself not.

165

36

Outside, the rain is coming down hard this afternoon, raining like it only rains in New Orleans. The children were playing earlier when the first sudden drops fell, causing them to drop the orange tabby cat, who was still wearing doll clothes. Everyone ran inside, except the tabby; she ran under the house. The baby carriage that the cat had been enduring is left outside. The woman downstairs who is not the hired girl runs out to bring it in.

That summer was a rainy one, and it kept us from working as hard as we wished. The newspapers were reporting the events back in the part of the world where the war was still being contested. Grant had lost over seven thousand men in a mere twenty minutes. Before, I would have been sorry not to have been in that hunt. Now, I found myself shocked like everyone else. I was changing, and reading that account made me realize that I was. Seven thousand men. Seven thousand husbands, fathers, sons. Twenty minutes. Dear God.[41]

We were heading along the bayou toward our next job, somewhere down the way on the road to old St. Matthew. We passed an old farmhouse. A woman came out on the front porch and poured out a pan full of water. She looked at us for a moment before she went back inside. A few moments later she came out with another and poured it off the porch.

Honoré made a clicking sound to slow "All Tom." In the shade of an ancient sycamore tree was an even more ancient man. He sat smoking a pipe. Dense, bittersweet smoke scented everything as chickens spread out across the bare earth of the yard, small necks and beaks stabbing in choppy movements, sideways glances of yellow eyes, muttered clucking. A rooster sprinted a short, strutting race to a bug, which he pecked and juggled and swallowed.

We pulled up in the yard, and the old man took the pipe from his lips and told us, "*Bienvenue. Comment ça va?*"

"*Bien, ça va bien, merci,*" Honoré replied.

---

[41] The battle of Cold Harbor, Virginia, June 3, 1864

"*La couverture coule*[42]," the old man said as the young woman came out again and emptied a cast iron pot off the front porch. He wore a stocking cap, the top of it hanging down to a limp tassel. Gray hair wandered out aimlessly from under the edges. Some of his teeth were missing, perhaps all of them. He sat on a ladder-back chair in the dirt yard of his abode and watched us with his old hands perched on his cane, one nestled into the back of the other. His cheeks flapped as he puffed the long-stemmed pipe that exited the corner of his mouth.

"*Nous pouvons l'arranger*,"[43] Honoré said as he pointed to the roof.

"*Combien?*"[44] The old man, a Monsieur Broussard, said.

"*Deux poulet.*"[45]

Broussard motioned to the house with his pipe and tilted his head toward it, a gesture of agreement. Half of us scrambled up to the roof on a rickety ladder while the other half felled a cypress at the edge of the yard and began cutting it into new shakes. The old shakes flew down to the ground, spinning like heavy leaves. New ones were laid down, one course over the eaves, another course higher, another, another, overlapping up to the peak of the roof.

The old man spotted Prosperine on the buckboard of the wagon, and his eyes lit up. He pulled his pipe from his lips and smacked them as he gathered enough air to shout.

"*Viens assis près de moi, ma belle*,"[46] he said.

"*Je peux pas voir*,"[47] she said off in his direction somewhere.

André and Jacques were crosscutting a length of cypress. Broussard called to them with the propriety of a father ordering his sons.

"*Eh, garçon, aide la jeune femme. Amener les ici pour ça sire adroite un vieux homme.*"[48] He pointed to the ladderback chair beside him.

André left the saw in the kerf and slapped his hands together to release a small blur of dust. He moved to the wagon and reached up to help

---

[42] The roof leaks.
[43] We can fix it.
[44] How much?
[45] Two chickens
[46] Come sit by me, my pretty.
[47] I can't see.
[48] You there, boy, help that young woman. Bring her here to sit by an old man.

Prosperine down from the wagon. He walked her over to Monsieur Broussard and sat her in the chair. Broussard was delighted.

From the roof, Honoré kept up a conversation with the old man in the simple ladder back chair in the yard. Honoré only paused to listen or to pull a nail from his apron or rap the nail home.

"*Quel âge avez-vous, monsieur?*"[49] he shouted down. A nail sunk in, clack-clack-clack.

The old man shrugged his shoulders. "*Plus de cien ans,*"[50] he replied.

"Gaaawww," one of our men said.

"*Comments que vous vivez si longtemps?*"[51] Honoré shouted down as he fished for another nail at his waist.

"*J'ai fume ça tout les jours depuis j'ai huit ans,*"[52] the old man said, lifting up his pipe.

"*Perique?*" Honoré asked as he paused to straighten his back up into the summer sky.

"*Oui,*" the old man said.

A dog wandered up while we were working and Broussard was enjoying the company of a pretty blind girl. The dog was a tan dog, barely past being a puppy, a dog that seemed to go wherever his feet wanted him to go. He sat at Prosperine's feet and put his head under her fingertips. He seemed as taken with her as Broussard was.

"*Il a un nomme, monsieur?*"[53] she asked.

"*Non,*" he said. "*Il a arrivé un au deux jour passé.*"[54]

She sat in the shade with the man and the dog, while the chickens scoured the yard and we men changed out the roof. We worked quickly, felling a second tree when the first was used up. When we were near finished, the old man in the shade of the sycamore croaked out a surprisingly robust, "*C'est jolie!*"

When we were finished, the old man invited us inside his small dwelling, offering his arm to Prosperine and escorting her inside. Honoré

[49] How old are you, sir?
[50] Over a hundred years old.
[51] How do you live so long?
[52] I've smoked this every day since I was eight.
[53] Does he have a name, monsieur?
[54] He just wandered up a day or two ago.

stooped to scratch the dog's head and flank, but when the dog tried to follow him in, the young woman of the house held the dog back with a broom.

"You, dog, outside, *en-dehors pour chiens.*"[55]

It was not a cold day whatsoever, but still a fire burned at his hearth. His granddaughter or great-granddaughter or great-great-granddaughter made coffee over it, and we sat around under the low ceiling and listened to him, passing the same two or three demitasse cups (all he owned) back and forth among us. His voice was quiet and fragile, and no one said anything as he told a tale. I understood very little of it, it was too soft and in French, but when it was done, Te Jean told me in a reverent tone that it was a tale of Old Broussard's earliest memories, of British soldiers and fire and mothers with babies in their arms and the babble of bleating and lowing livestock and sailing ships. It was a tale of an exiled people, told by someone who was perhaps the last surviving exile.

When he was done, he stood in what for him bordered on something athletic. Honoré rose and then we all rose from where we were sitting on the old plank floor. Broussard kissed Honoré on one cheek and then the other, and then we filed by one by one and he did the same to us, including Prosperine. A smacking speck on each cheek, each accompanied by a *merci*, or a *merci beaucoup*. When he had greeted each of us, or blessed each of us, really, he took his cane and jabbed up toward the ceiling and the roof above it.

"*Merci beaucoup, merci,*" he said in a graveled, pressured wheeze. "*Prendre deux poulets, et un troisieme comme lagniappe.*"[56]

The three chickens were gathered in a flutter of wings and feathers and cackles. Honoré and old Broussard spoke in low voices, the French only a murmur. The old fellow was tiring. I know the feeling now. Honoré leaned his ear down to the old man to listen, and the two continued the conversation in little more than a whisper.

We left them to their discourse and set the old, rotted shingles to burn in a fire at the edge of the yard. Our tools were loaded up. Honoré emerged from the house with Broussard right behind him, hunched over

---

[55] Outside for dogs
[56] Take two chickens, and a third extra.

his cane. Broussard said something to the young woman who looked after him. She disappeared into the house and came back with a canvass sack. As the bonfire of old shingles smoked up into the summer sky, mingling with the bittersweet smell of perique, she made the rounds and gave each of us an orange from the sack. Maybe the best orange I've ever had in all my years.

"Take that dog, too," the woman said. "I don't trust him around these chickens."

The dog followed us down the road, a serious look on his face as he smelled everything and marked everything with a lift of his leg and then beat a quick double-time to catch up with us. He loved the girl and the rest of us, but it was clear that he loved Honoré the best.

37

I awake to the bitter-bright smell of a satsuma, and I see them there, the little girl with the immense bow in her hair, like wings. I used to tease her, telling her to stay indoors on breezy days, or she would take off into the air. She would giggle and later I would see her on windy days making small leaps, testing my theory. That would make me chuckle.

There is another girl there, a colored girl. They are different, but each is beautiful. They are sharing a satsuma. They take turns feeding me sections, as if they were feeding an old dog or a billy goat. I suppose that isn't far from the truth. The colored girl calls me Nonc Pierre.

On the mantle of the fireplace in this room, a candle is lit, some saint performing a miracle of some sort. The woman downstairs who is not the hired girl lights them when she needs a special favor, especially when someone is sick. In such cases, she prefers the votives with scenes of miracles depicted on them. The great painters portray these things as something lithe and graceful, angelic and full of light. In actual practice, it is rough work and leaves both the healer and the healed exhausted. At least, that was the case when I saw them performed.

The cane rose out of the wet, black earth. It grew over a man's head, lush and green from the summer rains. With the first meager waves of cool air, it rustled and shivered and swayed. Mice scurried through it, wary of snakes. And the men sharpened their cane knives and waited.

And then the cutting began, lines of men in saggy clothes, chopping and sweating and singing and stacking. Mules strained against the heavy wagons that cut ridges into the earth. The road was full of them, wagons heading to the grinding sheds. We would pause and let them pass, "All Tom" pulling at clumps of grass as the heads and necks of other mules bobbed and nodded against their burdens.

"If a man got rich just from hard work, these men cutting cane would be millionaires, them," Honoré said as we walked along the side of our wagon and "All Tom." "*Les chanceux, les canailles,*[57] they the ones that get rich. Hard work is rarely enough."

Prosperine rode in the wagon, her hands pressed flat onto the buckboard to steady herself. She was the only one of us who could have seen over the tops of the cane. If she could see.

I was beginning to wonder why Honoré never offered to treat Prosperine for her blindness. Perhaps she had to remain blind in order to change us. It seemed like such a price for her to pay for whatever good it might do the world. Or, perhaps, it was something that was beyond his abilities as a *traiteur*. Or perhaps, he was afraid of what she might see.

The answer, in fact, was very simple. She first had to ask to be healed. He couldn't offer it. No *traiteur* could. Maybe she knew this, maybe she didn't. Maybe she was content with blindness. But, finally, she asked.

We were breaking for dinner at noon. She had been cooking that morning, humming to herself, feeling her way around the noonday meal she was preparing for us. After we had all eaten, Honoré had taken our tin plates and forks and was washing them in the big washtub Prosperine used.

She floated toward him and coasted into him with a hand on his shoulder. Then she caressed his temple and forehead and then his face to verify that it was him. She rolled up the sleeves of her dress and began helping him wash the dishes. At last, she asked him.

"*Monsieur*, will you treat me?"

---

[57] The lucky, the crafty

He thought for a moment as he scoured something under the water. He lifted it up, a tin plate, and handed it to her, and she dried it.

"*Oui*," he replied. He didn't ask if she wanted him to treat her for a wart or a headache. He said it as if he had been waiting all along for her to ask. "*Quand?*"

"When we're done here," she said.

They said nothing else to each other while they worked side by side. We were all quiet, everyone of us quietly thinking our own thoughts in the thoughtful quiet. The angle of the sun was changing in those days, moving south.

When the dishes were done, stacked away neatly in a chest where she kept them, she wiped her hands on the apron at her waist and put her hands on Honoré's shoulders to place herself. Then she turned her face to him. She was smiling, but only because she was trying. I'm sure that she was scared. Such is the way of impediments. You do not like them, necessarily, but you are used to them. You have developed a certain comfort for them.

He took her head in his hands, his fingers winding through her wiry blonde hair. His thumbs pulled up the lids. Her eyes were scaled, opaque, cloudy. He regarded them with the same air that he might appraise any other task, as if he were checking a board for trueness or the integrity of a joint.

"You will be able to see," Honoré finally said, "but it will hurt."

"What will hurt?" she asked. "What you gonna do to restore my sight or what I see will hurt?"

"Both," Honoré said.

He had us lift the washtub from the back of the wagon and place it on the ground, and he bid her kneel in front of it. Then he made a paste with sandy black earth and held it up to her on his fingertips. She raised her sightless eyes to his face in the stillness. Their blankness reminded me of a bust that my Uncle Horace had in his study in Mount Lebanon, some Greek or Roman somebody, a poet or a philosopher.

"If you will it, I can see," she said.

He shook his head. There was a look of seriousness on his face.

"*Ma fille*, ain't me that wills it."

His fingers pried open her right eye, and he used his thumb to scrub it.

172

Certainly, it was just as painful as it looked. She stifled her cries as the sandy paste scraped away the disease. The dog Honoré had named Pistache fretted and whined, and Jacques had to hold him as Honoré worked. His lips bounced silently around his prayer.

At one point, she raised her hands as if signaling that she had changed her mind. Her long, lean fingers wrapped around his hands, prying at them as they held her head like a vise, the nine fingers woven and pressing into her coarse, straw-colored hair. She whimpered and gave up.

He did the other eye, shutting his own eyes tight as his thumb found her cloudy pupil. Her hands grasped his forearm, honey-colored fingers on the stout muscles of the carpenter. I looked away and saw the rest of us looking away. We heard the slow smack of the surface of the water being broken and the ring of the metal washtub.

He had plunged her head under water. Her hands clawed at the edge of the tub. Pistache whined and then broke into a howl. Someone held his muzzle to silence him.

We looked back. Her hair was wet and dripping into the washtub. She was looking into the surface of it as her hands clutched the rim. Honoré took a towel and dried her face and hair.

"Somebody bring me some bread," Honoré said wearily. Phillipe searched through a towel and found the heel of a loaf, and held it out at arm's length. Honoré took it and broke it into two pieces.

"Make the sign of the cross over each of your fingers with the bread," he directed her in a low voice. "Then give the bread to a dog or a cat to eat, but don't watch him eat it, no. Because you can see him do it now."

She looked at her fingers, seeing for the first time since she was a small girl. Her hands shook as she made small crosses over each fingertip. When she had completed the last one, she looked around the clearing and saw Pistache. Weakly, she tossed the bread to him. He moved his snout over the ground, moving in on the bread halves. We all looked away and to Honoré, who was kneeling over the washtub with his hands clasped. His shirtsleeves were wet and his knees were pressed into the muddy ground. He moved to the side of the tub and vomited.

Prosperine sat looking at her fingers. Perhaps she was contemplating what would be painful to watch. She and Te Jean would be there to see it. I would not be.

173

38

Cold air filtered down from the north and with it came something equally chilling for those who had been holding out for their own country. The newspapers brought the frigid news that Lincoln had been reelected.[58] The North would not tire. There would be no deal made by the Confederacy to be left alone. It would be a fight to the death.

The territory along Bayou Lafourche had long since been in pocket for the Union. Life was going on just as before. Cane was still grown and cut by brown hands, and it was still ground by machinery powered by mules that trotted circular paths, working for hours on end and winding up at the same spot just like the cane cutters. Now, however, there was a new concept called "debt" to keep them tied to the earth and the commissary.

Work had fallen off for us, and we spent days idling in the cold. We sharpened our tools and then resharpened them. We told every joke we knew. I had read every newspaper from every town, both in French and English. It was so much like camp life in the army.

The campfire smoldered in between the diet of logs we fed it, its appetite leaping up in orange and yellow tongues with each new armful. We had acquired surplus tents from the army quartermaster in Donaldsonville, and we napped in them. Honoré and I shared one of them. Everyone had someone bunking with him except for Prosperine.

She spent a lot of time with a looking glass, a lot of time fixing her hair, making faces, pursing lips, batting her green eyes. All the things that sighted girls do when they are younger. She was catching up.

I sat on a log and read the *St. Matthew Compass*. Honoré sat next to me and amused himself with the new dog.

"Pierre, *garde ça*,"[59] he said, holding up a piece of chicken between his thumb and middle finger.

"Pistache." The dog sat.

"*Marteau*," Honoré said.

The dog nosed for the morsel of chicken. Honoré pulled back his

---

[58] Lincoln was re-elected November 8, 1864.
[59] Watch this

hand and repeated, *"Mar…teau."*

The dog turned and nosed through a collection of tools. His nose bounced over several things before finding the hammer. He worked his jaw over the wooden handle, snapped his jowls to reposition it, and carried it over to Honoré and laid it at his feet.

"Bon chien," Honoré said, and he handed Pistache the chicken. The dog ate it in a gulp and then tenderly teethed Honoré's fingers.

"I don't want to lose one more finger, me," Honoré laughed and shook his hand.

"Now. Pistache. Pistache." The dog sat politely and tilted his head. *"Scion. Sci-yon."*

The dog turned and rummaged through the tools. His tail wagged thoughtfully as he sniffed this item and that. He picked up a bit brace.

"Sci…yon," Honoré repeated. Pistache dropped the bit brace and picked up the saw by its wooden handle and brought it to Honoré. Honoré gave the dog another morsel and wiped his hand on his pants. He stood up and warmed his hands over the fire.

"A demain, allons,"[60] he said.

The cold air raised a fog from the bayous and the canals and the swamp, and the puffy, wet air hovered white and low over the black ground. The cypresses disappeared up and into it, the spiky, gray tops unseen in the fog. Crows sat in them, obscured up there, and called out at the folly of it all.

We made our way down a road that paralleled a bayou, I wasn't sure which one at the time. The fog was on us thick. "All Tom" was pacing ahead of the wagon he pulled. Prosperine and the dog rode in it, while the rest of us walked along side. Every so often I thought I recognized something. An unusual tree, an old live oak with huge limbs that dipped and rose and dipped, and a trunk that had a knot that looked like the tree was howling. A sad, squatty farmhouse here. A bateau half-filled with water and tied to a cypress knee there.

Word had come that a man down the bayou needed a water tower built and that his wife wanted some sort of elaborate dance hall. Another

---

[60] Tomorrow, we go.

crew had been hired, but either quit or were fired. And Honoré liked a challenge. We needed the work, and we were headed there.

The fog lifted a little on the fields that had been cut and now were black and smoldering again. Familiar barns passed by to the rhythmic clop of "All Tom" and the jangle of his traces. Grand homes passed by. More fields in the process of being cut. The chop of knives on stalks and the rustle of armloads and the bray of mules struggling against wagonloads. And then another grand home.

Mount Teague.

39

The woman downstairs who is not the hired girl loves her holidays. She celebrates *Réveillon* each year with a midnight feast, including the lighting of the *café brûlot*, a feat that I used to perform when my health was better. Now the Spaniard carries it in, and I sit with the others in the darkened *salle manger* and watch as his merry face is up lit by the momentary flames across the surface of the punchbowl.

At Christmas time, this house is trimmed from one end to the other, green boughs and red velvet bows. People come in and out, some years out of the cold and some years out of the warmth. It is a festive place, all because she makes it so. We go to Midnight Mass at St. Louis in our finery. She frets and straightens my tie, no matter how straight I already have it, and I sit close to her, and my old spotted hand holds her honey-colored one, still lovely as a day long ago, and the people of this house sit around us, and we listen to the Old Miraculous Story of how a loving God inexplicably thought us worthy again.

Mount Teague had been done up that way the year before, the month that I had left. A whole year had passed since then. This year, there was no wreath of woven cedar boughs on the front door, no garland along the handrails of the stairs. No red velvet bows, no bowls of "Christmas Cordial" at the doorway, no crystal glasses to drink it from.

"Come with me, Pierre, *s'il vous plaît*," Honoré said. "My *anglais, mais*, it ain't good, sometimes."

We ascended the stairs together. My legs felt heavy. My palms were sweaty, despite the cool, wet day. When we got to the porch, he put his arm around me and said, "*Mais*, this a big job for us, if we get it."

He knocked on the door, grasping the knocker with three fingers. My heart rose a little when I thought that the woman Mathilde might answer it. I still thought about her, sometimes. She was that beautiful.

The door was answered not by Mathilde, but by a lumpy Negro woman whose lips flipped as she talked and who walked with a shifting, side-to-side motion that swayed her massive backside like a wave on the ocean.

"Marse Sam," she called out and into the house, "some mens about that water tower."

The hall lamps glowed amber against the gloom of the day. There were new oval mirrors that distorted our reflections. On an easel, the portrait of *le baws-man* had been worked on. Upstairs, a fiddle scratched and whined a tentative tune, and a woman's voice, a northern voice shouted, "Jesus Christ, will you stop that? If you have to play that thing, go outside. Go outside, far, far away!"

The music stopped.

Downstairs, in the room that I knew as the study, a young girl read, not from *McGuffey's Primer* or some other school book, but from the *St. Matthew Parish Compass*. She read surprisingly well for a girl her age, her small voice pronouncing big words. *Armament. Fortification. Capitulation.*

The Negro woman paused at the doorway and waited for the girl to stop reading.

"Marse Sam," she said. "Some mens 'bout that job." *Jawb*, she pronounced it.

And then I heard his booming voice.

"I'll wait on the porch," I quickly whispered to Honoré. He looked at me, and instead of leaving, I put my hat back on and tilted the brim low.

"Thank you, that will be all," Teague said to the little girl. She exited the room, a pretty little thing, really. Long hair, carefully done up, a nice dress with small printed roses on it. She curtsied to us and then went up the stairs.

And then he was there. He extended his hand, and Honoré shook it. Teague looked at the missing finger and stared into Honoré's face.

"Carrick?" he said incredulously.

"No, *monsieur*. Mouton. Honoré Mouton. *Un carpentier.*"

I pulled the brim of my hat a little lower. My left hand was tightly in my pocket. I could feel Teague looking at me. Some men can do that, give you the feeling that they are staring at you.

"Pierre," I muttered as I tipped my hat and extended my hand, the one with a full complement of fingers. He took it in his big, soft hand. In the mirror, I could see him looking at me, looking at us, Honoré and me. Teague looked at us as if he were seeing double in the amber gaslight. Our reflections in the oval mirrors made us look like three fat men. Perhaps, if the light had been better, he would have recognized me.

"You remind me of someone," Teague said to Honoré. And then to me, "Can I take your hat…Pierre?"

"*Merci, no, Monsieur.* War," I added to make him think that I had been disfigured or something like it.

"Shall we adjourn to the Gentlemen's Parlor? Can I offer you a cocktail…*monsieur?*" I knew Teague well-enough to hear the doubt in his voice.

"*Merci, monsieur,* but let us speak now of this *jawb* you have for us."

Teague paused. "Certainly." He paused again. We remained in the central hallway. "Certainly. The wife wants herself one of those ballrooms. A great big one. Bigger than the one they have up at Nottoway in Iberville Parish. Massive thing. Biggest in the South, is what she wants."

Honoré was listening and thinking. And when he did that, he generally rested his chin in his three-fingered hand and his elbow on his chest.

"*Oui,* we can do this *jawb*. And the water tower. How high do you want it, *monsieur?* And how big?"

"Oh, about twenty feet across and twenty feet high. Whole thing a hunnert *[sic]* feet off the ground."

"Hmm," Honoré thought as his three fingers massaged his neck and he pursed his lips. "*Oui.* Yes. We can do it. But we must agree on a price, of course. For it is a big jawb. Pierre will write a price, and you will say if it is to your liking."

Honoré had Teague there. The girl who could read had been dismissed for the evening. The written word was secret code to Teague, and I knew it. Honoré produced a scrap of paper and a pencil from his coat pocket. He whispered a figure in my ear. I kept my left hand firmly in my pocket and wrote the figure in awkward, broken letters, not my usual flowing ballet of letters. I slipped the note across the sideboard to Teague. My incomplete hand stayed in my left pocket as if sewn there.

Teague stared at the quote. His nervous tongue wet his nervous lips. Then he forcefully launched into a bluff.

"This is robbery, sir! This figure will break me!" He slid the note back to me.

Honoré whispered a figure a little lower. But I could not resist. I wrote one even higher and slipped it to Teague. He looked at it with satisfaction.

"Now, this is more like it," he said.

"*Très bien*," Honoré said with a nod of his head. "Please sign, then."

"Won't a handshake do?"

"A simple mark, *monsieur*. As gentlemen," Honoré said. This I knew of Teague: to assert that something was what a gentleman would do was to throw down the gauntlet to Teague. It was to challenge him to a duel in which manners were the weapons.

Honoré handed the pencil to Teague. Teague looked at it like Cleopatra might have looked at the asp. He hesitated. His tongue wet his lips. He swallowed. He swallowed again. Then he put the pencil to the paper. He pushed hard and the lead broke. He smiled a relieved smile.

"Well, I guess we'll just have to shake on it, then, won't we?" Teague said.

But Honoré produced a spare from his coat pocket. Teague held it. His fingers rolled it. Then, applying it to the paper, he traced a clumsy backward S that looked like a dying swan, and a big-hatted T, two wavering sticks set at odd angles.

He handed the pencil to Honoré, who signed a fluid *H. Mouton*. It was as fine a hand as mine.

40

The next day we were up before first light and on the road behind "All Tom." It was a cold, bright morning. The eastern sky was blushing to life. We assembled in the side yard of Mount Teague, our tools ready.

And we waited.

We waited as the field hands trundled off in wagons for the last of the cane. We waited as the coopers stumbled off for the cooperage. We waited as the dairymen, the grinders, the boilers all went off to their duties. We waited for instructions from Sam Teague.

The prior crew had laid out the dimensions of the ballroom, but then they had moved on or been asked to move on. Honoré paced the area, his pants legs tucked into his boots like always, counting to himself with each step, *un-deux-trois-quatre-cinq*... Some of our crew smoked, all of us waited. Pistache nosed around the yard as Serbus barked furiously and strained against his chain and slobbered through bared teeth. Pistache cast a perplexed look at Serbus and then at us, and then he moved on to an azalea bush and marked it.

Teague appeared about mid-morning, well-fed and well-rested, complaining about the noise that Pistache had forced Serbus into making. Then he and Honoré toured the foundation of the ballroom, Teague again saying that it would be the biggest in the South, fully ten feet bigger in every dimension than the one "that Randolph feller" had up in Iberville Parish. Finally, with an idea of what he (and the new Mrs. Teague) wanted, we began.

It took us a week to set the posts to complete the foundation, then another week or so to set floor joists. It would have taken less time, but Teague would come out and look over our shoulders constantly. So did Mrs. Teague, the busty, copper-haired woman who had worn the green satin dress that night a year before. She seemed heavier to me now, and I thought she might be expecting. But no, she was just enjoying the rich lifestyle of being a planter's wife, so much richer than being an army officer's.

They would stand together, the two of them, and watch us shuffle planks into place and rap them home, Honoré nudging them forward with gesturing fingers and then a palm and a *droit-là*. And then a flurry of hammers. And then the planing and sawing of the next, and so forth.

The ballroom was really a freestanding wing connected by a breezeway, which the prior crew had already completed. Judging by the area it occupied, it was certainly destined to be something grand. After the floor joists were completed, we began constructing the walls on the winter-yellowed grass of the lawn. When "All Tom" pulled them to vertical, they would be twenty feet tall. Taller than the ones at Nottoway, of course. It would be a magnificent room, and, truthfully, we were excited to be a part of it.

One day, Honoré and I were hammering the plank flooring in place. We always gravitated to one another. Or, perhaps, I gravitated to him like a smaller planet seeks the sun. After the final clop of a nail, he looked up to where Serbus was sleeping in front of the mausolée.

"Pierre," he said as he took a nail from his apron. "You think it's odd that there's a mean dog tied up in front of that mausolée? You don't think somebody would be wanting to get out of there, do you?"

I paused between nails.

"No," I said. "Nor in."

We chuckled. Honoré pulled the next nail from between his lips and set it in place.

"I guess Teague don't want nobody to pass either way."

"Suppose not," I said as I set my nail in place. Honoré had taught me to set them with my palm facing the hammer. That way, if you miss, you hit your palm, which hurts less than the bony back of your hand.

We finished our nails at the same time. Honoré looked up and said, "And that sign says, 'BEWARE OF DOG,' no?"

"That's right." I held a joist in place while he nailed it home. "The woman who used to be the housekeeper here would tend the mausolée on All Saints' Day. She gave that dog a pork chop that was rigged up with laudanum to keep him quiet."

"I bet that dog made hisself some *do-do*, no?"

"Oh yes. *Oui, monsieur.* And he made even more *do-do* with the chloroform she gave him to sniff."

Later that day, the oldest Teague girl came out in the yard with a chair and her violin and her bow, balancing all three. She sat under a tree and practiced in the cold. She had cut the fingertips out of her gloves so she could work the strings. It was noontime for us, and Honoré walked over to watch her play. I went with him.

When we drew near, she grew nervous and began making small mistakes. She apologized to us, and Honoré said, "No, *sha*, you play good." It was charitable of him. It really was pretty awful, a squawking rasp.

"Why you play out here and not inside?"

"Miss Polly..." she paused and corrected herself, "*Mother* doesn't like us playing in the house. She naps a lot."

"Play me something," Honoré said. And he leaned back against the trunk of the live oak tree and closed his eyes. The girl took a deep breath and began to play a Christmas carol, "Hark the Harold Angels," I believe it was. Honoré listened with closed eyes and a look of rapture on his face that was fit for a fine opera house. His head nodded peacefully with the tune. The playing was horrible. I don't see how he stood it.

When she came to the end, a sudden screech of the bow, he opened his eyes and clapped his hands lightly.

"*Mais*, I enjoyed that, me." Then he said, "Here, *beh*, hold the bow *comme ça*, with just your fingertips. Now, make a sound, pull it across easy. Let it float."

She did. The improvement was sudden and dramatic.

"*Comment t'appelles?*" he asked her as her face fell in wonder at the sound her violin was now making. I believe mine had fallen in wonder, too.

"Jenny," she said.

"*Comprende Francais, ma belle?*"

"*Oui, monsieur, un peu. La femme Mathilde*," her French failed her, and she continued in English, "Taught me."

"Whatever happened to her?" I asked her. It had been in the back of my mind.

She became suddenly shy, almost sullen. "We're not to speak of her. Miss Polly...*Mother*...says we're not speak of her ever again."

I did not press her, but I did not stop wondering.

We returned to our work and listened to the music she played under the live oak, music that seemed to grow more beautiful and elegant with each pass of the bow.[61]

Over the next weeks, the floorboards were all laid in, durable white oak that would stand up to years of the quadrille and whatever other dances would be invented in the next decades. The walls went up, "All Tom" hawing and straining against the ropes that pulled the walls to the vertical, up to the sky.

As the weather got colder and grayer, Jenny Teague's playing became a thing of beauty in the midst of the bleakness. And we celebrated Christmas again.

It was on a cold, misty day. We had assumed that the day was free, and we had slept in. Honoré read from the Missal, and Prosperine supervised us in the production of a meal. We were in an irregular circle, enjoying the meal and each other's company, when Teague rode up on his black mare. I excused myself to my tent when he did.

"Why aren't you working? he asked.

"Because it's Christmas, *monsieur,*" Honoré replied.

"I'm aware of that, but I expect the work to continue."

"You expect wrong, then."

"What did you say to me, Carrick?"

Honoré must have thought that "Carrick" was some sort of slur. At any rate, he ignored it.

"I said, you expect wrong. We work tomorrow, same as yesterday. We work hard and in good faith. Your water tower get built. Your dance hall get built. One day ain't change that. You run off one crew already. You want to run off another, *monsieur?* Your reputation keep everybody away."

"When I get back to the house and look out my window with my field glasses, I expect to see you men gathering up your tools and headed over there to work." He pointed to our wagon and our tools and then in the direction of Mount Teague. Then he turned his black mare with a whirl of swallowtails and cantered off. Some of the men made faces and rude gestures.

---

[61] Chip, in searching through the archives to verify Carriere's tale, I just happened to come across this story in the *St. Matthew Parish Compass,* June 20, 1878: "Violinist Jenny Teague Set to Depart for New York, Paris."

Honoré took out his violon and began playing, and we danced the rest of the afternoon.

41

Out across Prytania, I see them. Angels, a city of them, brick and marble houses where people will sleep until the Judgment. Then some will rise and others, I suppose, will continue sleeping. There are old ones who died after long, full lives, filled with joy and sorrow and beauty and sadness. Young ones who died prematurely and were mourned violently. Married couples who were separated by it, lifetime companions, one put to bed while the other continued to live, not even sleepy yet. I have carved many of their monuments and then watched the departed, *les defan*, placed beneath the white stones.

Frequently, when I look out over the final, eternal homes of my across-the-street neighbors, I think of the first monument in marble that I made. No sculptor ever forgets that sort of thing.

The new Mrs. Teague wanted a marble statue of a Roman goddess as the centerpiece of a formal garden she envisioned. The rectangular slab of white marble had been delivered, along with the tools of the sculptor, but, alas, the sculptor himself never arrived. I seem to recall that he was stabbed by a prostitute in New Orleans, though I may not be remembering that correctly. Meanwhile, the block of marble sat in a nest of weeds, and the tools sat in a store room.

Honoré had stood his ground plainly about not working on Christmas Day, and Teague had had to accept it. He knew that no one else would take the job after two crews had walked away from it. It was a bitter pill for him, but, in this case, he had no choice but to swallow it.

And Honoré, being the kind of man he was, put out an olive branch to Teague.

"*Monsieur*, I got a man who can make you your statue," Honoré told Teague. "He ain't never worked in stone before, but he's good in cypress. Very good. You give him a chance, *monsieur?*"

Teague wanted to wait for another sculptor to arrive, from back east, or Europe somewhere, but the impulsive and volatile Mrs. Teague insisted she wanted the work done right away. The block was righted by a team of Mount Teague oxen, urged on by swearing in multiple languages and whips. The sculptor's tools were retrieved from the shed where they had waited for their original owner. And I carved my first ever statue in marble. It would be one of many in my lifetime.

Prosperine was my model, or, I should say, my memory of her blind and wet in the moonlight, reclining on the bank of Bayou Pigeon, that was my model. I could probably still sculpt it, entirely from memory, if I still had my physical faculties. It was so clear to me, as it still is, that I never once had to pause and sketch it.

I stared at the block of marble, and it stared back at me. I looked at it from this angle and that. I walked around it, stalking it. Are you in there, Venus? I silently asked it. I traced the outline of her on one face and then the other. Prosperine rising in the moonlight, smooth and naked, hair wet and hanging over her shoulders. The swale of hips and breasts, the dimple in her stomach. The smile on her lips, her blank eyes.

And then suddenly, I could see her, buried beneath a rubble of marble chips. I chipped away with secondhand tools, frantically, as if she had been buried in an earthquake. The marble fell, and I stepped on it as I wound around her. My boots crunched on the deepening layer of white chips. My mallet rapped the chisel, the chisel gouged the stone, my gouge chiseled the marble. The lie fell, the truth began to emerge.

My eyes adjusted to the fading light. And there was a startling tap on my shoulder.

"*A demain*, eh, Pierre?" Honoré said. And we put a canvass sheet over her and tied the base with a rope, to protect her from the elements and from prying eyes.

That night, he told me something that I remember to this day. "I watched you work today. You can do the job, I am confident, Pierre. But mind the measure, Pierre. Don't play the tune too fast. Mind the rhythm."

The next day, I slowed down. I slowly chipped away the stone, at the pace of a confident and considerate lover. The woman, the goddess, Venus was beginning to take shape. Honoré erected a barrier to shield us, she and I, the stone woman. To preserve the intimacy we shared. And, at the end of the day, we covered her emerging nakedness with the canvass and the rope.

Panama was still held, and, that Sunday, I attended, though I kept quiet with my hat pulled low with a cloth curtain under it, like a legionnaire, and my hands in my pockets.

The horse races were held. Of course, Hollyfield was now defunct and had no entry. And, as usual, the Mount Teague horses prevailed. And everyone who toiled on behalf of dear old Mount Teague was happy and proud.

And then it was time for the fights. When I left Mount Teague, Virgil Reeves had taken my place as the champion. His earlier transgressions in the ring had been forgotten, and he had been allowed to fight again.

The champion of the Parris place waited in a circle formed by spectators, waiting for Virgil to show up. But a few minutes became a half hour, and a half hour became an hour.

Someone called out, "Where's Reeves? Where's Virgil Reeves?"

A murmur went through the crowd. Some of the men had money in their hands.

"Where is he?" someone said.

"He don't ever miss a scrap," someone else said.

Someone spotted Eugene D'Ormeaux. I would never have picked him out of the crowd. He looked worn, exhausted, weighed down with worry. He looked like he had aged twenty years in the year since I'd seen him. He looked old.

"Say, Eugene! Where's Virgil?" a man's voice in the crowd called out.

Eugene answered in a nervous, agitated manner.

"How should I know? I mean, what do you mean? I don't know where he is. He left. He's gone. Gone away. I don't know where he is. Am I my brother's keeper?"

With that, Eugene pushed his way through the crowd, which dispersed in exasperation. As he stalked away, his eyes met mine. And they grew large as if I had returned from the dead. Which, I suppose to him, I had.

A few days later, Virgil turned up.

I was working more slowly on the marble statue of Venus/Prosperine. The rest of the crew was working on the ballroom. The roof was up, and the walls of the place were going up quickly. They were framing the large windows that would look out to the garden and the statue I was completing.

A rider galloped down the lane of oaks and dismounted, not even pausing to tie up his horse. He ran inside. Moments later, Teague had the bell rung, and everyone was summoned to the field in the courtyard that was central to everything at Mount Teague in those days.

Teague proclaimed in a loud voice, "I regret to inform you that Mr. Virgil Reeves, who used to work in the dairy, was found dead today."

A rushing gasp moved through the crowd, and faces turned to each other and then back to Teague. Someone asked him a question that I could not hear, and Teague pointed to the person and listened. Then he answered it.

"Floating in the river below Donaldsonville."

Another anguished murmur rippled through the crowd. Men took off their hats, women put fingers over their mouths. Some people genuflected.

Someone else asked a question. From where I was, it was a murmur. Teague pointed to that person, a woman with a gray shawl over her shoulders. He loudly answered her question so that everyone could hear.

"It would appear that he took his own life by gunshot and then fell into the river."

Another gasp moved through the crowd, and everyone genuflected.

"Let us pray for the tormented soul of Virgil Reeves," Teague proclaimed. "That is all. Please return to your tasks."

As soon as he reentered the house, murmurs sprouted among the crowd. He was found with a bullet hole over his right ear, the women said. The men were less circumspect and more graphic. He had floated out into the channel of the river, a gray-green bubble nudged into the path of a steamboat headed upriver with a boatload of St. Louis well-to-dos. Several of the women on board had fainted, and one had to be grabbed before going over the railing and into the water. A gaff was used to corral Virgil, poor wall-eyed Virgil, perhaps the second-meanest man I've ever met.

If it were true that he had a bullet hole above his right ear, then his suicide made no sense. I knew for a fact that Virgil shot left-handed.

I turned back to my monument, thinking of the perplexity. I chiseled and the marble fell in smaller chips now. Now it was simply a matter of smoothing corners, flattening ridges, rounding contours. The ringing of the chisels and gouges on the marble was music to me now. And then, there she was. Venus, a Roman beauty with the blank marble eyes of a blind girl.

Mrs. Teague hurried out of the house to see it, wearing a gaudy hat that was adorned with peacock feathers. I realized that I had not heard the birds' cries since my return. I looked around for one of their enormous fan-tails as Mrs. Teague began gushing over the statue. She was enthralled with it. She wanted to know my name. She said that she would be my patroness, my benefactor. But such is the way of people like the second Mrs. Teague. They are all cackle and no egg. Nothing ever became of it.

A garden was planted around it, a wash of vivid colors lining pathways laid out so that the statue of the Goddess of Love could be viewed from different angles. It stood there for quite a long time, as I understand it.

Years later, however, the third Mrs. Teague would have it unceremoniously dumped in Bayou Lafourche. She said that she found it vulgar. She also had the magnificent ballroom razed, as she was vehemently opposed to dancing and merrymaking. Besides, someone determined that the one at Nottoway was still bigger. The crew before us had measured wrong.

42

A New Orleans policeman named Corrigan comes by today with a ham. He thanks me for something I don't remember, something that happened some time ago, but he still seems very, very grateful for it. It is always a delight to get a visit from Corrigan, a man with a gift for stories and who occasionally sings with the Spaniard over coffee in the sitting room. And, on special occasions, like St. Patrick's Day, they take a splash of bourbon in their coffee.

Late that winter, early 1865, we all received a visit from another man in blue, a man named Potts who was the new Union commander. He came to pay a call on Sam Teague and the man he had employed. The man named Carrick.

Potts had worked his way up from the ranks in the Union Navy, a simple deckhand on the gunboats that patrolled the river, then as a pilot, someone who knew the shifting channels and sandbars and snags that populated that great, fluid beast, the Mississippi. He had a funny way of walking, with his toes splayed out, kind of like that Chaplin fellow in the movie house, but not as bad as that.

He arrived at Mount Teague unannounced, attended by a squad of Union Calvary. They clattered down the shell lane between the oaks. We watched them, blue wool and brass buttons, one of them carried a guidon, a small triangular flag that fluttered with the forward movement of the group. When they reached the house, Potts dismounted, but the others stayed in the saddle.

We had long since completed the ballroom. The statue of Venus was in place and the albino gardener was working with a crew to landscape the garden around it. We were nearing completion of the water tower. The timbers went up quickly, and the crew was delighted to see their work soar up into the sky. I suppose the Babylonians must have felt the same about their tower.

I was up in it that day, painting a huge MT on the tank of the thing, which was twenty feet tall and twenty feet across. Everyone had urged him to have something else painted on the side of the tank. They all told him that people would joke that the MT would imply that the tank was "empty." But he refused to listen. And, of course, the joke took off before the paint was dry.

I paused for a moment with the paintbrush in my hand and looked down. And then there he was. Potts. He did not stop at the house, but rode directly to the base of the tower where Honoré and the rest of our crew were working, hauling away scraps, *les boutailles*, Honoré called them. When Teague saw him, he rushed out with a napkin still tucked into his shirt. Potts stood up and said in a loud voice, almost a shout, "As commander of this precinct, I will speak with whomever I wish, wherever I wish, sir. You are excused."

Teague balked, and then Potts actually shouted, "You. Are. Excused, sir."

And then one of the mounted men moved his horse between Teague and Potts. Teague yanked the napkin out of his shirt front in a gesture that was pure frustration. He stalked back to the house, looking back suspiciously at Potts a few times.

Potts scanned the crew that was working below me and pointed to Honoré. Honoré pointed to his own chest, and then took off his apron and draped it over a cross-timber of the tower. He approached Potts, and they shook hands, and Potts looked at Honoré's hand after they let go. Then they sat on the gnarled roots of a live oak. The Union man had one polished black boot crossed over a knee and his hat in his lap. He mopped his bald head from time to time, that universal gesture of northern men in the South, even in the winter. Honoré sat across from him with his hands clasped together. Potts kept looking at Honoré's hands.

Potts summoned a man, an aide, to join the conversation, I'm assuming to translate for Potts, or at least to help with Honoré's accent. At last, they stood up and shook hands again, and they parted. Potts returned to the house, where Teague stood looking out of a window. They spent some time inside, talking, I suppose. Then the entire squad departed with their leader, the guidon flapping in the breeze as they galloped away between the lane of oaks.

Later, after Potts and his retinue had departed, Teague appeared on the catwalk of the water tower. I smelled the cigar smoke before I heard or saw him. I had just put away the brushes and had come up again to see if the paint was dry.

We stood leaning out a few paces apart, looking out from our perch.

"I thought you had died," Teague said, examining his fingernails and his cigar. "We sent out a party to find you, but you were gone."

Teague was always a smooth liar.

"No sir. I lived," I said.

"Well, good for you, son," Teague said. He looked at his fingernails and then said to them, "A very clever ruse."

"What's that?" I asked.

"Posing as some sort of French carpenter. Very clever. But don't worry. Your secret's safe. I know it's you, Carrick."

I said nothing to confirm or deny it. The silence swirled around us, up there a hundred feet off the ground. Teague inhaled deeply and blew out the smoke.

"Something, isn't it?" he said out to his empire. He took a cigar out of an inside breast pocket and gave it to me as he appraised his kingdom. I took the cigar but said nothing.

"I read somewhere that in India they have little darkeys who sit around in diapers with turbines[62] on their heads playing tunes on flutes to coax these spread-natters out of a basket."

How preposterous, I thought. *You didn't read it, you never read a word in your life*, I said to myself as my eyes narrowed on the near tip of my cigar. I clipped the end of it with my teeth and puffed the tip out. It fluttered to the ground far below.

"Same thing goes on here, in a way," he continued as he lit me. I was braced on my elbows looking out on the sunset and the cane. He adopted my posture and spoke out to the cane and the sun. "Boldness is the tune that charms wealth out of the basket. And then, wealth charms everyone and everything else. Whether you love it or loathe it, it is fascinating, wealth is. Wouldn't you agree, Carrick? Regardless of what that silly old saying says, the meek don't inherit the earth. They only inherit the dust of it."

I didn't say anything. Instead, I spit off the side. The white speck trailed away to the ground. The silence must have been pushing on him, and I was enjoying it. I was.

"I could set you up, Carrick. You'd have a stake in this place. The Hollyfield place is empty. It could be yours. A mansion, just for you. No more hard days, working your hands into blisters and callouses."

"That so?" I asked out to the cane.

"Sure. Only thing I'll need you to do is to sign a statement saying it was Mr. Reeves who was responsible for those certain nightly errands. My man's got the papers all put together. They're in my study down there in the house. Sign it and you could be a rich man, Carrick."

Down below, the small figures of Te Jean and Jacques and the other men were loading the wagon. "All Tom" waited patiently in the traces for his time to pull us back to our camp on the Twelve Arpent Canal. Then I told Teague something that I had heard Aunt Cora say in English and Honoré say in French.

---

[62] Certainly, he meant turbans. This is most likely Carriere's representation of Teague's mis-speech.

"Ain't it easier for a camel to pass through the eye of a needle than for a rich man to get into heaven?"

Teague straightened up and looked at me. "What the hell does that supposed to mean?"

I spit again. The white dot drifted in the cross breeze and hit the ground in the silence down below.

"I don't know," I said. "Just some silly old saying, I suppose."

I looked at him and then back out to the cane. I could feel his desperation. He was trying to wrestle his composure back into himself. He succeeded, though barely.

"What did you tell him, Carrick? What did you tell Potts?"

It was then that I realized that he thought Potts had been interviewing me and not Honoré. Out before us, the cane fields said nothing. The silent sun glared at us in a winter light. Only the wind spoke, cooing like a dove. Up there on the catwalk of the water tower, it was quiet. Down below, things rattled softly as the rest of our crew loaded up. I watched them, honest men cleaning up honestly after a day of honest toil. I pushed back from the rail of the catwalk. I had nothing to say to Teague, but he had one more thing to say me. It was not a good-natured request. It was a command.

"You tell him it was Reeves' idea, all of it. Virgil Reeves directed all of it. You understand me?" He sounded like he was beginning to feel the crushing weight that a half-pound of noose exerts on a man. He turned to me, pulled his cigar out of his mouth, held it in his left hand. He extended his right. I kept my gaze on the cane and the orange horizon.

"So, what say, then, partner? Deal?"

His smile and his hand reached out for a mate from me. I pulled the cigar into a glowing ember. I tilted my head back and let a mouthful of smoke escape into a blue-gray cloud.

"I decline your offer, sir," I said. "For what good is it a man to gain the whole world but to forfeit his soul?"

I ground out my cigar on the railing of his new water tower and threw the butt of it past Teague and over the railing. As I climbed down the ladder, his voice seethed invisibly: "You'll regret this, Carrick. Continuously. You'll regret it."

43

Our work was done at Mount Teague, and Honoré and I went to settle up with Teague.

The large, lopsided Negro woman met us at the back door and told us that Marse Sam was at the boiling sheds. Then she quickly went in to see to a crying baby, her footsteps drumming heavily on the wood floor as one side of her and then the other dipped with her walking. The baby cried like a toddler, trying to form sounds that might be words. I looked around for Mathilde, wondering if it were her baby, though her baby would not be a toddler just yet. I thought I might have seen her by now, with or without her baby. She must have moved on, sold perhaps, run off, perhaps, but gone all the same. Possibly in having her baby, she had suffered the same fate as the first Mrs. Teague, and, for that matter, my own mother.

I turned to go out to the boiling sheds, but Honoré tarried, and so did I, for a moment. The servant came down cradling a long-legged toddler, the child whose birth had hastened the death of her mother. In that moment, I felt an odd kinship with that little girl. I knew the doubt and the guilt that she would feel. I felt the vacuum that would follow her around. I saw the empty silhouette that the girl would gaze into, especially at those singular moments in her life, those moments when she herself would become a woman, a wife, a mother.

Perhaps Honoré sensed it, too. He took the child from the woman. He held the child, and she stopped crying. It was such a tender moment, his love for that child whose name, whose situation, whose future he did not know and did not need to know. I could not intrude upon that moment. I thought I might begin weeping, something I had never done before. I went out to the boiling sheds by myself.

Teague and his overseer, Mr. D'Ormeaux, always left a couple of hundred acres in the field to see if it would sweeten further. It was a bet they would make with Mother Nature. And, if there was a freeze, it was only the loss of a couple of hundred acres. Now it had been cut and ground and was being boiled. D'Ormeaux and Teague had cut it close-the new cane in the fields was already pushing out and ankle high.

I paced across the field with my hands in my pockets and my arms close to my sides. It had turned cold again in the night. The smoke from the fires of the boiling sheds billowed into a clear late-winter sky. When I arrived, there were three or four men who were working, turning the bubbling liquid over and over and skimming the top. Normally, there would have been lighthearted conversation or singing or jokes in French or English and laughter. But *le baws-man* was there, and everyone was silent. I have seen more animation at a wake.

Teague stood there observing the men with his hands clasped together behind his back over the tails of his swallowtail coat. The three kettles bubbled and popped in the cold air, the long stirring paddles swirling the molten liquid into eddies and whirlpools. One of the men opened the firebox door and tossed a couple of sections of wood into the orange fire-scape. The fire sizzled angrily in receiving the wet wood. Teague looked up from the work.

"Hello...*monsieur*," he said to me sarcastically. "I guess you've come to get paid."

"We have."

"Money's in an envelope on the desk in my study. But before you go, I'd like another word with you. Man to man." To the men manning the boiling, he said, "Will you boys excuse us?"

"But *monsieur*, the sauce will burn," a man said.

"I'll stir it," Teague said. "You boys go take a break."

"But *monsieur*."

"Goddam it, it's my sauce, and I'll stir it!"

The man reluctantly handed him a paddle, and the two other men left with him.

Teague leisurely stirred the sauce.

"Something," Teague paused as he turned the paddle. He looked into the kettle as if he could see the paddle scraping the bottom, "Something I need to know. I need to know what you and Potts talked about. If this is a matter of blackmail, Carrick, if you're holding out for money to keep quiet, well, that's certainly no object for a man like me. Especially dealing with a man of your...station...in life." He tapped the paddle on the edge of the kettle, and it rang a metallic, black-iron note. The liquid in the kettle was making a roiling, slobbering sound. I could feel the heat of it several steps

194

away.

Teague leaned the paddle against a post and approached me with an amiable expression on his face, a good-hearted grin, a sociable smile. He put his arm around my shoulders. We looked out to the fields of ankle high cane. There was a silence. The only sound was the bubble of the kettle behind us.

"So, what was it?" he asked, as if I had posed a riddle to him that he couldn't solve, and now he wanted the answer.

"I didn't say anything to Potts," I said as I shook my head. "I ain't never said a word to him in my life. And we both know it wasn't Virgil's idea to go on your coon hunts."

I should have stepped away from him before I said that last thing, because it caused something in him to snap. He turned quickly and pushed me toward the kettle. I stumbled and fell toward it. It seemed to rush toward me, an immense black half-shell, glowing red-orange at the edges. My face stopped inches from it.

"What did you tell him? What did you tell him, Carrick?"

Teague was on me, his palm pressing into my cheek and temple. The surface of the kettle popped and smacked. The heat of it was boiling away at my beard. His hand strained against my head as he pushed it closer to the red hot, black iron sugar kettle. My neck tensed violently, shaking in resistance against the force he was applying.

"What. Did. You. Tell. Him?" Teague's red face growled through his exertion. The hot black iron grazed the small hairs on my cheek. If he hadn't been trying to put my head directly in the boiling liquor, he could have easily burned a gash across my face or my eye. My hands were braced on the hot bricks of the fire box. They seared into my palms, not enough to burn them, but still uncomfortably hot. I could only imagine how hot the sugar kettle was.

Teague's expression strained. His teeth were bared down to the gums. His eyes were wide, the gray pupils large and rimmed in white, his nostrils flared. He was as strong as any man I had ever wrestled. I couldn't hold on much longer. I could smell the burning hairs of my beard.

There was a sudden snap, and I thought that the straining of my neck had snapped something in me. Then Teague tumbled past me. The kettle hissed like a snake against his face as I rolled away, barely missing the fire.

Teague rose quickly with his hands on his cheek as if he was trying to push it back in place or keep it from falling off. There was a barrel of rainwater by the post of the shed. He stumbled past me and thrust his head in it. His face had been so hot, it hissed in the cool water. He kept it under for as long as he could, then his head burst out of the water for a quick, desperate gasp, and then he plunged it in again. On the next gasp, he paused a second as he saw Honoré with the broken stirring paddle in his hand. Then Sam Teague put his head in the barrel again. By the time he pulled it out again, Honoré and I were gone.

Honoré ran straight to the wagon where "All Tom" and the rest of the crew waited in front of the house. I stormed through the back door, and now my steps were the ones that thumped on the wood floor. I went in Teague's study and rifled through the papers there, including a sheaf of his sad attempts at literacy, misshapen letters on a slate and infantile reading assignments. Among them I found it, an envelope written in the hand of a young child.

For Mistir Carruck.

Inside was some money and a note I didn't have the time to read. I tucked it in my shirt pocket and dashed out the front door. Prosperine was sitting on the buckboard next to Honoré, her hands neatly under her skirts. Honoré shook the reins, and she made a small exclamation and put her hands further out on the buckboard.

We pulled out from the lane of oaks, Honoré snapping the reins and "All Tom" cantering away swiftly, for a mule. The other men trotted alongside. We made the bayou road, the wagon rattling and jangling and creaking. We did not look back until it got dark.

We decided to make camp in a pecan orchard several miles up from Napoleonville. It was not the last we saw of Teague. Oh, no.

44

The girl is no more than five. She comes in my room, waking me from a nap in which my daddy, Uncle Ransom, and Big Eight are tanning hides in Lafayette Square. (I think Big Eight might have come to see me today, but certainly I just dreamed that, too.) Anyway, she puts her finger over her lips, in that way of secret enterprises, and shuts the door quietly behind her. The dog on the rug by my bed stretches to a sitting position.

"*Bonjour*, Papere," the girl says in a low voice, barely more than a whisper. Then she gets a chair, wrestling it with her small weight to keep the legs from scraping against the floor, and she looks up on a high shelf in the armoire where she and I keep them hidden. She reaches under an old quilt to retrieve them, a box labeled *Producto de Havana*. She knows she will get in trouble for this, but not much. A scolding, perhaps, but certainly not from me, even if I had a voice. The woman downstairs would come up and tell her, "*Pichouette!*"

She opens the box, and there they are, stacked like miniature cordwood. Cubans, my favorite. She takes one and puts it to my mouth, and my lips fumble with it like a horse going after a carrot. It takes her five or ten tries to flick the lighter, but when it catches, she holds it to the tip. I puff in and bring it to life. The dog is grinning with pride. She takes the cigar from my lips and holds it to the dog's.

"Here, Zipper," she says.

Zipper sniffs the cigar politely and then goes back to a smiling pant. She puts the cigar back to my lips, and I am happy for her kindness, the kindness of a small child. I smoke for a while and manage to wink at her. As much as I would like to, there is no associated smile. She shrugs her shoulder and grins.

Outside, automobiles sputter down Prytania, and people and their conversations float down the street. Some have laughter in them and some don't. A mule passes, pulling some sort of a wagon, hoofs on the cobblestones sounding like the fall of coconuts, over and over again with the rattle of harnesses and the squeak of the buckboard that diminish down the street.

A breeze lifts the lace curtains. The cigar is half its length now. The girl is petting the dog's head. Zipper, that's right, I named the dog Zephyr, like the wind, but she pronounced it Zipper and it stuck. Zipper.

Then the door opens, and it is the woman. She takes the cigar from my mouth. I have smoked more than half of it this time. I am satisfied. The woman lightly scolds the girl.

"Pichouette!" she says. Her anger seems to quickly dissolve into chagrin and then amusement.

"Suzette, the doctor says Papere can't have his cigar no more," the woman says with a forced frown. I think she is trying not to laugh. Only a smile breaks through as she turns from us. She parts the curtains, grinds the cigar out on the outside sill, and throws it out.

"Let Papere rest, bebe," the woman says.

The girl hugs my old head and kisses my scraggly-whiskered cheeks and tells me, "I just love you, Papere." She pronounces it *wuuuv* you.

And then the woman takes her hand and leads her back down the stairs, and the dog Zipper and I resume our naps. Downstairs, someone strikes random keys on the piano, and there is a shush.

And I am content in a diminishing aroma of a Cuban cigar.

The smell of cigars always reminds me of Carnival. Men who would normally refrain from it were prone to take it up for a while, as it was a time of celebration, a time when people did what they normally would not. And, for those who didn't particularly care for cigars, it was something easy to give up when Lent came.

That year, St. Matthew Parish was getting ready to celebrate Mardi Gras, the first in its history, I believe. It was modeled after the ones in Mobile and New Orleans, a spectacle that Marse Sam had promised the parish of St. Matthew, a party he had vowed to hold, and to not hold it would have been an admission that he was scared, cowering in the presence of the Union Army.

Men who believe themselves to be big men generally must always be showing themselves as larger than life. It is as natural a thing as rain in the spring and heat in the summer. A man who sees himself big must constantly pretend to be even bigger.

And so it was that Sam Teague was always king of Carnival in St. Matthew Parish, the *Krewe de Jupitre*. He was not Catholic and only nominally Episcopalian (or, as my daddy would call them, pissers). I'm sure that he had no idea what Lent was and probably wouldn't have observed it, anyway. Mr. D'Ormeaux had dreamed up the name.

Teague's burn was concealed by a bandage that was incorporated into his sequined mask. He maintained that he had had "a little accident with a sugar kettle." His bandage-as-mask concealed it. In the years that followed, there were things that you didn't mention at Mount Teague. At the top of the list was *le baws-man's* scar.

The day after our meeting in the boiling shed, we made camp in the pecan orchard after several long months of work at Mount Teague. It was a peaceful morning, and we spent it under the bare branches, sharpening saws and chisels and plane irons.

I gave Honoré the envelope, and he opened it.

"Pierre," he said, handing me the note and the envelope, "Read this, *s'il vous plait.*"

There was money in it, but not near what we had agree upon. The accompanying note was written in the hand of a child, and the misspellings led me to believe that it was his younger daughter who had taken his dictation. I've always considered it a taunt:

In closed is only haff of what we agreed upon. I refuse to pay full price for substandud, shotty work.
Samule Teague

Teague had shorted us for more than two months of work.

We were young men then, all of us, even Honoré. Older men would have left it at that, or gone to court, perhaps. We young men stormed about the pecan orchard, the branches still bare but the ground turned the lime green of spring and dotted with yellow and white wildflowers. Our mood was gray and black, however.

"Son of a bitch," some of us said.

"*Miche-en-flute*[63]," others said. We were incensed. Honoré quietly sighted down a saw, checking for trueness. So serene, always so serene. We were all young men then, good men (and I speak for the rest of them and not for myself), but men who still found it easy to take up a grudge (and I speak for all of us except for Honoré. I don't think he was capable of a grudge).

We ground our teeth and clinched our fists. Jacques took a windfall

---

[63] Chip, my parrain used to say this of pretentious people. Literally, it means, "Shit in a fancy glass."

limb and beat against the trunk of a pecan, striking it over and over again until the limb shattered in two. We had been taken advantage of in a big way, and almost three months' worth of work had vanished.

Honoré sat through all of this, quietly sharpening the saw, drawing the file over the small teeth. At last he put away the saw and took up his fiddle.

"Lent begins tomorrow," he said. "Let's make us a little merry, for tomorrow is ashes."

A jug of new wine was brought out. It made its way around our camp where it was met with thirsty mouths that pulled and then were wiped on the backs of hands. After several passes, the sting of our gullibility was dulled a little, and, after a few more, it was felt a little less, though not forgotten.

We all began dancing, and our dances became more erratic. Prosperine danced, grasping and lifting her hem off the green grass. She had spring flowers in her hair, stepping lightly this way and that as her skirts lilted and swayed. We would lift the jug to Honoré, who would play a long note as he took a long swig, and then the music would fall back into rhythm.

We drank the jug of wine and then another. We were still thirsty, so we brought "All Tom" into town, and we bought another jug. Across the way, one of the regimental bands of one of the occupying regiments was playing, and a procession was lining up. We came up with an idea.

There were some empty sacks out by the side of the building. We each took one and cut holes for our eyes and mouths and put them over our heads. We even took one and placed it over "All Tom's" head, cutting holes for his ears. We bought several sacks of dried peas, the cheap food of a St. Matthew peasant. We insisted that Honoré ride "All Tom." We hoisted him up on the wide back, and slipped a palmetto stem down Honoré's shirt so that the rays emanated out from his head. Then we hung a sign around Honoré's neck that said, "Prince of Peas." And then we headed down and joined the parade right behind the wagon of the King of Carnival, Good King Sam Teague, *Le Roi de Jupitre.*

He rode on a float, a wagon dressed up as one, wearing his sequined bandage-mask and tights like some Shakespearian actor. The livery capes that the big draft horses wore were purple and gold with green lettering over the rumps. Occasionally, unusable fodder would be ejected from under their stubby tails. *Good King Sam* was written right over the muscular backsides, the tails cropped and wrapped like the handles of a whip over the twin horse-asses. Perhaps it was someone's joke on this illiterate man. Maybe whoever made the capes knew of *le baws-man's* secret.

We were right behind him, throwing handfuls of peas to the crowds as the regimental band played "Marchin' through Georgia" the whole parade, as it was the only song they knew well, that, and the "Star-Spangled Banner" which you could sort of recognize with a little imagination. Silver honking, shining in the chilly spring sun.

The crowds chanted,

Cet homme-ça a jamais travaillé un jour de sa vie!
Cet homme-ça a jamais travaillé un jour de sa vie!
Cet homme-ça a jamais travaillé un jour de sa vie!

Over and over again, they cried lustily in full-voiced French, "That man there never worked a day in his life!" They also shouted the rejoinder, "*Vive le baws-man!*"

An oblivious Sam Teague smiled and waved to them, accepting what he thought were their wishes for a bountiful harvest. We rode behind. Though we did not realize it, we were a parody of the night men that *le baws-man* could not see, as he was intoxicated with the heady aroma of adulation he was drinking in from atop his cane wagon throne. While wearing the tights, tunic, and mask of a court jester. And a brass crown.

He had the wagon driver make several passes through town, but we peeled off and returned to the pecan orchard after the first one. Teague found the crowds thinner and the cheering less robust with each pass. Finally, when there were only a handful of people left, he was persuaded to return to Mount Teague.

The sun was setting in peculiar orange as we settled in the pecan orchard. Most of the men were getting an early start in sleeping it off, some of them still wearing their hoods. Honoré sat at the base of a tree and stared into the western sky. Night fell with the orange sun, and I made a fire that illuminated the undersurfaces of the pecans. Embers floated up among the gray, bare pecan branches and coasted up into the sky like fireflies.

In the morning, we were set to get up early and head up the river road toward Plaquemine and look for jobs up there. I assumed he was thinking about that, worrying about finding work there, worrying about our welfare. He looked especially pensive. Maybe he was hungover like the rest of us.

"Stay up with me a while, Pierre," he said. "*Je suis un peu triste.*[64] Stay up and keep me company."

But I was powerfully tired. My eyes kept closing. I kept nodding, falling over onto his shoulder where we sat side by side at the base of the pecan tree. Each time I woke, the fire had burned down a little more, and, each time, Honoré was still awake, his head in his hands. My head was on his shoulder when I finally went to sleep for good.

I woke up to a hovering torch light. Several of the others woke with startled shouts. Men who had fallen asleep with hoods over their heads pulled them off. Wild hair and red eyes emerged.

I looked at the rider who had entered our camp. He was a Union officer I had seen before, though sleepiness kept me from placing him right away. When he spoke, I knew who it was. It was Captain Harris, the Union captain whose daughter Honoré had healed of the snakebite.

"They're coming for you, *monsieur*," he said to Honoré. "Two whole companies, mine and another. They mean to hang you, sir. They think that you men are the night men. I've sent my company off on a wild goose chase. We'll ride around for a while and then call it a night. But I can't speak for the other company, Company D."

We were all getting up now. Across the embers of the fire, the gray shape of Prosperine looked up from her cocoon of blankets. Her green eyes were puffy and sleep-encrusted.

"It won't be long," Captain Harris said. He pointed to the river with his torch. "I'd head that way, to the river. Try to cross."

He wheeled his horse around. The horse pranced for a moment and bobbed his head. We began loading and hitching up.

"You don't have time for that," he said. "Leave now or risk getting hanged. Make for the river and cross it. There's an old johnboat tied up there. That's your best chance."

He threw the torch, an old pine knot, into the embers of our fire.

---

[64] I'm little sad.

202

"God be with you men," the captain said, and he rode off into the night. The darkness devoured the galloping hoofbeats.

As soon as the hoofbeats diminished, others began from down the bayou road. We ran, all of us, Prosperine ran, too, embracing herself over her shawl to keep herself warm. The river was about a mile away or so. We stumbled through ravines, slogging through knee-deep cold water. Panting, we stopped to pull each other up, and then we took off again, stung by brambles and limbs.

The levee loomed above us. Honoré's silhouette was on top of it, his hand outstretched and tapping the air. He was counting us. Pistache stood by him. His tail was wagging anxiously.

The bateau, what Harris had called the johnboat, was tied up to a willow. Under the moonlight, the silver current tugged at the boat and the willow. When Honoré was sure we were all there, he put us in it, Prosperine first, then the rest of us. It was sitting low, dangerously low. I'm convinced it could not have held one more person. I suppose Honoré was convinced as well. He shoved us off.

"Honoré!" Te Jean called.

"Go!" he said, and he gave the boat one last shove with his boot. He shouted, "*Allez!* I'll catch up later! I swear I will."

We pulled out into the river, taking turns paddling as there were only two or three paddles in the boat. The hangovers we had forgotten were suddenly remembered again, and someone was sick over the side. I looked back to the riverbank. Honoré's figure was getting smaller and smaller.

Lights were emerging from the dark of the woods, splinters of light that grew larger as Honoré's shadow grew smaller, shrinking on the levee. He let Pistache free, and the dog-shadow hesitated, and then ran the length of the levee. The lights converged where Honoré was.

A horn blasted on the river. We all looked up at once. A steamboat was on us, a passenger boat, a towering carnival of gleaming light. It narrowly missed us, splashing water up into our boat. It passed by us and cut us off from the bank where we had come from. It was close, close enough that we could hear a man on the bow call us a bunch of damn fools. *You coulda got yerselves kilt,* he yelled.

The immense boat eased past us, leaving the rhythmic racket of its paddlewheel slapping at the water and the rush of it falling from the top of the wheel. I could see well-dressed men and women in the salons, smoking and drinking in the amber light. When it passed us, we were almost to the other side. I looked back to the west bank, where we had come from. My eyes strained. The torch lights were fading off. I caught a brief glimpse of Honoré with his hands clasped together at his waist. And then I didn't see him anymore.

We reached the other bank and pulled up the bateau. The display of lights across the river had moved on, leaving only a swath of sleeping black willows under the milky moon that admired its reflection in the black water of the river. We tied the boat up to a fallen log and set off for the interior.

We traveled all night, single file, I at the head and Te Jean at the end, Prosperine in the very middle. We had left everything in the orchard, the wagon, "All Tom," our tools. Without them, we were just ordinary men.

The sun came up after several hours, and we kept going. Finally, we rested in a dense thicket. Every sound, every snapping twig, every sway of a limb, was an alarm that prompted us into motion again.

Prosperine was tired, and I wished that "All Tom" were there so she could ride on his back, or, even better, that we could ride on his back together, the small of her back pressing into me, my arms around her and holding the reins, my nose in the scent of her hair like a field of lavender, coarse and yellow like straw.

As night fell again, we found a weedy farmstead. The house seemed abandoned, no furniture in it. A breeze pushed and pulled at tattered curtains. A note on the door said, *Aunt Cille and Uncle Jesse, we gone west to Texas.* The others looked in the windows as I stood and pondered whether the note was to or from Aunt Cille and Uncle Jesse. In the end, we decided to sleep in the barn, just in case Aunt Cille and Uncle Jesse changed their minds and came back, if they had gone in the first place.

We slept that night in the barn loft, trying to ignore our growling stomachs and sore heads and dry mouths and aching hearts. It was a fitful night of gray sleep. In the morning, we looked into the empty smokehouse and the empty corncrib. Everything had been taken. The house was a shell.

Te Jean and Prosperine and I went into town to get us all something for us to eat, our shadows leaning out from us in the morning sun as we traveled west. Houses became more numerous. These were inhabited, and their dogs barked challenges at us. I thought about Pistache. We would all feel just a little bit better if he were around.

The houses became more frequent, and soon there were the markings of a town. A man was plowing near the road.

"What place is this?" I asked him as he made the turn of a row.

"Why, Baton Rouge is up that way just a mile or so," he said, and he shook the reins. The mule pulled the slack out of the traces and the plow pulled the slack out of the man's arms. The handles wobbled in his hands.

The road had side streets branching off now, and the houses were closer. The roofs of two and three story buildings stretched down to the river and the smokestacks tied up there. We bought several baguettes and some salt pork, and when we came out of the store, people were streaming down to the river.

The town was in some sort of an uproar. We followed the crowd down to the low bluff overlooking the river and the set of buildings that marked a complex called the Pentagon Barracks. There were gaps between the buildings, which were laid out in the shape whose name it bore. The crowd seethed between them. Prosperine held my hand so we could stay together in the jostle of shoulders. There was a gallows constructed there, a simple post-and-beam affair, built for one simple task, built to be dissembled when that task was completed. On the gallows, I saw him.

The boy Eugene D'Ormeaux was there with his hands tied behind his back. Union soldiers were everywhere, including several on the platform at what we called parade rest. An officer was reading a proclamation that I couldn't hear over the excitement of the crowd.

Someone in the crowd said that this D'Ormeaux fellow had been involved in that business down in St. Matthew Parish, and that he had fled upriver, trying to make it to a large city to blend into, Memphis or St. Louis, probably. But he was arrested in Natchez and brought back downriver to Baton Rouge. With very little prompting, he had confessed to the murder of Virgil Reeves. A military court, which had jurisdiction at that time, as Louisiana was a conquered province, found him guilty, a formality owing to his confession. He must have thought it would bring him mercy. It did not.

The prisoner was given a chance to speak. The crowd shushed itself, the sound like a fire being put out with water. Everyone fell quiet. This was salacious, the speech of a man about to be hung, something to tell your children and grandchildren about on cold nights around the fire.

His voice sounded less bright, more haggard and worn. In the time since I first met him, he seemed to have aged, but I think I have already said that. He had wet himself, and he blubbered and wailed and begged forgiveness. He shouted out to the crowd.

"Teague put me up to this. It was all his idea. All of it. All of it. He made me shoot Virgil. Teague made me do it. He told me that I had to do it to prove myself. What did I prove? What? What did I prove?"

A voice sounded from the crowd, a booming voice that I recognized instantly.

"Might as well hang him for lyin', too," it said.

The sack went over Eugene's face, over the red eyes that were leaking tears, over that boyish face with the snapping turtle nose, over the quivering lip. This sack had no holes for eyes and mouth, and the dingy canvass snapped in and out with his troubled respirations. His body trembled with his sniveling.

I looked around the crowd for Old Mr. D'Ormeaux and his wife, but I didn't see them anywhere. And then there, tall in the saddle with a top hat and a swallowtail coat, was Sam Teague. He spat and turned his horse. He trotted a few steps and turned to listen to the trap door slap and the rope sing and Eugene undulate like a worm in the spring breeze.

Eugene had gotten the sin off his soul, and he died an honest man. It just wasn't very pretty. And, while he may have died with a clean conscience, he most certainly did not die with clean britches.

The wind picked brown holdover leaves off the trees and threw them north, tumbling and whirling. A newspaper whirled with them and curved around the pillars of the Pentagon Barracks. I picked it up and read the headlines. Anything to keep from watching Eugene dangle.

The newspaper was from a couple of days earlier. The fall of Charleston was announced in big block letters. But under that in smaller print was a bigger story for me.

A man named John Simon Carrick had been captured just upriver from Donaldsonville by Union cavalry and taken to Baton Rouge. He was to be tried for the murder of Colonel Cass Hutchison (and hence, insurrection), as well as the murders of Robert and Octavia Lowe, and

206

robbery, and the rape of a girl named Odile Blanchard. I let the newspaper fall to the mercy of the wind.

The crowd waited with excitement. They wanted more. They knew that a trial was going on right above our heads in one of the rooms in the barracks, away from the anxious public. I listened to their accents and recognized them. They were the people of St. Matthew and all the surrounding parishes that we had visited on those nightly raids.

They showed up to hoot and catcall at him, one of the *hommes de nuit* that had terrorized them. To them, he was already guilty. People are generally more interested in vengeance than in weighing facts. For the defendant to be guilty was important, for if he was found innocent, he would be set free, and then there would be no retribution, and retribution is the most important thing. The crescendo, the ecstasy, the climax of boiling anger, that tender, sweet plum, Retribution.

A door opened, and our heads craned around from Eugene. A man came out of the room where the deliberations were taking place. A couple of reporters asked about a verdict. The man said there was one, but he wouldn't say which, guilty or innocent. The crowd came to a boil again.

I waited for the door to open again. I waited for Honoré to come out with his hands free, rubbing his wrists where the shackles had been. I waited for him to shake hands with the guards, thanking them for their kind treatment, and telling them that there were no hard feelings, he would just move along now, *merci beaucoup*. Prosperine and Te Jean and I all waited for the right thing to be done.

At last, the door opened. Potts came out with his shuffling walk, wiping red ink from his hands with a towel. It was a practice of some officers in those days to sign documents in red ink. Another officer held the document in his hand. He, in turn, was followed by two Union soldiers, and then two more, one on each side of Honoré.

His hands and ankles were still in shackles.

I could have stepped forward. I could have said, no, it was me, I am to blame. Look here, I am missing a finger. I have a semicircle of punctures from the bite I received from the girl that night, the one we raped, Maurice Berteau and Virgil Reeves and I. I delivered a satchel of serpents to Colonel Hutchison. It was I, I am John Simon Carrick. Set this man free, he is innocent. Hang me, instead.

But I said nothing. Oh, dear God, I said nothing. Nothing, nothing, nothing.

Honoré hung his head as the crowd hurled insults at him. To them, he was clearly one of the night men, *les hommes de nuit*, the ones who had kept the countryside living in fear for so long. He apparently never divulged his true identity. He protected me, he had taken on the burden of being John Simon Carrick. Some would call that stubborn. I would call it steadfast. [65]

He lifted his face. His eyes instantly found my face out of the dozens, hundreds in the crowd, and he focused right on me. It was a face of such profound sadness and resignation that it made the hubbub of the crowd fade into a dead silence for me. A soldier nudged him forward with the butt of his rifle, and Honoré hung his head again, and they surged through, past the insults and jeers and shouting.

I turned and pushed my way through the crowd, away from Prosperine and Te Jean. I ran down the streets, away, away, past the barking of dogs, through a brood of hens that were strutting back to their roost as a storm moved in from the south. Their rooster startled into a chuckling flutter of brown wings and alighted on a fence post. I ran as the rain came down and the dusty streets quickly became muddy. And I slogged down them as lightning lit up the eastern sky and the shapes of houses and trees flashed and faded. I ran breathless, helpless, small. A small man, a weak man. The marble rain beat on me and washed out my small tears. And I ran. I ran.

I ran until I saw the barn in a flash of lightning. I climbed up the ladder to the loft, dripping, soaked. I knocked on the door we had placed there. Someone opened the hatch. It was André, kind-faced André.

---

[65] Chip, I had the Tulane library obtain Potts' own memoirs, *Collections and Recollections of a Navy Man*. It includes this passage on pp. 121-122: "After my years of piloting the river ended, I found myself in St. Matthew Parish in the position of having to decide the guilt or innocence of a man on trial for insurrection, murder, and rape. I suspected the man of really being a French-speaking carpenter named Mutton, so I asked him, 'Son, you're not really Carrick, are you? Just say so and you're a free man.' He refused to say anything, so I had no choice but to accede to the weak facts of the case and the frenzy of the citizenry. Otherwise, I am convinced that a riot would have ensued. I have always been suspicious that an innocent man was sent to the gallows. May God forgive me if he was."

Several arms pulled me up and in, and the latch was secured behind me. Questioning faces looked at me.

"They're going to hang him," I said.

"Who?" they asked.

"They're going to hang Honoré."

45

In the loft behind a post, we found a demijohn of rum, perhaps one that Uncle Jesse had squirreled away from Aunt Cille and then forgotten about. We sat and watched the rain through the loft door that looked out onto the pasture. The cattle from the neighboring place were formed up in knots under trees. The dark day merged into night. And then, as the rain pattered on the roof, there was a knock on the trap door.

"*Qu'est-là?*"

"*Te Jean. Et Prosperine*," came the reply.

They were soaked. We pulled them up. The baguettes were soaked also, but we ate them mechanically in the darkness, chewing shadows against the rectangle of dim gray light. No one asked what had happened. We were all so hungry. So we sat in the darkness and ate wet bread. Perhaps we thought that, if we didn't bring it up, then it hadn't really happened. But eventually it had to wake up, that sleeping bit of bad news.

"Well?" someone asked.

I could see her outline against the loft opening. It buckled, and she leaned forward. She dropped the heel of bread she had been holding, and she put her face in her hands. She began wailing softly, the loving grief of a loving woman, a kind, simple heart, a beautiful face, green eyes gray in the darkness, all crumpling under an unbearable weight. We all began crying, sharing the sorrow, bearing the weight that was still too heavy, still too immense, still too crushing. Our heads were in our hands and we held each other and we shook together. We grieved in the shadows of despair and rum.

"What did they do with him?" André asked.

"The funeral man from the parish came and got him," Te Jean said.

The undertaker in St. Matthew in those days was a man named Joe Matthea. He was a nice enough man, but it was widely known that he had a weakness for the drink. He came up to fetch the body, paying for the trip out of his own pocket, to take it back to "the parish," as St. Matthew people called it.

They pulled Honoré's body out of the mud and put him in an old ammunition box, the ones that could hold a dozen rifles or the shells for the big siege guns. They loaded the box into a wagon pulled by a swayback mare and took him down to a steamboat that was tied up in the river. Hired men carried it onboard. It backed out into the current, the rain stippling the flat surface of the water, and then disappeared around the wide, sweeping bend of the river, the opposite back glowing with the flash of each spray of lightning.

Prosperine and Te Jean had watched as the torrent beat down on all of it. Then they returned to the barn loft, and we sat in the emptiness together. Rain and lightning and thunder droned all night, liquid and sharp and grinding.

By the next morning, the rain had let up and passed on. We made a fire and dried our clothes, which took most of the day. Te Jean, André, and I took Prosperine back into town and bought her passage on the next steamboat downriver. It took almost all the money we had, but we wanted someone to be there when he was buried, as he had no family that we knew of, only us. We figured that she would arouse less suspicion than we would. We were all wanted men.

We walked her down to the gangplank that rested in the mud of the river bank. She hugged Te Jean and André, and gave them kisses on the cheek. Then she hugged me, a tight, long hug, and I smelled the smoke on her clothes. I kissed her cheek, but she gave me her lips instead. She kissed me on the lips, a full kiss like lovers would exchange. Her green eyes were red and wet with tears.

"I will miss you, Pierre. Almost as much as I will miss Honoré," she said.

"Maybe your boy will be back from the war soon," I said. I was trying to be cheerful, hopeful, but it sounded as hollow as it was. I had stopped wishing him dead a long time ago. Perhaps I had succeeded, and I didn't know it.

"How many years has he been gone?" she asked as she put her hand to my cheek. "I don't think he's coming back, Pierre. Maybe he's found another girl and started a family up there in that place." *Virgineeya*, she called it. Without emotion, she shrugged her shoulders, as if the emotion of such a sentiment had long burned away, and she said, "Maybe he's dead. I don't even remember what he looks like. The shape of his face, I mean."

Her hand slipped from my cheek. She turned away and went up the narrow incline to the boat. She disappeared among cotton bales and crates, and then she was gone. The gangplank was taken up, and the bowline was thrown aboard. The boat made the channel, and then it was gone, as well. We turned back to return to our hideout in the barn loft.

There, the demijohn of rum was empty, and we were hungry again. We needed to work, but we could not stay together. We knew that if they had hung Honoré, the best of us, they would have no trouble hanging those of us he had left behind. We knew that we had to split up. There was nothing to load up. We had only the clothes we were wearing.

We stood in the barn yard around the doused embers of our fire, cold, wet ash. We were all around it, staring into it, as if it might tell us something.

"Where will you go?" I finally asked Te Jean.

"I may head back to St. Matthew to look after Prosperine."

"They'll hang you if they see you there," I said. For a moment, I thought about going there myself. "They'd hang any of us."

"So they may, Pierre. So they may."

We paused in that way that we paroled soldiers did when we came home from the army. We said we would see each other soon. We said that we would look out for each other. We said that we would send word when we got to where we were going. None of us believed any of it.

We shook hands all around, and then we simply began walking, walking in paths like the exploding tendrils of a firework, out, out, away, our heads down so that we could not see each other. Without my friends, the world was a vacuum. I felt both empty and heavy at the same time.

46

The dog downstairs barks. If you spend enough time around a dog, you begin to understand him. You know what each of his barks means- happiness, delight, anger, curiosity. His barks become speech.

From his bark now, I know that there are visitors downstairs. This house gets them on a regular basis. I believe they come to see the woman downstairs who is not the hired girl, but they always come up here to see me as well. Most of the time, I do not remember them, but when I was able to speak, I would try to play along as if I did. With time, their puzzled glances told me that they knew my mind was slipping. Now that I can no longer speak, I am relieved of the pretense.

My path headed north, up into a place called the Felicianas. I walked for several days, making slow progress, going nowhere in particular. It was May, and the war was over now. At night, I gleaned from gardens, the first produce beginning to come in. During the day, I walked and napped by the side of the road. It would have been a pleasant idyll had my heart not been empty and aching. I wandered until I came across the sound of hammers.

A crew of men were building a house. I stood for a moment and watched them. At last, one of them said, "You there, Frenchy, grab the end of that board for me, there, pleasir."

I helped him carry it. It felt good, reassuring, to bear the rough weight of wood. Then the man in charge said, "Cut them yonder like we did them other ones yesterday."

"Sir?"

"You got a short memory, don't ye? Cut 'em here, here, and here," he said making small ticks with his knife.

And so, I fell in and worked silently with them all day. Hard work was a balm for my soul. That evening we sat and ate out of a communal pot. I was hungry. I ate like a soldier.

"Damn, boy, you eat like that cur dog of yours," the foreman said.

"Yes sir," I said just to agree with him. "Reckon I was hungrier than I thought."

"Where is that dog a yours, anyhow?"

"Dog, sir?"

"Sure, that peanut-colored dog."

"Ain't got no dog," I said.

"Hmp," the man shrugged it off. "Well, I'll say one thing. You're English is a sight better today," he said. "Hardly got no accent at all."

I was too hungry to take stock of it. The sparse talk moved elsewhere, to Lee's surrender and then to Lincoln's murder, what we had sung about so longingly for those years, the thing we all wanted to personally accomplish.

"Son of a bitch. Got what he deserved," someone said in between the sound of scraping tin spoons on tin dishes.

"Just like that Carrot feller they hung down in Baton Rouge."

"Yeah," someone said.

"Yeah," someone else said.

I worked the rest of the week, but, when we were paid, I was given pay for a whole week, even though I had only worked two days. I asked the foreman, "You may have overpaid me, sir."

"Man does a full week's work, he gets a full week's pay. Unless you want me to take it back." He laughed a loud chuckle. He was missing three or four teeth.

"No sir, I'll take it. I just didn't want to take advantage of you."

He looked at me in a sidelong stare, as if it was odd to want to avoid taking advantage of someone. I took the money, six dollars, but I had the lingering suspicion that I was being paid for another man's labor.

I took my pay and went to the tavern there in that little place. Every little town had one in those days, not down on the town square, but safely located away from decent folk, out at the edge of town. There was talk of the hangings down in Baton Rouge a while back, and talk of what the Yankees and their Negro minions had in store for our conquered people.

I was getting comfortable with my jug of whiskey when someone exclaimed, "Say, you there, where's your fiddle? We thought you had left for the night. Render us another tune or two, *monsieur!*"

"Excuse me?" I asked.

"Sure! Play another one for us, we enjoyed it so!"

"I'm sorry, but you're mistaken," I mumbled.

"Oh, come now!" he insisted. "How many nine-fingered men can there be out on a night like tonight?"

I looked at my fingers, and I looked at the door. I went to it, beginning to float in the whiskey haze. The night was dead quiet, like it always was back then in the country. I looked up and down the road, both directions.

I went back in and spoke with the men in the tavern. Some men playing cards in the dim ivory light of a lantern swore they had seen a man who looked just like me, though he spoke with a French accent. We could be brothers, twins, even, they said over their hands of cards.

I went outside again, this time with the jug as a companion. I heard a dog bark, and not just any dog, but a familiar bark. It was Pistache's bark.

I left the light of the tavern behind me, and I took the jug with me. I moved down the moonlit road at a pace between a run and a walk. In every bend of the road, I would see something, the momentary blur of a man making a turn in the road. Not the sight of a man, but the sight of his motion. My pace picked up, my stride quickened, and I ran desperately through the dust, looking for the cloud the stranger might have raised. I threw the jug to the side of the road and I ran as if I was chasing or chased. The dark world blew by me as I huffed and my arms pumped and my feet kicked up a gray cloud into a gray night.

The road narrowed. When I got to where it merged into deep woods, there was nothing. No dust cloud, no footprints. I listened for the dog or the man or the music of a *violon*, but there was nothing. Only the drowsy night and its crickets.

I decided then to return to St. Matthew. I had to see if the tomb with my name on it was empty.

47

There is one thing I know from being in the monument business for as long as I have. When someone has his stone commissioned before he dies and he comes to see it, there is always a pause. He gazes upon it, and his fingers sometimes trace his name. There is nothing so chilling as seeing your own name chiseled into the cold, hard stone. Dickens knew this and showed it to Scrooge, and it was the moment that old Scrooge fell off his hinges. So it was when I saw my gravestone. My first one, I mean.

The next morning, I went to tell the foreman that I was leaving. It was a Sunday, and he was by himself, looking up into the rafters of the building. He was watching the weather and planning the next week's work, which, by the look of things, would be the roof and the walls. Around the clearing, a breeze stirred the new green leaves. Spring was hinting at summer.

"Shame," he said. "You do good work. That lap joint you made is the best I've seen." He pointed to the *trait de Jupitre*. "Strong as the gates of heaven and hell," he said. We both stood there for a moment with our hands on our hips, looking up in admiration. Then he turned, and we shook hands. I turned to the road south, with my hope hand-in-hand with my curiosity. And with what was left of my six dollars in my pocket.

I began walking back to St. Matthew. I followed a river called the Emmit[66], crossing it in a bateau with an old woman who was checking fish traps. I kept to the south, with the breath of the south wind in my face, light and soft. I slept under the boughs of the live oak trees, or in barns when it rained, which it did a time or two. The days were beginning to get warm, but the nights were still comfortable.

On the third day, I crossed the big river with a man in a bateau that was barely big enough for the two of us. He whistled the whole way across, unconcerned with the big steamboat that crossed our path, or the enormous logs coming down on the spring rains up north. He whistled and coughed and spat and paddled, as merry as can be. When we arrived at the other side, I offered to pay him for his trouble, but he declined with an upturn palm.

"I was headed over to see my mama anyway," he said.

In St. Matthew Parish, as in most of south Louisiana, most vaults are above ground, owing to how wet the ground stays. Otherwise, the coffins and their occupants have a tendency to ride up out of the earth, the corners

[66] Carriere almost certainly means the Amite River.

nosing up and out at odd angles, especially after a good, soaking rain. An above-ground vault solves that problem.

And so it was with the cemetery in Napoleonville. It was, and is, a city of the dead, much like the Lafayette Cemetery across from the house here on Prytania. Streets and side streets run through it, every occupant of every dwelling sleeping off his life like a reveler on New Year's Day.

I waited in a grove of cedars. Night fell, and the moon rose and threw dim white light on everything. Clouds were racing in on the exhalation of a warm south wind, casting shadows that slid by in the moonlight. I went down the streets of the cemetery, pausing for the moon to emerge and reveal the writing.

I had been through most of the graves and was nearing the periphery. I began to wonder if he had been buried in Labadieville or Paincourtville. But at last there it was. My name. *John Simon Carrick*, and the date of my death, *March 8, 1865*.

I knelt in front of it with my knees in a puddle of moonlight on the warm spring ground. The wind rushed through the trees, pushing the clouds through the night sky. I was scared, but I had come this far. I was determined to see if this grave had anyone in it.

Someone had spared no expense in that vault. I pushed on the top but found it too heavy to lift by myself. I tried several times and only provoked a meager stony complaint from the granite. I had moved it at most a quarter of an inch. Finally, I went to rest under a cedar while I contemplated my next move.

A lantern appeared. It moved closer, going up and down the rows. It stopped in front of the grave. There were two people sharing a single light. Had they not had it, I could have seen who they were in the passing moonlight.

They set the lantern on the headstone, and their shadows stretched over me. They were a man and a woman. Their silhouettes pushed and strained against the top. They succeeded in moving the stone into a quick rolling grind, but they could move it no further than an inch or so.

They had a brief discussion. I listened to them, hissing in whispers. *Wait here*, the man said in French. Then the man and the lantern drifted down one of the lanes in the cemetery, leaving the woman in the moonlight. And then I recognized her.

I called to her in a whisper, "Prosperine."

"Pierre?" She asked, looking around her at the dark. "Where are you?"

I stepped out of the cedar's moon-shadow. She embraced me.

"We saw him," she said. "We thought it was you. We had to come and check. To see."

Te Jean returned whispering to Prosperine, "I couldn't find us no bar or limb…" He stopped short when the light of his lantern found me.

"Honoré?" he asked.

"No, Te Jean, it's me, Pierre." Prosperine held up the light to my face. Te Jean grasped my hand and pulled our chests together. He put his hand to my neck and kissed me on both cheeks.

"People, *mais*, they think they been seein' him. The ones that know both of you, they think it's you that they see. That's what we thought, too, that it was you. Now we gonna see for all and once."

He always got that expression, "once and for all," backwards. We stood there in the deep shadows of a spring night in Louisiana, when the air gets thicker by the hour and by the night. We were quiet, listening to the crickets chatter. Finally, Te Jean said, "We gotta fine out, Pierre."

We rose, and together, we were able to move the granite top. The stone rasped a deep, scraping, gritty sound. We pushed it over and leaned it against the side of the vault. There was the Union Army crate, marked *One Dozen Enfields*. They hadn't bothered with a coffin. They had buried him in the box they carried him off in. It was a little shorter than he had been. They must have had to put him in it a little diagonally or curled his body up some.

We looked at each other's yellowed faces and nodded. Grabbing the rope handles, we lifted the box out of the low vault. It was heavy, like there was a man was inside.

We examined the lid and found that, while it had once been nailed shut, the nails had been pried out and the top simply set in place by pushing the nails back in their holes. Te Jean and I looked at each other in the lantern light. We worked our fingers under the lid, and the nails made a small squeezing sound as they gave up their wooden holes. The lid was resting on its box.

The three of us paused and took deep, forceful breaths. The inside of the box was still dark. Te Jean lifted his lantern. Prosperine turned her head and hid her face in her shawl. I opened the lid back toward me.

Te Jean looked in the box as if reading something, his hand holding up his lantern, his head tilted. He set down the lantern by the box and jumped in it on his knees. He began laughing, tilting his head up to the black night sky. He laughed up to heaven, and then down into the coffin-box. He shook with laughter, his hands on his knees. I set the lid aside and looked in.

There was no body in the box, only a thick layer of sand. Te Jean was on his knees in it, and written there was a message, *Pouquoi churche.* The rest of the message, if there had been any more of it, had been disturbed when Te Jean had jumped in.

"What does it mean?" I asked Te Jean.

"How should I know, Pierre? I don't read, me. It just means he ain't here. He's alive, Pierre. He's alive."

Prosperine and I studied the sand and looked around the nightscape and studied the sand again. Finally, we set the lid back on the box and placed it back into the crypt. Then we pushed the granite lid back into place. It did not seem to weigh as much now.

48

I hear the woman downstairs who is not the hired girl speaking with someone. I believe it is one of our neighbors, a woman with whom I have spoken on a daily basis for many years but whose name I cannot recall just now. I don't have even a wisp of it in my mind. I can see her, though, a woman with a pile of thick brown hair with gray streaks. Her children have spent a lot of time in this house, and the children of this house have spent a lot of time in hers. They are all grown now, I believe, but that thought, that memory is only a shadow for me at present. And likely to only grow dimmer.

They speak of someone they know as having been taken "to Jackson." Whoever it is has had some break with the real world and has been taken to that place where everyone inhabits his own little world. Most of those worlds seem tormented places. Or, that is what I suppose, having visited Jackson once myself.

We waited until first light and then Te Jean and I adjourned to a wooded area while Prosperine went to pay a call on Mr. Matthea, the undertaker. He had been the man who had fixed up the first Mrs. Teague. He was an odd duck, a loner who never married, a man who wore a headful of slick pomade which always failed at keeping a thick strand of hair from falling between his eyes.

A little while later, Prosperine came back and said, "Anybody who dies now got to go through Thibodaux to get to heaven. They took Monsieur Matthea up to Jackson. His housekeeper say he done loss his mine, him."

We agreed that we had to find him. He was the last person to see Honoré. Dead or alive.

The three of us spent the day within the grove of cedars, in secret. Prosperine and I cuddled close, with Te Jean nearby. If he had not been there, we might have satisfied our thirsts, though that is debatable.

That evening, we started off as the sun sank into the waist-high cane fields. We walked all night until we came to the midnight barking of the dogs of Donaldsonville. We "borrowed" a boat and crossed the river.

She would reach out for my hand, like she would do when she was blind. I liked the way it felt in mine. As we got further from St. Matthew Parish, we began traveling in the day time, even stopping to ask directions.

"Which way is Jackson, sir?"

"The one in Mississippi, or the one in Louisiana, the one with the madhouse?"

"One with the madhouse."

"That road yonder."

We were passed a day or two later by a wagon with a crate in the back. Through a space in the crate, a pair of wild eyes watched us. A pair of dirty hands grasped the slats. On seeing us, shrieking erupted from the crate.

"Quiet back there," the driver scolded the person in the crate. "I don't want n'more trouble from you. We almost there."

The wagon trundled on, the driver jostling from side to side. And then, less than a mile down the road, there it was. The State Asylum.

It was, and is, a magnificent edifice, grand columns in the Greek Revival style, two multistory wings that run in each direction from a central portico. The wagon and its crate were being unloaded. A small man emerged from it and was taken by two orderlies on each side. The man began writhing and bucking. His new keepers wrestled him to the ground in front of the steps, binding him in some sort of canvass wrapper and stuffing a gag in his mouth to silence him. One of the men put the poor little fellow under his big arm and carried him up the steps and into the building.

We paused at the base of the steps and looked up to the columns supporting the triangular pediment. Before us, a woman with a square face sat on the front steps, her hair cut short, but still wild. When we got close, she smiled at us. We smiled back, and she put one foot on the step and lifted her skirts. Her feet were bare, as was everything else. Her hands grasped her inner thighs on either side of the shadow of hair. We hurried up the steps as she laughed maniacally at our backs.

Inside, along the main corridor, men in a hodgepodge of uniform pieces slumped in unique postures. Mouths that once breathed the fire of secession now sat and mumbled nonsense at the opposite wall. Laughing and weeping and screaming and shouting and babbling and screeching erupted from different rooms off the main hall. It sounded like the bird house at the zoo. As the mentally unfit sat and stared away the days and years of their lives, dust floated in the sunlight like snowflakes on a moonlit night.

Some sort of clerk sat and scratched away at a ledger with a pen that was a long feather. The beak of the feather dipped into the inkwell, and he scratched some more. Prosperine cleared her throat, and the man looked up.

"Yes ma'am?" he said.

"We're looking for Mr. Matthea. From St. Matthew Parish."

He consulted his ledger, flipping back a page or two.

"Joseph Ransdale Matthea, St. Matthew. All right. This way. But men only. There are things down there that may be upsetting to ladies."

"Please, *monsieur*," Prosperine said. "He is my uncle," she lied. She was as anxious to hear what Matthea had to say as we were.

"All right," the clerk sighed.

We walked through that bedlam, the sounds of the inconsolable, the smells of the unwashable, past the uninhibited stares of shuffling, wild-haired men. Men engaged themselves in secret dramas, private conversations, all separated from the world and from each other. A gust of asylum laughter erupted from a room as we passed. Then, just as suddenly, an anguished cry of *no, no, no, no!* pealed out from the room across from it. A door down from that, we found him. If Matthea wasn't insane already, he certainly would be now.

"They he is," the attendant said unceremoniously.

Matthea was sitting on the floor against the wall. His head was in his hands, his arms were on his knees. He looked up and saw us. His eyes locked on me.

"It's you. You!" he wailed.

"No, *monsieur*," Prosperine said as reassuringly as she could, "That's his brother."

Matthea ignored her and launched into an oration of sorts.

"I, the prophet, saw it with my own eyes." He pointed to his eyes and passed his hands over them. Someone cackled and shrieked down the hallway. Matthea ignored that, too.

"The dead have busted open their coffins and risen, risen up, speaking in the tongues of foreigners from foreign lands. This, I, the prophet, have seen." He raised his hands and tilted his head back.

"If salt loses its flavor, it is just dirt. Sand." He began sobbing uncontrollably. "It is just sand. Just sand. Just sand! Sand!" He yelled and his face fell into a peculiar shape, the shape, perhaps, of some sea creature living at the bottom of a lightless ocean. The man in the waistcoat ran in with another man. We were asked to leave, and we did.

We weighed what Matthea had said, and we chose to believe that it meant that Honoré was alive. It is human nature to agree with someone, even the insane, if they tell you what you want to hear. And the more you want to hear it, then the more allowance you are willing to give them, the more credence they have, no matter how mentally unfit they are. Sanity is no object at times such as those.

We left the asylum with no clear plan. Perhaps that was our first mistake. We spent a good month walking, asking, searching, all the while aware that Te Jean and I could be rounded up as members of the night men, the band of outlaws once headed by the now-defunct John Simon Carrick. "And may God have pity on his low, murdering soul," was often the rejoinder.

We would tell people that he was my twin and that I had come back from the war and was looking for him and for the rest of my family. There was certainly nothing unusual about that. A lot of people were in the same situation.

But no one knew anything. Te Jean and I worked here and there, working just long enough to make enough money to keep moving. The only place we did not go was St. Matthew. Te Jean proposed that we look there, but I told him it was out of the question. It would have been suicidal to go there, as that was is where most of our mischief had been conducted. It was fine if they hung me. I was guilty. I didn't want Te Jean to get hung innocently.

Prosperine had given up on the boy who went off to war, and so had I. I was tired of searching. I wanted to move on with her. I wanted us to marry and enjoy the conjugal urge and raise perfect little blends of ourselves, each of them getting the best of our qualities. But, for now, we were consumed with searching for this man whose body had been lost or stolen from his tomb. Te Jean and Prosperine were convinced that he was around the next bend, or in the next town, or having a glass at the next tavern. I could not dissuade them to the contrary, even if I tried. So I didn't.

Spring was now as hot as summer. The river had cleared the spring rain and melting snow up north, and that meant we were in for the hottest four or five months of the year. We had just followed another dead-end trail, one that led us to the river at Bayou Sara. We sat watching the brown current coast by. I had a bottle that I drank from by myself. My drinking was becoming an issue with our little expedition. I found it to be the only thing that was predictable. Open, tilt it back, and pretty soon, things will start looking better, even if better is only tolerable.

Te Jean and Prosperine were just as optimistic as always.

"We've got to keep looking," he insisted. "We're so close."

"Why don't we just put a safe distance between us and St. Matthew and Teague and start our lives?" I said.

"But Pierre, you can't mean that!" Prosperine said, and she knelt down on the sandy bank and put her arms around me. I was in no mood for it. I shrugged her away and took another sip.

"You keep looking," I slurred. "Maybe he is dead. Maybe the resurrectionists[67] came for his body. Maybe some young university gadabouts are dissecting him right now while we go off looking for him like he was some kind of goddammed will o' the wisp or Santy Claus. You two go on, if that's what you want to do. I've had enough of it. Enough. This…this is just hare-brained. This is crazier that Mr. Matthea."

Te Jean and Prosperine looked hurt, as hurt as I had intended to make them. I gave the bottle another pull and added one more insult to the heap.

"If he is alive, he sure ain't looking for us. Some friend he is. Was."

I sat by the bank of the river and watched it coast by. I emptied the bottle and threw it. The river plunked a thank you and carried it away.

After a time, I looked back. Te Jean and Prosperine were long gone. I looked back across the river, and I thought I could see the dim and distant form of the man I used to be. And I think he could see the man I had become.

49

My Aunt Cora was fond of the saying, "the man takes a drink, then the drink takes a drink, then the drink takes the man." It was very simple to her how that could happen, as logical as nighttime following the sunset. But in reality, it is much more complicated than that.

The drink seduces a man, coming to him cooing and whispering, *Things are so hard for you, come, nurse a while from my glass-nippled breast. You are my favorite.* Then she beguiles you, coaxing you into the horizontal, and you wake to find that she has left with the pocket change of your dignity. She returns later with apologies and the offer of her breast and you take it. The pain is too great. You have no other choice.

There, she says, *just look at you, you old drunk, you will never amount to anything.* She says it as if it is the thing she finds most appealing about you.

---

[67] Nineteenth century men who would steal recently buried bodies and sell them to medical schools for anatomic dissection.

No one else cares for you, only I do. I am your only friend. And you cling to her. You must. She is everything.

Shame is her companion, a thing that watches you from the shadows. Its gaze is unflinching, gray and flat like the stare of a dying child. It is tethered to you, hollow-eyed and blank. You can pretend it doesn't see you and that you don't see it, your shame, but it does, it sees you. In darkness and in light, it sees you, it sees the part of you that you would rather not admit exists. Without a word, it reminds you of that thing that you did or failed to do. Drinking doesn't dull it, sleep doesn't soothe it into rest. It simply waits for you to awaken or sober up. It will outlast you, confound you, infect you and everything you try to do. It is a pebble in your shoe. It is a thorn in your flesh. It does not relent. It does not look away.

Shame and Drunkenness became my only companions as we traveled together along the lower stretches of the river, following jobs that were fleeting because of my drinking. If I was hired in the first place, I rarely lasted a week. Sometimes just a day would pass before the foreman would yell at my tottering form, "Clear out! Now!"

In towns where there were others, I was *a* drunk. In towns where there were no others, I was *the* drunk. In towns where French was the predominant language, I was *le soulard* or *le chamandeur*.[68] But, in any language, I was a mendicant, a wastrel. A vagrant, a beggar. My odor became that of my childhood days, and possibly worse. Townspeople requested that I occupy a position at the periphery of town. I would gather my dingy hat and my sign that read, "Veteran, CSA, P. Ridge, Iuka, Corinth, V'burg."

Church ladies would come with a few scraps brought out of a sense of charity. They would almost always be delivered by a young boy who would drop them quickly by my upturned hat and run off pinching his nose. It was all in the manner that one would feed a mangy stray. After a time, a week or a day or a month, time then having only hazy gradations for me, I would move on at the insistence of the townspeople, or simply from the urging of my master, Shame.

Drunkenness and Shame insist that you have no other friends, and so I had forsaken them, or they had forsaken me. One day, they simply weren't

---

[68] The drunk or the moocher.

there, none of Honoré's old crew. Te Jean and Prosperine had moved on. I wondered where they were, and I worried for their safety in those rare interludes in which I was neither drunk nor hungover. But sobriety was fleeting, and my master and my mistress would drive me off from wherever I was.

I would emerge again, hungover, in another town, to follow the same script of pity, charity, tolerance, and disgust. And then I would move on again, stowing away on steamers loaded with cotton, as a stowaway or as a passenger paid for by the previous town to get me off their streets and out of their hair, with a sigh of relief and good riddance.

And so, I washed up again in a new place on a foggy day. I moved into town, ascending a hill in the mist. A castle loomed in the fog. It was the capital, which meant that I was in Baton Rouge, the place where the mischief had been done. If only one bold and courageous man had said the right words in the legislature, perhaps I would never have gone off to war on behalf of a failed country and a flimsy excuse, and my daddy would never have died refusing to hoorah for its president, and the widow Lowe would still be alive and married.

But no one had said those words, whatever they might have been, and the war had pressed its weight on us. And here we were. And here I was. Back in Baton Rouge, where they had hung my friend, Honoré Mouton. Who had died because I had not been a bold and courageous man with the right words.

On this foggy day, there were a great many men there in suits as I pressed on up the hill.[69] I found myself in the midst of the Pentagon Barracks. The gallows had long since been dissembled. I sat in the square where it had all taken place. After a few minutes, one of the soldiers who was stationed there came out and told me to move along.

I stumbled on and decided that I would go and pray. It is what my Aunt Cora would do. I found the nearest church, which I believe was the Catholic one. I went and knelt down. And then I laid down.

I woke with a shake of my shoulder.

"You can't sleep in here," the priest said. I ignored him, presenting him an offer instead.

---

[69]Chip, I'm thinking this may have been the legislature.

"I can carve you a new crucifix for your altar, Father," I told him in a slur. "I'm a sculptor."

"Oh, a sculptor, are you? Well, isn't that something. We should give you a chance, then."

I was too drunk or hungover or both to detect the sarcasm in his voice. I might as well have told him I was Andrew Jackson or Robert E. Lee.

He took me out back where a pin oak tree had fallen. The caretaker of the rectory had a saw that was dull, and I spent a full day cutting it to size, an upright and a cross member. Part of the delay were the naps I needed to take. Finally, I had them cut, and it took me another day of work, punctuated again by napping and swearing, to join them into a cross.

The priest and the caretaker watched me from the rectory window as I used the dull saw to cut away at the stinking green oak. At the end of the day, the priest would bring me a little dinner, and I would sleep out in the night heat. Late the next morning, I would wake, cuddling with my work like a hideous lover, and I would arise and begin beating away at it with the borrowed tools of the caretaker.

When I pronounced the crucifix complete, the priest gave me a small token sum, enough for a meal and passage downstream. I bought the ticket, but decided instead to take my nourishment in liquid form, a bottle of rye whiskey. As I left the churchyard, the crucifix was being hauled away to the woodpile, a lumpy, grotesque thing that reeked of stinky green oak. I had created it in my own image.

I walked down to the riverfront, where I had said goodbye to Prosperine months before. The man turned his head away and took my ticket. The boat pushed off and headed downstream.

Night fell beyond the west bank, a low, sprawling thing in black against the orange evening sky. I watched the receding riverbank until it fell to darkness. A man had been watching it with me. In the last of the day's light, I recognized him.

"Potts," I said, "Aren't you supposed to be in St. Matthew Parish?"

"I've resigned my commission. Mrs. Potts and I are just returning from St. Louis. Going to Europe. She wants to see Rome." He said it very genially. He had been facing the river but speaking to me. He turned to me. We were perhaps twenty feet apart on the railing. The light of a half-moon was shining off the water. I looked up from it in time to see Potts' eyes narrow and then flare in recognition.

"Carrick," he said, "aren't you supposed to be-" It was an odd question, but I suppose he had to ask it. And I answered it.

"Dead?" I took the last pull from my bottle. "Yes sir, I am." I threw the empty into the river. "I should be."

He backed away along the railing as the moon and the current slid by and the paddlewheel slapped at the water. He kept his eyes locked on me and his hand locked on the railing. But before he could ask me anything else, the steward came and got me, reaching out for my arm and letting it go when he got a good whiff of me.

"Let's put you back by the wheel. But if the wind changes in the night, I'll have to come and move you."[70]

I did not see Potts the next day. He kept to his cabin, claiming to be overheated and not feeling well. I was out of whiskey and fell to panhandling fellow passengers for any stray liquor they might have. Apparently, it was a bother to them, that and my insistent aroma, and I was put off in the next town, a place that I faintly recognized.

Donaldsonville.

50

I can hear them out there. The woman downstairs who is not the hired girl is cracking pecans with the children on the front balcony. Every so often, one of them shows her their efforts, and she says, "Ooh, *sha, mais,* that's a nice one. You got it all out together." She says it with the same beatific voice that guides the girls through tatting lace and cooking. She is patience personified.

Later, she will take the pecans and the girls will chatter at her heels as they go down the stairs to the kitchen. They will ask small-voiced nonsensical questions of the woman, and she will answer them patiently

---

[70] Chip, there is no mention of this encounter in Potts' memoir, *Collections and Recollections of a Navy Man.* I find that a little strange, don't you?

and sincerely. Their voices will recede down with them, and I will strain to hear them. Then the sweet, butter smell of pralines cooking will fill the house. But, for now, the sound of the shells cracking brings back painful memories.

The streets of Donaldsonville were beginning to bustle again. Though the war had been won, Union soldiers were still everywhere, bored and homesick and generally milling around. I tottered down the gangplank and wandered down to Mississippi Street and slumped down on the porch of one of the businesses. The sun was hot, but the shade was merely warm. I deployed my sign and my upturned hat for alms in a splash of that tepid shade and lapsed into a dream about my daddy and the mama that I never met, or that perhaps I met and cannot remember.

Looky here what I got for you, ol' gal. A whole sack a pecans, my daddy tells my mama in that dream which began so pleasantly. She looks so much like the first statue of the blessed mother that I did, the one out of that cypress log for St. Lazare. Then I heard it.

I heard it before I felt it, the sound like something cracking, and in that half-awake state I dreamed of my daddy, the way he would crack a sack of pecans or walnuts or hickory nuts against a tree trunk to loosen their shells. And after that split second of half-sleep, I felt it, and it summoned me from deep, drunken sleep. And after I felt it, I saw the heel of the shoe grinding down on my hand, the right hand, the one with a full five fingers. It was a woman's shoe, a row of imitation pearl buttons up the side of the ankle.

And when I felt it, I didn't shout. Instead, I howled like a dog. She, whoever she was, was bracing her weight with one hand on the hitching rail I had passed out next to. The other hand held her skirt hem up enough so that she could watch her shoe do its work on my hand.

"Lady, please, lady," I moaned, too weak, too hungover, too drunk to escape her heel with her weight on top of it.

"Please," I begged her again, until her other shoe hit my groin, once, twice, and again and again, until my moans leaked into a whimper, and the tears leaked down onto my dirty, smelly face. I clutched myself with my hands, one pointer-less and one mangled and swollen. I protected myself, already feeling my groin swelling from inside myself and from outside with my hands.

I looked up through gummy eyelids to see who my attacker was. It was a woman with narrow eyes and dark hair, a girl who looked so familiar to me. A girl who was pretty and on the verge of beauty, a girl with full eyelashes.

Then her shoe found my face, striking it again and again and again and I could feel it swelling, lips swelling, eyes shutting. The footsteps of men came running, and the kicking stopped but the pain didn't, nor did my weeping, which was like that from a cheap theatrical, only it was real.

"Easy-easy, Miss," a man's voice said in a low, reassuring voice. "He's just an old drunk."

Someone helped me up, and then I heard them slap their palms across each other, trying to rid them of my smell. I tottered down between buildings, one of them belonging to the Jew tailor who had made me a splendid suit once. As I cleared the alley, stopping only to vomit between swollen lips, I heard the voice.

"No, *monsieur*, he raped me," her voice said.

"Oh, you're *that* gal. Well, the man what raped you got hung for it."

My Aunt Cora liked the Bible verse about the guilty running when no one is chasing them, or something like that.[71] That's exactly what I did. I wandered through the alleys and streets, trying to run but only stumbling through the shadows of buildings, some of which I had helped build, some of whose views I had stood upon to see the whole of the town and the river.

But now I could not see anything. Everything about me was swollen, including my eyes. Though it was day, the world was dim to me. I wondered if Prosperine could see this much when she was blind. I staggered out of town and down Bayou Lafourche. After a while, I collapsed on the slope of its bank.

I thought I was alone, but I heard low singing and then someone spat and it made a light speck sound in the water. I opened my eyes to mere slits to see that an old Negro woman was fishing under a wide brim hat down the bank from me. I could hear her better than I could see her. She

---

[71] Proverbs 28:1, "The wicked flee when no man pursueth: but the righteous are bold as a lion."

saw me looking at her and pointed to a wooden bucket next to her.

"*Onze sac-a-lait!*" she said proudly. Her lips flapped over toothless gums. She tilted her pole back and then forward. The line swung out, and the cork landed with a plunk. A moment later there was the sound of stirring water and splashing and the desperate flapping of a fish.

"Heh-HEH!" she exclaimed. "*Un douze!*"

I tried to look through my swollen eyelids, and I only saw the black speckles on silver scales as her old brown hand grasped the fish and the other twisted out the hook. The tailfin slapped at her. She tossed the fish into the wooden bucket. I could hear it swim in a frantic circle before settling in with the others. I listened for the sounds of the town but only heard the squeaking warble of birds on distant limbs.

Then a hand grasped mine. My swollen eyes strained to see who. I could see the old Negro woman, so I knew it was not her. The hands began undressing me.

"What are you doing?" my swollen lips mumbled.

There was no reply. Each layer of clothing let off another scent, each one more foul than the one before.

"I can wash myself," I muttered. There was a quiet chuckle, and the hands kept bathing me. *Yes, but why haven't you done it already?* The hands seemed to ask.

"You gone have to wash that man head and hands, too!" the old woman chuckled. "He show ripe."

The hands pushed my head under and the world was liquid and my head seemed to swim in a frantic circle and then there was air again and then I knew to get another breath and my head went under. Then I was out again, my eyes shut tight against soap and water. I waited to be dunked under again, but I found that I was alone. There was only the sound of birds.

After a while, I emerged naked from the water. On the bank, there was a towel and a bundle of brand new clothes. The person who had bathed me was gone. And I could see much better. Much, much better.

I dried with the towel and dressed quickly. The old woman kept watching her cork and payed me no mind. I dressed in the clothes, a fine suit of light blue seersucker. The woman spoke.

"That man he say meet him at the Planters Hotel in Dawsonville.[72] Room 21, then look out the window."

I went into town, clean and in new clothes. At the hotel, I stepped in. My face was still bruised, the color of an autumn sunset over a cane field. The man at the desk looked at my face and said, "Aren't you the man in Room 21? How'd you get so beat up? You want that I should call the police?"

I shook my head no.

Instead, he took me up to the second floor, and opened Room 21. There on the floor by the neatly made bed with the chenille bedspread was a tool chest. The tool chest of the carpenter, Honoré Mouton.

A breeze from the river toyed with the lace curtains in the window. I waited most of the morning for him to return. Every footstep in the hallway, every opening door, every sound, I was sure was Honoré. But none of them were.

I sat by the window and the first wind of fall pressed through it and the sun set and threw gold and orange light on to the blue surface of the river. Lanterns were being lit along the levee. I got up to lie down on top of the bed. The wind pushed, and, in the distance, the trees sighed and something metal rang quietly, pushed by the wind, rhythmically against something else metal. I shifted on the bedspread, and I noticed that my body did not hurt anymore. I touched my face. It was no longer as swollen, though it was a little sore. And then I fell asleep.

Rays of sunlight slanted in when I woke. Cold air hung about me, that first breath of cold air in the fall that signals that the heat is over and the cane will be cut soon, but for now, you can all rest a while. I sat up and looked out to the river. A steamboat was tied up and the gangplank lowered. I felt like I had been asleep a thousand years. It was the first time that I had slept indoors since I left the garçonnière at Mount Teague, not counting barns.

I rose and went to the window, and the fresh breeze tugged at my hair and beard. Down below on the street, a man and a woman sat huddled in the shade of a tree. The man had a slouch hat pulled low over his face.

---

[72] Certainly, he means Donaldsonville. Of course, this is how so many pronounce it.

231

The woman wore a shawl over her hair. I studied their movements, they moved in a way that was familiar to me. At last, I called to them.

"*Monsieur et madame*," I said down to them. They looked up to the window of the hotel where I stood. And then I saw them clearly. Te Jean and Prosperine.

"Come up," I said, as quietly as I could to their upturned faces. "*Vingt-un*."

I waited at the door and answered it on the first knock. I embraced them, the tobacco smell of Te Jean and the lavender of Prosperine. I could not say I was sorry, but I think that they knew it without me saying it. I wanted to cry, but I did not. She looked into my face.

"Pierre?" she asked. Then she examined my hands, checking for the missing finger on the left hand.

"Yes."

"Forgive me, but I was making sure that you weren't Honoré. People have seen him. We thought they might have seen you instead."

I didn't say anything. I just pointed down to Honoré's tool chest. Te Jean fell to his knees and examined the tools in it, the bit brace, *le scion, le marteau*.[73]

No one said anything. We were all so quiet. We could hear each other breathe. Outside and on the river, a steamboat was huffing and whistling and belching, getting up steam for the trip down river. We sat on the side of the bed on the chenille bedspread and looked out the window. The morning sun had changed things.

Prosperine got up and stood at the window with her hands resting on the sill. The breeze picked at her hair like straw. The sun illuminated her green eyes. She closed them and enjoyed the feel of the breeze, a sightless, pure joy like when she was a blind girl, before she had seen things that are hard to see and impossible to forget. She opened them, and then she opened them even wider. She looked back to me to make sure I hadn't left the room and gone down on the street.

"Pierre. Te Jean," she mumbled as she kept her eyes locked on the street. "Go down to the street. Go," she murmured. "He's there."

We sprang up from the bed and to the window. Prosperine pointed

---

[73] The saw, the hammer

down to a figure in a white linen suit and a wide-brimmed hat, what they call a Panama hat nowadays. The man was waiting near the gangplank with his hands in his pockets. At his feet was a peanut-colored dog.

We took off down the hall and past a woman with an armload of sheets coming up the stairs. The desk man looked up from sorting messages as we dashed by. We clattered across the planks laid down across the muddy street. The man in white turned, and we slowed as he did. The dog barked merrily moving from one of us to the other, nosing us and whimpering.

I ran to the man and fell to my knees and embraced his legs. And I sobbed. Oh, how I sobbed, a great, heaving cry, the kind that makes you think you will break in two. My shoulders pushed into Honoré's legs.

He looked around and scooped his hands under my arms and pulled me up, a gesture that spoke of his concern over my losing my composure in public. Then he put his arms around me and embraced me and said to me quietly, "You a good man, boo."

"No," I said. "I betrayed you. I've betrayed everyone who's ever meant well for me." My face twisted in grief over the man I was, my cheeks were hot, my eyes squinting with tears, my words were choking on themselves.

He looked at me, my own image looking into itself. Our faces were close. "Pierre. Pierre." He sounded embarrassed by my behavior -not embarrassed *by* me but embarrassed *for* me. "You a good man, Pierre. There's a spark of something good, a mustard seed, in even the most foul, *le plus pire, le pécheur plus bas.*[74] Only the blessed can see it. And only the very blessed can make others see it. You let this shame stay inside you, and you won't be able to work. The work you got left to do, you ain't gonna be able to do it, no."

I looked around me, and I saw that we were all there, all of the old crew. The others had slowly emerged from the alleys of Donaldsonville and from the wooded bank upriver and downriver, Phillipe, André, Jacques, and all the others. We were together with Honoré.

The dog had made his rounds, and Honoré and I reached down to pet his head and neck, each of us with our incomplete hands. We straightened

---

[74] The worst, the lowest sinner

up, and Pistache returned to Prosperine.

"Pierre, *garde ça*," he smiled and looked both ways. He would do that whenever he had something funny to say or was about to play a practical joke on someone. He pulled his collar back, and under it was a mark. I put my fingers on it. It was a scar. He pulled his collar open to show me all of it. He had a look of mischief on his face, as if he was showing me a clever trick.

"I axed that hangin' man if he knew what he was doin'. Axed him 'twiced' as he say. Guess he didn't, him. I fall asleep, and, next thing you know, I wake up in that box. *Mais*, I push and I push. They nail that thing down some good." His eyebrows and the corners of his mouth raised. "But I got out, as you can see.

"But I was a little stunned, me, so I got out and walked around town for a while. It was night, not a soul out. Then I thought, well, maybe I should go back to tell ol' Matthea that, *merci non*, I wouldn't be needing his fine box after all. He woke up from his shovel and his bucket of sand and his bottle and saw me. I opened my mouth to speak, but I couldn't yet, because of the necktie that them blue-suit-men made for me. Matthea ran out, so I left a message in the sand he had put in the box."

We all shook our heads. Like a lot of Honoré's tales, it was wildly preposterous. But it must have been true. Here he was among us.

We were in a circle around him. A few other passengers were getting on. Honoré made the rounds of us one last time, speaking quiet words to each of us. When he got to Prosperine, she asked him what he had written in the sand. He smiled and whispered it into her ear.

"Where are you going?" André asked him.

Honoré looked around and said in a low voice, "Cuba. Havana. Maybe I fine me a Spanish angel, and we have ourselves some Honorés and Honorettes." He looked to Te Jean. "You keep my tool box until I get back?"

"How long?" Te Jean said.

"I don't know. Just keep it. And use it. Keep everything sharp for when I come back."

At last, he came back to me. Even though I was standing, he told me, "Rise, Pierre, go and pay the debt. Rise." I wasn't sure what he meant. Then he pressed two keys into my palm, a large key and a small key. From the other pocket, he pulled a bottle. *Tincture of Laudanum*, it said. "You remember how Teague's dog likes his pork-*chop*? Pay the debt, Pierre."

I looked at him, and I'm sure my face was a question mark. He just patted my cheek and turned. He walked up the incline past the sign nailed to a piling in the river, hand scrawled letters on a cypress board, *Port of Donaldsonville, Parish of Ascension*. The morning sun was behind him and his long shadow stretched over us. He walked up the gangplank in his white linen suit and Panama hat. Then he disappeared among the bales of snow white cotton. He appeared again on the hurricane deck.

"Split up, spread out," he called down to us on the bank. "There's plenty left that needs to be rebuilt. The dwellings and the people that live in them. Beaucoup heartache, beaucoup want, beaucoup sadness. Go and do what you can, even if it ain't much, no. Just do what you can."

Pistache stood poised on the bank by the gangplank. Honoré whistled to him, but the dog lifted a paw to test the plank and then withdrew it. He twisted his head and then came and sat by my feet.

"I guess he don't wanna go," Honoré shouted. "You keep him for me, Pierre. I think he likes you best, anyway. Dogs are a good judge of character, they say, no?"

The boat shrieked a shrill whistle to announce its departure. Deckhands pulled up the gangplank. The wheel was slapping at the river, and water was cascading from the top slats. The boat made the channel and pushed down river, pulled by the current into the morning sun. That was the last I ever saw of Honoré Mouton. And that was almost sixty years ago.

We were lost then, in that weightless moment, the way a boat must feel lost when the anchor is pulled and it begins to drift. A wind was pushing in off the river and snapping at the American flag, stretching it out in rippled red-and-white stripes. Someone had to say something, but we all knew that, once that something was said, the departure of one from another would be set in motion. The silence was crushing, and finally we decided to go in pairs. We could look out for each other that way.

I asked André, who was next to me, "Where will you go?"

"West, I believe. Phillipe and me. Opelousas, I think. The prairie."

And then, the ice broken, everyone began to choose a place and a companion, like we have always done in this country, since the day we stepped off a boat and headed into the woods and down a rutted path. Or we simply made our own path. We chose where we were going, not weighing any long-term consequences, large or small, but by a whim.

Te Jean went up to retrieve Honoré's tool box from the room. He came down, and we all admired it. The dovetail joinery, each compartment with a purpose, a reflection of the man who made it and used it. Written in chisel marks across the handle was one of his favorite sayings, the thing he told us so many times, *Ton Travail Est Ta Prière*.

Your Work Is Your Prayer.

"What about you, Te Jean? Where?" I asked him.

"St. Martinville. I have people there," he said.

Prosperine looked from Te Jean to me. She was torn, trying to decide. She loved Te Jean like a brother. Perhaps she loved me more than that.

"Where will you go, Pierre?" she asked quietly.

"I have a job to do in St. Matthew," I said. "It will be dangerous. I will need to go alone, I'm afraid. Go with Te Jean. He'll look after you."

Te Jean nodded.

We began drifting away, André and Phillipe, all the others, off in pairs like the animals coming off the ark after the flood. Off into a world that had almost drowned and was trying to catch its breath again.

I looked back to see them, the men I had worked with, sang with, joked with, eaten with, slept with. We melted away from one another. Only Prosperine looked back, her face sad, so sad, wrestling with an impossible choice. I put my hands in my pockets, my left hand resting on the bottle of laudanum there. I moved away through town, down Bayou Lafourche, along the bayou road. Pistache ambled along with me, pausing and marking, marking and sniffing the wind. The cane was tall, the tops twitching in the wind. It whispered its autumn song, murmuring in a rustle of green fronds, *we green stalks, we are not long for this world. We will all be cut down. All of us.*

A whisper emerged from within the cane fields, a whisper of my name, insistent, distant, and then closer, *Pierre, Pierre, Pierre.* I turned, and there she was, running, a handful of skirt, a handful of shawl, running, running after me, down the road that bordered the cane. *Pierre, Pierre, wait, Pierre.*

"I will come with you," she said. It was not a question. It was not a request. It was a statement, a fact.

"It could be dangerous," I reminded her.

"Yes," she said. "Yes."

And so we walked on together, hand in hand, to the south, on an errand with an uncertain outcome. The others, Te Jean and Jacques and André and the rest, had slipped away. Some of them I have seen since then, some of them I have not. But I have not seen any of them in years. Perhaps they are all asleep now.

51

The woman downstairs who is not the hired girl comes up to my room. She gets in my bed with me and puts her hand on my chest where the gray hairs wander through the pajama shirt. It reminds me that I am more than a shell. I am still a man. Her closeness kindles a memory for me. Yes, I remember. We shared a bed for many, many years. Her scent triggers another memory. It is sweet like fresh cut cypress on a crisp fall morning.

Her hand is old but still lithe and yellow-brown and graceful. There is a ring on her finger. Yes, I remember the day I bought that ring, from the jeweler down on Canal. She coos to me, "Pierre, you're still my hero, my knight."

Prosperine and I walked hand in hand through the fall breeze, through the cane, the tops well over our heads. This was the fall of 1865, mind you. The men from the armies who were coming back were all home and trying to resume lives in which killing was no longer acceptable. Certainly, her love, this boy Leesie, was not coming back, not this late, the better part of a year since the war was over. She had not mentioned him. And I surely had not.

I began to think of the life we might live together, the couple we would make. The children we would have, wonderful amalgams, perfect blends of each of us. I thought of how we would look together in portraits we would have made in ten, twenty, fifty years, each portrait with more children around us. I wanted to live to see it. But I knew that I had a job to do, and to fail to do it or to fail to even try to do it, would be to invite Shame and possibly Drunkenness again. I would not fail this time. I would pay the debt, though I wasn't sure what the debt was. I only knew that it was on the other side of Teague's dog.

We walked a while, and then we walked some more. Prosperine was tiring, and so we pulled off onto a rutted lane used to ferry wagonloads of field hands in and wagonloads of cane out. The cane was so tall now that it was like a canyon of green. We lay there with the green fronds and the blue sky above us, her head on my chest, her straw-yellow hair falling over light caramel skin. Her eyes were closed and her breathing was small, lifting and falling.

I looked at the keys and the bottle of laudanum. I knew that whatever debt I had to pay was in the mausolée at Mount Teague, and that the big key would let me in. But what was the second key, the smaller key, for? I held it up against the sky-blue heavens.

Prosperine shifted and put her hand on my chest. What I wanted more than anything was for her to live. I was trying to devise a plan for her to stay behind, some ruse, some small errand like, *stay here with Pistache. I'm afraid he will get in trouble where I'm going.*

We tarried a while longer while the wall of cane sheltered us from the wind, and its shadow, waving and serrated, crept over us. Her body was nestled into mine, her breast pressing through the bodice of her dress and my shirt and against my ribs. I was contemplating waking her and giving her a kiss, a real kiss, a lover's kiss. The kind that raises excitement from a dead sleep.

Then, behind us, something moved through the cane. At first, I thought it was Pistache. He had been nosing in and out of the cane, his sound lost in the rustle of the wind. The tops of the cane cast shadows that twitched and danced in the breeze to the song the wind stirred through it. And then there was another shadow.

The silhouette of a man's head bobbed above the weaving silhouettes of the cane tops. When the wind gusted, his shadow arm would reach up to hold down his hat, a top hat. His outline stopped and pivoted, and then there was the sound of the hocking of phlegm and then a spit. The smell of cigar smoke filled the breeze and was carried off.

The man's head-shadow exhaled wisps of smoke that lifted into the lane and disappeared. He was behind us, just a pace or two, but he couldn't see us.

Across from the wagon lane from us, Pistache nosed through the cane, sampling the smells of the creatures that had passed through before him, rats and mice and snakes. He emerged into the rutted lane. The man on the horse whistled to him. And I recognized the whistle of man-for-dog. I had heard it before. When Sam Teague called to his dog, Serbus.

Pistache flashed a friendly grin to the man behind us in the cane. The man clicked to Pistache, and the dog lowered his ears and smacked submissively. Prosperine awoke and sleepily called to the dog to come. And the shadow man heard.

The black mare with the blonde mane quietly parted the cane, and there he was.

Sam Teague.

And I panicked. I jumped to my feet and grabbed Prosperine by the hand. We ran across the wagon lane and into the opposite field.

"Stop there!" Teague called.

Prosperine and I took off into the cane, a dark world where the sun could not easily penetrate. We heard a shot, and I wondered if it had been intended for us or for Pistache, and if it had found its mark. I could hear the horse and its rider over the rustle of cane. We stopped and hunkered down low in the darkness of cane stalks.

And then they rustled again. Teague passed by us, his head floating above the cane as if it had been disembodied. He called out to us.

"Come on out, you two. Let's just talk about why you're in my cane field."

His head bobbed past us, over the tops of the cane, his top hat set in the blue sky. When he had moved on, Prosperine and I quietly, slowly eased back to the wagon lane. We paused at the edge of it and waited. When the only sound for some time had been the cane sighing, we emerged again into the wagon lane.

I looked over my shoulder and forward and then back again. I could see the bayou road and the trees that marked the edge of Bayou Lafourche. Just fifty yards away and we would be safe. Her hand was in mine, and we walked at a pace that made the keys in my pocket jingle. The trees along the bayou were getting taller as we neared. But then at our backs was the voice.

We stopped in the lane and turned around. There he was, towering into the sky on his black mare. Her blonde mane shimmered as she nosed over to nibble a stalk of cane. He quickly jerked her head back as he steadied the revolver at us. Its round black eye stared at the space between mine. It seemed as big as a siege gun. I put my arms back to keep Prosperine behind me.

"Honest to God, boy, it baffles me yet how an innocent man could go to the gallows for a wretched bastard like you."

I closed my eyes, and I heard the shot. It clipped the tops of the cane. I heard him wheel his horse around, and I opened my eyes to see Teague raise his revolver and look out to where the shot had come from. Then there was another. With this one, I could tell that it had come from the tree line of the bayou.

And with this one, Teague whirled about on the black mare, clutching his thigh and cursing. He seemed dizzy. We watched him as he fell forward onto the neck of his horse. Blood was dripping down his pants leg, into and around his boot. He slipped from the saddle, but his foot caught in one of the stirrups, and he dangled from it. The black mare turned by instinct and cantered back to the house, dragging her rider through the muddy lane. Teague's swallowtail coattails slid under his back and around his head.

We turned back to the bayou as a figure emerged from the bank. He came running across the Bayou Road and down the wagon lane. There was a burden on his back, and he ran awkwardly with it, like we used to do when our officers had us double-time somewhere. He had a rifle in his hand, one of those long Enfields that we all had coveted. As he neared, I remembered him. It was Ulysse Hebert, my friend from the army, the one who had told me about St. Matthew Parish in the first place.

"Prosperine!" he shouted. "Prosperine. *Ma tout-tout!* Where have you been? *Mais,* I've been looking for you! I've been following you for months!"

He slid the knapsack off his back and laid his rifle down.

Prosperine seemed confused. "Ulysse?" she asked. "Ulysse?"

"*Ma Prosperine, ma tout-toutsy.* Your eyes. *Mais,* they clear. Can you see me?"

She closed her eyes and put her fingers to his face. I realized that she had never actually seen him. A single word signaled the end of any courtship I might have with her.

"Leesie," she muttered as her fingers danced over his features. "Leesie."

They looked at each other, and then they kissed, the long, pulling kiss of reunited lovers. I looked off into the cane. Their hearts were mending to a new strength, a bond that could never be broken. Mine was breaking instead. The wind pushed and pulled at the trembling tops of the cane, and I watched them rake against the blue sky. It was a beautiful moment. Really it was. But it was their moment and not mine. Then they must have realized I was still there.

"*C'est Pete?*" he asked as he gave me a closer look. "*Mais, neuf-doigt Pete!*[75] *Mon bon ami!* I ain't seen you since we were paroled at Vicksburg! How you know *ma tout-toutsy?*"

"Old friends." I said, and then I added the sad, bitter truth of it. "Like a sister to me."

I shook his hand, but I did not thank him for saving my life. There are really no words for that. Instead, I left him with his prize, his girl. But in that moment, that tender, crushing moment, she looked at me. A look tinged with the bitter myrrh of regret at how things must be now.

I did not explain to him why Sam Teague was about to shoot me. There was not time for that, nor would there ever be. Leesie only knew that Teague had threatened the only thing that had kept him sane in the years since he had left St. Matthew Parish. His *Tout-toutsy.*

I felt for the bottle of laudanum and the keys. They were still there. I was determined to pay the debt. I turned and left them and followed the blood trail toward Mount Teague.

52

The Spaniard sits with me this afternoon, his gray eyes studying the

---

[75] Nine-fingered Pete

Times-Picayune. I believe he sees me as his father. I do not remember the day he was born, though I remember the days that my other children were born. But he is as much a son to me as my other children.

We sit on the porch, and I scratch this paper with this pen, and he reads and the lazy traffic of Prytania comes by infrequently, mostly automobiles today, though I believe a horse and wagon has passed as well. A few streets up, the bell of a streetcar dings, and I think I can hear the mechanical slap as the door opens and then closes. It rumbles off as I gaze across the street into the city of sleepers, housed in marble and granite, all slumbering without turning or snoring.

They all fell into this world as babies, in a rush of bright light and cold air, into the arms of someone who loved them at least enough to feed them and clean them and teach them to walk and speak. They grew up and fell in love, and then they fell into the madness that their bodies made them feel. And then they fell in love again, this time with the little creatures that they begat from the madness. Then they fell into old age, and they fell ill. And then they simply fell asleep. And I am getting sleepy.

But I was not sleepy that night. I lay down under the chill of the fall night sky, no blanket, no food. Prosperine and the man Ulysse, *Tout-toutsy* and *Leesie* as they called each other, had drifted back to Donaldsonville with plans to cross the river and into a new life, the one that she had given up for dead but that now had come back as not just a possibility, but as a certainty.

I lay awake that night and looked at the hard points of stars and thought of the nights that she and I lay under them, our bodies naked and wet in the moonlight, my body yearning for hers, but her body simply naked and wet. I thought of the life we might have had, a life that was now an impossibility.

I tried to sleep, but my mind raced. I wondered about what debt I would pay and how I would pay it. I wondered about Serbus and how I would deliver his dose of laudanum without a pork chop to put it in. I wondered if Teague had died. I wondered if Honoré was on a ship for Havana yet. I wondered if Leesie and Tout-toutsy had engaged in bodily madness. Then I fought off self-pity. I wondered about Pistache. He was nowhere to be found, and I wondered if he had turned around and left with the new, old couple. I finally fell asleep at first light when the eastern sky was pink and orange, the colors of an intense fall sunrise.

I woke midmorning from a dream in which old blue Maybelle, my favorite of Uncle Ransom's coon hounds, was nuzzling and snuffling my face and ears. When I woke fully, I saw the peanut-colored fur of Pistache. I rose and composed myself. I had two keys and a bottle of laudanum in my pockets, and only a vague idea of how I would use them to pay this debt that Honoré had spoken of.

As I stood and took my morning relief, a sound came to me on the brisk air, the sound of a *violon* and the bubbling sound of merrymaking. I paused for a moment to make sure I wasn't imagining it. But there it was. And then there was a smell, a good smell that Pistache smelled, too. I climbed the tree I had just watered, up from branch to branch. From that height, the cane seemed soft and green, all the way to a line of trees. It looked like you could walk across the surface of it. I climbed a few branches higher. Leafy green extended for several hundred yards to a line of trees, a line that wavered in the shape of the bayou. Across that, smoke rose up into the hard, clear air and trailed up into the colossal blue sky.

The smoke carried the aroma of cooking meat. Pistache's nose bounced on the air and his eyes narrowed as if trying to concentrate the scent. We were hungry. We set off along another of the wagon lanes, down between the towering cane. We followed the smell of roasting meat and the merry lilt of a violon. At last, the trees towered over the tops of the cane. We kept walking, and then the bayou was there, and then the back of a house with a fairly new cypress shake roof. An ancient sycamore tree rose from the front of the house and over it. Large brown leaves hung from its branches.

Across the bayou, in the yard of the house, a pig carcass turned, splayed on a spit. A young man was scratching out parts of tunes on the *violon*, practicing, tuning up, getting ready. A man stood stiffly in a suit of saggy clothes, and a woman, his bride, stood at his side with a veil over her face. I stood on the opposite bank and watched it all.

A girl, about ten years of age, saw me across the bayou.

"Bienvenue, monsieur!" she called. *"Ma Tante Nita, se marie aujourd'hui!"*[76]

---

[76] My Aunt Nita got married today!

243

She scrambled into a bateau and poled over to get me. Me, a stranger. I stepped into the boat. Pistache paused as he contemplated getting in. He balked for a moment, and then he made a quick, tentative leap and turned and sat at my feet.

"Tante Nita, she don't truss dogs around her chickens, no. Keep an eye on that one. We keep him tied up, no?"

The bateau nudged up onto the bank. The girl and I lured Pistache out and secured him to the ancient sycamore tree. I knelt for a moment and scratched Pistache's head. The tree, the house, the new roof. I recognized them then. It was the house of the old man, *l'ancien*, Old Monsieur Broussard. With all the meandering of the bayou, I was surprised that from the edge of Sam Teague's cane fields, it was only half a mile or so from Old Broussard's home.

The couple had just been married that morning, and now a celebration was being held, what we would call a reception nowadays. I looked around for *l'ancien* but did not see him. The young man was talking to old men and women, aunts and uncles and neighbors, all of them reliving their days of romance and courtship, remembering the days of the anticipation of a night of desire finally permitted to burst into bloom.

My French had come of age, and I followed conversations about family and friends and who was doing well and whose health was ill and who was expected to get married next. A jug was passed through the crowd, and, while I don't remember my last drink, I do remember the first time I refused one.

"*Merci, non*," I said as I passed it on to the priest who had performed the ceremony. But I stayed and I ate, and as the young fiddler scratched out waltzes for us on his *violon*, I danced with every woman and girl there, the young, the old, the fat, the thin. And I laughed in the crystal air of fall, a remarkable sound escaping from me. I laughed, and I knew from it that my heart would not stay broken forever.

Finally, I danced with the bride. When I took her hand in mine, she recognized me, and through her veil, I recognized her.

"Monsieur Mouton!" she said from behind the gauze. Her face was small and dark and pretty, like if someone were to draw a fox as a person in a story book for children. "*Mais*, thank you again for *la coverture* that you and your crew put up. Such a good roof, that. Never leaks even in the heavy

244

rain. For three chickens, it was a bargain. Merci."

I did not correct her. Instead, I asked her, "Where is old Monsieur Broussard?"

"Papa Joseph? *Pauvre bête, defan.*"

"I'm sorry to hear that," I said.

"*Mais,* we all head home, sooner or later, no?" she said as she ducked under my arm to give herself a twirl.

We finished our dance. Noon had come and gone, and the older ones and the younger ones were beginning to nap in the shade of the trees. I wished the bride and groom a long life, filled with children and the abundance to feed them. Then I went to collect Pistache, who was sleeping in the shade of the sycamore. I paused to think back to the day that Old Broussard had sat in the shade of this very tree with a pretty blind girl.

They offered me a sack of *grattons,* and Pistache and I got in the boat. The same young girl poled us back across, and I realized that this was one of her chores, to ferry people across the bayou and back. She chattered on in French, still excited about the day, a day she would remember forever. I offered a *gratton* to Pistache, but he only nibbled it politely. I believe the children of that gathering had gone out to the sycamore and fed him all day.

On the other side, I lifted Pistache out of the boat. He felt quite a bit heavier. The girl leaned on her pole, and I kissed her on both cheeks, which she gave to me with a grin.

"You will make a beautiful bride one day," I told her, and she blushed. Pistache and I scrambled up the bank, and the girl pushed off, back across the bayou, her small voice singing brightly, a song in French about true love.

The afternoon cane greeted us, tall and beginning to cast the small skirts of afternoon shadows. We found the wagon lane and took it, and then we came to the Bayou Road and followed it. The cane was tall, and the cypresses were beginning to rust again at their tops. The air was still cool, the sky intensely blue.

A carriage passed us, wheels and spokes turning, horse hoofs clopping. A short while later there was another. Then a man cantered by on a chestnut mare. And then another carriage. They all seemed to be heading to the same place.

I came to one that was stopped. A Negro attendant was setting out a picnic lunch for a couple.

"Say, what's the occasion for so much traffic today?" I asked innocently.

"Haven't you heard? Mr. Teague down at Mount Teague is gravely ill," the woman said.

"What happened?" I asked, though of course I knew.

"Shot through the leg," the man said. "They don't expect him to live."

"Do they know who it was? Who shot him?"

"No one knows. Whoever it was just drifted away." The man dropped an oyster in his mouth from one of those tiny utensils that have always reminded me of Neptune's pitchfork.

"I hope they catch him," the woman said as she took a sip of champagne, "so they can give him a medal."

The Negro servant, who was wearing white gloves, said, "Oh, now, Miss Nancy!"

The husband paused with a slick, gray oyster dangling from the fork. "Darling, we shouldn't speak ill of the dead," he said. The black man nodded his head in agreement.

"But he's not dead yet." The woman held her flute to the servant who filled it from a bottle that he held with white-gloved hands.

"Still, a little Christian charity," the man said. And I swear I think I saw him suppress a smile.

She hastily finished a sip and said, "Really dear, don't you think St. Matthew Parish and the world would be a better place without him?"

"That will be enough, Nancy. So many share your sentiments, but really, that will be enough. God rest the poor tormented soul of Sam Teague."

"If there is such a thing," the woman said, and the servant fell to chuckling, white teeth breaking out behind brown lips.

"God rest Sam Teague," the husband said again.

I only knew him for a moment, and I never got his name, but I believe that man was the most charitable I have ever met.

I continued down the road in the afternoon sunshine, and then I saw it again. A white citadel in a sea of cane-green. The gleam of Mount Teague in the afternoon light.

53

We have visitors today, our friends the Heberts from Côte Française.[77] Leesie and Tout-toutsy.

We sit in the front parlor. The woman who is not the hired girl and the woman Tout-toutsy both have green eyes and white hair. They also have the same olive skin, caramel skin, skin that ages well, only the slightest hint of wrinkles. As they have gotten older, they have looked more and more like sisters, though I know that they are not sisters. They behave like them, though, talking for hours on end, laughing, whispering, fixing each other's coffee without asking how they take it. Just knowing.

Leesie and I have been friends since our CSA days, and, again today, he talks about them. He does not talk about lifeless bodies and blood and shrieks of the wounded at night. No one who was there speaks of things such as that. He talks about the practical jokes we played on each other, the bawdy saloon ditties we sang, the secret, funny names we had for our officers. He asks about the boy named Sidney Fisher from Natchitoches Parish, the one everyone called Re-Pete, the boy who talked all the time. "Whatever happened to him?" Leesie asks.

Shot in head, Vburg, I write on the margin of the *Times-Picayune.*

"That's right." We have discussed this before. I do believe that Leesie's memory is fading like mine.

Our wives are sharing a joke and a giggle like two schoolgirls, leaning forward and grasping hands and touching foreheads. Perhaps we, their husbands, are the butt of their jokes, but that is no matter to us. It is far too late for us to begin courting new wives. Besides, we know any merriment at our expense is just a sign of love.

Leesie and I go down the muster roll of our friends from the old war days. There will be another Confederate Veterans Reunion soon. We attended one, once. It was held east somewhere, I can't remember where. We left it early, however, when a man appeared in a gray uniform, with wide cuffs and fancy piping traced up the sleeves, the uniform of a Confederate officer. He had a limp, and a scar on his face. We took one

---

[77] Chip, I believe this is the old name for French Settlement, Louisiana.

look at him and saw his fraud. Leesie and I left a day early and returned home.

But back to that day that I returned alone to Mount Teague.

Carriages were coming and going, lined up along the lane of oaks. They sat parked under the branches as the people milled away the afternoon, the poor, the well-to do, all of them. They were like townspeople waiting at the train depot for the circus to arrive. If you were to ask one of them, any of them, they would have said that they were there to pay their respects. Certainly, more than a handful were hoping for his demise. Perhaps most of them were. Well, all right, all of them.

Word percolated through the crowd that it wouldn't be long. Catholics genuflected, Protestants bowed their heads or raised them to heaven. Then the vicar appeared on the porch. He held up his hands, and the babble of the crowd was hushed. He announced in a loud voice, "Samuel Teague is as near to death as to life. Let us pray for the soul of Samuel Teague."

Someone in the crowd of death-watchers said in a stage whisper, "I didn't know he had one," and there was a ripple of inappropriate laughter that was stared down and out of existence by some of the more pious in attendance. One of them scolded, "He's a child of God like everyone else."

"That'd be news to me...and God!" someone else said, and there was a bigger rush of laughter that caught the vicar's attention and made him scan the crowd with a scowl.

The hubbub served my purposes well. I pushed my way through the crowd of bowed heads. Pistache moved with me, his tan tail swishing against the black trousers and dresses of the people who called themselves mourners but who were really more along the lines of sightseers and gawkers. We headed for the mausolée.

And there he was, Serbus, jealously guarding the dead under his BEWARE OF DOG sign, only pausing from his phlegmy barking to lift his leg and water it and scratch the ground with his hind paws. As we approached, he became more agitated, more challenged.

From the grease-mottled bag, I threw a *gratton* to Serbus. He ate it in a quick, crushing bite and the backwards gulp of a reptile. I threw another. Same. I sprinkled a little laudanum on the next one. Same. Another.

More laudanum. Another. Another. I think I could have offered him a whole pig like that, and he would have eaten it.

His growling became muttering as he stared at the bare ground. His eyes were saggy and red. At last, his front legs buckled, and he wilted to the ground. He sprawled out and slept with his eyes half-open. He dozed as though he would slumber through the Second Coming, snoring a guttural canine snore under the sign that read, BEWARE OF DOG.

Pistache moved closer and sniffed Serbus. He kept his eyes on the big dog and gingerly stepped within the sector of earth that Serbus' chain described. When Serbus remained inert, Pistache merrily marked every vertical surface within the arc of chain. He squatted and relieved himself not in one, but in two different places, his face grinning, his tail quivering.

While he put his signature on every corner of the watchdog's territory, I moved quickly. I compared the lock with the key. The big one was for the crypt. I put it in the lock, and it took two hands to rotate it. I opened the complaining door to an intense darkness. The air smelled of shadows and dust and mold. Veils of cobwebs pulsed with the draft of the door. It was a place where even mice and roaches would not venture.

There were coffins on either side of the narrow aisle, and in the aisle was another body, a woman laid out without a coffin. The body was holding a baby to her chest. As the light cut into the darkness, the body rose. The woman put up her hand to shield away the new light that was coming directly through from the west. She rose from an exhausted, defeated sleep. When she turned, I recognized her, though she was thinner than I remembered her.

"Mathilde?" I asked.

"*Oui*," she said with her hand over her eyes against the brilliant light that I was silhouetted by, that I was coming from. "Are you Jesus?"

"No. Pete. Monsieur Carrick. What are you doing in here?"

"*Monsieur* is getting ready to take us away, to Cuba or Brazil. He is going to sell us there. He is ashamed of the boy, and the new wife wants no part of us, especially with how much the boy looks like him."

I could see the child now, a light-skinned boy, even lighter than Mathilde. He blinked against the light. His eyes were nickel gray. There was no mistaking who his father was. And there was the cruel irony. Sam Teague had finally sired a male. With his mulatto mistress.

"I'm here to get you. Take you away. You and the boy."

I made a motion to her, and she handed the boy to me. She was hesitant at first, but she was also exhausted. I don't think that they had eaten in some time. I took the child in my arms, and he molded up against me. And I had never had such a feeling as that. You fall in love when you hold another person next to you. That love is so much deeper and truer when that other person is a baby.

"Well, I don't see why he should be so ashamed," I said. "This is perhaps the most beautiful child I have ever seen." That was no exaggeration. Then I said, "We had better go."

I still wasn't sure about the second key. Until I saw the chest behind her. It was a lockbox on a stand, really. I gave the boy back to her, and I took the second key from my pocket. The lock clicked, and I opened the lid. And I have never seen so much money in one place in all my life. It could have passed for Laffite's treasure, if it were filled with Spanish doubloons and not US gold and silver dollars.

Mathilde handed me the baby and scrambled out to a shed and brought a basket, much like the one she used to bring us bread in. In fact, it may have been the same one. We emptied the lockbox into the basket, a rush of clinking, glimmering metal in the darkness of the tomb. I scratched through the basket and pulled out a nickel. One small nickel. I put it in the lockbox and locked it again. I didn't want to leave *le baws-man* completely destitute. If he lived.

"We ought to go," I said. "While people are still preoccupied with Marse Sam's passing."

She paused for a moment, cradling her son against her as she leaned forward. She kissed one of the coffins, the one with the placard, *Joseph Savoie*.

"*Au revoir, Papa*," she said.

Mathilde placed her apron over the basket, arranging it with one hand as she held her son. It took all I had to carry it. I stepped over Serbus, who was snoring on his side. His red eyes were blank.

We circled around the back of the big house to avoid the crowds. The sheds, the workshops, the cooperage, all of them were empty. Everything at Mount Teague was in chaos. We passed by the grinding sheds. And then we spotted him.

He wore blinders and stared forward. He looked like he had been beaten. His neck sagged as he stood there tethered to the beam of the grinding wheel, the clock that faced heaven and revolved with the hours.

I set down the basket and stripped "All Tom" from the traces, leaving only a leader over his muzzle. I rubbed his withers and scratched his ears. I gave him a handful of oats from a trough nearby. Mathilde took the leader, and I picked up the basket of money. It seemed even heavier.

The afternoon sun was casting shadows on the faraway crowd. The darkness spilled out from the lane of oaks, out beyond them and up into the yard. We skirted them, keeping the simmer of their conversations distant. We were headed to the commissary.

It was still open for business. It kept hours both early and late, always ready to accrue more debt and add weight to the anchors that kept everyone and everything in place. I walked in, struggling with the basket. Mathilde was next to me, the baby wrapped up against her.

"I've come to pay the debt," I announced to the clerk.

"Whose debt?" he asked.

"Everyone's," I said.

He cast me an uncertain look and retrieved the record, the chain that tethered everyone to their anchor. It was not a thin ledger by any means. There were over three hundred names in it, over three hundred souls who were in debt to *la commissaire*, all in varying degrees. And we paid it all off. Every. Last. Cent.

The clerk went down the list, crossing out each name. When the last name was crossed off, the clerk asked me, "Who should I say has rendered this service? Paid off these debts?"

He took a stub of a pencil from behind his ear and held it over a slip of paper. An elaborate MT was embossed at the top. Only the best at Mount Teague. The clerk looked at the paper, waiting for me to tell him.

"Tell everyone, including Marse Sam, if he lives, that it was Honoré Mouton, the French housejoiner, what done it."

"Hon-or-ray…" he wrote out carefully.

"Oh, do not feel compelled to write it down for him," I said. I leaned in and over the counter toward the clerk, and I said in a chuckling whisper, "For *le baws-man* cannot read. Not one lick."

The clerk gave me a raised-eyebrow look of delighted surprise at this juicy bit of information. Then I told him the one thing that would ensure that the information would be broadcast far and wide, in low tones and whispers, as quick as the telegraph.

"But do me a favor. Don't tell anyone, hear?"

"Oh, no sir, heavens no," the clerk said, and then I knew that the news would soon be on its way, clear across St. Matthew Parish by midnight and in St. James, Ascension, and Iberville Parishes by morning.

I looked around the commissary at the items, trying to remember what had been stolen from whom, trying to figure a way to get everything back to its rightful owner. It would have been impossible. I bought Mathilde a tin of crackers and a tin of cane syrup, *Mount Teague Brand, Sweetest-Purest.* I bought her a pound of ham, all the peanuts in the roaster, an entire block of cheese. I bought her baby a calico and a gingham blanket. And then, behind the clerk on a shelf, I saw it.

There was my daddy's satchel with CARRICK stamped on the side.

"May I see that satchel, sir?"

The clerk took it off the shelf behind him and handed it to me. I opened it, and there were my daddy's tools. Also in there were the tools of the sculptor.

"How much for this satchel of tools?"

"Twenty dollars. Would you like to set up an account, sir?" He knew I could pay, but he had been trained to offer debt to anyone who would possibly take it on.

"That won't be necessary," I said with a smile.

Into his hand, I put four five-dollar gold pieces, each stamped with a seated Lady Liberty on it. I laid them in his palm, one-by-one, slowly, carefully, so he would see the missing finger on my hand.

The basket was much lighter now, so we laid the blankets in it and put the baby in among them. We set the groceries, the peanuts and the ham and the cheese and the syrup and the crackers, in with him. Then we set off for the quarters, knocking on doors and telling the people that their debts were all paid, that they could leave. Some refused to believe it and thought it was a trick, so we began giving each person a silver dollar to leave. By morning the rows of two-room shanties were vacant, their doors left open to the fall cold.

With a shortage of workers that fall, Mr. D'Ormeaux, acting for the convalescing Marse Sam, had to pay top dollar to get the cane in. At first, he offered two dollars a day. There were few takers, and he had to offer three dollars a day.

When Marse Sam finally recovered enough to go out at night to check on the lockbox, I'm sure he was quite shocked to find that the *defan* of the mausolée and old Serbus had failed to safeguard his treasure. The Savoies were already dead, and he had no recourse against them. That left Serbus. In a fit of anger, he kicked the dog, which was a mistake. The dog bit him on the leg. And that was the dog's mistake. Teague put him down on the spot.

Due to *le baws-man's* illness, grinding season at Mount Teague was delayed that year. A great deal of the cane froze and was useless for grinding. And Marse Sam took a loss.

54

I happened to meet Mark Twain once when he came to New Orleans to see our mutual friend, Mr. Cable. This was before Mr. Cable was forced out of town for espousing the radical concept of racial equality and celebrating miscegenation in some of his stories. I've always wondered if the woman downstairs who is not the hired girl and I were his inspiration. He never said one way or the other. I seem to recall that he died earlier this year, in Florida of all places, but my mind does not answer its rudder very well these days.[78]

Mr. Twain was discussing his former editor, a man named Bliss[79], who had bilked him out of some money. It was quite a sum, though Twain never said how much.

---

[78] The author George Washington Cable was a resident of the Garden District in New Orleans until the mid-1880's, when public opinion forced him to move to Massachusetts. He died in Florida in January of 1925.

[79] Chip, I found this quote from Twain's autobiography: "Well, Bliss was dead and I couldn't settle with him for his ten years of swindlings. He has been dead a quarter of a century now. My bitterness against him has faded away and disappeared. I feel only compassion for him and if I could send him a fan I would."

"Well, Twain," Cable said, "I hope he gets what's coming to him, here or in the beyond."

I had something to say about that, and I spoke up.

"I really don't think any of us wants the justice we have coming. No, the best we can hope for is mercy."

I seem to recall that the three of us raised our glasses in a toast to that sentiment.

Sam Teague did not die that fall. He was still fairly young then, and only the good die young. I know this to be true, as I'm old, too. He came very close to dying, however.

His horse had dragged him down the lane of adolescent oaks, Teague's head bumping over his coattails and the ground. At last, horse and burden pulled up to the front porch of Mount Teague. He was put to bed, and the doctor was called. And then several doctors were called. They came from Thibodaux, Baton Rouge, New Orleans. Each did the best he could. Each left shaking his head.

Finally, he lingered to the point that the Episcopal vicar was called. There was a great deal of pacing and hand wringing. But finally, the patient pulled through. Everyone knew that Teague was on the mend when he told the vicar to "get the hell out of my house."

He didn't lose his life, and he didn't lose the ability to walk, though he did so with a limp for the rest of his years. He was unashamed of it. He called it his "war wound." No one questioned him on it, including at that veterans' reunion that Leesie and I attended, though no one could ever remember seeing him in camp or on the march, let alone on a battlefield. No one in St. Matthew Parish ever said a word about his leg wound, even those who knew better. It was on the list of things that weren't talked about, right up there with how *le baws-man* got the scar on his face.

After his brush with death, he did not repent and he did not vow to become a better man. Those kinds of things only happen in stories, particularly the Horatio Alger, rags-to-riches-type foolishness that my Aunt Cora favored. Real life is much more brutal and unforgiving than that. Tigers do not change their stripes. Lions do not lie down with lambs. Nor do wolves.

After firing Mr. D'Ormeaux for mismanaging that season's crop,

Teague simply waited and plotted and schemed. He took a loss the first year, made a small profit the next, and within a year or two more, he had reestablished his leafy, green empire.

He kept Mount Teague, but he did lose another Mrs. Teague. The second Mrs. Teague continued to spend prodigiously, unconcerned with her husband's financial woes. Her spending went on unchecked until she left abruptly in the middle of the night and was never seen again. After being "abandoned," Teague waited the required period of time and then divorced her.

I have always found it odd that a striking, red-haired, big-bosomed woman like Polly Teague could go missing and never be seen again. But so it was. The next Mrs. Teague, number three, was installed when the ink was barely dry on the divorce papers. She was the one, you may recall, who had my statue of Venus dumped in Bayou Lafourche and the ballroom razed. But she would not be the last Mrs. Teague, either.

Teague lived to be an old man with a limp in his stride and a scar on his cheek. His death occurred years later, about ten or twenty years ago, I'm thinking. He died not of old age, but in some sort of agricultural accident.[80]

His son, the one they call Junior Teague, hired the best man to sculpt his tomb and monument, the one in the family plot behind Mount Teague by the Twelve Arpent canal. Inside the vault, just above the door upon that cold-flat surface, in a place only the dead would be able to see is an inscription, put there by that sculptor:

CAVETE A DEO

You may have guessed that it was I who chiseled that inscription into the dark red porphyrian marble, imported from Italy and worked by the best artist in the city of New Orleans, Pierre Carriere. Only the best at Mount Teague.

That inscription was my idea and mine alone. None of the Teague

---

[80] *St. Matthew Parish Compass*, Oct. 15, 1915: "Mount Teague Patriarch Dies in Cane Mishap"

family knows it is there. Only one could. If he were alive in there. And if he could read. But I'm sure that even without being able to read it, the illiterate occupant of that fancy tomb now knows the saying to be true:

Beware of God.

I understand it now, the parable about the camel going through the eye of a needle. We all die penniless. When the undertaker closes our eyes, it matters not how many four-in-hand carriages we own, how many swallowtail suits are in our armoires, how many acres of cane we plant in the spring and cut in the fall. When we die, all of that is left behind. None of it fits in the coffin with us, let alone on the back of a camel testing the eye of a needle. There is no baggage car for that train that sits at the station for us with the curtains drawn, waiting to take us to a place we cannot fathom. We are all destitute then. We all become beggars, as the old German said.[81]

And then we are all equally dead. Though, I suppose, in some cases, like Sam Teague's, some may be more dead than others. He left behind everything, as he had no need for any of it where he was going. Well, no, I take that back. I imagine that a fan would be pretty handy for him about now.

55

The woman and the Spaniard take me to the doctor. The doctor has me stretch my hands in the air. My arms are scrawny, but they are heavy for me, and they wobble a little in my effort to raise them. The doctor takes some kind of picture, a tintype of the inner man. Then I wait by myself in another room, sitting in a wheelchair staring at the blanket draped over my legs. The woman comes back in the room with the Spaniard, who I think is her son. Their eyes are red. They've been crying like they've just been given bad news. Whatever it is, they don't tell me.

"Let's take you home, Pops," the Spaniard says, wiping his eyes with the back of his hand.

---

[81] "We are all beggars before God."-Martin Luther

I know what the news is. This old body is closing up shop, much like on winter evenings when the woman would come and get me and tell me that supper was ready. The dark had invaded the city, but the lights of my workshop were holding fast against it.

She would critique my work. The nose is a little big, don't you think? I love this angel's hair, so real. This frown, it looks like a smirk. I would redo it. No one else could tell me these things. I have always valued her opinion.

I would turn out the lights, one by one, by turning a key in the gaslight days, then by flipping a switch when the city was electrified. At last, I would turn out the big light, the one over the monument I was working on. Then I would lock the door behind us, and we would go in the house.

Supper would be ready on the table, usually one plate for me, as everyone else had already eaten. Some nights, I would find that the children had been sent to sleep over with their cousins at their Aunt Nissy and their Uncle Etienne's house. We would leave supper on the table, and she and I would ascend the stairs.

Her dress would fall from her shoulders in the dim gaslight, floating amber and pale. She would do the same with my suspenders and my shirt. We would try to restrain ourselves from wrenching the clothes off our bodies, try to keep a slow, even pace. After what seemed like a splendid eternity, we would be naked before each other, our skin the same color in the hazy light. And then we would lie together and enjoy the blessing that even a good man barely deserves, let alone a man like me.

56

We left Mount Teague, and I have only been back once since then, to complete the monument of *le baws-man*. It was one of the last major projects I did. I insisted that Teague the son pay up front. I had known his father, you see, and I also knew of the old saying about apples not falling far from trees.

Mathilde and I and the baby and "All Tom" headed north to the spot where several of the departing hands said we might find the man we called Big Eight. I was convinced that Big Eight would take one look at the little quadroon baby and assume it was mine and kill me, but I had resolved to stop running from my consequences.

I wasn't sure if I could take him. Since our last meeting, I had been shot, beaten, kicked in the groin, the face, the hands. Oh, and hung, though that one is only a technicality. I would plead innocence with the big blacksmith and ask for mercy. Or take the consequences.

"All Tom" seemed to be enjoying the pleasant weight of Mathilde and her son, Joseph, named after her father. As night fell in earnest, we pulled up into a flat dotted with scrubby oaks and palmettos. I whistled as I had been instructed. There was an answering whistle like a bird. I whistled again, twice, two quick bursts. The bird whistled again twice. I whistled once again, as I was told. The bird whistled three times. And then he was there.

He and Mathilde embraced. The big man, whom I had known as Big Eight, was crying, silver moonlit tears on midnight black cheeks. He took my hand in a shake, and he pulled me to him. This is it, I thought. I will now see if there is a God. When this big man is done with me, I will know.

He embraced me tightly. "*Merci, merci, merci,*" he said. "*Merci pour avoir la ramener.*"[82]

He released me, and he whistled into the night. Another bird returned the whistle. And then a woman almost as dark as he was emerged holding a baby, a little wooly head nestled in a blanket. The woman showed the little face to Mathilde. Mathilde looked into the new baby, the little one still unencumbered by the nonsense of the world, and she made that gesture, that universal, *let me hold him gesture*, and the black woman gave her the bundle. And Mathilde held the baby and kissed the little dark forehead and swayed with the small, agreeable weight. And she cried happy tears.

Big Eight put his hand on Mathilde's shoulder.

"*Garde-là,*" he said to the little bundle with a big, wrought iron finger pointed at Mathilde. "*Ça c'est Tante Mathilde.*"[83]

"Where will you go now?" Big Eight asked us.

---

[82] Thank you for returning her.
[83] Look there, that's Aunt Mathilde.

"New Orleans," I said. "It will be easier to blend in."

"We will go with you," he said.

And we went, with a mule and a dog. We traveled together along the west bank, as cane wagons began rumbling out in the cool fall air and groaning back full and the air was filled with the first smoky wisps of burning cane and the cane cutters sang and chopped and shouted and dropped armloads of green stalks that were picked up and thrown into the wagons.

At Algiers, we crossed over on the ferry, with a baby sleeping in a basket with a nest egg big enough to get us set up as a blacksmith and a stonecutter. Enough to provide food and shelter for our families. A chance, an opportunity.

I stepped off the Algiers ferry and into New Orleans. And so began my life as Pierre Carriere.

57

Today the young man reads from Luke's gospel. He comes to the very words I have chosen for my epitaph, but he doesn't know it. They are chiseled into the stone that is in the corner of my workshop under a burlap cover among half-finished angels and crosses and lambs. Mr. Bourgeois knows the granite marker is there, however, and when I pass, he will have a man retrieve it for my final resting place among others of my kind, the sleepers waiting to be raised. They are the words that were written in the sand of my first grave, and now they will preside over my second grave, my true one.

Downstairs are the sounds of our household. I hear her, the woman downstairs who is not the hired girl. The sound of her old voice talking to the dog, the sound of her making *pain perdu* for the grandchildren. The sound of the dog whining for a scrap.

The dog Zipper is one of the descendants of "Pistache," a *tayaut de carpentier*, a carpenter's hound, a breed of dog that can tell a hammer from a saw from a bit brace. A dog bred for things such as that, but mostly a dog bred for companionship. I have outlived many dogs. I believe that this one will outlive me.

I used to look at the world as an unbearable burden to whoever had created it, unless it had simply fallen out of some larger sky, brushed off the shoe of an immense giant walking the road at midnight in another universe. The woman's faith is deeper than mine, however, and she has always seen to it that we attended Mass regularly, not only Sundays, but also the holy days of obligation and the saints' feast days. I have gone, not because of an unshakable belief in God, though my hope is that He exists and readily forgives. No, the main reason I have always gone willingly to Mass is because I have craved her company.

As this household breathes and speaks and sings this afternoon, I think again of my old friend, Honoré Mouton. Sam Teague once said that he wouldn't be bested by a half-a-man. I know now that that was exactly what Honoré was, a half-a-man. The other half was not of this world but rather something divine and forgiving. Someone who saw a mustard seed of something good and was determined to make it grow, because he could. He could make it grow.

I'm losing weight, and the doctor says I have a spot on my lung. How I wish Honoré were here now, to treat me and maybe give me a little more time with the woman downstairs. Perhaps he could restore my speech for a few minutes, and in those few minutes, I would tell him and the people of this house how much I love them.

A large man comes to visit me today, black as midnight but with graying hair. I am glad to see him. When I could talk, he and I would trade stories about Mount Teague and the cooperage. Even the time I pinned him, *"Par bon chance"*[84] he says, when he attacked the man called Old Tuck for insulting his sister. He laughs again, small, pitiful, old man chuckles, at how I thought he was saying "My, sir!" when he was actually saying *"Ma soeur!"*

My sister.

Neither one of us could pin anyone now, and haven't in a long time. Old age is kind like that.

He repeats the old stories, of how he was taken across Confederate

---

[84] By luck

lines by Teague and D'Ormeaux and sold to the Texas slave men, and how he slipped off one night and came back to the swamp to live and wait for the world to change.

Again, he repeats the old stories, as if he is telling them to me for the first time. Of how he has made everything from wrought iron gates and balconies to mule shoes in the decades he has been a blacksmith here in the city. One of the last now.

I know, too, that he has also made duplicate keys to mausoleums and lockboxes. I would not mention it, even if I could speak. I am enjoying listening to my brother-in-law, my *beau-frère*. He repeats the stories as I always repeated mine, when I could talk, each of us listening politely to the other, lapsing into and out of French to English and back. Repeating them every time we saw each other, sometimes multiple times in each visit. Old age is cruel like that.

I find myself thinking about the story of the Hollyfield Negroes and the Texas slave men who fell victim to the Rougarou in the swamp, though none of them saw it. They swore that seeing the Rougarou and not dying would bring you the worst luck imaginable. But those who caught the faintest glimpse of it, enough to get away with just one's ordinary luck, describe it not as scaly or furry, but as something big and black. It was always a wonder to me that twenty people shackled together could somehow free themselves from their chains without any help. Help, say, from a blacksmith.

I never asked Big Eight about it. I didn't want to hear the truth about what happened to the Texas slave men, and I didn't want my *beau-frère* to have to lie. So we never spoke of it. In sixty years of partnership making stone and iron monuments, we never spoke of it.

If I could speak, I would thank him for saving my life that night when I was shot, thank him for scooping me up, thank him for wading through the swamp with me, thank him for taking me to *le traiteur*, Honoré Mouton. Thank him for saving my soul, for saving it when I didn't even know I had one.

He holds my hand in his big black hand as I lay there, now bedridden. Perhaps he thinks this is the last time we will see each other. Perhaps it is.

When he leaves, pushing up his immense, black body like a ton of coal, up on a cane that is dwarfed by his size and bows slightly on his rising, he leans down to kiss me on both cheeks.

"*Mon frère,*, thank you for being…" he lapses into French again, "*Un bon mari pour ma soeur, Mathilde,*" he says.[85]

Like a light coming on in the darkness, with one word, the flip of a switch.

The woman Mathilde. I remember now. The woman downstairs is named Mathilde. My wife, the mother of my children, the grandmother of my grandchildren.

I must not forget again.

I've never seen the ocean, not once in my life. Not once. I've always wanted to see it. Years ago, I was traveling east on the train. I don't remember where. I had plans to get a look at it, the ocean, when we passed over the railroad bridge at Pass Christian in Mississippi. But I fell asleep, and, when I woke up, we had passed into flat, coastal plain dotted with pine trees and grass. On the return trip, it was night, and, though I knew it was out there, it was merely a dark, brooding thing out beyond the bright windows of the train.

But tonight, I'll see it, I'm sure of it. Phosphorescent greens, cobalt blues, rising and fading and rising, the contour of the water changing, fascinating. Blue, green, a wash of white bubbles. Blue, green, white. The kaleidoscopic crash of the Gulf and, on the other side, Old Havana and Honoré.

I look out onto the city of the dead over the high brick wall. People passing by on Prytania can't see them, but I can. Columns, elks, logs, angels, all made of stone. Mine will soon be among them. And I have chiseled it myself. This will be my second gravestone, but this one will truly be mine. It's a lovely spot in the shade of a sycamore tree, where the clop of the last of the mules in New Orleans and the whir of autos and the distant clang of the streetcar bells will sing me to the rest I don't deserve but that nevertheless I still hope for.

It will say *Pierre Carriere, son of John Carrick the tanner, friend of Honoré Mouton le traiteur.* Under that will be the date of my birth, ironically the date of the death of my mother, and the date of my death to be chiseled by the hand of another, the work of a hired man.

---

[85] Thank you for being a good husband to my sister, Mathilde.

C. H. Lawler is a lifelong Louisianan and writes stories set in his home state. He is also the author of *The Saints of Lost Things* and *The Memory of Time*. You can read a sample of them at Amazon.com.

For more information, visit
https://www.facebook.com/chlawlerstories/#